ALRENE I.
Belfast and now lives in Manchester. She is a member of
Manchester Irish Writers and her short stories and poetry have
been published in anthologies and broadcast on radio. She was
an English teacher for twenty years and now writes full time.
The Golden Sisters is the sequel to her bestselling first novel
Martha's Girls, published by Blackstaff Press in 2013. Both
books are inspired by a scrapbook of concert programmes and
newspaper cuttings about her mother and her aunts, the real
Golden Sisters.

The Golden Sisters

ALRENE HUGHES

BLACKSTAFF PRESS

Acknowledgements

Many thanks to everyone at Blackstaff Press for enabling me to continue the story of the Goulding family, and especially to Patsy Horton for her insightful editing. Thanks to Heather Hart for all her encouragement and advice on the American characters; to Rose Morris for her friendship and support over many years and her knowledge of Dungannon and farming; and to Carolyn Baines for her musical expertise, and especially helping me understand what it feels like to sing well. Finally, I am grateful once again to Brian Barton for his definitive book *The Blitz* – my 'go to' source for understanding life in Belfast in the war years.

Published in 2015 by Blackstaff Press
4D Weavers Court
Linfield Road
Belfast BT12 5GH

With the assistance of
The Arts Council of Northern Ireland

Supported by
The National Lottery®
through the Arts Council of Northern Ireland

Typeset by KT Designs, St Helens, England

Printed and bound by CPI Group UK (Ltd), Croydon CR0 4YY

A CIP catalogue for this book is available from the British Library

ISBN 978 0 85640 939 4

www.blackstaffpress.com
www.alrenehughes.com

For Jeff, Adam and Dan

Chapter 1

Martha Goulding carried the bucket of soapy water out the back door and round to the front of the house. The smell of burning hung in the air and white dust from a thousand fires had settled on every surface. She wrung out the rag and started on the windows – wiping, dipping, wringing, over and over.

She tried not to think of streets just down the road where they were still pulling bodies from the rubble. Instead she pictured Irene, beautiful in her wedding dress, next to Sandy in his air force uniform. The two days leave he had been granted was no way to start married life, but she'd be glad to have her eldest daughter home from honeymoon and all her girls together tonight.

As she cleaned, she thought of other women sluicing away the debris from their homes – those who still had homes. Please God, don't let them bomb us again, she prayed as she carried the dirty water to the drain. A charred piece of paper was caught behind the drainpipe. She gently pulled it out and saw it was a page from a child's jotter with the title 'The End of the World'. The rest was ash and crumbled in her hand.

*

When Peggy arrived for work at the music shop in Royal Avenue, her boss, Mr Goldstein, was outside on a stepladder, putting the finishing touches to the sign he had painted on the window. 'Business As Usual' it proclaimed and underneath 'No Bomb Damage Here.'

'Peggy, at last! Where have you been?' His Polish accent thickened with agitation. 'There is dust everywhere in the shop. Esther has made a start mopping the linoleum, so make sure you walk on the newspaper. You must dust all the gramophones, wirelesses and instruments.'

'Mr Goldstein, there are no buses or trams running – I've had to walk all the way here. There's so much bomb damage, rubble in the streets, roads closed because of ruptured gas mains, and water everywhere. I could do with a sit down and a cup of tea before I start.'

'Humph … you may as well make one for Esther and me too.'

In the kitchen at the back of the shop Peggy put the kettle on. She removed the flat brown shoes she had borrowed from her mother to walk to work and replaced them with her black patent high heels. In the mirror over the sink she powdered her nose, and added another layer of lipstick. She smiled at her reflection, but her mood was no lighter by the time she had made the tea and carried it into the shop.

'It doesn't help when you're dog-tired after being up half the night with these false air raid warnings. I'm sure the Germans have done their worst here, they must have plenty of other cities to bomb.'

Goldstein reached for his tea and shook his head. 'No, they will be back for sure, Hitler has unfinished business in Belfast. Tuesday night's raid was bad, but he will regard it as a failure.'

'Failure! With all that damage, all those people killed?'

'It wasn't what they came for,' Goldstein explained. 'They meant to destroy the shipyard and aircraft factory, instead they lost their bearings and bombed people's homes. You mark my words, they will be back.'

'So we're expected to spend every night under the stairs freezing in the pitch black and listening to air-raid sirens?'

'Either that, or you could go into the hills like half the population are doing.'

'I don't think I'll be climbing the Cave Hill to sleep in a ditch. I'd sooner take my chances with the Germans.' She wiped the smear of lipstick off her cup and smiled. 'Well, at least we've got some concerts to look forward to. I can't wait to get rehearsing and performing again. Lisburn Barracks next, isn't it?'

'I'm afraid not, Peggy, I've had a phone call cancelling all concerts for the military. They've been put to work clearing unsafe buildings and I doubt civilian concerts would be well attended while there's a threat of more bombing. I am sorry to say I have no idea when there will be another Barnstormers' concert.'

'Well, that's just great. As if the bombing wasn't bad enough, now we've got to live a miserable, boring existence as well!'

'Now, now Peggy, be thankful that you and your family are safe and that you've still got a roof over your head, not to mention a job. Speaking of which …' Goldstein nodded towards the shelf of wirelesses covered in dust.

Peggy rolled her eyes, piled the cups and saucers on the tray, marched into the kitchen and dumped them in the sink.

The motorbike, driven by a young man in an air force uniform and with a pretty dark-haired girl riding pillion, pulled up outside Short Brothers and Harland aircraft factory. The girl, dressed in a pair of men's trousers, jumped off the bike, pulled out a headscarf and in one long fluid movement bent over and wrapped it turban-like around her head. Neither of them spoke. She looked over her shoulder at the workers swarming through the factory gates and absent-mindedly twisted the rings on her finger. He caught her hand and whispered in her ear. She smiled and he pulled her close to kiss her goodbye.

Irene passed through the factory gates feeling she'd rather be anywhere but there and praying she would get through the day. She had no desire to speak to anyone and she certainly didn't want to deal with any questions. She'd been off work less than a week and during that time Belfast had been bombed, her best friend had been killed and she'd married a man she loved with all her heart even though she hardly knew him.

She clocked in and went through to the hangar. Robert McVey, his face pale and anxious, had obviously been looking out for her. 'Glad you're back, Irene. You heard about Myrtle?'

She held back the tears. 'I heard. She didn't turn up to the wedding and someone came to tell us that she'd been killed in the bombing. When's the funeral?'

'Don't know.'

'But surely– '

'There's a bit of a problem,' Robert looked down and scuffed his boot across the floor as he spoke. 'You know she went to stay with some cousins in Thorndyke Street after her house was bombed last month? Well, the cousins' house took a direct hit this time. Everyone inside was killed. When they brought the bodies out, there was no one there who could identify her.' He raised his head and saw Irene's puzzled look. 'The unclaimed bodies were removed, but we don't know where they've been taken.'

'Well, if it isn't Miss Skivvy, or should I call you Mrs Skivvy now?' The foreman stood in his office doorway and sniggered at his own joke. 'Come 'ere, there's someone I want ye to meet.' Without a word, Irene followed him.

A young woman dressed in heavy blue trousers and a green checked shirt was standing in the office. Her hair was a mass of red curls and she towered over Irene.

'Hi, how'ya doin'?' She shook Irene's hand.

'This is Miss Macy. You'll be looking after her today, showin' her the ropes, so to speak.'

'It's Macy, just Macy, an' I'm guessin' you're Irene.'

'You're American?'

'Well spotted, accent throws a lot of people.'

'Not me, I've watched enough American films to recognise it anywhere. Are you going to be skivvying with me?'

The foreman interrupted. 'Not this one. She won't be sweeping floors; she's something different altogether,' and he sniggered again.

Macy ignored him. 'I'm a riveter. Gonna be workin' on the Stirling bombers.'

4

'A riveter?' Irene was amazed. 'But you're a woman!'

'Certainly am. How about that … a riveter *and* a woman?' and she threw back her head and laughed.

The foreman ignored her and went on, 'Yer to take Miss Macy to the stores to pick up her tools, ye can show her around a bit too, then she's to come back here and report to Robert. Tea and lunch breaks, take her to the canteen.' He looked straight at Macy and added, 'She's to sit with the women.'

On the way to the stores, Irene had a job to keep up with her charge. As she strode through the factory, the workers stopped what they were doing to stare.

'Do you always move this fast?' Irene shouted as Macy ran up the stairs two at a time.

'I do when there's a job to be done. Heard you lost four planes in the raid Tuesday night, saw their carcasses out near the runway first thing, damn shame!'

'Is that why you're over here? To help us?'

'It's one reason.'

'But America isn't in the war. Why would you risk coming over here?'

'Maybe I'm looking for some adventure.' She laughed again. 'I heard so much about Ireland when I was growing up, figured I'd come take a look. Managed to get cheap passage on a convoy; guess most of the traffic goes the other way.'

'Have you family in Belfast?'

'Don't know, might have. My grandmother used to talk about how her family came over from Ireland.'

'So where are you living?'

'Checked into the YWCA, just next to City Hall, for now, same as I did in New York when I worked there. Good way to meet people.'

Irene's eyes widened. 'You've been to New York city? What was it like?'

'Like Belfast, only a thousand times bigger, on a river close to the sea. You've seen it in the movies, right?'

'Yes, but …'

'Well, that's just what it's like, only bigger and noisier and more

5

people than you can imagine.'

The store man, usually miserable without two words to say to anyone, was unexpectedly talkative. 'You're that Yank girl, aren't ye? Got your stuff ready here.'

Macy looked through the canvas tool bag and picked out the hammer, weighing it in her hand. 'Hey, what's this, a joke?'

'It's the lightest one we've got. You'll just have to manage the best ye can.'

She tossed it back on the counter. 'Then you'd better get me the heaviest.'

Robert was waiting for them when they got to the hangar where there seemed to be a surprising number of men standing around taking a breather. There were a few wolf whistles and someone shouted, 'Howdy, pardner'.

'Sorry about that,' Robert looked embarrassed.

Macy shrugged. 'It happens, don't worry. If they're still doing it in a couple a days, I'll be surprised.'

'I'd better get back to work,' said Irene. 'See you at tea break, Macy.'

'Sure thing.'

As Irene walked away there was a noise behind her and she turned to see Macy running up the ladder and disappearing into the Stirling bomber to the sound of clapping.

Every day, as Pat Goulding arrived for work at Stormont, home of the Northern Ireland government, she felt her heart lift at the sight of the elegant white building on the crest of the hill, surrounded by sweeping lawns. But this morning she was surprised to see a small crowd outside watching workmen erecting scaffolding across the façade.

'What's going on?' Pat asked a woman she knew by sight.

'They're going to paint it with pitch and cow dung. Why on earth would they want to do that, do you think?'

Pat could guess why and what's more she had a good idea who had given the order.

Inside the building she made her way to the offices of the

Ministry of Public Security where several of the clerks in the air-raid precautions department were already hard at work gathering information on Tuesday's raid and writing reports. The deadline for the comprehensive report of bomb damage and defence response was fast approaching and Pat got to work quickly – collating, reading, précising reports from Air Raid Precautions posts around the city. The minister expected the report by two o'clock, which meant William Kennedy, his permanent secretary, would want to see her draft before noon. William Kennedy ... Pat closed her eyes and allowed herself a few moments to remember the touch of his hand, the smile just for her and the joy of singing with him at Irene's wedding. Was that only two days ago?

At 11.30 a.m. precisely she knocked on his door. He was sitting behind the mahogany desk, head in his hands. He looked up as she came in and attempted a smile. She saw at once that he was exhausted, knew instinctively that he would have been all over the city to see the damage for himself and would have listened to numerous horrific accounts, all the time feeling responsible and desperate to make a difference. She had no doubt it was William who had ordered the camouflage of Stormont.

He took the report from her and scanned it quickly, but said nothing. Instead he went to the window and stared out over the immaculate lawns. Pat waited. When he finally spoke, she felt a stab of disappointment at his clipped tone.

'The prime minister is to make a statement about the state of emergency. Our priority is of course to restore normality – gas, electricity and water supplies' – he pointed at the report – 'but this will also help us understand how people reacted to the bombing. You've mentioned the fear felt by the children, so maybe it's time to try another evacuation programme to get them out of harm's way. Then there's the worry of thousands of people sleeping rough every night.'

Pat was surprised. 'We had no reports of such huge numbers.'

'You only have the numbers of those sheltering in designated buildings – church halls and the like. Those people are the lucky ones. The cumulative damage to housing equates to twenty thousand homeless and add to that the people leaving their homes to spend the night in the hills because they're terrified of being bombed.' He managed a fleeting smile and his voice softened, 'I wanted to speak to you about that.' He indicated that she should sit down. 'I'm getting together a group of people to go up the Cave Hill tomorrow night to find out about conditions and to talk to people about why they're not going to the shelters. I'd really like you to come with us.'

The thought of being out at night with William both excited and disturbed Pat. 'I'm not sure about–'

'Pat, I've always valued your common sense when it comes to understanding why people react as they do.' There was a pleading in his voice she'd never heard before.

'But to be tramping around up there in the dark ...'

'There'll be six of us. I'm hoping three men and three women. I'm thinking the mothers with children might talk more freely to another woman.'

Pat bit her lip. His reasoning was sound, but what would her mother say about her being out all night?

William leaned across the desk. 'This is important work, Pat. The ministry needs information so we can make the right decisions about how to protect people. Please say you'll join us.'

Martha was in the front bedroom cleaning the inside of the windows when she caught sight of Betty Harper from next door leaving her house. Something about the way she was moving – head down, small quick steps and clearly out of breath – made Martha call out, 'Are you all right, Betty?' The woman stopped and looked around her. 'I'm up here,' shouted Martha. The look on her neighbour's upturned face sent a shiver through her. 'Wait there,' she called, 'I'm coming down.'

Up close, Martha could see Betty was struggling to catch her breath between sobs. Her hair hadn't been combed and she'd probably slept in her clothes. 'What on earth's the matter? Come inside.'

'I can't. I have to find my sister.'

Martha put an arm round Betty's shoulder. 'Sure come in for a minute and talk to me.'

Martha busied herself boiling the kettle and setting out the cups and saucers. 'Am I right in thinking you haven't eaten for a while?'

'Aye that's true enough, maybe not since yesterday afternoon.'

Martha set a plate of soda bread on the table. 'Help yourself, you'll be able to think better with something inside you.'

When she was calmer, Betty began to speak. 'After the raid Jack and I went to check on my sister and her family. The street was closed – they said it was a ruptured gas main, but we could see her house had been destroyed. One of the ARP men said the dead and casualties had been taken to hospital and everyone else had gone to church halls or relatives' – she blinked and brushed away the tears with the palm of her hand – 'so we went looking.' She paused, stared at her hands in her lap. A minute passed, Martha waited. 'I never dreamt there were such sights. We couldn't find her anywhere. Then we heard they'd set up temporary mortuaries in the swimming baths and we went there first thing …'

'And did you find your sister there?'

Betty shook her head. 'Jack's exhausted, he's having a lie down. I was just reading the paper and it says unclaimed bodies have been moved to St George's Market. There's a last chance to identify them before …' and she began to sob again.

'Is that where you were going?'

Betty nodded. 'I was, but I don't think I can face it. I know I have to go, if she's there I can't just leave her, but I'm so scared. I can't bear to see any more bodies …'

'Just you sit there while I wash my face and fetch my coat. Then we'll go and see if we can find your sister.'

St George's Market was a large red brick Victorian building at the end of May Street in the city centre. It was normally busy with people shopping for fruit and vegetables, meat and fish and household bits and pieces, but today there were no stallholders shouting their wares, no hum of conversations filtering through the wrought iron gates. There was only the sound of weeping and a stench that overpowered the smell of disinfectant.

Betty stopped suddenly. 'I can't go in there. I can't!' and she turned to walk away.

Martha caught her arm. 'Yes you can. Think about your sister. You're doing this for her.' Martha held out her hand and Betty gripped it tightly. 'We'll go in together and find the person in charge.'

Inside, the smell was unbearable. Martha felt in her pocket for a handkerchief and passed it to Betty. 'Put this over your nose.'

If anything, the sight that met them was worse than the smell – row after row of rough wooden coffins, maybe two hundred or more, many lidded, but some with their lids pushed to one side. A young man in a St John's Ambulance uniform directed them to the far end of the building where two men sat at a table taking details.

Martha was aware of Betty turning her head from side to side taking in the scene, one moment holding the handkerchief over her nose, the next using it to wipe her eyes. At the table, however, she seemed to regain some composure and gave details of her sister – address, age, physical description. They were assigned a Red Cross nurse who explained she would take them to view the remains along with a young man whose job it was to remove the coffin lids. Martha felt comforted by the calm presence of the nurse, a middle-aged woman like herself. 'I'll take you to the ladies who were found near your sister's house,' she said.

As the first lid was removed, Betty squeezed Martha's hand. Together they looked quickly at the body, before turning away to retch at the appalling sight.

'Is it your sister?' the nurse asked. Betty shook her head. 'Let's move on, then.'

Behind them, a man who was using a watering can to spray disinfectant joined their slow procession. Martha lost count of the number of bodies they saw. Eventually, their nurse suggested they stop for a few minutes and took them to a mobile canteen set up by the Salvation Army.

'I don't know how you can do this,' Martha said to the nurse.

'Someone has to,' her smile was kindness itself. 'But I'll tell you true, I was a nurse in the last war, served in France so I did, and

I never saw sights like this before. There are some girls, and boys too, from the St John's sent here to help and they don't last an hour. I shudder to think what memories they'll carry with them for the rest of their lives.'

'How long will the bodies be kept here?' asked Martha.

'Until Sunday, then they'll all be buried in a mass grave at the city cemetery,' she sighed. 'It'll be a long weekend.'

'Is it always nurses who take relatives around?'

'Mostly, but there are some volunteers, sympathetic people, you know.' Then with a wry smile she added, 'With a strong stomach!' The nurse tilted her head and looked at Martha. 'Somebody like you could do it.'

Martha shook her head. 'Oh no, I wouldn't be able to …' Her voice trailed off, she could say no more; the thought of the hideous bodies becoming familiar and of trying to console the inconsolable overwhelmed her.

'I'm sure you could. Why don't you think about it? We need all the help we can get.'

They sat a while and drank stewed tea from tin mugs and the nurse explained that there were some other bodies that could not be visually identified, though clothes or personal possessions found on the body might still provide a means of identifying them. 'Will we look for your sister among those people, Betty?' she asked.

Betty nodded. 'I've come this far and looked at all this. I'm not going to leave until I'm sure she's not here.' She turned to Martha, 'Will you stay with me?'

'Indeed I will.'

The unidentifiable remains were together in one corner of the market hall. To help with identification, these coffins had chalk markings on the lids listing possessions found on the body and within minutes they had found her. 'This is her,' Betty shouted. 'Apron, knitting, four needles, I know it's her!'

The lid was pushed back just enough to retrieve the personal effects. The apron and a scrap of knitting on four needles were put into Betty's hands. 'Yes, they're hers – best apron and socks in double rib, always double rib. Never got the hang of four needles myself, but she'd have a pair of socks done in an afternoon.'

'I'm glad you've found her.' The nurse put her arm around Betty. 'I'll write your sister's name on the lid and give you the coffin number. You'll be able to contact an undertaker now to arrange the funeral.'

'Excuse me,' said Martha, 'What does it say on this coffin here?'

'Oh that's an odd one, so it is. We were discussing it earlier. We think it says "taps stage costume" though what taps have to do with the stage …'

'Can you open it?'

The nurse pushed the lid to one side to reveal a woman's legs. Martha bent down and looked at the soles of the shoes. 'Taps,' she said. 'Tap shoes – see the metal tips on the toes and heels? She's a dancer. What's she wearing?'

The nurse pushed the lid a little more, revealing a dusty red taffeta skirt and the lower half of a white embroidered gypsy-style blouse. Martha stifled a cry.

'Do you know who it is?'

'Yes,' whispered Martha. 'It's Myrtle, my daughter's friend.'

Chapter 2

Martha took the large soup ladle from the hook at the side of the range and stirred the broth, making sure the pearl barley wasn't sticking to the bottom. The ham shank she'd used for stock had no meat to speak of on it, but the nourishment in the bone marrow would do them all good. That and the soda bread made from a bottle of soured milk. Waste not, want not.

Sheila was first home and rushed into the kitchen, threw her school bag on the floor and grabbed a glass from the cupboard. 'I'm dying for a drink.'

'The water's off again,' said Martha, 'and have you forgotten we've only to drink boiled water? There's a pan full in the back hallway, nice and cool out there.'

'That's just one more thing we've to thank the Germans for, is it?'

'Either that or typhoid, take your pick. Did you call at the McCracken's as you were bid?'

'Aye they're fine, but the bombs came close, only a couple of streets away. They've been busy cleaning the shop, getting it ready to reopen. I've to be there before eight. Saturday's always busy, but John says it could be heaving tomorrow because people will have

13

run out of food over the last few days with all that's happened.'

There was the rattle of the gate and Peggy and Pat came round the back of the house, arguing as usual.

'If Goldstein says there's going to be no more concerts, there's nothing we can do about it!'

'But he formed the Barnstormers to raise money for the war effort and to keep up morale,' Peggy snapped. 'That hasn't changed and, when you think about it, concerts are needed more than ever now.'

'And what did he say when you told him that?'

'He said I didn't understand. According to him, the military are too busy for concerts and everybody else just wants to hide under the stairs or up the mountain.'

'Well, there you are then!'

'You're home earlier than I expected,' said Martha, 'and in good humour I see.'

'There were buses running up the Oldpark Road,' said Pat. 'Packed, mind you, but we all squeezed on. What's for tea?'

'Broth.'

'Tell me you haven't put any of that barley in it,' said Peggy.

'It'll fill you up more.'

'No it won't.'

'Yes it will,' argued Martha.

'No it won't, because I'm not eating it!'

'Where's Irene?' asked Pat, changing the subject. 'She's coming home tonight, isn't she?'

'As far as I know, she and Sandy were leaving the hotel in Bangor early this morning and he was dropping her off at the factory before reporting for duty at his base.'

'She'll be really sad saying goodbye to Sandy, won't she?' said Sheila.

'I'd have thought that was obvious, seeing as they've only been married two days!' snapped Peggy.

'Not necessarily, she might be happy because she's back home with us.'

'What, back to no water, air raids every night and broth for tea!'

'Will you two stop bickering and let's have a quiet meal for a change,' said Martha as she served up the broth, pearl barley and all. They ate in silence for a while then Martha asked, 'What's the news from Stormont today, Pat?'

'You'll never believe it, but they're going to paint the building with pitch and cow dung!'

'What?'

'Aye, that beautiful white building.'

'Why would they do that?'

'Because it gleams in the moonlight and the Germans can use it to pinpoint anything they want to bomb.'

'It's a bit late now, isn't it?' laughed Peggy.

Pat gave her a withering look. 'They're doing it for the next time they come. The ministry's making plans to keep people safe.'

'Like I said, it's a bit late now!'

Pat ignored her and turned to Martha. 'We're going to try another evacuation programme – Sheila could get on it. I could put her name down if you like?'

'I don't know, Pat. Maybe she's better here with us than with strangers in the back of beyond.'

'Ach, Mammy, you're the one listens to the wireless: the Luftwaffe will be back any day now.' Pat was into her stride. 'We'll coordinate the evacuation at the ministry, the transport will be laid on and inspections made of those willing to take the children.'

There was a clatter of cutlery at the end of the table and Sheila was on her feet. 'I'm not a child, I'm fourteen and no one is going to tell me I have to leave my home! It's like we're giving into the Nazis. You're all going to stay here and so am I!'

Pat was about to answer, but Martha stopped her. 'Hold on a wee minute, Sheila, this isn't like it was before. Now there are bombs falling on us and there are hundreds being buried as we speak. Next week it could be thousands.'

'But, Mammy–'

'No, Sheila, this is something I'm going to have to think seriously about.'

They were just clearing the table when Irene came in. Martha could see she'd been crying, but the others didn't seem to notice as they plied her with questions about her trip to Bangor. Soon, she was telling them all about it.

'The weather was lovely and so was the hotel. We went swimming in Pickie Pool and dancing at Caproni's. They had a really good resident band with two girls singing all the latest songs. Some of them would be good for us to learn, if you could get the sheet music, Peggy.'

'You make a list of the titles and I'll see if we've got them in the shop.'

Martha disappeared into the kitchen and returned with Irene's tea on a tray. 'Now give her a chance to eat, will you?'

Peggy waited until Martha was back in the kitchen then said, 'You know, if Goldstein can't organise concerts, maybe we could sing in a dance hall.'

'No we couldn't. Those people are professional singers,' argued Pat. 'We're just amateurs.'

Peggy was affronted. 'Amateurs! We're not amateurs.' She turned to Irene and demanded, 'How good were those girls in Caproni's? They weren't better than us, were they?'

Irene paused, a piece of soda halfway to her mouth, and considered. 'They had style, you know, hair, make-up, beautiful dresses. They seemed to move very well; a bit like you'd see in a film.'

'Yes, yes,' Peggy interrupted, 'but what about the singing, the harmonies, the sound?'

'Well …' Irene returned the soda to the tray. Her sisters leaned forward in their seats.

'Well, were they or weren't they?' shouted Peggy.

'What?'

'Better singers than us?'

Irene laughed, 'No, they weren't a patch on us!'

The whoops and cheers brought Martha from the kitchen. 'Bless us all!' she said. 'What on earth are you about now?'

'Nothing,' said Peggy calmly, 'we're just very happy Irene's home.'

Later, as they sat in the front room with the blackout curtains drawn, Martha told them of her visit to the market with Betty and her belief that Myrtle was there.

'Right enough,' said Peggy, 'the Templemore Tappers were dressed in gypsy blouse costumes for their final dance routine and we all left the concert without changing because of the air-raid warning. So, unless there's another member of the Tappers missing, it probably is Myrtle.'

'God love her,' Pat was close to tears. 'We can't leave her there. We need to tell her family.'

Irene, who had listened to the news about Myrtle with her head bowed, spoke softly, 'I'll talk to Robert McVey at work; he's in touch with her family. What do they need to do?'

'They should go to the market tomorrow and ask to see the unidentifiable bodies—'

'Unidentifiable? What does that mean?' The panic rose in Irene's voice.

Martha realised her mistake. 'No, no it's all right, it's all right.'

But Irene was on her feet. 'I'll go there now! Sure, I'll know if it's her.'

Martha caught her arm before she reached the door. 'You mustn't go! You don't need to.'

'Yes I do. I can tell them it's her.'

'There's no need. Just make sure her family come to the market tomorrow and I'll be there waiting for them. Tell them I'll stay with them until they're sure they've found Myrtle.'

Irene looked puzzled. 'Mammy, why would you be at the market?'

'Because … because I've volunteered to help them with the relatives.'

'Why would you do that?'

It was a question Martha had been asking herself all afternoon and she struggled to explain. 'I was asked and I couldn't say no. Somebody has to …' Now, looking at Irene's tear-stained face, Martha knew she'd made the right decision.

'Irene, why don't you go to bed now? You're exhausted, love. I'll be with Myrtle tomorrow until her family comes, so don't you worry. Maybe we should all go up and get a bit of sleep, for there'll surely be another air-raid warning tonight and when it happens I want all of you down here under the stairs and that includes you, Peggy – no staying in your bed like you usually do.'

*

17

Pat couldn't sleep. There had been no opportunity to talk to her mother about the plan to spend the night on the Cave Hill and maybe that was as well, because she couldn't trust herself to explain it without being embarrassed. She could always wait until tomorrow night then simply announce where she was going, but what if her sisters were there? The last thing she wanted was to be teased about being out at night with William.

She waited until she was sure Irene was asleep then slipped out of bed. The light was still on in the front bedroom. She knocked and went in. Martha was sitting up in bed, totting up the week's expenditure in her housekeeping book.

'Mammy, can I ask you something?'

'There's no harm in asking,' said Martha, but something in Pat's tone put her on her guard.

'There's a team from the ministry going to talk to the people spending their nights up the Cave Hill and they want me to be a part of it.'

'Is that so?' Martha waited for the rest.

'They're going up there tomorrow night and I wanted to ask you if I could go?'

'And who exactly are "they"?'

'There'll be six of us – three men and three women.'

Martha raised an eyebrow. 'Oh aye, and is William Kennedy one of the men?'

Pat felt the blush burn her face and bent her head. 'He is, Mammy.'

The seconds ticked by, Pat looked up. Her mother was staring straight ahead. Eventually she spoke. 'I don't like it, Pat. William Kennedy is a good man, but even good men …'

Pat blushed again.

God help me, thought Martha. It was easy when they were wee girls and she knew where the boundaries were. Was she being unreasonable, unfair?

'You like William, don't you?'

Pat nodded and bit her lip.

'Has he said anything about how he feels?' Pat didn't answer. 'I'll take that as a "no" then. Look, Pat, I don't want you hurt.' Martha struggled to find the right words to express her fears. 'You mustn't do anything foolish, but you know that, don't you?'

'It's important I do this so the ministry can find out why people go up there. You're going to the market to help – it's the same thing.'

Martha sighed. 'You see there on the dressing table … the big hatpin? Get that and put it in your lapel when you go tomorrow night and remember to keep your wits about you.'

Pat laughed. 'A hatpin?'

'Aye,' Martha could see the humour of it. 'Well it's better than nothing and make sure you put plenty on you, it'll be cold up there.'

Saturday morning dawned grey and wet and Peggy was soaked by the time she arrived at the music shop. She would be on her own all day because Goldstein and his niece Esther did not work on the Jewish Sabbath. Peggy hoped that, with a bit of luck, the weather might even keep the customers away, giving her the time to set her plan in motion.

She began with Irene's list of songs. They had three of the records in stock, and sheet music for the others. By the time she'd played the records a few times she had the tunes in her head and sat at her favourite upright piano and picked out the melodies. She had been taught to read music by Martha, but preferred to play by ear – listening and playing over and over until she had it exactly right. The few customers who ventured into the shop were given brisk service and little in the way of pleasantries since Peggy's head was filled with the songs and the harmonies needed for three voices.

Goldstein expected her to work through lunch, taking a short break only when there were no customers, but today at one o'clock she hung up the closed sign, pulled the blinds and locked the door behind her. The rain had stopped and a watery April sun peeped from behind the clouds as she walked up Donegall Place to Robinson and Cleaver's department store. She went straight to the first floor and scanned the signs for the one that read 'Ladies' Cocktail Dresses'.

Style, she told herself, that's what we need.

She went through the racks at speed, having in her mind something she'd seen in a Bette Davis film: slim shape, with a scooped, off-the-shoulder neckline. And there it was … the colour of kingfishers, it caught the light and shimmered first blue, then green. On a stage under spotlights the colour would dance. She headed for the fitting room, curtly dismissing the salesgirl's offer of help.

The dress fitted her like a glove. She held her hair up and turned from side to side seeing herself utterly changed from every perspective. She stepped back from the mirror and moved to the rhythm of the song she'd had in her head all morning. Perfect. The price, of course, was ridiculous, two weeks' wages for the dress and they needed three. No matter. Up Royal Avenue she marched and into the fabric shop to search through the dress patterns. The shape of this one, the neckline of that, and maybe some added darts at the waist. Yes, she could see it clearly. She bought the two Butterwick patterns and wandered around the shop looking at bolts of cloth. There was a display of shot silk draped over mannequins. A quick calculation told her the material for each dress would cost one weeks' wage. All she had to do was find the money.

The doors of the Plaza Ballroom were chained up, but Peggy was undeterred. At the back of the building she found an open door and three men sitting on upturned beer crates playing cards.

'Y'all right there, love?' asked one of them, hat tipped back and a cigarette hanging from his mouth.

'I'm looking for the owner.'

'You wouldn't catch the owner in this place,' he laughed. 'What is it ye want?'

'I've come about a job.'

'Have ye now?' He stood up and flicked his cigarette out into the street and nodded towards a dark corridor for her to follow him. Peggy didn't hesitate.

She'd been to the Plaza once before, to the Christmas Eve dance in 1939, and she remembered it as an elegant ballroom hung with garlands and huge paper bells, with a mirrored ball reflecting the spotlights that swept the room. She remembered, too, the romance of it, dancing all night with Harry Ferguson, the touch of his lips, the words he whispered. Now Harry was gone, away to England to join the army, leaving her and his debts behind. She pushed the image away.

The man led her to a double door and ushered her in. She could see immediately how run-down everything was: paint peeling from the ceiling; dirty, brocade-covered chairs; a stale smell in the air.

'Somebody here wants a word with ye, Devlin.'

The man was behind the bar with his back to them, stacking bottles of lemonade on the shelves. 'I'm busy,' he shouted over his shoulder.

Peggy stepped forward. 'I can see that,' she said. 'In fact, I've not got a lot of time myself so I'll get straight to the point. I'm here to enquire whether you're looking for new resident singers for the band.'

'Nope.'

'I think you'll find that the act I'm speaking about – they're called the Golden Sisters – could really add some style to the Plaza.'

He carried on stacking bottles. 'Got all the style we need.'

'They've all the latest songs from America in their repertoire.'

'I'm not interested.'

'Well you should be!' Peggy raised her voice.

The man turned and stared at her. 'What do you want?'

'I told you. I want the Golden Sisters to be resident singers with the Plaza band. We're very good. You should hire us.'

'Listen, love, I don't need any singers.' He came out from behind the bar and walked slowly round Peggy, looking her up and down. 'But I'm short of a cloakroom girl, since the last one took fright of the bombs and went back home over the border.'

'Do I look like a cloakroom girl?'

'Well you could if you tried.'

For a split second Peggy thought about storming out, but instead she asked, 'Would you be needing a pianist at all?'

James Devlin shook his head in disbelief. 'Are you always like this?'

'Like what?'

'Pushy, persistent.'

Peggy looked him in the eye. 'If you never ask, you never get.'

'You've certainly asked, but I'm telling you I don't need singers or a pianist. I need a cloakroom girl for tonight. The pay's five shillings and, if you're a bit nicer to the customers than you've been to me, you might get a few tips as well.'

Peggy opened her mouth to argue, closed it again and thought about the five shillings. 'What time do I start?'

'Right, I think you're all set,' said John McCracken when Sheila arrived at the shop on Saturday morning. 'I've brought a couple of sacks of potatoes round the front. It seems like that's all some people are eating these days, so you should sell plenty. Now there are two boxes of Armagh apples fresh in, so try and sell as many of those as you can. I don't mind if people buy them in ones or twos, as long as they go. The carrots are on their last legs, so drop the price after dinner. If anybody asks for tick refer them to Aggie. I don't mind if they're regular customers, but I'll not give credit to people we don't know.'

'That's grand, Uncle John. Are you going to be away all day?'

'Lord only knows. The situation's desperate and they've asked our group to work on the Unity Street ARP post. You know, the one that took a direct hit. Thirteen good men lost, some of them still unaccounted for. We'll be shifting rubble 'til the light goes at least.'

'But Aggie'll be working with me, won't she?'

'She'll do her best, but Aunt Hannah hasn't been that good these last few days. Had us up all hours of the night, thinking it was morning and asking for her breakfast.'

'Still a bit confused is she?'

'A bit? Lord save us, some days she thinks I'm her father and other days she doesn't know me at all and wants me out of her house. I tell you it's the strangest illness I ever saw.'

'Uncle John ...' something in Sheila's tone made him stop stripping the wilted leaves from the cauliflowers. 'Mammy's been talking about sending me away to the country.'

'What, evacuated?'

Sheila explained about Pat wanting to put her name on the

22

ministry's list. 'I don't want to live with strangers. Will you tell Mammy I'm needed in the shop?' she pleaded. 'I know she'll listen to you.'

'Now, now, young Sheila, your mammy will want to do the right thing. She'll think long and hard before she makes a decision. Remember the scriptures: "Honour thy father and thy mother." You know what that means?'

'Aye, I've got to do what she tells me.'

'Precisely. Those bombs the other night were the work of the devil …' John shook his head to clear it of the sights he had seen. 'God forbid, you're caught up in anything like that.' He arranged the cauliflowers in a pyramid, closed his penknife and almost smiled.

'What is it, Uncle John?'

'I'm minded of a time when I was close to your age, the summer of 1900. There was trouble on the streets for a while then and our mother sent us away to some cousins in Cavan. Ha! Thought we'd landed in the back of beyond. The girls cried themselves to sleep every night, wanting home.' He paused a moment, remembering. Sheila waited. Eventually he blinked a few times and said quietly, 'Happiest months of my life.'

He was suddenly animated. 'Come with me!' he shouted and Sheila followed him through the shop where Aggie was sweeping the floor.

'Hello Sheila, how are you?'

'No time for niceties, Aggie,' shouted John over his shoulder, 'we're on a mission!' Sheila followed him through the back kitchen …

'Hello Father,' shouted Aunt Hannah.

… out into the yard. 'Wait here,' said John, and he disappeared into the shed.

It sounded like he was wrestling in an ironmonger's and after a few minutes the door opened and a large wicker basket appeared followed by a pair of handlebars.

'What do you think?' John sat astride the delivery bike, his ARP uniform covered in cobwebs.

'I don't understand, Uncle John.'

'When I was sent to Cavan I learned to ride a bike and spent all summer riding the country lanes. It was such an adventure.'

Sheila walked round the bike. The tyres were flat, the saddle was mildewed, and the black paintwork was dusty – but she saw the possibilities.

At seven o'clock precisely Peggy walked into the entrance hall of the Plaza on Chichester Street, past the ticket booth and the cloakroom and straight into the ballroom. It was transformed from the shabby, draughty hall she'd seen a few hours earlier. Wall lights cast a soft golden glow and, from the ceiling, the mirrored ball reflected fragments of light that chased each other around the room. The stage was hung with red velvet curtains and the band was tuning up.

'You're here then, cloakroom girl.'

'My name's Peggy. I said I'd be here, didn't I?'

James Devlin came out from behind the bar. 'Glad to see you've reported for duty looking smart.'

Peggy's eyes widened at the sight of him in a tuxedo with a white dress shirt and black bow tie. His hair was brushed back and gleaming. 'I'd say the same about you, but you're a bit over-dressed for a barman, aren't you?'

He raised an eyebrow. 'I could be the barman. In fact, as I'm the manager, I could do most of the jobs here.' There was an edge to his voice.

'Peggy gave him her brightest smile, 'Would that include cloakroom girl, Devlin?'

'Of course.'

'What about pianist or resident singer?' It was Peggy's turn to raise an eyebrow.

He looked at his watch. 'I think it's time you started work,' and he walked away calling over his shoulder, 'and only my friends call me Devlin. You just call me Boss.'

One of the barmaids who had experience of the cloakroom showed Peggy how the ticket system worked. 'You should be able to manage on your own. We haven't had that many in since the bombing; people are afraid it'll happen again, I suppose.'

For the next two hours, Peggy felt she was rushed off her feet. Goodness knows what it's like when it's busy, she thought. Then almost instantly there was no one wanting to check in a coat. On cue, the barmaid returned to relieve her. 'Nothing much happens for the next hour until people start to leave, so you can have a bit of a break. Get yourself a drink at the bar.' She nodded at the saucer on the cloakroom counter. 'Take your tips. You've done quite well there.'

The band was playing a waltz in a lively enough style, but the drummer was a fraction off the beat. Peggy bought a lemonade and sat at the bar watching the dancers move round the floor. The singer was introduced; a thickset man in a dinner suit that had seen better days. The opening bars played and she instantly recognised 'Let's Put Out the Lights (and Go to Sleep)'. Might as well do, she thought, because there's no life in his delivery – another two-a-penny crooner. The second song was a quick step, 'I Get a Kick Out of You', but his phrasing wasn't quite right …

'Excuse me, would you like to dance?'

He was a sailor, not that old, not that tall, but she took his hand. He was a passable dancer who concentrated on his steps, rather than his partner, but she didn't mind. When the music ended, he thanked her and moved away. There was a tap on her shoulder and she turned, smiling, to face her next partner.

'What do you think you're doing?' Devlin's eyes were blazing. 'I'm not paying you to pick up men!'

'I'm not picking up men. I'm on my break.'

'No, you're on my time and the rule is no mixing with customers!'

'You didn't tell me that!'

'I'd have thought it was obvious.'

Peggy could have raised her voice and made a scene, lost a job she didn't really want, but she was so struck by the squareness of Devlin's jaw and the cleft in his chin … He really had the most beautiful face …

'I'm sorry, Boss. It won't happen again.'

'Aye well, it had better not.'

'I'll get back to work,' she whispered.

Martha knew that she smelled of death even though she had ceased to be aware of it hours ago. All day she had met relatives, shown them decaying bodies, comforted them and cried with them until the light began to fade and they closed and locked the doors of St George's Market. It had been the bleakest day of her life, but she was glad she'd volunteered, not least because she would be able to reassure Irene that Myrtle's body had been claimed by her family. Before she left she agreed to return the following morning, the last day the unclaimed bodies would be on view. Don't think about it until then, she told herself, and hoped that the walk up to McCracken's shop on Manor Street would clear her mind and freshen her clothes.

Sheila was serving a customer when she arrived. 'We'll be closing in a minute, Mammy. Go through to the back, Aggie's in there with Aunt Hannah.'

'How is she today?'

'Ach, she's had us in stitches. Keeps calling me Martha, so she'll be really confused when she sees you, but sure she's happy enough.'

'Well, that's all that matters.'

'Oh, and she's going dancing later.'

'Dancing?'

Sheila giggled. 'You'll see!'

Martha went through the chenille curtain into the cosy kitchen that also served as a living room. The McCrackens were her cousins on her mother's side; the three siblings John, Aggie and Grace had never married, nor had their elderly Aunt Hannah. Aggie was at the sink, engulfed in steam, draining a pan. 'You're just in time for something to eat, Martha, if you're partial to wilting cauliflower and plenty of it.'

From behind the door, hidden from view, Aunt Hannah shouted, 'What's that awful smell?'

'Cauliflower!' shouted Aggie.

'I think it might be me,' said Martha, peeking round the door.

Then, catching sight of the old woman, her jaw dropped, 'What on earth!'

Aggie, still clutching the huge steaming pan, started to laugh. Sheila came in, looked from her mother's shocked face to Aunt Hannah's, which was made up like a Hollywood starlet, and howled with laughter.

Martha had to smile. 'What's going on?'

Neither Aggie nor Sheila could compose themselves long enough to explain. Then Martha noticed the rows of beads round Aunt Hannah's neck, the jangling bangles on her wrists and the dandelion corsage on the shabby ballgown. By now Aunt Hannah was laughing too, looking from one face to the other. Martha resisted the urge to join in. 'Is she …'

'Yes, I'm going dancing,' and the old lady smiled in delight showing her false teeth smeared with bright red lipstick.

'Sheila, open the window, will you, and let that smell out while I get the tea on the table,' said Aggie, 'and, Martha, get the herrings out of the oven, they'll take away the taste of the cauliflower.'

Around the table, Aggie explained Aunt Hannah's appearance. 'She thinks she's eighteen again. Talked this morning about someone called George taking her to a dance and how she needed to get ready. Before I know it, she's found that old dress in the bottom of the wardrobe and, would you believe it, a pair of gutties for her feet! I ask you, what can you do? When she appeared with the lipstick in her hand, Sheila put it on her and a wee bit on her cheeks. The oul dear's had a great day. Mind you, we'd better get her shipshape before John gets home. You know what he's like. He'll be reading us the story of Jezebel and asking awkward questions about where she got the lipstick!'

They were doing the dishes when there was a knock on the shop door. 'Away out, Sheila, and tell them we're closed,' said Aggie. 'You can't even get your tea in peace these days.'

Seconds later, the sound of Aunt Hannah's delighted laugh and clapping broke the silence and Aggie and Martha turned from the sink to see Sheila had returned, followed by a portly young man with a florid face. 'This is Reverend Taylor from St Mary's up the road. He's invited us to a prayer meeting tomorrow to raise our spirits.'

'George!' shrieked Aunt Hannah and with the support of her stick she was on her feet reaching for him. 'I'm all ready to go.'

He took a step backwards. 'But it's not 'til tomorrow.'

But it was too late. Aunt Hannah began to sing 'Come into the garden, Maud' and stepped forward. One hand gripped his shoulder, the other took his hand and she waltzed him round the room.

Someone should have stepped in and rescued him, but none of them had the heart to upset Aunt Hannah. Besides, he'd said he wanted to raise their spirits.

Chapter 3

Pat stood in front of the mirror and held her navy dress with the sailor collar against her, then threw it on the bed and picked up the floral with the three-quarter sleeves. If she was going to be spending several hours with William she needed to look her best, but what exactly was suitable attire for tramping over a hillside in the middle of the night? Get a grip, she told herself, it isn't a date, it's work and you'll be out in the freezing cold.

She eventually settled on her green woollen dress; it was old but warm, and chances were nobody would see it under her coat. She took her chrysanthemum scarf, went to put it on her head, changed her mind, slipped it round her neck and arranged her thick auburn hair over her shoulders. Finally, she stepped into her well-polished, sensible lace-ups.

As arranged she walked to the end of her road where Joanmount Gardens met the Oldpark Road. William, who was already there, leaned over to open the car door and, without any greeting, he explained, 'I thought we'd drive up the hill part of the way and watch the people go past, see what their mood is and what sort of things they've brought with them. Then later we'll follow them up on foot and talk to them. I've thought of some questions to ask …'

He handed her a sheet of typed paper.

'Where are the others?' Pat asked.

'Others?'

'You said there were six of us.'

'There are, but you and I are doing the Cave Hill and the other two couples have gone up the Black Mountain and the hills behind Holywood … that way we'll cover the main areas of high ground around the city.'

Pat was thrown by his use of the word 'couples'. 'Oh, I didn't know.'

'It's not a problem is it? This is an official survey on behalf of the ministry. What we discover tonight will be part of a formal government report.'

'No, it's not a problem.' Pat stared out the window, uncertain whether to feel relieved or snubbed.

Beyond Ballysillan, on a lane Pat recognised as Buttermilk Loney, the land began to rise steeply and William stopped the car and reversed into the entrance of a field. Was it really over a year since she was last up here? She'd been sledging with her sisters when Jimmy McComb, in a fit of jealousy, had told her that William was a married man. She remembered the disappointment and distress she'd felt when she had realised how much she loved William. So much had happened since then: Jimmy was dead, killed at Dunkirk, and William's 'wife' turned out to be his sister. Even so, nothing had come of their relationship. William was a work colleague and it seemed that was all he would ever be.

They watched the setting sun disappear behind the mountain and as the twilight gathered, William broke the silence. 'Do you remember the first time we sang together?'

Pat detected the change in his voice, no longer the senior civil servant speaking to one of his clerks. 'The duet from *La Bohème*, she said softly. He was quiet for a while and Pat wondered if, like her, he was recalling the tingling excitement of expressing such passion.

'Pat, I'm glad it's just you and me together here tonight. Every day there's so much to be done, isn't there? Sometimes I can't help feeling that I've failed. Those people who've died … if I'd been able to get more shelters or searchlights, they might still be here …'

'You mustn't think that. No one could've done more than you.'

'But Pat, sometimes I wish I could shut it all out just for a while to think about other things ... like music ... and you.'

His face was close to hers and she saw the softness in his eyes and the line of his jaw that she was desperate to touch ... his face moved closer. His lips hesitated above hers and she closed her eyes, a kiss ... so simple, so sweet. He moved back and looked at her in wonder, reached out and took a strand of her hair, caressed it, let it fall and kissed her again.

He held her tight and her heart beat faster. She felt his breath in her ear as he whispered, 'We have to make time for each other. I need to be with you.'

A sudden noise made them jump. A boy of six or seven was kicking a stone up the lane. He bent to pull up his socks then noticed the car and stood watching them. He was joined by a woman with a baby in a shawl balanced on her hip and an older woman carrying blankets.

'Our first arrivals, I think.' William moved away from her, business-like once more. 'A mother, two children and probably the grandmother – no man at all.' He turned to Pat, 'Would you say they looked distressed or frightened?'

'They look like they're wondering what we're doing here,' and truth was she beginning to wonder the same, but by then William was already scribbling down notes.

A man went past with a handcart containing an old woman who was sitting on a chair, rag rug over her knees, nursing a clock; a woman pushing a Tan-Sad with three small sleeping children inside; two young men dragging a mattress behind them; endless weary people, backs bent into the climb with blankets under their arms or on their backs.

A grey pock-marked moon hung low in the sky when William eventually put away his notes. 'I think it's time we followed them up the hill. You remember the sort of questions to ask?' Pat nodded. 'Now we'll stay together as much as we can, but you try to get the women to talk to you.'

On the higher ground, the air was chilly and Pat was glad of her warm dress and coat. Within five hundred yards they came to the first small encampment.

'We'll start here,' William whispered. 'I'll explain who we are.'

Pat could make out a family group, the mother and father, similar in age to her and William, and two, no, three children – the youngest, a baby, held close to the woman's breast.

'Good evening,' William held out his hand to the father who didn't take it. 'We're from Stormont, Ministry of Public Security, trying to find out what conditions are like up here and, er, we'd like to ask why you've chosen to spend the night out of doors.'

The man looked at him as though he were mad. 'Stormont ye say? Wantin' to know why we're here? That's a good un.' The man stood up, moved closer and William instinctively took a step back, almost fell, then righted himself. 'If you'd been to Duncairn Gardens and stood on the pile of rubble that was our home, ye'd not be askin' such bloody stupid questions.'

'You were bombed out, were you? Why didn't you go to one of the emergency shelters set up in schools and church halls.'

The man shook his head. 'Ye've no idea, have ye? Them places is full to burstin'. An' every night the air-raid warnin', frightnin' the wife an' weans.' His voice rose and he stabbed a finger at the city below. 'Away back to bloody Stormont and tell those bastards we're livin' hand to mouth, worse than gypsies we are!' and he turned away, shoulders heaving.

Pat could sense that William was shaken as he took her by the arm and they followed the path further up the hill. In a clearing, a group of about twenty people of all ages were sitting around a small campfire and children were running in and out of the trees. There was the smell of meat cooking. William touched Pat's arm and nodded towards a group of women chatting. She moved closer, her heart pounding. What if they were angry too? She thought of her mother and Sheila who, only a few nights before at the height of the raid, had climbed this hill to get away from the bombs. If they were here now, how would she approach them? They would be very wary of a government employee, but she knew they would welcome someone from a church concerned about their welfare.

Instinctively, she went over to a woman close to Martha's age who was with two young girls. 'Hello, I'm Pat from the Cliftonville Church. There's a group of us who've come up here to find out how we can help people like yourselves. Have you been bombed out?'

The woman moved over and invited Pat to share her blanket. 'No, praise be to God, we were lucky; three streets away was flattened.' She swept her hand to take in the group, 'We're all neighbours; we know it could be us next time. Why sit there waiting for bombs to drop on ye, when ye could be up here out of harm's way?'

'And what do you bring up with you?'

'Ach blankets, a few bits an' pieces – personal, ye know – and a bite to eat and drink.'

'So you have all you need?'

'I wouldn't say that! If it rains we'll be soaked, no doubt, and to tell ye the truth there's not much food at all in the shops. My man's still workin' an' he leaves here at six an' walks to work wi' nothin' in him.'

'So some shelter and warm food is what's needed, you think?'

The woman laughed. 'Can't see the WRVS setting up a mobile canteen, or Belfast Corporation puttin' up tents, can you?'

'So you stay up here all night?'

'We do, but there's some of them wait 'til two or three in the morning and, if there hasn't been an air-raid warning by then, they start makin' their way home.'

Pat noticed that William had left the men and was making his way up a path beyond the clearing. She'd follow him in a moment, but first she wanted to ask about the children and why they hadn't been evacuated. It was as she thought, no one had really expected the Germans to bomb Belfast so the mothers chose to keep them at home. 'And what about now, after Tuesday's raid, would you be interested in having them evacuated given the chance?' Pat asked.

'I'd put my girls on the first bus out of here if I was sure someone would take them in.'

The path was well worn, but overhanging branches meant no light from the moon touched it. There was the sound of voices above her, so she assumed William was with a group higher up the hill. She had her head down, picking her way carefully, when a noise caused her to look up. Three men stood about ten yards away, blocking her path; silhouettes with a faint light behind them.

'Now I wonder who this is, all on her own up here?'

'One a those askin' questions maybe.'

For a split second Pat hesitated, weighing up whether to stand her ground or run back down the hill. Then one of them shouted, 'Or wantin' a bit a fun!' Suddenly they were running towards her, covering the ground in seconds. The weight of the three of them knocked her to the ground, arms pinioned, legs grabbed, impossible to move or struggle. She filled her lungs and screamed at the top of her voice, held the note and when a hand covered her mouth she bit down hard, and screamed again. One of the men gave a yelp and loosened his grip on her. Pat managed to free one of her hands and felt for the hatpin in her collar. She plunged it into soft flesh, felt it snap. Then there was shouting above her and the sound of people slithering down the slope. In an instant she was free, someone lifted her to her feet, but still she screamed.

'Pat! Pat, are you all right? Stop screaming, you're safe, they've gone.' And then she was shaking, trying to catch her breath. William held her tight and when her knees gave way he lifted her and carried her down the path to the women she had been with only minutes before.

The first thing Martha and Sheila noticed when they arrived home from the McCrackens' was that the house was in darkness and the blackout curtains hadn't been drawn.

'I know where Pat is, but where are Irene and Peggy at this time of night?' said Martha.

'Where's Pat?' asked Sheila.

Martha ignored her and unlocked the door. She still felt uneasy about agreeing to Pat going up the Cave Hill and she certainly didn't want to answer any embarrassing questions from Sheila.

On the kitchen table there was a note scrawled in Peggy's hand. 'Gone to the Plaza, will explain when I get home. Irene out with a friend from work.' Martha pursed her lips, said nothing and busied herself with the dirty dishes the pair of them had left in the sink.

It was almost eleven, Sheila had just gone to bed and Martha was listening to the news on the wireless when there was a sharp rap at the front door. 'Who is it?' she called out.

'William Kennedy – I've Pat with me.'

They came into the light and Martha gasped at the sight of her daughter. Pat's head was bowed, her hair dishevelled, her hands and legs were dirty.

'What's happened?' Martha took Pat by the shoulders and bent to look at her face. It was streaked with tears and a scratch across her cheek was smeared with blood. 'Dear God–' Then she saw the ripped dress. 'What's happened? Who's done this to you?'

Pat tried to speak but, seeing her mother's face, she burst into tears.

'Are you responsible for this?' Martha turned on William.

'No …' he hesitated. 'Well, indirectly …'

'What have you done to her?' Martha demanded.

'It wasn't him, Mammy! It was other people.'

'Who? Who was it?'

'I don't know who they were!'

'Mrs Goulding, I can explain–'

But Martha ignored him. 'Pat, come in the kitchen where it's warm and we'll have a proper look at you.' She took her daughter by the arm and sat her in the armchair next to the range. She emptied hot water from the kettle into a bowl, knelt down and smoothed Pat's hair, then bathed her face and washed her grazed hands and knees, all the time talking to her – calm reassuring words – while William stood in the doorway.

Eventually, Pat began to speak. 'Mammy, it's not what you think. I'm all right, just shaken up. Some young fellows thought they'd have a bit of sport. I was walking up a path, it was dark and they grabbed me.'

Martha turned to William. 'And where were you when this was going on?'

'I'd gone on ahead to speak to some people.'

'You left her!'

'Just for a minute.'

'Where was the rest of the party? There were six of you, weren't there?' Martha looked from William to Pat and back again – neither of them met her eye. 'I see,' she said.

Pat breathed deeply. 'They had to go to different areas. It was just me and William up the Cave Hill. It's my fault, Mammy, I should have been more careful,' and she began to cry.

In a moment William was across the room, kneeling next to her, stroking her hair. 'No, no, it was my fault. I should never have left you.'

'But you rescued me. If you hadn't heard me scream …' Pat laid her head on his shoulder and he kissed her forehead.

Oh my, thought Martha, what have we here?

'Mr Kennedy, it's time you went,' she said sharply. 'You can tell Pat's supervisor that she won't be in work next week; she's had a severe shock. In fact, after what's happened tonight, I'm not sure if she'll be back at all.'

There were loud protests from both Pat and William. 'Mammy, I'm fine, nothing happened! I have to go back on Monday, there's so much to do!'

'Mrs Goulding, I can assure you–'

The back door opened and in came Peggy. 'What's all the noise about? I could hear you from the street.' In a split second she had taken in the scene – Pat and William on one side, her mother on the other. 'God, Pat, you look a right mess! What happened to you?'

'Never you mind,' Martha snapped. 'Away to bed with you or I'll start asking where you've been to this hour.'

'Ask away, sure I've nothing to hide,' she said defiantly, eyeing up Pat and William.

Just then Sheila appeared in her nightclothes, blinking at the light. 'What's all the noise? You woke me up.'

'Nothing, go back to bed!' said Martha.

'Pat, if you're sure you're all right, I'll go,' said William, 'and if you're not well enough to come to work on Monday, I'll understand.'

'I'm fine now, just tired, but I'll be in work, don't worry.'

He squeezed her arm and nodded curtly at Martha, 'I'll see myself out, Mrs Goulding.'

Outside, he passed Irene on the path without a word, jumped in his car and raced away.

'Was that William Kennedy in high dudgeon that just stormed past me?' asked Irene as she came in the back door. Then she realised that her entire family were standing in the kitchen, in an atmosphere crackling with anger and recrimination.

Chapter 4

Sunday morning dawned with clear skies and the promise of a fine day, but it did nothing to improve Martha's mood. She had to be at St George's Market for eleven o'clock, but before that she had the worry of Pat, then questions for Peggy and Irene about why they'd been out so late. Lord, what was she to do with them? She'd no idea what they were up to half the time. The fire in the range was nearly out and she had to coax it with a few sticks and bits of coal before she could get the porridge on. Irene was the first down and Martha was glad to have her on her own to explain about Myrtle.

'Her father came with someone called Robert, said he knew you from work.'

Irene sat at the table, eyes down, tracing the pattern on the tablecloth. 'Aye, Robert McVey, he said he'd go.'

Martha didn't mention the fact that they'd identified Myrtle by the ring she always wore that had been her mother's. 'The funeral's on Friday afternoon and Robert said a few of you might get time off work to go.'

Irene covered her face with her hands. Martha sat next to her and stroked her back. 'It's hard, love, I know.'

'Why Myrtle? She was a good person and she was only twenty. It's not fair!'

'God only knows why some are taken.'

'It could've been me, or Pat or Peggy; we were out in the bombing too, coming home from that last concert. Why not us? Or will it be us next time?'

'We can't know what's going to happen,' Martha reasoned, 'but we should try and keep ourselves out of harm's way. You know, being out at night you could be caught anywhere, that's why I can't be doing with all the coming and going of you and your sisters.'

But Irene wasn't listening. 'Do you want to know what the worst of it is?' Her voice was rising hysterically. 'Myrtle was expecting a baby, so that's the two of them dead – a wee baby, Mammy!'

Martha hugged her close. 'Ssh, ssh now,' she whispered over and over, for there was no other comfort she could offer and she couldn't trust herself to say much else.

Irene pulled away from her. 'I didn't want to be in Bangor, you know. I wanted to come home as soon as I got there. I tried to tell Sandy how I felt and about Myrtle, but all I could do was cry. I don't think he knew what to do.'

'What did he say?'

'Nothing really, left me to it and went for a walk. That's when he came back with the tickets for Caproni's. I told him he was cruel.'

Martha was suddenly alert. 'Was he? Did he upset you?'

'Ach no, he was kind, but I wasn't myself, was I? And now he's gone and …' She gripped Martha's arm. 'What's it meant to feel like when you're married, Mammy? Please tell me, because I'm just empty inside and I know that's probably because of Myrtle and the baby' – her tears were falling again – 'but I don't really think about Sandy at all.'

'Oh, Irene, marriage isn't some sort of secret feeling that comes with a ring. It's a hard slog, believe you me, and you have to work at it.' She smiled then, remembering something her own mother had told her years ago. 'Being married is like baking soda bread; you make it fresh every day and some days it tastes better than others. You'll find your own recipe, but don't forget, sometimes you have to make it with sour milk, if that's all you have.'

'Aye, maybe you're right.'

'Of course I am. Mammies always are!'

Irene smiled in spite of herself, dried her eyes and fetched the bowls for the porridge. 'But, you know, I'm glad to be home. I don't think I could go off and live in some RAF base even if Sandy asked me to.'

'It might not come to that. With a war on they can't be thinking about housing wives and families.'

'You're probably right, and when this war ends maybe Sandy will leave the air force and we could live in Belfast.' She seemed to brighten then and stirred the porridge and filled the bowls. 'Have we any honey left?'

'Aye, Betty gave me some. I don't think I'll ever get used to thousands of bees living next door, but I do love their honey.'

'Jack makes me laugh, every time I see him out there in his beekeeper outfit. What will he think of next? We've had vegetables, chickens, and now bees – could be a few pigs, you never know.'

'Please God, no. I don't think I could stand the smell!'

'Mammy, you know I was out last night with somebody from work?' Martha thought it better not to voice her annoyance. 'Well, it was a new girl and she's on her own, living in the YWCA. I felt a bit sorry for her. So, you can say no if you want to, but could I ask her to come for her tea one night?'

'Aye well, I suppose so, but you'd better tell her it won't be great; there's less and less in the shops every day.'

'She won't mind whatever you give her, it'll be a novelty. She's American.'

'God bless us,' said Martha, 'sure she'll be used to steaks and ice cream and things like that!'

'Who would?' said Peggy, who'd appeared in her candlewick dressing gown.

'Irene's American friend.'

Peggy's eyes widened. 'Where did you meet him? What's he called?'

'It's not a he, it's a she and she's called Macy.'

'What kind of a name is that?'

'An American one, of course.'

Martha handed Peggy her porridge. 'And what were you doing at the Plaza last night?'

'Aah … I was earning some money.'

'Were you indeed?' Martha looked sceptical. 'Doing what exactly?'

'Hat-check girl, I think the Americans call it,' and she giggled at her cleverness.

'You never asked me if you could work in a dance hall.'

'There wasn't time.' She reached for the honey and stirred a large spoonful into her porridge. 'I was walking past at lunchtime and there was a notice on the door. I went in on the off chance just to ask about it. The manager offered me the job there and then; only Saturday nights, mind you, and I get five shillings. I did come home to ask you, Mammy, but you weren't here.' Peggy looked sideways at her mother as if to imply it was her fault that permission wasn't given. Then she pressed home her advantage. 'You can have the five shillings towards the housekeeping, if you like.'

'I'll have to think about it,' said Martha and she busied herself setting a tray with porridge and tea.

Think all you want, thought Peggy, but I'll certainly be there next Saturday, for the tips and to see Devlin again.

'I'll take this up to Pat, she's having a lie-in today.'

When Martha had gone, Peggy leaned across the table. 'Did you find out what happened to her last night? Was she out with William Kennedy?'

'Seems they went up the Cave Hill to talk to the ditchers–'

'The what?'

'Ditchers – the people who've been sleeping out in the open – anyway I think she slipped and fell down a–'

'Ditch!' Peggy laughed. 'And did Kennedy push her, catch her, or fall on top of her!'

'Whatever happened, he's in the doghouse with Mammy.'

Upstairs, Pat lay in bed staring at the ceiling. 'How are you today?' asked Martha.

'I'm fine, just a few cuts and bruises.'

'Pat, did those young fellows …'

'Mammy, I've told you it was horseplay and William was there as soon as I shouted.'

'He should have been there the whole time. Leaving you alone in the dark, I ask you. Well, you can take a week off on the sick. They'll manage without you, I'm sure.'

'I'm going in as normal tomorrow. There's work to be done.'

'Well, I can't stop you, but I'll tell you this for nothing, my girl, I don't expect to see Mr Kennedy back here any time soon!'

After breakfast, Martha and Irene sat on the back step watching Sheila wash and polish the bike she got from the McCrackens.

'You mean to say she pushed that ugly article all the way from Manor Street?' asked Irene.

Martha laughed. 'She certainly did. The conductor wouldn't let her on the bus with it.'

'But she can't ride a bike, can she?'

'Not to my knowledge, but do you think that'll stop her?'

'Maybe a few cut knees and lumps on her head might.'

'Do you know your tyres are flat as a pancake, Sheila?' shouted Peggy from the bedroom window.

'Of course I do. I just need a pump. Do you know who's got one?'

'Try the McKees – the boys used to have a bike.'

Sheila returned a few minutes later with a pump, oil can, several spanners and Brian McKee.

'We'll soon have this chariot on the road for you,' he said and pumped up the tyres, then tightened and oiled the brakes. 'Now sit on the saddle, Sheila, and put your feet on the ground, so I can adjust the height for you.'

Sheila wobbled from side to side, but couldn't get both feet on the ground at the same time.

'Hop off,' said Brian and made the adjustment. 'That should do it.'

Sheila sat in the saddle and balanced the bike perfectly. Brian opened the gate. 'Right, off you go!'

Sheila looked up at Peggy, then at Irene and Martha on the step, and pushed off. Within a turn of the wheels she had over-balanced and fallen against the wall of the house and grazed her arm.

Brian picked her up. 'Have you ridden a bike before?'

'No,' said Sheila and pedalled off again. This time the front wheel veered sharply from side to side as she tried desperately to stay upright. Brian ran after her and caught the saddle. 'Come on, you,' he said. 'We've got the whole day; let's find a flat stretch of road.'

Peggy waited until Martha had left for St George's Market before sitting down at the piano to play 'Boogie Woogie Bugle Boy', one of the songs she'd been practising in the shop. The sound immediately brought Irene and Pat in from the kitchen.

'You've learned one already!' Irene exclaimed.

'Said I would, didn't I?'

'Have you the words too?' asked Pat.

Peggy handed them a sheet. 'Are you ready to run through it? Don't worry about the harmonies, we'll work those out later.'

Irene and Pat looked at each other and laughed. 'Let's do it!'

Peggy played the lively intro while her sisters clicked their fingers, moved in time to the rhythm and nearly came in on cue. At the end of the second verse Peggy held up her hand to stop the singing while she played a riff improvised in a blues style. Her sisters danced in the circle between the piano and the rest of the furniture. In the next verse Pat sang the melody while Irene did her best to harmonise with the sound of a trumpet. By the last verse, with Peggy singing too, the song filled the house and escaped through the open window and into the street.

'Brilliant!' said Irene. 'We could have it ready for the next Barnstormers' concert.'

'That's if there is a next one,' said Pat.

'Doesn't matter if there isn't,' said Peggy. 'There are plenty of other opportunities to perform.'

'You're not still thinking of a dance band are you?' Pat was sceptical.

'Oh you'd be surprised by what I've been thinking.'

'Don't be so mysterious,' said Irene. 'Tell us.'

Peggy hadn't intended to reveal the full extent of her plans, but she couldn't resist showing off. 'Apart from another excellent song I've learned, I could also show you something I've bought.'

'What is it?' said Irene.

Pat said nothing.

'Wait here!' and Peggy ran out the door and up the stairs.

'You shouldn't encourage her, Irene, Lord knows what she's up to.'

'Ta-da!' shouted Peggy waving the Butterwick patterns. 'We have the songs, next the style!'

Irene was delighted. 'They're gorgeous! Imagine being on the stage in dresses like these.'

'I think we could combine the two, you know, get the best of both. This neckline, but with these sleeves would really work. We'll look like professional singers.'

'But we're not,' said Pat. Her sisters turned to look at her. 'Well, we're not! Besides, there are two problems with your plan, Peggy.'

'Oh … only two?'

Pat ignored her sarcasm. 'These are just pretty pictures and bits of paper. So tell me – how will we pay for the material and secondly who's going to make them for us?'

'You're such a spoilsport!'

'I'm a realist.'

'Oh, for goodness sake, you two,' shouted Irene.

But Pat was getting into her stride. 'And Goldstein isn't organising any concerts, so where do you think we're going to sing, even if we had the dresses? Answer me that.'

'I've somewhere in mind, but I'm not saying where.'

'Ach, catch yourself on!' said Pat.

It was late afternoon when Irene lit a fire in the sitting room. They sat around reading magazines waiting for Martha to come home. When she hadn't arrived by six, Pat went to the kitchen to get the potatoes on. There was still no sign of Martha when Pat mashed the potatoes and added the scallions and butter so she carried the steaming plates into the front room and the girls sat warm and content eating their champ and listening to the wireless.

They had drawn the blackout curtains and added a small shovel of slack to the fire when they heard the back door open and moments later Martha came into the room. Sheila was first on her feet. 'Mammy, are you all right? What's happened?'

'I'm fine, just a bit tired. It was a long day, so many people looking for their relatives.' Martha's shoulders were slumped and she looked pale and worn.

'Sit down and I'll bring you your tea. I kept it warm in the oven.' said Pat.

'I'll away and have a bath first, ease my bones.'

'Wait a minute, I've something for you.' Peggy ran upstairs, returning moments later. 'Here you are, the bath salts I got for my birthday. They'll make the water softer for you.'

'Thanks, love, you're a good girl.'

'Why does she look so ill?' asked Sheila when their mother had gone.

'She's not ill,' said Irene, 'just exhausted, I think.'

Later, they all sat together in the sitting room listening to the Sunday service followed by the news. Ever since she had been given the wireless set by her sister Anna, Martha had never missed the news before going to bed. Tonight there were reports about the British attempting to stem the German advance in Greece.

'Why would the Germans go to Greece?' asked Sheila.

'Dictators will go anywhere to frighten people and take their country. It's what they do,' said Martha, 'until someone is brave enough to stop them.' She eased herself out of the chair. 'I think I'll take a couple of Aspros and go to bed. Make sure you lock the doors and see to the fire.'

Under the eiderdown, with her feet on the hot-water bottle, Martha lay perfectly still, trying to ease her aching body and thumping head and desperately hoping sleep would come. But the images of the day were lodged in her mind: the old woman shuffling down the rows of coffins searching for her son; the girl, not much older than Sheila, with not a mark on her still there at the end of the day, unclaimed. Until, at last, memories became nightmares and she found herself running in a landscape of ruins, desperate to escape the deafening noise that pursued her.

'Mammy, Mammy, get up quickly!' The room was pitch-dark and the ruins had gone, but the noise remained. 'It's the air-raid siren,' shouted Pat. 'We have to get under the stairs!'

They had long since worked out the routine to fit all five of them into the cramped space with blankets, pillows and a torch to hand.

'This is nearly every night now. I'm really fed up with it,' moaned Sheila. 'It'll be another false alarm, you'll see.'

'Better false alarms than bombs,' said Pat. 'They'll be back soon, we can't risk staying in our beds. Anyway, if you don't like it, why don't you agree to be evacuated?'

'How many more times do I have to tell you? I'm not going!'

'That's enough! There isn't room in here for arguments.'

'But Mammy– '

'No, Sheila, I heard today that Lord Haw Haw said– '

'You can't believe what that traitor says. He's just trying to frighten people!'

Martha carried on regardless. 'Lord Haw Haw said they're going to attack Belfast again as soon as we've buried our dead. And I'm telling you there's a wee girl, just like you, who'll be buried in a mass grave tomorrow and she'd still be alive today if she'd been evacuated to the country. Now that's an end to it, all of you, try to get some sleep.

Chapter 5

Peggy stood at the window watching Goldstein hurry across Royal Avenue and walk briskly towards his club, where he'd spend a couple of hours having lunch and a fine cigar with a few business acquaintances as he did every Wednesday afternoon. No doubt they would grumble about the slow trade since the bombings and their falling profits.

When he had disappeared, Peggy turned to Esther. 'We'll try a little experiment while your uncle's away, to see if we can persuade people to come into the shop and maybe even buy something. This is what we'll do ... '

The shop door was open wide and Esther stood just inside with a welcoming smile, greeting each person as they ventured inside to see what was going on. Peggy was sitting at one of the pianos, playing one popular song after another. Before long the shop was full of people lingering and browsing and – once Peggy had nodded to Esther to return to the counter – buying. As they left, they were replaced by others attracted by the lively music and the sight of a shop full of people.

Peggy had just finished 'Zing! Went the Strings of My Heart' when a dapper-looking gentleman who had been standing next to the piano asked, 'Can you play "I'll Take You Home Again, Kathleen"?'

Peggy hesitated, it wasn't her style at all, but she managed a smile. 'Of course.' Four bars in, the man began to hum, after eight bars his rich baritone voice was filling the shop and people were crowding in the doorway. He finished to warm applause, whereupon Peggy stood up and announced. 'A wonderful song and you can buy the sheet music or a gramophone record right now.'

'What about "We'll Meet Again"?'

'Yes, you can buy that here too.'

'No, will you play it?'

Peggy gritted her teeth, she loathed the song, but needs must, she thought. Several people quickly crowded around the piano to sing along and so it went on. Peggy would play, people would sing and some would buy. Eventually, she announced there would be a break while she helped serve the queuing customers.

'Sure that's a pity, I was enjoying the sing-song.' The voice was unmistakeable. It was Devlin looking like he'd come straight from a tailor's shop – and an expensive one at that.

Peggy touched her hair, shaping it round her ears, knowing it would accentuate her high cheekbones and took a step towards him. 'Were you here when I was playing the Glenn Miller?'

'No, I missed that.'

She was so close she could see the neat hand-stitching on the lapels of his pinstripe suit. 'That's a pity. I don't usually play these sing-along tunes. Not my style at all. I could play something else if you like.'

'I really need to get back to the Plaza – things to do.' He turned to leave.

'What about some Ella Fitzgerald or the Inkspots maybe?' she called after him, but he was already at the door and didn't look back.

Almost as soon as Devlin had gone, Goldstein came hurrying in, his eyes wide with surprise at the sight of the queuing customers and the lively atmosphere. 'What's going on? Why are all these people here?'

'They're shopping of course,' laughed Peggy, 'and we could do with a hand.' For the next half hour Goldstein, Esther and Peggy served customers until they found themselves alone once more and staring at the open till, bursting with copper, silver and notes.

Goldstein gathered up the money. 'What on earth happened? I've not seen anything like that since last Christmas Eve.'

Esther began to giggle.

'What have you two been up to?'

'Peggy had an idea, she—'

'Ssssh!' said Peggy, but she was laughing too.

Goldstein folded his arms and stared at his two assistants. 'Come on, out with it.'

'You have to promise not to be angry,' said Esther.

Her uncle lifted his shoulders and raised his hands, palms upwards. 'You have put money in the till. Why would I be angry?'

'Because we opened the door and Esther invited people to come in,' Peggy confessed.

'And Peggy played the piano.'

Goldstein studied their faces. 'And ...'

Peggy and Esther looked at each other and giggled again. 'And we all had a good sing-song!'

'A sing-song! In my shop?'

'You said you wouldn't be angry.'

'I'm not angry. I'm confused,' and he took himself off to his office to count the takings.

Martha had stripped the beds and put the sheets to soak in the bath with a bit of bleach. She was just going back upstairs to tidy the girls' rooms when there was the slap of the letterbox and a brown envelope landed on the mat. It looked ominous, official, and must surely be a bill of some kind. Martha sat on the bottom stair and scanned the letter quickly. How had this come about? She read it again and, as realisation dawned, anger rose within her. How dare she! And without a word to anyone!

Just then there was a shout. 'Are you in, Martha?' It was Betty from next door. Martha shoved the letter into her apron pocket and went quickly through the sitting room into the back kitchen.

'Jack's been clearing out the vegetable beds ready for summer planting,' said Betty. 'I brought you a few cabbages, they're good enough for soup,' and she put them on the draining board.

'Ach, that's kind of you, Betty. Don't know what we'd do without your Jack – he's a one-man Dig for Victory campaign!'

'Sure he loves it, gets him out of the house. He's tried for an allotment, you know, but you can't get them for love nor money.'

'Well any time he wants to come round and dig up my garden he'll be very welcome!' laughed Martha.

'Thank heavens we were able to sleep right through last night, first one without an air-raid warning since the bombing.'

'Aye, be thankful for small mercies. Do you stay in your bed when there's an alert?'

'Not any more I don't, not after last time. I wish to God we had somewhere else to go, well away from Belfast.'

'Would you leave your house?'

'Certainly would.'

Martha touched the letter in her apron pocket. 'They're going to start evacuating children again, you know. There's a chance Sheila could go, but I'm not sure ...'

'Away on with you! Why would you keep her here?'

Why indeed, thought Martha.

Betty went on, 'And it's not like she's a little one who'd fret and pine. She's a big girl.'

'Aye, maybe you're right.'

When Betty had gone, Martha rinsed the sheets, put them through the mangle and hung them on the line. Later, when they were dry, she took them down, ironed them and put them back on the beds, and all the time she wrestled with the problem of what to do about Sheila and what she'd say to Pat.

The cabbage soup proved an unexpected success thanks to the floury dumplings and an accidental slip of the hand when Martha was adding the pepper. It was Peggy and Sheila's turn to do the dishes but, when they stood to clear the table, Martha said, 'Leave all that, we need to talk about something.' All four daughters turned to her, struck by the strange tone in her voice. 'I've had a letter today,' she told them, 'telling me that Sheila is on a list to be evacuated.' Suddenly she was bombarded by questions, only Pat said nothing.

'That's not fair,' shouted Sheila.

'Where's she being sent?' Irene wanted to know.

'When's she going?' asked Peggy.

'I'm not going!' snapped Sheila.

Martha held up her hands. 'Just stop a minute, will you? We're going to discuss this without anybody getting annoyed and you'll all have your say. The letter says the evacuees will leave on Sunday and Sheila is to go to Coleraine.'

'Evacuees?' said Peggy.

'It's what they call people being evacuated.'

'Where's Coleraine?' asked Irene.

'God knows, somewhere out in the country.'

Sheila folded her arms and scowled. 'I'm not going!'

Martha spoke gently. 'Sheila, think carefully please. Remember we talked about it being an adventure, a chance to go somewhere different and meet new people?'

'That's just it! I won't know anyone. And what about school?' Sheila was close to tears and searching her sister's faces for some support. 'I'll finish in the summer and I'll find a job and earn some money.'

'God save us,' said Martha. 'We could be bombed out by then and there'd be no jobs for any of you.'

'If you go, I'll have the bedroom to myself,' said Peggy.

'What kind of a thing is that to say to your sister!'

Sheila sat bolt upright at a sudden thought. 'Wait a minute. Why is my name on a list? How did it get there?' The questions hung in the air.

Pat, who had listened in silence to the increasingly angry argument spoke softly, 'I'm just going to say what I think,' and she paused to collect her thoughts. 'We know there'll be more bombing very soon. Don't we all want Sheila to be safe? This chance has come her way and if we refuse it and something happens to her ...' Pat struggled to find the words to persuade them. 'She just has to go.'

Irene knew Pat was right, but sending Sheila away against her will would be heartbreaking for them all. 'Maybe there isn't a perfect answer to this,' she began, 'but what if Sheila could go and stay a wee while, until the beginning of the summer holidays, that's not too long. Then, if there have been no bombings in the meantime, she could come home. What do you think?' She looked around at her family.

Martha was the first to speak. 'And, Sheila, maybe I could visit you after a few weeks.'

'You could take your bike.' Irene was warming to the idea.

'You'd get well fed in the country,' said Peggy.

'Perhaps that's a solution,' said Martha. 'A holiday in the country, then come back here and find a nice job. What do you say, Sheila?'

Sheila said nothing, just left the room and went upstairs to throw herself on her bed.

'I see she's got out of doing the dishes now,' grumbled Peggy.

'Irene, will you give Peggy a hand?' said Martha and went into the sitting room, nodding at Pat to follow her.

'Well, miss, what have you to say for yourself?'

'Honestly, Mammy, I did it for the best. They had this list in work where we could put forward names of children to be evacuated. They're trying to get the programme going again. You remember last time when hardly any children went? This'll be the first evacuation since the bombings and they want it to work, so the first buses will be full of Stormont workers' relatives.'

Martha shook her head. 'That's as maybe, Pat, but you'd no right to do that without consulting me.'

'And in the meantime all the places would have gone!'

'You girls forget sometimes that I'm the mother in this house, so don't let me catch you going behind my back again. Do you understand?'

'Yes, Mammy.'

Martha knocked on the door to Sheila and Peggy's bedroom and went in. The room was in darkness. She went to the window and closed the blackout curtains before switching on the light. Sheila was lying facing the wall. Martha sat on the edge of the bed.

51

'Sheila, I can't drag you down the town and push you on a bus and make you go. But maybe this is for the best. You know we just want you to be safe.'

Sheila didn't respond so Martha went on, 'Sometimes things happen for a reason. They're just meant to be. You're on this list to be evacuated and, to tell you the truth, I think it's God's will that you should go.'

It was still dark when Sheila and Martha made their way through the deserted city centre. Sheila had said goodbye to her sisters the previous night. Irene gave her half a crown, Pat some handkerchiefs still in their box and Peggy a new hairbrush. Sheila was the only one who didn't cry; she'd slowly reconciled herself to the idea of being evacuated over the preceding days. 'You'll all write to me, won't you?' she'd urged them and they said they would. 'Promise you're going to come and visit me?' she'd pleaded and Martha promised. 'I can take my bike, can't I?' she'd asked and Martha had said, 'Why not?'

In Great Victoria Street, they joined the procession of people walking towards the bus station, many of them laden with cases and trunks, some pushing prams piled high with children or household items. As they got nearer, they saw a crowd of people sitting on the pavement, many wrapped in blankets, all looking exhausted and cold.

Just then a bus pulled into the station and all around them people leapt to their feet, gathered up their belongings and rushed towards it. Amid screams and shouts, the strongest and most ruthless pushed their way to the front. A fight broke out next to Martha and close by a mother was desperately trying to hold on to her child's hand, while the force of people moving forward dragged him away from her. Within minutes the bus was full and pulling away from the kerb, leaving those behind crying or cursing in frustration.

Martha spotted several policemen standing nearby, none of whom had made any attempt to control the crowd. 'Was that the bus to Coleraine?' she asked them.

'Who knows?' one laughed.

'Who cares?' said another. 'Most people aren't bothered where they end up as long as they get as far away from Belfast as possible. The driver'll take them where the majority want to go.'

Martha showed them her letter from Stormont. 'But I was told my daughter was being evacuated to Coleraine, now you're telling me she could end up anywhere?'

'Ah no, missus, this is different. Go down the side street here and you'll see there are special buses laid on for the unaccompanied children. Just show your letter to the evacuation officer.'

Around the corner, the sight of a hundred or more children and their parents saying goodbye stopped Martha in her tracks and all her fears surfaced again. What was she doing, sending Sheila away to God-knows-what? How easy it would be to turn on her heel and take her daughter back home.

'Mammy, what is it?' Sheila's face was full of concern. 'Are you all right?'

'No, I ...' but the moment of doubt had passed. Martha struggled to hold a smile and say something positive. 'Sheila, remember you're going to the country because that's where you'll be safe, but if you need me, just write and I'll come.'

'I know, Mammy, I know.'

The evacuation officer checked the letter, ticked Sheila's name on his sheet and directed them to join the queue for the first bus. All around them the children's faces reflected their fear and excitement. Few of them would ever have spent a night away from their own beds and a Sunday School excursion once a year would have been the longest journey they had ever made. The parents' faces were strained with the worry of it all. The last few days would have been filled with the practicalities of choosing, then washing, ironing and finally packing the clothes in the recommended pillowslip with a drawstring top. Now there seemed only trivial things to say at this dramatic moment. 'Don't forget to wash behind your ears.' 'Remember your manners.' 'Say your prayers.'

Martha hugged Sheila and kissed her cheek, 'You look after yourself, love. Remember to speak up and be afraid of no one.'

'I will, Mammy,' and Sheila lifted her bike on to the platform and climbed up after it.

'Hey you!' They turned to see the driver rushing towards them. 'Get that contraption off my bus!'

Sheila didn't move. 'Why?'

'Is she not allowed to take it?' asked Martha.

'No, missus, I'm not taking bikes on the bus. There's no room.'

Sheila pointed to the roof of the bus. 'You could put it up on the luggage rack for me.'

'I'm not struggling to put a bike up there.'

'Why not?'

'Because it's not safe! Now are you gettin' that bike off the bus or not, because we're ready to go?'

'I'm not going without it!' Sheila was ready for an argument, but Martha could sense her child's panic.

'Then you're not going,' said the driver.

'You can't stop me!'

The break in Sheila's voice brought Martha close to tears, but the last thing she wanted was to have a scene there on the pavement. She could insist Sheila leave the bike, but it was likely she meant what she said about not going without it. The only alternative was to follow the voice that screamed in her head, 'Take her home!'

'Now then, if you were wanting to go on my bus to Dungannon I could certainly take a young lady and her bike because I've got plenty of room.' It was the driver shouting from the cab of the bus behind.

'Dungannon?' said Martha.

'That's right, the grumpy oul fella who won't let you on his bus is going to Coleraine. This is the Dungannon bus.'

Martha turned quickly to Sheila. 'I think Dungannon sounds a good place to ride a bike. What do you think?'

'Dungannon it is then,' said Sheila and she bumped her bike off the platform.

As the Dungannon bus pulled away Sheila slid back the top half of the window, stuck a hand out and waved. 'Bye, Mammy!'

Martha felt the tears chill on her cheeks, but didn't wipe them away. She simply smiled and blew her youngest daughter a kiss and waved until the bus disappeared round the corner.

Chapter 6

The bus up the Antrim Road to Bellevue Gardens was crowded with people from the city off to spend a Sunday afternoon in the late April sunshine. Pat managed to get a seat downstairs next to an elderly lady who told her she was meeting her daughter and grandchildren to visit the zoo.

'And what about you, dear, meeting someone are you?'

'Just a friend from work.'

'I'm sure he's very handsome.'

'Oh it's not like that,' Pat blushed.

'But it might be after today,' the old lady smiled.

William was already there at the entrance. He looked different dressed in a sports jacket, flannel trousers and an open-necked shirt – younger, less earnest-looking. He waved and she walked to meet him, keeping her eyes on the ground, knowing he was watching her. It was the first time this year that she had worn a summer dress. She was conscious of the thinness of the material and was glad to have a cardigan draped over her shoulders and fastened with the top button at her neck.

They joined the throng of people walking up the steep hill to the entrance. All around them there was chatter and laughter. Pat and

William walked in silence, both feeling awkward about what to say. Now and again, they glanced at each other and smiled.

The previous night Pat and Irene had sat in their bedroom, talking in whispers about what Irene had insisted was a first date. 'Just relax and be yourself. Let him do the worrying. If he's interested in you, he'll have to find a way to tell you.'

'But I won't know what to talk about.'

'Pat, when have you ever been short of words? Look, if you're stuck, talk about singing or work … best of all get him to talk about himself. Oh yes, and if he offers to pay for anything, you're definitely on a date!'

They joined the queue at a kiosk next to a turnstile and Pat took her purse from her handbag.

'No Pat, this is my treat.'

'That's very kind of you, William,' and with a rush of confidence she added, 'have you been here before?'

'Never,' he replied and took her hand. 'Have you?'

They walked through the formal gardens, cut and trimmed with geometric precision, and past beds of daffodils, where Pat asked how he'd become interested in singing. He'd been a boy soprano in the school choir, he told her. On past the cream narcissi, while he talked about amateur operatic shows, Gilbert and Sullivan mostly. By the time they reached the tulip beds, Pat knew this would be one of the most memorable days of her life.

They sat for a while on a bench, where he let go of her hand to put his arm around her. 'What did your mother say when you told her you were meeting me today?'

Pat knew she ought to tell him the truth – that her mother didn't know she was with him – but that would break the spell of this warm April day, heavy with the scent of flowers and the touch of William's fingers caressing her neck. 'She said I should take a coat, because it's going to rain.'

William didn't detect the nervousness in her laugh; he saw only the blush on her cheeks and the pink of her lips and bent to kiss her. The kiss lingered longer than she could ever have imagined. She gave herself up to the moment: his fingers in her hair, his arm on her back pulling her towards him and above all his lips so intimate she could hardly breathe.

His mouth left hers, but she didn't move; her head remained tilted, her eyes still closed, her breath came back, quick and shallow.

'Pat,' he whispered.

She opened her eyes. 'William, I ...' but she had no words.

'Yes I know, I know,' he said and kissed her again.

They lost all sense of time passing as they held each other on the bench by the tulips, but Pat in her thin dress eventually became aware of the cool shade as the sun moved behind the clouds. She shivered.

'You're cold,' said William and he rubbed her bare arms. Then he undid the button of her cardigan. 'Here, put this on properly and we'll have a warm drink in the café.'

They sat at a table by the window, drank tea and ate buttered scones with raspberry jam and the conversation flowed easily.

'You know we have a summer garden party at Stormont every year?' he told her.

'I didn't know that.'

'Oh it's a really grand affair – the great and the good turn up in their finery and the Civil Service choir and orchestra provide the entertainment. You know, like we did at Christmas. You enjoyed that, didn't you?'

Pat nodded, remembering the wonderful evening when she'd sung in the choir in the great hall at Stormont. 'Yes, Aunt Kathleen came to watch us and she said we should have been the soloists.'

'Aah, those Saturday afternoons when we went to her house for singing lessons ...' his voice trailed off. 'You know, I really miss all that.'

'What, Aunt Kathleen shouting at you because you'd forgotten you had a diaphragm and your breathing was all wrong?'

William laughed, 'And you being told to sing with passion.' Then he was serious again. 'It all seems so long ago, not just that concert but the performances with the Barnstormers and Goldstein knocking us into shape. Remember when he wanted you and me to be like Jeanette MacDonald and Nelson Eddy, Belfast's sweethearts he called us.'

Pat lowered her eyes; she had always been embarrassed by that role. 'But it wasn't to be, was it?' she whispered.

William reached out and lifted her chin. 'But it could be, Pat, you and me – sweethearts.'

She couldn't meet his gaze, couldn't acknowledge what was in her heart, couldn't be certain of his intentions. 'You're not suggesting we sing again as the Mountie and the Indian squaw? That was never a success, was it?'

His fingers fell from her chin. 'No, no,' he said quietly, 'I wasn't suggesting that.'

At once Pat felt awkward but she could see no way of bringing back the moment and William, too, sensed its loss. He cleared his throat and said briskly, 'I think it's brightening up. What about having a look at the zoo while we're here?'

Pat had been to the zoo once before as a child when her father had taken her and Irene as a treat. Her abiding memory of the day was of her father trying to persuade her to have a ride on the elephant – an enormous beast with dusty grey skin that hung from its body in folds. He had held her high above his head towards the arms of the zoo keeper on the elephant's back and she had screamed and kicked in fear, more terrified of the strange man trying to grab her than the animal.

William held her hand as they walked the paths, looking in paddocks and identifying the animals, before moving on to the cages of the more exotic inmates. Finally, they followed the path signposted 'Cats'. The crowd was bigger there, the more exotic the animal the longer people lingered. The leopard lay comatose, its mangy coat dull and scabby. Before the war there had been a furrier in Donegall Place and Pat recalled seeing a crowd outside it one Saturday and, curious to know what they were looking at, she had crossed the road. In the window was a solitary white mannequin draped in a stunning leopard-skin coat.

There was a railing across the front of the cage to keep people away from the animal but, as they watched, a man ducked under it and ran a walking stick across the bars. 'Wake up,' he shouted, 'we've come to see ye!'

In a split second the leopard was on its feet and had launched itself against the bars, teeth bared, claws scrabbling at the stick and the man. There was a loud crack and the bars bent outwards bringing a chunk of the metal, in which they were anchored, away from the roof of the cage.

The screaming and shouting that followed seemed to enrage the animal even more. Those at the railing turned in their panic and pushed into the crowd behind them. Pat pulled William away, but he resisted and continued to stare at the leopard as it charged again at the bars.

'William, come on!' she shouted and they joined the crowd hurrying away from the scene.

Further along the path half a dozen keepers ran past them with pitchforks and spades and Pat was astonished to see one of them carrying a shotgun. Moments later a single crack of gunfire reverberated across the hillside.

'They've shot it!' Pat cried. 'That poor animal.'

'It's a good thing they did; it could have killed somebody.'

'No it couldn't, it only reacted because that man frightened it. It was a pathetic creature, just like the rest of those animals in cages.'

William was staring down the hill at the streets of houses far below. 'No, they're dangerous. Given a set of circumstances where their cages became damaged and they felt threatened, they wouldn't only escape, they'd be capable of killing, I'm sure.'

'William, what are you talking about? It was one scared animal and they shot it.'

'But don't you see? If this area was bombed, these animals could escape. They'd be on the streets below here in minutes. Can you imagine the scene?'

'Don't be ridiculous. That's not going to happen.'

'Pat listen, this is serious. I'm going to have to talk to someone at the ministry about this. And sooner rather than later.'

Pat saw the look on his face. 'Do you mean now?'

'I'm afraid so. Something needs to be done quickly. I think we were about to go home anyway. I'll walk you to the bus.'

Pat gave him a withering look. 'Don't trouble yourself, not when you've more important matters to deal with.'

William hesitated. 'It's just that ...' and he began to walk away from her. 'Look, I'll see you tomorrow at work.'

Pat shook her head in disbelief and at that moment raindrops as big as florins began to fall. Faster and faster they came and by the time she got to the bus stop at the bottom of the hill she was soaked through. Perhaps she should have listened to her mother.

Sheila was glad to find a seat on the bus next to a girl her own age who introduced herself as Lizzie.

'Looks like we're the oldest on the bus,' Lizzie said. 'Have you been to Dungannon before?'

'No,' said Sheila, 'Have you?'

'No, but I think it's a long way away.'

The roads out of the city were busy for a Sunday. 'Where do you think all these people are going?' Sheila asked.

'My daddy says lots of people are trying to get away from Belfast. They're going to stay with family or friends in the country, away from the bombs, but sure we don't know anyone, so he got me evacuated.' She sighed. 'I just hope a nice family pick me.'

In all the upset and preparation around leaving, Sheila had never thought about how the evacuees would be paired up with a family. What if she didn't like the people who picked her? Worse still, what if nobody picked her?

They left the city behind as the sun came up and soon the road was edged with hedgerows of hawthorn and wild fuchsia, beyond which the patchwork fields spread over the gentle hills into the distance. They passed through villages, glimpsing neat rows of little houses, a few bars, and in some, a shop or two. On and on they travelled through the morning with the heat rising. One by one the passengers discarded their coats, jumpers, cardigans. They stopped once at a mission hall with a tin roof and women gave them each a sandwich and a drink of water. Then they were back on the stifling bus.

Around midday the woman in charge made her way to the front of the bus and spoke to all of them. 'We're coming into Dungannon now and the bus will drop us at the dispersal centre. Remember to be on your best behaviour. Don't let yourselves down.'

The centre turned out to be a church hall. Inside, wooden chairs were set out as though for a meeting and at the front stood a man with a sheet of paper. There was some confusion at the door, a few of the little ones were reluctant to be the first to step into the hall and walk under its echoing roof. They were herded in and, with sterner voices than necessary, were ordered to sit down quickly.

The man in charge spoke rapidly. 'I'll check yer names, see if youse is all here. If youse is all here that'll be fine. Then youse'll wait 'til someone comes tae take ye. If nobody takes ye youse'll be allocated to somebody later.'

'What did he say?' asked Lizzie.

'I don't know, couldn't make him out. Do you think they'll all sound like that?'

'If they do we'll need to learn another language.'

The man began to call out names and the children answered as though it was a register taken in class, but by the end Sheila's name hadn't been called.

'Should I go and tell him?' she asked Lizzie.

'I don't know. He might send you back if you're not on the list.'

'I'll wait a wee while, maybe tell him later,' said Sheila.

The children sat in the hall, alert and expectant, and a few minutes later an elderly couple came in. The man in charge spoke to them. They nodded and went to stand at the front to look at the children. It was evident they were discussing them. As Sheila watched they appeared to reach a decision and pointed at a girl of about eleven. She was well dressed in a coat with a velvet collar and a beret. She was brought to the front, her name was crossed off, the elderly man signed for her and all three left the hall.

And so it went on all through the afternoon. The younger ones and well-dressed ones went first. Sheila and Lizzie being the oldest were beginning to think they'd be sent back to Belfast. Then around four o'clock a red-faced man in a checked suit came into the hall. He nodded at the man with the sheet, stood in front of the few remaining children and addressed them all.

'Now then, where's the wee lad with the bicycle?'

Nobody moved.

'There's a bicycle propped up outside and I'm told it got here by bus from Belfast with a wee boy.'

Sheila stood up. 'I think that would be me.'

'You're not a boy.'

'No,' said Sheila sharply, 'but it's my bicycle.'

'Is it indeed?' he looked her up and down. 'And tell me, can you ride it?'

Sheila met his gaze. 'Of course I can, or there'd be no point in bringing it with me.'

'I wonder, are you as sharp with reckoning as you are with your tongue?'

'I am,' said Sheila bluntly.

'I'll have her,' he turned to the man in charge, 'where do I sign?'

Sheila came out to the front and the man consulted his list. 'What's your name?'

'Sheila Goulding.'

'No one of that name here,' he said. 'I've a Sheila Gardiner.'

Sheila imagined the long journey home, the shame of not being picked. 'That's me,' she said.

She followed the man outside, collected her bike from against the wall and wheeled it into the street. She glanced sideways at him. He was tall and heavily built with a long stride and she had trouble keeping up with him. They walked in silence a hundred yards up a hill to a square. As they waited for a horse and cart to pass he seemed suddenly to remember she was at his side. He turned and thrust out his hand 'McManus.'

'Pleased to meet you, Mr McManus,' said Sheila shaking his hand. 'Have we far to go?'

He pointed to the opposite side of the square at the sign across a double-fronted shop, 'Francis McManus and Son, High Class Butchers and Slaughter Men'. By the time Sheila had read it, McManus was halfway across the road and she had to rush after him. They went up the side of the shop and in the back door.

'Bridie!' he called.

'I'm coming.' There was the sound of movement above them, then a creaking of each stair as someone slowly descended. The door opened and a woman came into the room sideways, manoeuvring her huge frame through the door.

'Frank, I thought you said you were coming back with a messenger boy?'

'She is.'

'She is what?'

'A messenger boy.'

'Frank, she's a girl!'

'I know that, but she's got her own delivery bike.'

'And where's she going to sleep? She … I mean the delivery boy … was meant to be sharing Dermot's room.'

'Aye well, sure she can sleep in the outhouse, there's a bed in there.'

Bridie McManus sighed heavily and lowered herself into a chair. 'What's your name?'

'Sheila.'

'Well now, Sheila. Go upstairs to the hot press on the landing and get yourself a couple of sheets and blankets and a pillow. Then you and me will go and sort out a wee house for you to live in. How's that?'

The outhouse was a small whitewashed building at the end of the yard with a green door and a small grimy window. Bridie took a large, rusty key from the hook on the wall and opened the door. 'I'll stay here,' she said. 'Away you in and have a look and come out and tell me what you think.'

It took a moment for Sheila's eyes to adjust to the darkness. Over to the left was a recess with an open hearth and to one side some wooden shelves; in the middle of the room was a table with two chairs up-ended and stacked on top. To the right was another recess, this time with a raised area covered by a flock mattress. She moved into the room and felt the cobwebs catch across her face, under her feet the floor was gritty, hard-packed earth.

'Well?' said Bridie when Sheila reappeared. 'What do you say?'

'Can we boil some water, and have you a scrubbing brush and bucket?'

Bridie showed her how to work the pump in the yard. 'No running water out of a tap here,' she said. 'And there's the privy, no flushing toilets here either. You're not in Belfast any more!'

Sheila worked through the late afternoon and on towards twilight when Bridie brought her out a couple of Tilly lamps – 'No electricity here at the flick of a switch.' She carried on into the evening, sweeping, scrubbing, washing down, returning again and again to empty filthy water down the drain. When the moon was high over the outhouse, Sheila made up the bed and, without taking her clothes off, fell into a deep sleep.

She took her breakfast with the family in the main house. Dermot the youngest son took after his father. He was a big lad for fifteen, with a ruddy complexion, but unlike his father he seemed shy and blushed when Sheila said good morning. The daughter, Rose, looked like she might take after her mother for size, but then Sheila realised she was pregnant.

Rose greeted Sheila warmly. 'I hope you were all right last night in that oul shed.'

'I was except for all the beetles that came out in the middle of the night.'

'Argh,' said Rose, 'that's terrible!'

'They'll be in the crevices in the stonework,' said her husband John. 'We get them sometimes in the slaughterhouse. I'll bring some DDT home with me and spray the place.'

The breakfast was an enormous fry – two eggs, bacon, soda bread, and potato bread. Sheila had never eaten so much in the morning.

'I'll bet you don't get a good feed like that in Belfast,' said Bridie.

'No,' laughed Sheila, 'I'll be the size of a mountain when I get home!' and wished immediately that she hadn't said it.

When they'd all eaten their fill, McManus pushed back his chair and said, 'Now then, Sheila, time to earn your keep.'

In the shop he showed her a notice in the window that he'd made the previous evening. 'Free home delivery of meat over five shillings.'

Sheila nodded, 'Oh, I see … meat's heavy to carry home when you've got other groceries and people might spend a bit more to get it delivered.'

'Well, I'm glad you see the benefit. I'd a job getting the rest of them to understand. Now, when you're not out delivering on your bike, you can serve in the shop. Rose does that, but with her, er …' – he searched for suitable words to use – 'with her condition, she could do with more help. She'll show you how the scales and bacon slicer and things work.'

'Oh, I can work scales and a bacon slicer already,' said Sheila.

'Can you indeed?' McManus looked impressed.

Sheila served in the shop all morning and Rose was glad to have someone working with her. 'My mother helps out if we get busy, especially Saturdays. My father stays in the back most of the time doing the butchering, but then he goes to meat auctions or to farms some days. Dermot and John work at the slaughterhouse. You wouldn't catch them in the shop.

'You're quick at adding up aren't you?' said Rose after watching Sheila tot up a list of six items in her head.

Unlike Belfast, there seemed to be no shortage of meat in the window and not one of the customers was refused what they asked for. After lunch there were several orders to be delivered. Rose put them in order to create a sensible delivery route.

'Now the addresses are written on each parcel,' said Rose. 'I'll give you directions to the first house and you can ask there for directions to the next house. Easy!'

Easy enough if at each house someone was at home, firstly to take the meat and, secondly to give the directions. Within half an hour, Sheila was hopelessly lost, having left blood-soaked parcels on several Dungannon doorsteps in the heat of the day. She stopped at a crossroads that had no signpost, determined not to panic, and climbed a five-bar gate to see the lie of the land. The town was below her to the left. She would take the road straight ahead and look for a left-hand turning.

She rounded a bend and the road dropped steeply in front of her, she took her feet off the pedals and free-wheeled, gathering speed. The wind raced past, cooling her body through her cotton dress. She stuck her legs out … faster and faster … She opened her mouth and let the noise of excitement stream out of her.

She didn't see the sign for the junction.

The lorry had been delayed at its last delivery and the driver knew his tea was already on the table going cold. Sheila shot out of the lane on to the main Dungannon road. She passed in front of the lorry, missing it by a whisker, skidded on the gravel on the far side of the road and went head over heels across the handlebars.

The thud of landing took the breath from her body and the crack on her head took everything else.

Chapter 7

It was Pat's custom, if the weather was fine, to walk the length of the drive from Stormont to the gate lodge at the bottom of the hill and back again in her lunch hour. She liked to imagine herself in a painting of the grand estate in an earlier, more romantic era, a solitary figure in the sweeping landscape in a bustle skirt and a large picture hat. She had just passed Carson's statue in the middle of the drive when she heard footsteps and William fell into step beside her.

'Hello Pat, how are you?'

'Fine.' She didn't look at him.

'Look, I'm sorry I had to rush off on Sunday. I had things I needed to sort out.'

She stopped and gave him a long hard stare. 'That would be arranging for animals to be shot, I suppose?'

'Well, yes.'

'You invited me out for the day then ran off and left me. What was it you said just before that, something about wanting us to be sweethearts?'

'I'm sorry.' He stared at his feet. Pat didn't reply; she'd had enough of his half-hearted attempts to court her. 'I just can't seem to get things right when it comes to us,' he added.

Was she meant to feel sorry for him? 'William it's not just that. It's … I don't know … sometimes you're like a scalded cat! Rushing to paint buildings, shoot animals, spend an hour with Pat.' She shook her head in despair. 'You need to focus on what's really important and see that through. You get distracted by the small things.'

'I get distracted by you.'

Too late, William realised what he had done.

'So I'm a "small thing" then, am I?'

There really was no going back after that.

'Mammy, you don't need to go to all this trouble. Sure I told you Macy'll take us as she finds us.'

'I'm not having a Yank come here and think we don't know how to do things properly.'

'But you've spring-cleaned the whole house. She could eat her tea off the floor and she'd come to no harm.'

'And that's how it should be. Now just run the iron over those napkins before you go to meet her off the bus.'

'Napkins!'

The beef sausages were sizzling in the pan with the onions and the apple tart was in the oven. The potatoes were ready to be mashed and the scallions added to make champ. Milk for the custard just needed a light under it when they were ready for pudding. Martha heard the sound of raucous laughter as Irene and her guest came round the back of the house and she tutted because they hadn't used the front door.

'Mammy, this is Macy.'

'Good to meet you, Mrs Goulding.'

'Good gracious, aren't you tall!' said Martha.

'Am I?' Macy laughed. 'Thank you for inviting me to your beautiful home.'

Martha inclined her head at the compliment. Americans are such polite people, she thought.

'I brought you a present.'

'For me?' Martha was all flustered and blushed. She unwrapped the tissue paper to reveal a colourful scarf inside. 'Ach, it has pictures on it.'

'Sure has,' said Macy. 'That there's the Empire State Building and there's the Brooklyn Bridge.'

'And that's the Statue of Liberty, isn't it?' asked Martha.

'You got it!'

Martha had just put the scarf round her shoulders when Pat and Peggy, hearing all the noise, came into the kitchen. Irene introduced them and Macy shook their hands.

'So you're the rest of the famous Golden Sisters – heard a lot about you.'

Macy ate everything put in front of her, with, as Pat later remarked, only her fork, and declared it all delicious. 'You even baked an American apple pie for me!'

Martha couldn't stop herself. 'Oh no, it's an Irish apple tart, so it is.' And everyone laughed.

Later, as they sat in the sitting room chatting, Peggy turned to Macy, 'You know who you put me in mind of – Maureen O'Hara. You know, she played Esmeralda in *The Hunchback of Notre Dame*.'

'You do look like her,' said Pat. 'It's your colouring. It's definitely Irish.'

'Do you have Irish ancestors?' asked Martha.

'I think so, way back. Couldn't tell you exactly where they were from.'

'Well, I think we should make you our adopted cousin,' said Irene and everyone agreed.

The talk turned inevitably to music. 'Irene was telling me how you all sing. How did that start?' asked Macy.

'We've sung in the choir at church since we were little. Then when the war started we were asked to sing at some concerts to raise money. Not Sheila, of course, she's too young,' Pat explained.

Peggy took up the story. 'Then Mr Goldstein – he owns the music shop where I work – decided to form a troupe of entertainers.'

'That's the Barnstormers, right?' asked Macy.

'Yes, all different acts: singers, musicians, comedians. We've even had a magician and a ventriloquist and dancers, of course.'

'What kinda dancers you got?'

'There's the Templemore Tappers – a group of girls who do tap and high kicking routines.'

'Any solo dancers?'

'No, not really, but sometimes Pat and Irene dance a bit on stage.'

'So, no Ginger Rogers or Carmen Miranda?'

'No, nothing as modern as that.'

'Would a solo dancer get a chance to be part of the Barnstormers?'

Suddenly, all eyes were on Macy.

Irene laughed. 'Don't tell me you're a dancer! What? Like Ginger Rogers?'

'More like Fred Astaire,' said Macy and everyone laughed.

'So tell me all about your husband,' Macy said when she and Irene went upstairs to chat. 'How did you meet him?'

Irene explained about the day trip to Stranraer where she met Sandy, a Scotsman, who was based at an RAF base nearby and about how he'd written to her and sent her a present. 'You're sitting on it,' laughed Irene and stroked the orange silk sari that covered her bed.

'It's beautiful,' said Macy.

'He sent it from India when he was stationed there. We lost touch for a while after that, until he was posted over here.'

'And you got to know each other, fell in love and decided to get married.'

'It wasn't quite like that. I suppose it was a bit of a whirlwind romance. To be honest, we didn't get to spend a lot of time together before we were married. Nor since, come to that. In fact, I nearly …' Irene hesitated, uncertain whether to reveal the other marriage proposal she'd received before she accepted Sandy.

'You nearly what?' Macy leaned forward inviting a confidence. 'Tell me.'

Irene smiled at the thought of what might have been. 'You mustn't tell anyone. My family don't know.'

'Course not, I love secrets and I'm good at keeping them!'

'I very nearly went to America. A boy asked me to go there with him. Just think, you and I could have met there and not here.'

'Wow, an elopement? Who was he?'

'His name was Sean – very tall, dark and handsome. His sister Theresa was my best friend. But he was in a lot of trouble. The police were after him. He hadn't done anything, but no one would have believed him.'

'But you did?'

'Yes, I did and I helped him a bit – passing messages and letters between him and his family. Then the police nearly caught him. That's when he decided to get away to America and he asked me to go with him.'

'Why didn't you go?'

The one question to which Irene had no answer. 'I don't know. I wasn't ready … maybe I was scared. Sometimes I think …'

'What if you'd gone with him … but then you wouldn't have married Sandy.'

'No.'

'Did you ever hear from Sean again?'

Irene shook her head. She had often thought about him. Remembered how they had hidden in a dusty attic while the police ransacked the street searching for him. She brought to mind the touch of his lips on hers, knew instinctively that he thought of her too, wherever he might be. 'No, I never did.'

Chapter 8

Beyond the heavy curtains the clear sky was lit by a crescent moon in its first quarter. In the front bedroom above McCracken's shop the only light was from a bedside lamp draped with a scarf and casting an orange glow. The heat from the paraffin stove was stifling and the fumes hung in the air. Aunt Hannah lay in the bed. Aggie leaned over to her and trickled a little water into her mouth and wet her lips.

'I'm really grateful to you for sitting up with me, Martha. When the doctor came this morning he said she wouldn't last the night.'

'Sure Aunt Hannah's family, I've known her since I was a wee girl. I'm glad to keep you company while Grace gets a bit of sleep – I know she's to be up for work in the morning.'

'Will your girls be all right on their own?'

'Ach aye, they're old enough to look after themselves.'

'And what about wee Sheila? Have you heard from her?'

Martha felt the fear that had plagued her for the past week grip her again, but this wasn't the time to speak of it. 'No, not yet, sure it's only a week since she left. She'll be busy settling in and she could be miles from a post office.'

'So you haven't got an address for her?'

'Not yet. I'm thinking I'll be told where she's staying when they sort out the paperwork.'

'Well, we'll miss her in the shop, so we will. But it's the best place for her. Did you hear the cities over the water have taken a pounding? I wouldn't be surprised if we're next on the list.'

'Where do you normally go when there's an alert?'

'There's a shelter up the street. It's not too bad inside and we know everyone there with them coming into the shop.'

There was a soft moan and Aunt Hannah whispered, 'Where am I?'

'Sssh now, you're in your bedroom.' Aggie patted her hand.

'Who are you?' the old woman struggled to lift her head.

'It's me, Aggie, and Martha's here too.'

'Is it time to get up?'

'No it's night-time – go to sleep.'

The longcase clock on the landing struck midnight and as the last chime faded, Aunt Hannah's breathing changed to a soft rasping sound. Martha and Aggie sat listening to it in silence. Ten minutes later, another sound crept into the room and rose within seconds to an urgent scream – the unmistakeable sound of the red alert. Neither Aggie nor Martha moved.

Grace came running in, pulling on her dressing gown. 'Are we going to the shelter?'

'You go, Grace, and you too, Martha. I'll stay here with Aunt Hannah.'

'No, I don't think so,' said Martha.

'Me neither,' said Grace. 'I'm staying here with you two.'

'There's no point,' Aggie spoke sharply to her sister. 'Away to the shelter with you.'

At that moment there came a different, chilling sound. Aunt Hannah was struggling to breathe and each breath became a rattle that threatened to be her last.

In Joanmount Gardens, Irene, Pat and Peggy had spent the evening rehearsing two new songs – 'I'm Nobody's Baby' and 'Fools Rush In'. Peggy had borrowed the sheet music from the shop and scored it for three voices and a piano. As usual, she took control of the rehearsal.

'A couple of hours hard practice now and then we'll polish the songs every night and by this time next week they'll be in our repertoire.'

'But we already have a good repertoire,' argued Pat. 'What's the point of learning more songs when there aren't any concerts where we can sing the songs we already know?' and she threw herself down on the settee and picked up a magazine.

'This business is all about being up to date. People want to hear the latest songs and dance to them as well,' snapped Peggy.

'So that's what this is all about – your singing with a dance band idea again!'

'Not necessarily. I tell you, Goldstein's slowly coming round to the idea of organising a show, especially after Myrtle's funeral.'

'What's Myrtle's funeral got to do with it?' asked Irene.

'You saw how many performers were there. Well, quite a few of them spoke to him about getting the Barnstormers back together – they want to do their bit. Think about the money we've raised and all the troops we've entertained, we shouldn't just give up.' Peggy paused, 'There was even talk of doing it for Myrtle.'

'Myrtle loved the Barnstormers,' said Irene. 'She'd want us to carry on.'

'Of course she would' – Peggy held out the score she'd prepared – 'and we need some new material.'

Pat was gracious enough to accept defeat. 'In that case, we'd better get on with it,' she said and she took the score and joined Irene and Peggy at the piano.

Later, as Peggy lay in bed with the tunes going round and round in her head, she congratulated herself on taking another small step towards singing with a band. The previous Saturday she'd made a point of speaking to Devlin during her break and had managed to bring the conversation round to the resident singer and his lack of up-to-date material. She was careful not to be too pushy and resisted the urge to mention the Golden Sisters, but he listened without comment and she hoped a seed had been planted. She stretched out in the bed that was all hers, now that Sheila was in Dungannon, and brought to mind the sight of Devlin in his tuxedo. She yawned and imagined an orchestra playing … her heavy eyelids closed …

Peggy loved to dance a quick foxtrot, especially when her dancing partner was the handsome James Devlin. He held her close and whispered something in her ear, something she couldn't quite catch over the music. Then someone was pulling her away from him and shouting. Her brain desperately tried to focus on the dance steps, but her head was filled with a screeching sound.

'Get up, get up – it's a raid!' Pat had pulled the bedclothes off her.

Peggy blinked and tried to focus. 'Leave me alone. It's a false alarm.'

'You don't know that. We have to go under the stairs.'

'There are no guns, I'm staying here 'til I hear the anti-aircraft guns.'

'Oh, you're just so stupid!' shouted Pat.

'No, I'm just so warm.' Peggy yawned, pulled the eiderdown over her head and imagined Devlin's arms around her again.

In the warm bedroom above McCracken's shop, Martha, Aggie and Grace dozed in their chairs and Hannah too was sleeping soundly. Martha was the first to stir, moving her head from side to side to ease her stiff neck. Something about the room was different. The air-raid siren had long since ceased but she detected a soft undertow of sound. In the seconds it took her to walk on tiptoe to the window, the noise changed from a low hum to a steadily rising drone and moments later she jumped as the anti-aircraft guns erupted. Aggie and Grace joined her at the window and together they scanned the sky streaked with anti-aircraft fire. The drone deepened and they caught their breath at the dark shapes of the German planes moving across the sky, dropping threads strung with luminous crystal-flares. They needn't have bothered; bright moonlight already laid bare the city beneath them.

*

At the first crack of the guns Peggy was on her feet and pulling the heavy coat that lay across her bed around her shoulders. She took the stairs two at a time, but in the hallway she hesitated. The noise above the house was deafening and seemed to resonate through her body. She paused, thought about the cramped space beneath the stairs, then opened the front door and stepped outside. The planes had already passed overhead and she wandered out into the road to follow their progress towards the city centre. A minute later they were over their target and dropping bombs on the docks and factories. The drone from the next wave crept over the mountain behind her, getting louder and louder, until suddenly the planes crested the hill and swooped low overhead. Peggy covered her ears against the noise, feeling her brain vibrate with its intensity. Above her, she counted five planes, one after the other, all close enough to see the markings on the under-carriages, and felt a rush of excitement at the thought that they were looking at her, a solitary, defiant figure in the middle of the road.

Under the stairs, Irene could stand it no longer. 'Where's Peggy? She must have heard the guns,' and she began to crawl over Pat towards the door.

'You have to stay here, Irene. Remember "your home is your air-raid shelter". If Peggy wants to put herself in danger—'

'Oh shut up, Pat. I'm going to get her,' and she pushed open the little door and crawled out from under the stairs.

'They're dropping incendiaries,' said Peggy as Irene joined her in the street. 'Do you see the red glow?'

'The docks, do you think?'

'Worse than that, the fires are spreading; it could be the whole city. Why are they doing this to us? It's not fair.'

'Nothing's fair, Peggy.'

'What's going to happen to us?'

'We'll hide under the stairs and if we wake up in the morning, we'll thank God we're spared and if we've still work to go to that'll be something, won't it?'

'But how much more of this can we take?'

'As much as there is, there's nothing else for it.' From over the hill behind them the drone came again. Irene took her sister's arm, 'Come on now, we have to get inside,' and then put on Pat's voice, 'remember: our home is our air raid shelter!'

'For God's sake, don't you start!'

The thousands of fires sparked by the incendiaries caught hold in houses, shops, mills and factories. They joined together, devoured everything in their path and, within an hour, the sky across the city was one enormous conflagration. In Manor Street, close to the city centre, the upstairs bedroom was bathed in an eerie red glow and still the three women stood at the window waiting for the real damage to begin.

A soft whimpering startled them and they turned to see Aunt Hannah struggling to raise her head.

Aggie rushed to her side. 'There, there, everything's fine.'

But Aunt Hannah gripped her hand. 'Am I …' she struggled to speak. 'Am I dead?'

'Ach sure, no.' Aggie stroked the wisps of white hair from the old woman's face. 'Amn't I here with you?'

Aunt Hannah licked her cracked lips. 'Am I … in hell?'

'Of course you're not.' Then, realising she could see the glow of the flames, Aggie added, 'it's just a fire outside, that's all.'

'Is it a bone-fire?'

'Aye,' said Aggie, 'that's it – the bone-fire. Now you go back to sleep, for haven't we to be up early in the morning to go and watch the Orangemen?'

And Aunt Hannah closed her eyes, all the better to listen to the pipe band.

The night wore on and the incendiaries gave way to high explosives and parachute bombs and the area under attack widened. Soon the deafening noise of exploding shells encircled Manor Street. In the bedroom they had closed the curtains for fear of the windows blowing in. A bomb exploded at the end of the street, so close it shook the house and they thought their eardrums had burst.

'Is there anything under the bed?' asked Martha.

'Probably a week's worth of dust. Why?' said Aggie.

'Maybe we should crawl under it?' Martha suggested.

'But what about Aunt Hannah?'

The old woman's breaths were laboured and rasping again and Martha, embarrassed at her suggestion, sought to make amends. 'I'll go down and fill a hot jar; her hands are like ice. I'll make us some tea too.'

'Get a few broken biscuits from the boxes in the shop,' shouted Grace after her, 'We may as well eat something.'

The kitchen retained some heat from the range and while the kettle boiled Martha stood over it warming her hands and listening to the steady falling of bombs. She hoped that Irene, Pat and Peggy, being further away from the city centre, were safe. She filled the hot jar for Aunt Hannah, then poured the tea, found a tray and carried it up to them.

'Did you forget the biscuits?' asked Grace.

'Ach, my head's away. I'll go and get them.'

'Never bother yourself, sure it doesn't matter.'

'No, no, I'll go and get them.'

There was enough light coming through the shop window for Martha to find the Crawford biscuit tins behind the counter. She was just searching for some broken custard creams when there was a loud crump from outside. She froze in the moment of silence that followed and as the bomb exploded the air was sucked from her lungs and she was flung hard against the wall. There was a final shudder and the entire stock rained down on her head.

It was well past three in the morning when the last of the bombs fell on the city, but by then Martha's girls had already closed their eyes and, in the cramped space, had found a soft part of a sister on which to lay their head and fall into a deep sleep. The knocking on the front door did not wake them.

The knocking on the kitchen window caused Irene to stir a little, but it wasn't until there was banging on the back door and a man's voice shouting that she jumped up, wide awake, and banged her head on the step above her. She quickly shook her sisters. 'Wake up there's someone at the door!'

There was a sharp intake of breath from Pat. 'It sounds like William. What's he doing here? He mustn't see me, Irene. You'll have to get rid of him!'

Irene crawled out into the kitchen and called behind her, 'When I go to let him in, you two sneak away upstairs.'

William brought the smell of smoke into the cold kitchen with him and stood looking pale and drawn, twisting his hat in his hands. 'I've come for Pat, where is she?'

'She's upstairs. What time is it?'

'After six.'

'Time we were ready for work.'

'Ha!' His laugh was humourless. 'Don't bother yourself, there'll be no work today.'

'Is it really bad?'

He sighed deeply and rubbed his hand across his eyes as if wiping away the scenes he had witnessed. 'It's been burning all night. They couldn't save much.'

'The aircraft factory?'

'Gone.'

Irene covered her mouth, stifling a cry.

'Everything,' he went on, 'what the bombs missed, the fire consumed. It's burning still.'

'Did the firewatchers and the fire brigade not–'

'There was no water.'

'No water!'

'It was low tide – they couldn't get the pressure. And anyway the bombs had ruptured hundreds of water mains.'

'Mammy stayed down in Manor Street last night with her cousins. Do you know if that was bombed?'

'There's damage in that area, but I don't know the detail yet.'

The door opened and Peggy came in wrapped in her dressing gown. 'What's going on?'

'William says we can't go to work, it's all been bombed or burned.'

'Not Goldstein's shop?'

William didn't answer; he was looking past her to where Pat stood fully dressed in the doorway.

'Hello, William.'

'Get your coat, Pat.'

'I don't need a lift from you. I'll get the bus like I always do.' Her tone was dismissive.

Her sisters looked at her in amazement. 'Pat, the bombing–'

'Is Stormont still standing?' she directed the question to William.

'It is,' he said.

'In that case, I'll be in at the usual time to collate the information on the bombing and write you a report.'

'As your superior officer, I'm ordering you to get your coat and come with me.'

'You can't talk to me like that, I'm–'

'There's no time to waste. I'm not waiting in Stormont for reports! It's chaos out there and I need to tour the city first-hand to see the situation and I need you, Pat' – he spat out her name – 'I need you to record my findings in detail, so there'll be no delay in implementing effective emergency measures!' He paused, drew breath and, struggling to control his temper, repeated in a low voice, 'Now, get your coat.'

Outside the sky glowed pink, not the colour of dawn, but of disaster. They drove towards the city in silence and soon the first signs of the bombing were evident: rows of houses smouldering, their roofs all but gone; craters in the road; slates strewn everywhere, crunching under the tyres.

William stopped the car at the end of Manor Street. 'Irene said your mother was staying here last night. Go and check she's all right.'

The gable wall at the end of the road had collapsed, exposing the rooms with the wallpaper stripped and hanging like rags, and every window in the street had gone. Pat began to run, past the people sweeping up glass, and a man trying to board up a window with an old door. 'Please God let her be safe,' she whispered. The shop was on the end of a row of terraced houses. It was still there! She quickened her pace. The window had gone and the door was hanging off its hinges.

Inside, Pat picked her way through the stock that had been

hurled from the shelves – blackened cans, burst packets – past a set of scales balanced precariously on an upturned crate of apples, and towards the chenille curtain at the back of the shop. She stopped … listened … could it be her mother's voice?

She rushed into the room and there in the armchair was Martha, her clothes blackened and torn. Aggie was kneeling on the floor beside her, bathing a wound on Martha's forehead.

'Mammy, are you all right? You're bleeding!' shouted Pat.

'Ach, she's fine, aren't you Martha?' said Aggie.

But Martha was already on her feet. The sight of Pat had made her think the worst. 'What's happened? Is it Irene, Peggy? Where are they?'

'No, no, it's all right. They're safe.'

'But what are you doing here at this hour? Why aren't you at home?'

'I have to go to work; there are things to be done.'

Martha shook her head in disbelief. 'God have mercy, child, are you mad?'

'I wanted to make sure you were safe.'

Martha's tone softened. 'Aye well, I'm glad to see you. I'll survive. But mind you if I hadn't bent down to get those custard creams who knows what state I'd be in now. The counter took the brunt of the blast, praise be to God.'

'But that's a bad cut on your head, you'll need to get it seen to,' said Pat.

'There was so much flying about in the blast, something knocked me out, but sure the bleeding's nearly stopped now.'

'Grace has gone to get the doctor,' said Aggie. 'We'll ask him to have a look at it when he comes round. Oh Pat, you'll not know that Aunt Hannah died during the night.'

'Ach no,' said Pat, 'I'm sorry to hear that.'

'She slipped away in her sleep,' explained Aggie, 'with all hell breaking loose around us and your poor mother buried under our entire stock.'

'Pat, if you're sure Irene and Peggy are fine then I'll stay here a while to help clear up,' said Martha.

'Aye, of course they are. I'll try to find out what's happening at the aircraft factory and at Mr Goldstein's shop and whether they can go into work tomorrow.' She didn't mention what William had said about the damage. In fact, she thought it wise not to mention William at all.

Pat was dreading the hours that lay before her touring the devastated city. She wanted to be of use to William, but the firm set of his jaw and the fact that he didn't look at her when she got back in the car made her wish that they could at least be civil to each other.

'My mother's safe,' she told him.

'Good,' he replied, before slipping the car into gear and heading for the city centre.

For the next three hours, they inspected the major industrial areas. At the docks, the shipyard and aircraft factory, William dictated his findings and recommendations without a trace of emotion and Pat meticulously recorded them.

They left the car in Shaftesbury Square where the bomb damage was not so bad and walked towards the city centre. As the City Hall came into view their steps slowed then stopped altogether. A section of the roof was gone; only the black twisted rafters remained, silhouetted against the sky with a hundred spirals of smoke curling upwards.

Pat had been close to tears several times at the sights she had seen, but this was different. Soundlessly, the tears fell. How long did she and William stand there? Long enough to contemplate a frightening future where no one would go to bed with any certainty that they would be alive in the morning. She felt a touch on her arm, took the handkerchief William offered.

'It's lunchtime,' he said, 'let's try to find somewhere to eat.'

The Pam-Pam was surprisingly busy despite the scenes of destruction just streets away, but the solemn look on the faces of the diners and their subdued talk gave it an eerie atmosphere. Without asking her, William ordered sandwiches and tea and they waited in silence for them to arrive. How strange to be here with William, thought Pat, when this is where we first met. She looked at the table where they had sat and pictured them there. They had come straight from work – she from the linen mill; he from Stormont, although she did not know that then. Goldstein had been with them, chatting about his idea to pair them up – the soprano and the tenor – to add some culture to his troupe of entertainers. William followed her gaze.

'I was rude to you that day, wasn't I?' he said.

'Not rude, a bit unfriendly maybe,' she smiled.

'I forgot my manners. I was angry because I didn't even know you, yet Goldstein wanted us to sing together.'

'I was embarrassed when he left us alone to discuss it.'

'I know you were and I should have put you at your ease. I'd a lot on my mind, but that's no excuse.' For the first time that day William looked her in the eye. 'But we did it, didn't we?' He leaned across the table and said softly. 'Singing with you was so special. I wish …' He hesitated, shook his head, 'Pat I'm no good at this.'

The waitress arrived with the sandwiches and tea things. 'I'm sorry we've no sugar, the wee bit we had went this morning.'

William looked away.

'That's fine,' said Pat, 'we'll do without,' and busied herself pouring tea, then filling the half-empty pot with hot water. In the past she would have left William's words hanging between them, assuming she had no right to ask him to explain, but she'd had enough of his inability to express his feelings.

'No good at what, William?'

'You and me … I can't get it right. I want to, but then the work just seems to elbow everything else out of the way. How can I …' He struggled for the right words, 'How can I be courting you when all the time I'm thinking about shelters and searchlights and evacuating children? I can't be that selfish, do you see?'

'I do see, of course I do. There's nothing more important than the work you're doing. I know that because every day I see what you're trying to do.'

'But you know what makes it even harder?' He leaned forward searching her face, 'It's having you there by my side. Every day is a struggle to concentrate on what needs to be done when I just want to … oh, I don't know … just get in the car and drive away with you as far from Belfast as we can get. Imagine you and me in Donegal.'

'You're saying I distract you?'

'Yes. No. I feel as though I should be paying you more attention.'

'I've never–'

'I know you haven't, but … you mean so much to me and I want to show you how I feel. Trouble is, in the midst of all this' – and he waved his hand towards the window and beyond – 'it seems so …'

'Irrelevant?'

'I was going to say inappropriate.'

Pat turned away. The tears would surely fall if she looked any longer at William's anguished face. Misery settled in both their hearts.

William absent-mindedly picked up a sandwich and returned it to the plate uneaten. Pat smoothed the tablecloth. Time slipped away and left them alone.

Eventually Pat spoke. 'Maybe I should resign or get a transfer to another department. That way you won't be thinking about us.'

'Not that, Pat, please. I need you to support me in the work,' his voice cracked, 'and, God help me, I need you because I can't bear to be parted from you.'

She took a deep breath, 'Nor I from you.'

It seemed the discussion had reached an impasse and they sat in silence, the sandwiches and tea untouched, but both of them glad that their feelings had been shared. Again it was Pat who broke the silence. 'At work we can be together, for now that's the most important thing. But you must stop thinking about my feelings – I'll be your colleague and friend, but you need to focus on what this city needs.'

'And you'd be happy with that?'

'I would,' she said, 'until the chance comes along to escape to Donegal.'

They left the Pam-Pam and within minutes were picking their way along the middle of the road and past the main shops at

Donegall Place. The street was running with water from burst mains and on either side buildings were still smouldering. A police sergeant was standing outside Anderson and McAuley department store, surrounded by the shattered remains of the plate glass windows. William introduced himself and asked for an appraisal of the situation.

The sergeant stood to attention and delivered the information as though it was a report from his notebook. 'No electricity, water mains blown to hell, gas mains too with a danger of explosion. The engineers are shutting them down as quickly as they can. Some looting early on, but we've got officers on the streets now to deter them.'

On they went, towards Royal Avenue where they came across some shop workers half-heartedly picking over the debris, trying to salvage their stock. Here and there workmen had begun to board up windows. In the faces of the people they passed, they saw only despair and the realisation that such devastation could never be put right.

And then they were outside Goldstein's music shop. The windows were gone and, lying like a paper pathway, out of the shop and into the road, were scattered hundreds of copies of sheet music sucked out by the updraft of a nearby explosion. Inside the shop Goldstein was sitting on the piano stool in front of the baby grand, hands clasped in front of him, his head bent. Startled by the noise of them trampling over glass, he looked up, but didn't seem to recognise them.

'Mr Goldstein, it's me Pat Goulding. William Kennedy's with me. Are you all right?'

He stood up, gave an elaborate shrug of his shoulders and lifted his hands. 'The inevitable has happened, my shop has been bombed, but I thank God that I am still alive and, make no mistake, I will soon be back in business. Someone is coming this afternoon to board up the windows and tomorrow we will begin the clear up. You must tell Peggy to come in as usual and that she must wear her oldest clothes.'

'That's the spirit,' said William, 'I wish I could bottle that, it's exactly what's needed to get through this.'

'Well, I've been doing a lot of thinking sitting here this morning,' said Goldstein. 'The people of Belfast were stoic after the Easter bombings, but this is much worse and life is going to get a lot harder. You know, I met a young man last week at the synagogue; some friends helped him get out of Poland. He told me ...' He paused, then shook his head, as if the boy's words were too painful to repeat, and waved his hand at the chaos in the shop. 'This is nothing compared to what others are suffering who find themselves under the Nazi jackboot. Ways must be found to get through the anguish that's coming. I tried before to raise people's spirits when I formed the Barnstormers, but after the last bombing I lost heart. I thought people wouldn't want entertainment when they'd lost so much, but I was wrong. They do not know it yet, but music and laughter are exactly what they need and it is my job to provide them.'

'You're going to re-form the Barnstormers?' asked Pat.

'Indeed I am,' he smiled as he repeated the phrase he had used so many times before, 'and you two – Belfast's Sweethearts – will be the stars of the show!'

Chapter 9

On the wall at the side of the bed was a picture ... red ... a heart ... delicate hands ... the face of a man watching over her ... a kind face. Sheila recalled seeing him before when she awoke from a deep sleep. How many times had she closed her eyes on his face and slept?

'Sure there you are now, wideawake, praise be to God.' Bridie McManus was next to the bed.

'Where am I?' asked Sheila.

'You're in our Dermot's room. We couldn't a left ye in that wee house a yours on your own, could we? Not with ye being concussed an' all. We've sent him to sleep out there.'

Sheila tried to sit up and winced at the pain that shot from the tips of her fingers to her elbow. 'What's happened to me?'

'Ah, your wrist's in a bit of a mess, now. Not broken, but you'll have that bandage on it a while yet. Do you remember being knocked off your bike?'

'I think so, but I don't remember how I got here. I woke up a few times and went back to sleep. Have I slept in? Is it time to get up?

Bridie laughed, 'Aye, ye could say that.'

Sheila threw the covers back, 'Rose'll be needing me in the shop.'

'Not so fast, now,' said Bridie and she helped her sit up and propped the pillows behind her head. 'Sit a wee while, get your bearings. Shall I to make ye a bite to eat?'

Sheila realised she was starving. 'Yes please, but can I get up to eat it?'

'I don't see why not. You've got the colour back in your face. Get yourself dressed and come down.'

The fire was lit in the kitchen to take the chill off the damp day. Even so, Sheila was glad of the blanket Bridie offered her. She wrapped herself in it and curled up in the chair.

'I remember delivering the meat and then I got lost. Is that when I fell off my bike?'

'Aye, and just missed bein' hit by a lorry I'm told.'

'What happened to the bike?'

'To tell ye the truth I don't know. We were more concerned about you.' Bridie put a thick bacon sandwich in front of Sheila. 'We brought you back here; the doctor said you'd want careful watching. Powerful dangerous, you know, a blow to the head.'

'How long have I been here then?'

'A few days, you've been dozing on and off.'

Sheila jumped up, 'Oh I'll need to write to my mother to tell her I arrived safely and to give her your address so she can write to me.'

'Aisy now' – Bridie helped her back into the chair – 'time enough for writin' when your wrist's a bit stronger. Sure your mother knows yer here with us. The Evacuee Officer had to write and tell her about the accident, regulations you know. Anyway, he just said you'd fallen off yer bike bumped yer head and sprained yer wrist, nothin' to worry about.'

'So she knows I'm safe?'

'Of course she does. You'll probably get a letter from her any day now. In the meantime, yer excused shop duties. So you an' me'll just potter about 'til yer feelin' better.'

Over the next few days Sheila and Bridie fell into a routine that was both mundane and mysterious. After breakfast, when the rest of the household had gone to work, Sheila cleared the table while

Bridie washed the dishes. Then they'd settle down at the fireside, Bridie with her knitting and Sheila with a book. The McManus family weren't great readers, but they did have an oak bookcase with a set of Everyman's library books.

'You go ahead and help yerself, Sheila. Sure nobody's touched them there books since Frank brought them home from an auction in Pomeroy twenty years ago. Claims he waved at a fella across the room and it cost him ten shillings. He was half-cut at the time, if ye ask me.'

When Bridie got to the end of the ball of wool, she looked up and asked, 'What book is it ye have?'

'It's called *Jane Eyre*. I think it's her life story. She's only a wee girl now.'

'Tell ye what, why don't ye read it out loud, give me somethin' to listen to while I crack on with the knittin'?'

And so they whiled away an hour or two until dinner time.

'Would ye credit the badness of that John Reid gettin' Jane in trouble for no good reason? I'd take my hand to him, I'm tellin' ye!' said Bridie as they tucked into fried egg and potato bread. 'I'm dyin' to know what happens to the wee girl.'

Just before two o'clock, with Jane Eyre on her way to Lowood School, Bridie shoved the knitting down the side of her chair. 'We'll take a wee break there, I think,' and she heaved herself up and made her way over to the range to put the kettle on the hob. 'I'm expectin' a visitor,' she said. The hesitant note in her voice caused Sheila to look up from the book.

'Do you want me to go?'

'Ach no, there's no need.' Bridie crossed the kitchen and sat down. She clearly wanted to say something, but seemed to be searching for a way to begin. 'Give me your hands, Sheila.' Bridie took Sheila's hands in her own, closed her eyes and breathed deeply. After a moment she began to speak quietly as though reading something behind her closed eyelids.

'I see you crying. The room is very warm. There's a man nearby.' Bridie paused as though deciphering something, 'Aah I see … his soul has left his body.'

Sheila pulled her hands back, but Bridie held them fast.

'Something more …'

After a moment Bridie opened her eyes and released her grip. Then she lifted her hand to Sheila's startled face. 'Don't be frightened. What's happened to you can be known by others through you,' and she caught a lock of Sheila's hair as it rested on her shoulders. 'I saw you another time and your hair was cropped like a boy's. Why did you cut it?'

'The man was my daddy, I was the only one there when he died and I sold my hair because we needed some money. How do you know these things?'

'The same way I know how to breathe.' The kettle began to rattle gently on the range. 'Give me your hands again.'

Curiosity got the better of Sheila's fears and she didn't resist when Bridie took her hands and turned them palms upwards. This time Bridie did not close her eyes, but instead examined Sheila's hands, tracing her fingers along their lines

'I see you all alone in a bright light and there's music all around you.'

'I don't remember that,' said Sheila.

'Don't worry, you will.' The kettle began to whistle and at the same moment there was a soft tapping on the back door.

'Now Sheila, I want you to make a pot of tea and, when I tell you, bring three cups to the table for you, me and the visitor. The rest of the time you're to sit in the chair by the fire and be absolutely still.' With that Bridie opened the door and an elderly woman wearing an ancient hat of brown felt pulled low over her brow came in. Her coat was good tweed, but many sizes too big for her and on her feet were Wellington boots.

Sheila busied herself making the tea, but kept an ear open to the conversation. The woman had the strong Dungannon accent, but fortunately Bridie did most of the talking.

First she took the woman's rough hands and closed her eyes. 'Ye lost a beast, did ye?'

'Aye, aye. A pig …' The cause, though given, was indecipherable.

'Rows with yer son again – he's not tellin' ye the truth, ye know.'

And so it went on: Bridie seeing and the woman believing, until she released the woman's hands and called, 'Sheila, fetch Mrs McCann a cup a tea, will ye?'

All three sat at the table drinking, the two women swapping gossip, while Sheila tried hard to catch the gist. Mrs McCann drank noisily and drained her cup past the dregs, so they stuck to the side of the cup. Then she pushed it across the table to Bridie, who with an almost imperceptible nod of her head signalled to Sheila to move away. Bridie placed the cup upside down on the saucer and turned it three times before lifting it to examine the tea leaves.

'You've a store of apples from last year. You need to get them used or they'll not be fit to eat.'

Mrs McCann nodded. Bridie turned the cup.

'There's a letter here, from across water on its way to ye.'

'That'll be me brother in Manchester.'

'I don't think so,' said Bridie. 'This is from very far away.'

Mrs McCann opened her mouth to speak then closed it again. She glanced over at Sheila, who appeared lost in her book, then leaned across the table and whispered, 'Could it be from Amerikay?'

'Aye, it could, right enough,' said Bridie.

Mrs McCann's eyes opened wide. 'And is it good news I'll be gettin'?'

'Suffice it to say, there'll be money involved.'

'Well, I never, after all these years.'

When Mrs McCann had gone, Sheila went to the table where Bridie was sitting quietly. 'You saw those things in the tea leaves?'

'Not really.'

'So it wasn't true?'

'Ach, it might be. We'll have to wait an' see.' Bridie picked up a silver florin that lay on the table and went to the dresser.

'And she pays you to read the future?'

Bridie opened a cocoa tin and dropped the money inside. 'Not at all, she gives the money to me and I give it to the missionaries to help the wee black babies.'

By the end of the week, Jane Eyre had seen the death of her dear friend Helen at Lowood School and, with an authorial sleight of hand, had grown into a young woman – no longer a pupil, but a respected teacher. In the McManus kitchen Sheila had seen two more women drink their tea to the dregs and learn their future and Bridie had finished the matinee coat and was struggling to shape the matching bootees.

'Bridie, can I ask you something?'

'Ask away,' came the reply.

'Could you teach me to do that?'

'What ... knit bootees?'

'No, teach me to tell a person's fortune!'

'Sure what would ye want to do that for?'

'Well, those women come in and they look sort of worried and when they leave they seem easier in their minds somehow and ...' Sheila struggled to explain, 'I just thought it would be good to help people like that.'

'Aye, but maybe they're worried because they know they shouldn't be dabbling in things they don't understand and when they leave me they're relieved I've told them nothin' bad.'

Sheila's eyes widened, 'You see bad things too?'

Bridie raised her eyebrows as though surprised at Sheila's naivety. 'Look, I see what I see, but I tell them what they want to hear.'

'But how do you see it all? Will you not tell me?'

Bridie rested the knitting in her lap, 'Come over here and sit down, Sheila. Now then, take my hands like I take theirs.' Sheila took Bridie's large soft hands and held them. 'Close your eyes and try to clear your mind; the only thing you're to think about are my hands in yours. Sit quietly and wait for an idea of what to say to enter your head.'

Sheila did as she was told. Time passed, her mind wandered and she struggled to bring it back to Bridie's hands. In not much more than a minute she opened her eyes to see Bridie smiling at her.

'Well, what did you see?'

'Nothing, I saw nothing at all.' Sheila couldn't hide her disappointment.

'Ye must've seen something.'

'I didn't. Nothing to speak of anyway.'

'Ye can say anything that comes into your head.'

'Yes, but it wouldn't be seeing something from your past or something that's going to happen to you in the future, would it?'

'Sheila, ye asked me to teach ye how I do it and that's it, I've told ye. How to get it right can't be taught. I think it's something in my head that's switched on, but in other people it isn't.'

'Can I have another try?'

Bridie nodded. 'I'll be happy if you tell me these bootees'll be finished before my grandchild arrives.'

Sheila concentrated hard, her grip on Bridie's hands tightened, she felt them slip a little, and for the briefest of moments she imagined them smeared red with blood like Frank's when he carried the trays of meat into the shop.

'I can see you. You've been helping Mr McManus with the butchering,' said Sheila and opened her eyes.

'Have I indeed? Well that'll be a first!'

The Municipal Technical Institute was one of Belfast's grandest buildings with elaborate carved stonework and elegant turrets topped by copper domes, but the Goulding sisters had no wish to raise their eyes from the pavement to marvel at its splendour. Instead, as the rain beat off the streets, all three of them huddled under one umbrella and dashed across College Square, intent only on avoiding puddles.

At the heart of the Institute was a large auditorium with arched ceilings. Along one side of the room were tall thin stained-glass windows, giving it a church-like feel, but instead of biblical scenes they depicted the crafts studied by the students. Several performers stood around chatting, others were already seated and each new arrival was greeted with hugs or handshakes and a noticeable rise in the noise level.

'Mr Goldstein invited all the Barnstormer acts along, but there'll be new acts who want to audition as well,' explained Peggy. 'He's asked me to accompany anyone who needs backing music, so I'll go and get ready at the piano.'

'Peggy, you remember the songs we've agreed on?' asked Pat.

'What kind of a question is that?'

'It's an important one. I want to be sure you won't play the introduction to a song you prefer, rather than what we've rehearsed.'

'Ach, catch yourself on. Why would I do that?' and she flounced off.

'Because that's what you usually do!' Pat shouted after her.

The room was filling up fast and Goldstein was already at the front checking his watch when Irene caught sight of someone coming through the door.

'She's here!' she shouted and waved both hands. 'Macy, I'm over here!'

'I'm glad you came,' Irene whispered to Macy as they took their seats.

'Thanks for asking me to come along.'

'Are you going to audition?'

'Sure am, wouldn't miss this for the world.'

'Did you bring your music?'

Macy smiled, 'Yeah,' she tapped the side of her head, 'it's all in here.'

Goldstein had made his way on to the stage, where he straightened his dicky bow, put his thumbs in his waistcoat pockets and called for silence.

'Thank you all for giving up your Sunday afternoon and coming out in such awful weather. You will know from my letter that I am keen to get the Barnstormers performing again. You have only to look into the faces of your family and friends and people you pass in the street to know how badly affected they are by what has happened to our city. Some people might argue that it is the wrong time to be putting on a show – singing, dancing, telling jokes – but I say to them, this is exactly when shows are needed. You are talented young people with the power to help others through these dark days and I am determined to give you the opportunity to do so.' He paused to let his words sink in, then with a flourish he announced, 'I am proud to say that our next concert will take place in less than three weeks' time in this wonderful hall!'

The Barnstormer acts went through their usual routines and some like the Golden Sisters had new material. Peggy stuck to the agreed songs and they gave a good account of themselves. Pat and William sang a duet and it was clear they were under-rehearsed, but Irene also thought their performance lacked the connection between them that was so exciting when they first started to sing together. But the biggest disappointment was the Templemore Tappers. Their energetic dance routines always lifted the show; they weren't the greatest of dancers, but their sense of fun and enjoyment usually made up for their lack of precision. It was sad to watch them go through the motions: not quite achieving the straight line; an uncertainty in the changes of formation; high kicks a little lower than before; and fixed smiles that quickly faded away. The Tappers were dancing, but Myrtle wasn't there to lead them. Irene felt the tears prick at her eyes, she blinked and they fell, she wiped them away and they came again. Her friend was gone, leaving her and the dancers bereft. The routine ended and the Tappers, heads bowed, left the stage. Goldstein sensing the mood had altered within the hall called a break after which the new acts would audition.

'Come on,' said Macy, 'let's find somewhere where I can change and put on my make-up.'

In the ladies' toilets, no bigger than a broom cupboard, Macy quickly applied her make-up in front of a tiny mirror hung behind the door and finished with the reddest lipstick Irene had ever seen. Then she pulled a pair of black trousers and a white shirt from her bag followed by a pair of men's shoes.

'You're not wearing those, are you?' said Irene.

'Sure am.'

'But they're men's clothes.'

'Yep.' Macy changed quickly, then took a black tie from her trouser pocket, deftly tied it and straightened her collar. She put on the shoes and tried out a few tap steps – the metal tips rang out on the tiles. Finally, she pinned up her mass of red curls and covered them with a black homburg tilted forward at an angle. She held out her arms and spun round on her heels.

'How do I look?'

'Amazing!' said Irene.

Macy stood in the middle of the stage, hands behind her back, head bowed and her face hidden under the homburg. There was no music just the sound of one foot moving from side to side, tapping out a rhythm. A stillness fell and the audience held its breath. From behind Macy's back came the sound of clicking fingers. She slid one foot out to the side and spread both arms wide, then lifted her head to reveal her beautiful face – the audience gasped.

Later, when those who had watched Macy dance tried to describe what they had seen, they found only inadequate words. It was brilliant and astonishing and all those other superlatives, but none could explain how the combination of grace, rhythm and the simple sound of tapping metal had mesmerised everyone in the room.

Chapter 10

Two weeks after Sheila sprained her wrist, Jane had married Mr Rochester, Rose had taken to her bed exhausted and not a single letter had arrived from Belfast.

'Why doesn't Mammy write?'

Bridie stopped scrubbing the frying pan and gave Sheila a hard stare, 'I couldn't say, but there again ye haven't written to her, have ye?'

'She promised she would and she knows I've got a bad wrist, doesn't she?'

'Yer wrist's fine now. There's a writing pad and envelopes in the sideboard so you've only to write it and stick a stamp on it.'

'I'll do it on Sunday then.'

'Well, see that you do.'

But on Sunday morning there was a knock on the door of Sheila's little house in the yard and when she went outside there was no one there – just her bike against the wall. She sat on it and turned the handlebars from side to side testing the strength of her wrist. Something made her look up and there was Dermot at his window watching her. He made to step back out of sight, but she signalled for him to come down.

'Did you fix my bike, Dermot?'

He smiled shyly. 'Yes, me and me da. It wasn't too bad, just a buckled front wheel and a puncture.'

'It's great to have it back. I thought I'd never see it again.'

'Me da says you've to be more careful on it. You might not be so lucky next time.'

'I know. I'll maybe keep off the main roads for a while.'

'You could ride around the Black Lough – there's no traffic there. I could show you, if you like.'

'Would you?'

Dermot grinned, 'No problem, sure I'll get my bike and you can follow me.'

The path alongside the lough was narrow so they rode in single file. In places it was overgrown with trees and bushes. Every now and again Dermot would shout a warning for her to take care, but apart from that they did not speak. After a while the high hedgerows gave way to fields of oats and the path widened. Sheila quickened her pace and came alongside Dermot. He did not acknowledge her, but she felt him glance in her direction from time to time. The morning grew warm and they stopped in the shade of an ash tree to rest.

'Would you like a drink?' Dermot took a bottle of lemonade from his saddlebag and offered it to Sheila.

'No it's yours, you have it.'

'No, you take it. I brought it for you.' He set the bottle down beside her.

'We'll share it then,' said Sheila and unscrewed the top. It was warm, but felt good on her dry throat.

He took a white paper bag from his saddlebag and sat down next to her. 'Do you like Paris buns?'

'Sure, they're my favourite.'

He broke the bun in half and offered it to her.

'Just like a picnic,' said Sheila and handed him the lemonade.

Dermot hesitated.

'Go on,' she laughed.

He took the bottle and raised it to his lips.

'Good?'

Dermot smiled. 'Yes,' he said, 'very good.'

They sat in silence a while then Dermot asked, 'What's it like in Belfast?'

'Have you never been?'

'No, but I'm going to go.'

'Well, there's more people, houses, shops, buses and we have trams.'

'And the sea … have you been to the seaside?'

'Of course, have you not?'

'No, me ma and da have been to Bundoran, but that was years ago, before Rose was born. Now it's hard to leave the shop and the slaughterhouse.'

'You can see the water in Belfast, but that's just the lough. The real seaside is where there's a beach and you can paddle in the sea. Sometimes, we go along the shore to Carrickfergus, or Holywood, or even Bangor, where you can make sandcastles and paddle in the water. But that was before Daddy died.'

'You live with your mother and sisters, don't you?'

'Yes, there's Irene – she's the oldest – then Pat, Peggy and me. I'm the youngest.'

'Do you miss them?'

Sheila thought for a moment. 'Sometimes I do, like at night when I can't get to sleep, but in the day …' she sighed. 'It seems like they're so far away. I don't just mean the journey on the bus.' She picked some pebbles from the path and made a circle of them. 'I forget all about them sometimes.'

'You haven't had a letter from anyone have you?'

'No.'

'You should just write to them.'

'Yes, I know.'

She gathered up the pebbles, threw them out into the lough and watched the circles of interconnecting ripples spread and die.

They rode on together in silence until the path split in two. 'Which way now?' asked Sheila.

'Right will take us back to town.'

'And left?'

'There's a wee wood further on with a great rope swing.'

'The rope swing it is then,' said Sheila.

The sunlight shone through the trees, creating a dappled effect on the dry riverbed. On the bank of the river stood a tree and from one of its branches there hung a rope with a stick tied to the end. Polished dry earth marked the runway on one side of the tree and a similar patch – a kind of landing strip – was on its other side.

'Do you swing out over the riverbed and come back?' asked Sheila.

'Not exactly – I'll show you.' Dermot took the rope and placed his hands on either end of the stick, then he ran at full speed until there was no more bank and jumped into the air; the rope tightened and seemed to pull him back. At that exact moment he twisted and, by some mystery of force and counterforce, he flew in a wide semi-circle out over the riverbed and returned to the tree. Sheila watched in amazement and clapped to see him skid to a halt right next to her. His face was flushed, his eyes wide with the exhilaration of it.

'My turn, my turn!' Sheila reached for the rope.

'Whoa! Not so fast.' Dermot lifted it into the air above her head. 'You can't just do it. It took me two weeks and a lot of skin from my back to learn how to do that.'

'Don't be daft. I can do it!' Sheila jumped for the rope.

'Look, you don't want to have another accident, do you?'

'All right then, teach me.'

Dermot explained the need to build up speed on take-off, how to turn in the air, and how to brace against the hard landing.

Heart beating fast, Sheila took the stick, her eyes tracing the route Dermot had followed. She held her breath and ran until there was no solid ground beneath her. She felt her arms twist upwards past her ears and then suddenly she was hurtling backwards. Light and leaves flashed across her vision. She had no breath to scream, but screwed up her eyes and waited to come against something solid …

He caught her in his outstretched arms and, as one, they fell backwards on to the hard earth. He broke her fall, but nothing broke his. The stick flew from her hands and her head banged against his shoulder. Instinctively, he closed his arms around her and held her fast. They lay still for a moment, each acutely aware of their own body and its pain, and just as aware of the one they were pressed against.

'Dermot?'

'Yes?'

'Are you all right?'

'Yes.'

'I'm going to get up now.'

No answer.

'Is that all right?'

'Yes.'

She rolled off him and lay on the ground, still feeling the impression of his body beneath her.

'Sheila, are you hurt?'

'No.'

She sensed him sit up, felt his arm on her shoulder. She knew she had only to sit up and face him.

He kept his arm on her shoulder, his fingers just touching her neck. She turned and looked into his eyes and in one movement raised her head to bring her face level with his, neither moved. They came towards each other. A first kiss, unexpected, unforgettable.

'Irene, will you get up out of there!' Martha shouted from the bottom of the stairs. 'It's nearly ten o'clock.'

'I'll get up soon.'

'You'll get up now, young lady!'

Irene came into the kitchen still in her dressing gown and slippers, her parting had disappeared and her thick black hair stuck up at odd angles. Martha was busy ironing, but she kept half an eye on Irene who ate her breakfast in silence while staring straight ahead, as she had done every morning since the aircraft factory was bombed. Martha took a letter from the high mantelpiece and put it on the table. 'Looks like another letter from Sandy,' she said.

Irene left it where it was.

'Are you not going to open it?' Martha couldn't keep the sharp edge from her voice.

'Maybe later.'

'Did you answer the other letters he sent?'

'Mammy, I don't want to talk about it.'

'But he's your husband!'

'Sure, I know that.'

'Irene, what's going on?'

'Nothing.'

Martha stood the iron on its end and sat down opposite her daughter. 'Now look here, there's something amiss, that's for sure. Look at the state of you. You look dreadful, you've lost weight and, God knows, there wasn't much of you before.' Martha shook her finger. 'And if this is about your marriage, you'd better get it sorted.'

'What makes you think it's about him? Could it not be because I've no work to go to and no wage coming in?'

'Then why aren't you away down the town looking for work instead of lying in your bed? You know that factory won't be open again for months. And more to the point, why are you so low in spirits you can hardly be bothered to talk to people – answer me that!'

Irene slumped over the table, her head on her arms.

Martha sighed and smoothed her daughter's unruly hair. She tutted, but when she spoke her voice was softer. 'Irene, what's the matter?'

Irene raised her head. How pale she is, thought Martha.

'I just can't be bothered, Mammy, I'm so tired.'

'We've all been through a lot, you especially, first with Myrtle and then Sandy being away.'

'He's been posted to Ballyhalbert; they're setting up a new base there and he wants me to go and stay for a while. There's a wee house nearby we could rent.'

'And what did you say to that?'

'I said I'd think about it, but now he keeps writing and asking when I'm coming.'

'And you don't want to go?'

'I really want to see him, but I just can't face going away.'

Martha shook her head and tried again. 'Do you remember the time when your Aunt Anna was ill?'

'When she was rescued from the mailboat that struck a mine?'

'Aye, well you remind me of how she was after that – no interest in anything, not even her wee girls and Lord knows she loved them. I went to a herbalist and he told me to make onion soup every day for her – gave me herbs to put in it – and, right enough, she slowly got her energy back and a bit of spark. Maybe we'll get you some of that, what do you think?'

Irene gave a half smile. 'I think it'll take more than onion soup, Mammy.'

The windows were gleaming, the door was open and the sun had shown its face for the first time in a week. 'What more can we ask?' said Goldstein as he finished painting the words 'Grand Re-opening' on the window and added a flourish underneath.

'Now, Esther, remember the stock is limited, but if we haven't got the gramophone record or sheet music a customer asks for, you must suggest an alternative that we do have. Peggy, your idea to play the piano in the shop was a stroke of genius' – Peggy beamed in delight and gave an impromptu bow – 'it proved to me that even when things seem hopeless, it's possible to lift people's spirits by entertaining them. So I think you should stay on the piano unless it gets really busy. It doesn't matter what you play, as long as it is uplifting. No dirges today; people are miserable enough shopping in a bombsite, without us playing an accompaniment to it.'

Just before lunch, when Goldstein nipped out to the Belfast Institute to discuss the forthcoming concert with the manager, Esther and Peggy were at last able to chat.

'You promised to tell me about this boy who's just come over from Poland,' said Peggy. 'What's his name?'

'Esther smiled shyly. 'He's called Reuben and he's tall and slim with dark hair, a little long you might say, and lovely brown eyes.'

'What does your uncle think of him?'

'He introduced me to him. He plays the violin, so that's a good thing, and he is also an instrument maker which is even better. He attends our synagogue too, so my uncle thought it would be good for us to play together.'

'And you're going to perform with him in the concert?'

'Maybe,' she blushed. 'We're going to rehearse every evening and if we're good enough …'

'I can't wait to meet him.'

'He's a bit shy and his English is not good. So you mustn't ask him lots of questions, and you'd better not flirt with him either.'

'I never flirt,' Peggy pretended to be annoyed.

There was a shout from the doorway. 'Yes you do!' and Devlin strolled into the shop. Esther took one look at his serious face and whispered, 'I'll go and sort the sheet music.'

'Have you come for the lunchtime sing-song at Goldstein's music shop?' laughed Peggy.

'No. Are you coming to the Plaza to help clear up the bomb damage and get it ready to re-open?'

'Why would I do that?'

'Because you're one of my employees and I'm telling you to.'

'But I work for Mr Goldstein all week. You only employ me on Saturday nights.'

'Never mind Goldstein, you get yourself round to the Plaza first thing in the morning, or you can wave goodbye to your job!'

At that moment, Goldstein came through the door. 'What is going on here? You are shouting in my shop, young man, and I think maybe you should leave.'

'And I think maybe you should mind your own business,' snapped Devlin. 'I'm talking to one of my staff.'

'No, you are not, you are threatening one of mine and if you do not go now, I will call the policeman on point duty outside.'

Devlin ignored Goldstein and turned to Peggy. 'You'd better be there tomorrow,' and the look on his face left her angry and shaky for the rest of the afternoon.

Peggy finished work at six o'clock and stood on the pavement outside the music shop deciding what to do. Common sense told her she ought to go straight home, but an indignant voice hammered in her head, how dare he! And, before she knew it, she was pushing open the doors of the Plaza. The foyer was littered with broken glass and the smell of smoke hung in the air. She found Devlin in the ballroom, up a ladder, pulling down the charred remains of the stage curtains.

'How dare you come to the shop and speak to me like that!' Peggy shouted. 'You've no right to order me about,' and she marched the length of the ballroom to stand in front of him, hands on hips.

'Well, it's brought you here, hasn't it? So you can get to work right now if you know what's good for you. Start by sweeping up the glass in the foyer. Then come in here and mop the floor. After that you can sort out the smoke damage on the walls. Those bloody incendiaries damn near burnt us to the ground. Good job I was here fire-watching, or there'd be no Plaza left,' and he walked away.

'I'm not your skivvy,' she yelled. Devlin turned slowly, his eyes dark and menacing, and came towards her. She stood her ground.

'You're whatever I say you are – cloakroom girl, skivvy, cheeky madam,' and in one swift movement he reached out and grabbed her. His kiss was crushing and took her breath away. In her shock she didn't struggle. She knew how volatile his temper was, but this was something else. He set her down and released her arms. She raised her hand, hesitated, uncertain whether to slap his face. In a flash he had grabbed her wrist, twisted it and pushed her away.

'You've work to do!' he barked.

Her breath was coming in short bursts as she struggled to find words to hurt him. In the end she turned and ran across the ballroom into the foyer and straight out the front door.

Peggy threw down her knife and fork. 'Mammy, what is this we're eating?'

'Sprats.'

'What in God's name are sprats?'

'Fish, and don't swear please.'

'What sort of fish?'

'I've told you – sprats.'

'I'll have it, if you're not going to eat it,' said Pat and scraped the fish on to her plate. 'The ministry recommends eating plenty of fish.'

'It's bad enough having the ministry rammed down our throats every night, without having to eat their sprats as well!'

'Peggy,' said Martha sharply. 'I don't know what's the matter with you, but you've had it on you since you came through the door, and I'll thank you to keep a civil tongue in your head.'

'Talking of the ministry—' said Pat. Peggy groaned and rolled her eyes. Pat ignored her. 'I've got some good news, I've been promoted!' she beamed. 'I'm going to be clerk to the permanent secretary.'

'That's great,' said Irene.

'Aye, but I'll be expected to bring some work home to do in the evening. I was thinking I'll need a briefcase. I'm sure there was an old one up in the loft, wasn't there?' and she turned to Martha who didn't answer.

'Will you get a pay rise?' asked Irene.

'A modest one, but it should help us out 'til you start back at Shorts. Isn't that good, Mammy?'

Martha pursed her lips. 'Humph,' she said, 'and who might this permanent secretary be?'

Pat lowered her eyes and said quietly, 'William Kennedy.'

'Pat, be careful, only walk on the joists, or you'll end up coming through the ceiling,' shouted Irene from the landing.

'I can see the briefcase but there's so much stuff on top of it.'

There was the sound of something being dragged, followed by a sudden shout, 'Wait till you see what I've found!' Moments later, Pat's face appeared through the square hole in the ceiling. 'I'm going to pass it down to you so get ready, it's heavy,' and she momentarily disappeared.

'What is it?' shouted Irene, sensing the excitement in her sister's voice.

Pat's face reappeared and in her hands she held a heavy coil of rope.

'What is it?' Irene asked again.

'Don't you recognise it? It's our skipping rope!'

Together they carried it downstairs and into the sitting room where Peggy was filing her nails. 'Is that what I think it is?'

By this time the rope was beginning to sag and the ends were trailing. 'Grab it, Peggy, before it falls!'

All three of them squeezed through the door into the kitchen where Martha was standing at the sink. 'Let's get it on the table.'

'Away on with you, it's filthy. Take it outside!' shouted Martha.

They carried the rope into the garden and laid it like a snake on the grass.

'Do you remember when Daddy brought it home from the shipyard for us?'

'He had it over his shoulder and we didn't know what it was at first.'

'It had a funny smell, a mixture of tar and the sea.'

'Still does.'

'We took it out into the road at the front.'

'All the kids came to skip with us.'

'We were still there when it went dark.'

'Under the street lights.'

'Skipping and skipping.'

'I went to bed and skipped in my sleep!'

Irene picked up one end of the rope and without a word Pat walked to the other end and picked it up. Peggy took the slack in the middle and in procession they marched through the gate and out into the street.

The rope stretched the entire width of the road. Irene stood on one pavement, Pat on the other. After a couple of false starts they had the heavy rope turning and soon Peggy got into her stride and skipped effortlessly. All three instantly remembered the skipping rhymes as though the words were in their heads just waiting for the turn of a rope.

> Jelly on the plate, jelly on the plate,
> Wibbly, wobbly, wibbly, wobbly,
> Jelly on the plate.

Peggy wiggled and wiggled, never missing a jump of the rope.

'My turn now!' shouted Irene. Peggy took the end of the rope from her, but a hand immediately relieved her of it. It was Martha's. She had heard the singing and laughter from the kitchen and had come out to see what all the excitement was about. She smiled at Peggy and started another chant.

> Ingle angle silver bangle,
> Ingle angle out,
> If you'd have been where I'd have been,
> You wouldn't have been put out!

First Irene skipped then Peggy joined her and pushed her out. Irene ran quickly round Martha just in time to come in again and push Peggy out. Some girls playing jacks on the pavement further up the street came to join them and soon they too were dodging in and out of the rope. Martha and Pat quickened the pace until the rope was turning at speed with the skippers rushing in and out. Shrieks and laughter filled the balmy evening, drawing other girls and women into the road where they lined up to take their turn. Even Martha was persuaded to join in a frantic game of tig – in and out of the ever-turning rope.

'Heavens above, Martha, where do you get your energy from?' Mrs McKee, attracted by the noise, had come out to join the fun. Martha, her face red, left the skipping line and she and Mrs McKee went to sit on the kerb to watch.

'I must be mad. My heart's thumping. I'll give myself a stroke!'

'Ach, you're as fit as a fiddle, so you are, and it's good to see your Irene's got a bit more energy.'

'Aye, a wee bit – thanks to the platefuls of onion soup.'

'Have ye heard from your Sheila at all?'

'No, not yet,' Martha tried to keep her voice light.

'But you'll have written to her …'

'No.'

'No? Why not?'

'It's not that easy,' Martha sighed and wondered if it wasn't time to speak of her fears. As a mother, Mrs McKee might understand her worry. 'I don't have an address. She went to Dungannon, I know that, but she could be anywhere within five or even ten miles of the place. The truth is she seems to have vanished into thin air. I've no idea where she is.'

Mrs McKee heard the break in Martha's voice. 'Don't fret yerself, she'll be fine I'm sure. You know our Brian went missin' once. We looked everywhere; further and further afield we went. In the end, we found him in the most obvious place – fast asleep in his bed.'

'Well Sheila isn't in her bed, that's for sure.'

'No, but maybe she's where she's meant to be – right there in Dungannon. Can you not ask the people who sent her there where she is?

'Pat's been asking at Stormont, but the paperwork is very slow at coming through.'

'Surely to God they wouldn't give a child to someone as if they were a side of beef without asking who they were and where they were taking her.'

'You're right, I know it. It's just that with all that's gone on with the bombing and everything … '

'Martha, I'm sure she's there and safe, you'll see.' She stood up. 'Now, tell you what, me and you'll get this rope crackin' and see how fast these wee girls can move!' With that she went over and took an end of the rope and Martha did the same.

'Come on now, youse uns! All in together girls,' shouted Mrs McKee and they rushed to form a queue. Rapidly, one after the other, they timed their run, caught the rhythm and soon they were all jumping in time, jostling and giggling.

The rope quickened, but no one faltered. Their feet went faster and faster and the chanting grew louder and louder. 'All in together girls. Never mind the weather girls … '

Chapter 11

The early morning train to Dungannon was packed, but Martha just managed to get the last seat in a carriage. She stowed her old shopping bag containing a change of clothes, nightdress and toiletries on the luggage net drooping above her head. She thought it doubtful she would have to stay the night anywhere, but still … she didn't know what might – or, worse, might not – await her in Dungannon. She kept her handbag on her knee and her handkerchief up her sleeve just in case.

The day after the skipping Pat had come home from work with worrying news. 'I spoke to the woman who is responsible for information about evacuees. She'd had the return from Dungannon's evacuation officer – Sheila's name wasn't on the list.'

Martha caught her breath, 'Dear God, where can she be?'

Peggy, who had been on the floor cleaning her work shoes, stood up, a shoe over one hand like a glove, and shook a brush at Pat with the other. 'What kind of people lose a fourteen-year-old girl? I wouldn't trust a civil servant as far as I could throw them!'

Her malice was not lost on Pat. 'Look Peggy, that's uncalled for. There's a war on and it was a huge undertaking to evacuate all those children.'

'But you were supposed to keep them safe, not forget where you left them! If you ask me they'd be better off taking their chances with the bombs.' Peggy polished the shoe vigorously.

'Pat, is it possible that she's on the Coleraine list? You remember she was down to go there?' Martha asked.

'No, Mammy, she's not. On the Coleraine return it said "Did not travel".'

'What are we going to do, Mammy?' asked Irene.

'We're going to sleep on it,' said Martha calmly.

The night was warm and humid and trying to imagine where Sheila might be sleeping was enough to keep Martha tossing and turning until the house martins under the eaves began their morning chorus. Then, when on the cusp of dreaming and waking, she again heard Mrs McKee's voice – 'She's where she's meant to be.'

Martha left her bed immediately and, when the girls came downstairs for breakfast an hour later, she was sitting in the front room washed, dressed and ready for her journey.

She was due to arrive in Dungannon at ten. The last train back to Belfast was at four. Five hours to do what she could. How big was the town? Where should she start looking? From her handbag she took the photograph of Sheila taken at the Waterworks the previous Easter. It was a good enough likeness, although her hair was short then, but the eyes and the smile … surely someone would remember her if she'd ever been in Dungannon.

Martha felt the heat rise from the pit of her stomach and spread upwards; knew that her face was flushed. She resisted the urge to wipe the sheen of clammy sweat from her forehead.

The guard clipped her ticket and asked, 'You all right, missus?'

'Yes,' Martha forced a smile. 'It's very warm today, isn't it?'

'Aye 'tis. Tell ye what, I'll open the window a bit for you. How's that?'

'Do you know Dungannon at all?' she asked.

'I know you walk up the hill from the station to the main square, that's all.'

'Would there be a police station there?'

'Oh I'm sure there is.'

Martha found the square easily enough and when she got there she asked a young woman for directions to the police station. She soon found herself face to face with the sergeant. When she showed him Sheila's photograph, he examined it closely. 'Evacuated, you say? Don't think I've seen her, but she could be anywhere in the parish. There's many a young 'un workin' on the farms around here.'

'Is there anyone else I could ask? Maybe at one of the churches? I'm sure she'll be going to church on a Sunday.'

The sergeant handed back the photograph and scratched his chin. 'Now, let me see. Yer best bet would be the Church of Ireland. Go to the far corner of the square and follow the road to the left – look for the steeple with a clock, you can't miss it. I've a feeling someone from there was involved in sortin' out the childer from Belfast, matchin' them up wi' families an' the like.'

The church was imposing, with arched windows and doorways. She was relieved to find the door open and the interior as cool as marble. There was no one inside, but she wasn't worried; she would find the rectory once she'd cooled down and collected her thoughts. Sitting at the back, she marvelled at how elaborate the church was with its high roof and raised altar, but it was a stained glass window depicting Jesus blessing the children that gave her hope. The door opened and a thin white-haired woman emerged carrying two large vases full of delphiniums.

Martha watched as she made her way towards the altar. 'Excuse me.'

'Heavens above!' said the woman. 'I didn't see you there.'

'I'm sorry I startled you.' Martha moved up the aisle towards the woman. 'Can I help you with those? They look very heavy.'

'Yes, thank you. Here, take this one, would you? It goes over there,' and she nodded towards the pulpit.

'They're beautiful flowers.'

'Indeed they are and a wonderful colour,' said the woman and added, 'especially for a church. My husband says they're the colour of prayer.'

'Your husband?'

'Yes, he's the rector.'

'Oh, I was hoping to speak to him,' said Martha. 'Is he at home?'

'No, he's out visiting at the moment. I'm not sure when he'll be back.'

Martha's face fell.

'Maybe I could help?'

'I don't know. I haven't got much time. I've come from Belfast …' Martha's voice wavered.

'Look, it seems to me that both of us could do with a cool drink. Why don't you come to the house? It's not so far to walk and who knows, maybe he'll be back sooner rather than later.' She held out her hand. 'My name's Lynne.'

The rectory kitchen was vast, with a huge range and a tiled floor in a black-and-white checked pattern. Martha sat at the kitchen table and Lynne fetched two tumblers.

'And there's no record of her ever being here, you say?'

'Nothing, it's like she's disappeared into thin air.' Martha's lip trembled.

Lynne pretended not to notice her distress and disappeared into the walk-in pantry and emerged with a jug of apple juice. 'Now, as far as I know, the children arrived by bus at the church hall. I wasn't there that day. I'd gone to visit my sister.' She stopped pouring suddenly. 'I've just remembered there was someone in charge, an evacuation officer. I know his wife. Look, we'll have our drink then I'll take you round to their house. He'll be sure to know.'

They left the rectory and made their way back to the square. Lynne, aware that Martha was becoming ever more tense, kept up the conversation all the way there. 'You'll need to describe Sheila in some detail to him: what she was wearing; her height and build; something of her facial features.'

Martha stopped and opened her bag. 'I have this.'

'Good heavens, a photograph. That's splendid. May I have a look?'

Martha handed over Sheila's picture and Lynne squinted at it. 'It's no good, I can't see without my glasses.' She moved it further and further away, until at arm's length she gasped. 'Wait a minute.' She stared across the street. Martha followed her gaze and read the name of the shop opposite: 'Francis McManus and Son, High Class Butchers and Slaughter Men.'

'I know this girl,' Lynne was smiling. 'I bought some meat from her last week. We've only to cross the road and you'll have found your daughter!'

Martha hesitated at the shop door. She was overwhelmed with relief and knew when she went inside that she wouldn't be able to hold back the tears. She stepped to one side until she was partly hidden by the sheets of brown paper that hung from the steel butcher's hooks above the window display. She saw Sheila then, smiling and chatting to a customer as she weighed and wrapped, took money and gave change. How precious her daughter was, and what pride she felt seeing her now as a stranger might.

When the customer left, Martha slipped into the shop. Sheila was rearranging mutton chops on a tray.

'Hello, love.'

Sheila looked up and her eyes widened. 'Mammy!' she screamed in delight, ran round the counter, threw her arms around her mother and hugged her tight. 'What are you doing here?' She looked past Martha, searching. 'Where's everybody else?'

Martha stepped back and smiled as she took Sheila's hands in her own. 'I've come looking for you. Your sisters aren't here. There's only me and this is Lynne; she helped me find you.'

Sheila's voice was tearful. 'Why didn't you write to me, Mammy? Did you forget about me?'

'Bless us!' said Martha, touching her daughter's cheek. 'Of course not, sure I didn't know where you were. How could I have written? You didn't write and tell us your address.'

'But my wrist ... they told you about my accident, didn't they?'

'Accident? What accident?' Martha was alarmed, and looked her daughter up and down. 'Are you all right?'

'Of course she is. She's grand.' Bridie McManus hearing the excited voices had come through from the house and immediately realised what was happening. She crossed the shop with her usual slow gait, her hand outstretched. 'And you must be Martha Goulding.'

'Indeed I am.' Martha shook Bridie's hand.

'I'm Bridie McManus.' She looked past Martha to Lynne. 'Hello, Mrs Jones. Have you come for your meat?'

'No, I've been helping Martha to find Sheila. I couldn't believe it when she showed me a photograph and I realised it was the girl in your shop.' Lynne smiled at Martha. 'Well, now that you two have been reunited, I'll be getting back.'

'Thank you so much for your help,' said Martha. 'I'd never have found her without you.'

'Not at all, glad to help … so pleased it was a happy ending.'

Bridie wasted no time in locking up the shop. 'Sure, it's nearly lunchtime anyway and Frank's away to a cattle market so he'll never know if we have a nice long dinner.'

She ushered them into the kitchen. 'Come on in and sit yerself down. Now, Sheila, let's get the kettle on and some roast beef sandwiches on the table.'

Little by little, the whole story came out – Frank thinking he'd gained a messenger boy with his own bike and Sheila's decision to say she was Sheila Gardiner for fear of being sent back to Belfast, then the accident and the sprained wrist and the official letter sent to the wrong family. And finally, Sheila's feeling of being forgotten and Martha's desperate worry over her disappearance, though never openly expressed, were silently shared.

'Mrs McManus–' Martha began.

'No, no, yer to call me Bridie, please.'

Martha inclined her head slightly in acknowledgement of the connection between them through Sheila. 'Bridie, I can't thank you enough for taking Sheila into your home and for looking after her so well.'

'Aah, Martha, sure it's been a pleasure. She's great company, so she is, and she's been such a help in the shop. I've got to say, Frank picked a good 'un when he went along to the church hall that day, even though I'd sent him for a boy!'

Suddenly, from above them, came the sound of banging on the floor.

'It's just our Rose,' said Bridie. 'I'll go up and check on her. She probably wants a cup of tea. Sheila, put the kettle on again, would ye?'

'Rose is having a baby soon,' explained Sheila. 'She's not been very well, so the doctor says she's to stay in bed until the baby comes.'

From upstairs came the sound of raised voices and sudden movement. Martha recognised the sound of distress and, had she not been in a stranger's house, she would already have been climbing the stairs.

'Sheila, I think there's something wrong. Maybe you should go and see if Bridie needs help.'

Sheila replaced the unfilled kettle on the stove and, at the unmistakeable sound of a scream, she raced to the stairs, but Bridie had returned and was blocking the way. Sheila backed into the room and Bridie followed, her outstretched hands covered in blood, her face drained of colour.

'Go quickly, child, to the doctor's and tell him Rose is bleeding and he's to come right away,' she shouted.

When Sheila had left, Bridie turned again to climb the stairs.

'Bridie, would you like me to come with you?'

It was as though she had forgotten Martha was there and it took a moment for her to respond. 'Yes, thank you,' she said simply.

Within ten minutes the doctor was at Rose's bedside and, within twenty, the child, a girl, had been born. She died within the hour.

Martha opened her eyes and squinted at the bright square of light on the earth floor next to the bed. For a moment she frowned, then rolled over on to her back and followed the shaft of light to the small window set in the whitewashed wall. Next to her, Sheila slept on, dead to the world, and Martha was thankful to see her sleeping soundly at last.

Hard to believe it was less than a week since she'd left Belfast looking for her daughter only to find her safe, then within the hour to watch another woman grieve over a lost child? Things had moved fast after that. Sheila had been sent to the slaughterhouse to fetch Rose's husband, while she and Bridie bathed and dressed both mother and baby.

The wake for the child was like nothing Martha had experienced. The tiny open coffin lay in the parlour while the family kept vigil and friends and neighbours called to pray and pay their respects. The phrase 'Sorry for your trouble' repeated over and over was strangely comforting in its simplicity. Martha and Sheila made themselves useful in the kitchen, baking batches of scones and making tea for the visitors. Then the previous evening the two of them had sat alone with the baby while the family ate together. In the quiet room, heavy with the scent of stock flowers placed in vases on either side of the coffin, Sheila had wept softly and held Martha's hand, speaking only once to say, 'I wish we could have had Daddy at home and stayed with him a while.'

There had been concerns about Rose being fit enough to attend the funeral; it was clear that, mentally, it would be an ordeal, but the doctor then ruled that she was too weak physically and must not leave the house. The family faced the dilemma of who would stay at home with her and in the end it was Rose's wish that all the family should go to the funeral and that Sheila would stay behind to keep her company.

Martha left the little cottage, crossed the yard and lifted the latch on the kitchen door, intending to get the fire going and start breakfast for the family. In the half-light she saw Bridie kneeling by the hearth in prayer and, without speaking, she knelt beside her. After a while Bridie made the sign of the cross and, leaning heavily on the chair, stood up.

'Well, Martha, this'll be a hard day to come out the other side of.'

'Indeed it will, Bridie.'

'I'm glad you're here, you know. Sometimes God sends a stranger for a reason. I knew one was comin', but I never imagined why.'

Martha waited for Bridie to explain, but she said no more. Instead she left the room and slowly climbed the creaking stairs.

Just before eleven the family left by the front door of the butchers – the child's father led the way, carrying the coffin with its tiny lily of the valley wreath. Passers-by on the main street stopped and bowed their heads. Martha walked some distance behind the small procession, conscious of not being closely connected to the family and a little embarrassed that she wasn't wearing black. Inside the church she continued to keep her distance by sitting just inside the door. She had lived half a century and in all that time had never attended a Catholic Mass. Slowly her eyes adjusted to the dim interior and she was aware of a pungent smell wafting from the altar where the priest stood resplendent in his vestments. The stained glass windows were dramatic in their intensity of colour and images – but it was the gilded plaster Madonna that drew her eye, smiling reassuringly only a few steps away from the cross bearing her own lost child.

Martha sensed movement just behind her and was startled to see Sheila peer round the door and raise a finger to her lips. She crept in leading a figure in black by the hand, her face covered by a mantilla. Rose. Together the two of them slipped into the last pew.

Chapter 12

'What's for tea?' asked Peggy as soon as she came through the door.

'They're small and fishy and they're on toast,' said Pat.

'Not bloody sprats again!'

Pat put the plate in front of her. 'We've to be out of here in half an hour. Goldstein wants us backstage at the Institute and in make-up an hour before curtain up.'

'I can't go,' said Peggy without looking up.

'What do you mean?'

'I mean I can't go.'

'What? I can't believe you, Peggy Goulding!' Pat's voice was incredulous. 'Why can't you go?'

'I have to be somewhere else,' said Peggy matter-of-factly and carried on eating.

'Somewhere else! Where might that be?'

'I'm playing at the Plaza tonight,' she looked Pat in the eye and added, 'the piano, in the band.'

'You can't do that! We're booked to do this concert with the Barnstormers. You can't come along two hours before curtain up and say you're not taking part. We're on the bill, the Golden Sisters, three girls and a piano. Not two sisters and the third one with the piano down the road at the Plaza!'

At the sound of raised voices Irene ran downstairs and arrived in the kitchen to find Peggy sitting at the table, eating and Pat on her feet, red in the face and shouting loudly.

'What's going on?' asked Irene.

'Ask her!'

'What's happened, Peggy?'

'I can't be at the concert because I have to be at the Plaza tonight; the pianist has left and the manager wants me to play in the band.'

'Just tell him you can't do it, that you've got a prior engagement. He can't make you do it.'

Peggy thought about how angry Devlin had been when she'd told him just that. He had been waiting for her when she left work, stepping out from a doorway to block her path. He needed a pianist or there would be no music for dancing at the Plaza. His tone was soft and he'd stroked her arm. She'd told him she couldn't do it. He had sworn and threatened her.

'Yes he can. I'll get the sack if I don't.'

'So what?' said Irene.

'He's going to pay me ten shillings. Have you forgotten we need the money, now that you've no work,' snapped Peggy.

'That's not fair,' shouted Irene. 'It's not my fault the factory was bombed!'

Pat, having regained some of her composure, spoke up. 'Have you considered the fact that Mr Goldstein might well sack you for letting everyone down? You'd lose a full-time job and all the money that brings in.'

'Mr Goldstein won't know,' said Peggy.

'I think he'll notice you're missing tonight.'

'Not if you tell him I'm sick.'

'You've got to be joking. I'm not lying for you!'

'Then, if I get sacked, it'll be your fault.'

Pat gasped. 'I cannot believe what you're saying,' and she turned to Irene for support. 'Will you tell her this is ridiculous?'

'I'll do it. I'll tell him you're not well,' said Irene.

'You can't!' shouted Pat.

'I have to. We can't afford to lose any money.'

'Well, I'm having nothing to do with this deceit. It's a disgrace you are, Peggy Goulding, and make no bones about it either of you, I'll be sure to tell Mammy when she gets home!'

'You might have to wait a while,' said Peggy. 'She rang the shop today to tell me she's going to stay in Dungannon for a while longer.'

Goldstein was standing in the entrance hall of the Institute discussing the arrangements for ticket-selling with Horowitz, his assistant director, when Pat and Irene arrived.

'Good evening, girls', he greeted them. 'In fine voice I hope?' It was a moment before he realised that there were only the two of them. 'Where is Peggy?' he asked. 'I need to talk to her about an act that needs an accompanist.'

Pat walked quickly past muttering something about needing to talk to William, leaving Irene to answer the question. 'Er … Peggy's not with us, Mr Goldstein.'

'Where is she?'

'She's not coming, I'm afraid. She's sick.'

'Sick?' He looked more puzzled than alarmed, 'But she was fine when she left the shop.'

'She was sick on the bus home, nearly passed out, and sick again when she was getting ready.'

'So she's not coming?'

'She couldn't, she's so ill.' Irene felt the need to develop the story. 'She was sure she'd be sick on the stage and ruin the whole show. She's gone to bed.'

Goldstein threw up his hands. 'No Golden Sisters, but you are one of my best acts! You raise the whole show.' He paced to the door and back again. 'Right, Esther and Reuben will have to go on. It's probably too soon for them, but never mind, they'll have to do it.' He turned to Horowitz, 'Can you accompany a few acts instead of Peggy?'

'I can, but what about front of house?'

'That will become Irene's responsibility.' He glared at her. 'Seeing as she is not singing.'

'But I've never–' Irene protested.

'It's not difficult,' said Goldstein. 'Just put on a welcoming smile and sell the tickets.'

Pat found William warming up his voice backstage. He looked so handsome in his dinner jacket, white shirt with black bow tie and his smile, just for her as she came into the room, made her heart leap.

'I've something to tell you,' he said and took her hand. 'I'm going to Dublin, to speak to the government to ask them for more help. I'm leaving on Thursday and coming back on Saturday.'

'That's great,' said Pat. 'Maybe you can persuade them to–'

He put his finger on her lips. 'Sssh,' he said. 'That's not all – you're to come with me.'

'What? I can't go to Dublin.'

'But you have to,' he laughed. 'You're my personal clerk, remember?'

'I couldn't possibly … I wouldn't know what to do.'

'Of course you would. You'll do everything you do now: get me organised, take notes, save me from despair.'

'Oh William, you're really going to ask the Irish government to help us?'

'Sure didn't they send us fire tenders – twice? But keep all this under your hat. Nobody must know we're there. And best of all,' he kissed her cheek, 'we'll be able to spend some time together.'

In the entrance hall, Irene sat behind the table to check the tickets and the float before unlocking the door. She thought of everyone backstage surrounded by the excitement and tension before a show begins. She and her sisters had rehearsed every night at home, polishing their harmonies and routines, and all for nothing. She had wanted to sing so much. It was a relief from her miserable life with no work or company. At times she felt like she'd slipped into one of those bomb craters and had no energy to climb out and, worst of all, no one knew she was there. The sound of the entrance door rattling startled her.

'We're not ready to open yet,' she shouted. 'It'll be another ten minutes.'

'Irene, is that you?'

She gasped, 'Sandy?'

'Yes, let me in!'

Her hands were shaking as she undid the bolts and the heavy door swung open. He stood in the shaft of light that spilled from the open doorway and her heart melted at the sight of him in his RAF greatcoat. They stood looking at each other, not knowing what to say.

A shout from the street made them jump. 'Hey, what about the blackout – shut that bloody door!'

Inside, Irene said softly, 'What are you doing here?'

'Do I not even get a kiss from my wife?' His handsome face looked so sad.

She smiled shyly and kissed him on the cheek. 'How did you know I was here?'

'Husbands have ways of knowing these things. They have to, when their letters aren't answered.'

'I didn't know what to say to you.'

'Oh come on, Irene, you can do better than that. Since when have you been lost for words?'

'I haven't been feeling right, can't seem to concentrate on anything, and then you wanted me to come to Ballyhalbert and I … Oh I don't know …'

'You didn't want to come and see me?' There was hurt in his voice.

'I thought you'd make me stay there.'

Sandy shook his head. 'You don't know me at all, do you?'

Irene bowed her head and struggled to hold back her tears. Sandy moved closer and lifted her chin. 'I'd never make you do anything you didn't want to do.'

'But you said you'd found a house for us.'

'I have, and I thought that you'd want to come and see it, but there wasn't a word from you, not even after the bombing. You didn't even let me know you were safe. Didn't you realise I'd be going out of my mind? Thank God, your mother wrote and told me you were all fine.'

'My mother wrote to you!'

'Yes, and she told me you'd be here tonight. I was due a weekend pass, thought I'd surprise you.'

The entrance door swung open and a group of elderly women came in together chatting away.

Irene passed Sandy a pile of tickets. 'Two shillings each, tuppence for a programme, they can sit where they like.'

Goldstein stood in the wings, ready to give the signal to strike up the music and begin the show. The hall was just over half full, but it was enough to justify his decision to bring concerts back to the city so soon after the bombing. He raised his hand and the music began, the curtains opened and there were the Templemore Tappers in dramatic black and red costumes in a straight line, hands linked behind their backs, smiling broadly. Right on cue they began their routine with high kicks that drew gasps from the audience. At the back of the hall Irene and Sandy had slipped in to watch the show. She was glad she had suggested to Goldstein that Macy should work with the Tappers and help to direct their routines. It was clear she'd had an effect on them. Some of their old spark had returned and once again there had been talk of doing it for Myrtle.

The Tappers were followed by a crooner, new to the company. Pat had dismissed him during rehearsals as having a voice best suited to a public bar, but the audience enjoyed his choice of popular songs and even joined in with the chorus of 'We'll Meet Again'.

'And now, ladies and gentlemen, we have a change from our programme,' said Goldstein, coming onstage. Unfortunately, one of the Golden Sisters is unwell and we wish her a speedy recovery. In her place I'm delighted to introduce two young people, gifted musicians from Poland, who are performing together for the first time this evening. Please give a warm Belfast welcome to Esther and Reuben!'

Esther was dressed in a navy A-line skirt, a white blouse with broderie anglaise collar and cuffs and navy court shoes. Her hair was plaited and curled into coils on either side of her head. Reuben followed her on to the stage. He wore a suit, much too small for him, made of coarse black material, his dark hair touched his collar and long ringlets fell in front of his ears. They avoided looking at the audience and instead turned towards each other and placed their bows on their instruments. A hush fell over the audience as they waited to hear what sound this exotic young couple would produce. Reuben counted them in and the opening notes of Vivaldi's *Four Seasons* soared towards the arched ceiling. The audience were entranced, but Esther and Reuben were oblivious to everything but the music and each other. When the piece came to an end, the clapping startled them and they quickly bowed and left the stage with the same serious expression they had worn throughout the performance.

Macy was up next. Pat was already in the wings, watching her dance routine, when she felt a finger gently trace the scooped neckline of her gown across her back.

'I love to see you in this dress,' William whispered, 'it reminds me of our first concert.'

Pat adored the dress too, the feel of silk against her skin, the touch of coral beading across the bodice and, above all, the way it made her feel like a real opera singer.

A few minutes later, it was their turn to perform. They stood at the front of the stage, heads held high, while Horowitz played the introduction to '*Viene la Sera*', the duet from *Madame Butterfly*. William sang of his love in a voice so rich and charged with emotion that Pat believed absolutely every word. When she replied it was with every fibre of her being; he was by her side and her voice soared with the joy of it all. They came together, he held her hands, looked into her eyes and their voices blended in a declaration of passion, building an intensity they could never have expressed with mere words. The final notes soared out over the audience. There was silence, then applause erupted and Pat sank in a curtsey while William bowed. Together they left the stage and in the wings William crushed her in his arms and kissed her with all the excitement and drama of their performance.

After the concert the performers were in high spirits backstage – laughing and hugging each other. The audience may have been small, but the applause and cheering at the curtain call was enthusiastic and it was not just for the wonderful show they had seen, it was also for helping them to forget about the bombed buildings outside for two hours.

Outside, Sandy took Irene's hand as they strolled towards the City Hall.

'Where are you staying?' she asked. He raised an eyebrow.

'You don't have anywhere to stay do you?'

'Well, I was hoping …'

Ten minutes' walk away, in the Plaza Ballroom, Peggy was coming off stage for a short break.

'I want a word with you.' Devlin caught her by the arm, 'You're playing too fast.'

'I think you'll find the tempo is correct,' said Peggy. 'It's the singer who's too slow.'

'Must you argue about everything?' Peggy opened her mouth to protest, but Devlin held up his hand. 'I'm telling you to slow it down; you're making him sound ridiculous.'

'That's not my fault.'

'As far as I'm concerned it is and, if you want to get paid, you'd better do what I say.'

Any other time Peggy would have stood her musical ground, but her head was thumping and her stomach was queasy. She went to the toilet to rinse her hands and face in cold water but, as she turned to leave, she began to retch and within moments was vomiting. When she finally emerged from the toilet and made her way back to the stage Devlin was waiting for her.

'Where the hell have you been?'

'I've been–' she retched again.

'Oh for God's sake, you're nothing but a liability!' He reached into his breast pocket and took out a small silver flask. 'Here, drink some of this.'

'I don't think I could–'

Devlin shoved the flask into her hand, 'Drink it. It'll settle your stomach. Then get up there and play!'

The brandy burned her gullet and her head was spinning, but Peggy hadn't the strength to argue when he pushed her in the direction of the stage.

'And slower this time, do you hear?'

The crooner nodded in her direction. 'What happened?' he asked.

'I ate some bloody sprats.'

When Devlin placed the silver flask on the piano fifteen minutes later, Peggy reached out and drank it straight down and, for the first time in her life, her sense of timing deserted her, bar by bar, until the last waltz resembled a dirge. By the time the band played 'God Save the King' she had her head on the keys and was snoring gently.

She had a vague recollection of being carried across the deserted dance floor to Devlin's office where he laid her on a sofa and threw a blanket over her. She might have heard the screaming of the air-raid alert an hour later, but it's doubtful that she'd have registered Devlin manoeuvring her under his heavy desk and crawling in beside her.

At the Goulding house no one was asleep when the alert sounded. Pat's head was too full of the duets she had sung with William and the fluttering of excitement in her chest returned as she sang every word again in her head. Then, without warning, the notion that she might accompany him to Dublin would scatter her thoughts in different directions: the long journey; the two of them alone; dinner and maybe dancing. No, she chided herself, they were colleagues. William had vital work to do and it was her job to assist him, so she'd no business dreaming about it like a lovesick schoolgirl.

Across the landing, Irene was lying in Sandy's arms and in the darkness they were bold enough to speak of their hopes and fears.

'I want us to be together. Why won't you come and live with me in Ballyhalbert?'

'I won't know anyone and I'll be on my own all day.'

'There are other wives.'

'I'm needed here; I need to earn a wage.'

'But you don't know when the factory will open again.'

'I'll get another job.'

'Don't you want to be with me?'

'I do, but–'

'But what?'

The sound of the alert saved Irene from saying something that was bound to be hurtful. Instead she jumped out of bed and shouted, 'Quick! We need to get under the stairs.' And at that moment Pat pounded on the door.

'Did you wake Peggy?' asked Irene as they crept on all fours into the confined space under the stairs.

Pat, already embarrassed by the fact that she was squashed up against Irene's husband, a man she hardly knew, hesitated. 'Ah … she wasn't there.'

'Wasn't there? You mean she didn't come home from the Plaza? Where is she?' The question hung unanswered in the air.

Irene was grateful for the fresh eggs Betty had given them the day before which, together with the end of the pan loaf, meant that there was a decent breakfast to give Sandy before his long journey back to base. She walked him out to his motorbike and, when he pulled her towards him, she spoke the words she had rehearsed as they sat shivering under the stairs in the early hours before the all-clear sounded.

'I will come to Ballyhalbert for a while.'

'As soon as you can?'

'When I find out how long I'll be off work and when Mammy's coming home.'

He nodded reluctantly and kissed her again with the same intensity as he had when she awoke in his arms in the early dawn.

'I see love's young dream has been ignited once again.' Peggy called as she walked past them.

'Where have you been all night?' Irene called after her.

'Mind your own business.'

Pat was sitting at the table adding up columns in a jotter and Peggy was frying the last egg when Irene came back into the kitchen.

'We're going to be short this week with the rent money,' announced Pat. 'We'll have to cut down on food.'

'But we eat little enough as it is,' protested Peggy, 'and I can't be doing with the awful food you keep buying. I won't tell you what those sprats did to my insides.'

Pat ignored the moaning and asked Irene, 'When do you think you'll be back at work?'

'I've told you – nobody knows!'

'What about you, Peggy, any chance of doing an extra night at the Plaza?'

'I'm not going back there,' she said bluntly and tossed a ten shilling note across the table. 'That's the last I'll take from that place, you're welcome to it.'

Pat picked it up. 'With this we might be able to manage this week, especially as I'll be away from Thursday to Saturday.'

Her sisters turned to face her. 'Where are you going?'

'Government business, I'm not allowed to say.'

'Go on,' laughed Peggy, 'you're sneaking off somewhere with William Kennedy!'

Pat blushed to the roots of her hair. 'How dare you! We're not all like you, staying out all hours. So never mind me, where did you spend last night?'

'Don't change the subject,' snapped Peggy. 'Wait 'til Mammy gets back, she'll get it out of you.'

Irene could see Pat was deeply embarrassed, but she had no doubt she was telling the truth about government business, even though she hadn't denied William was somehow involved.

'Actually,' said Irene, 'I might be going away myself. Sandy wants me to go to Ballyhalbert for a while and I'm thinking I might as well if I have no work to go to. There'll be less food needed if I'm not here.'

Peggy whooped with excitement. 'I'll have the house to myself,' and she reached across the table and snatched back the ten shilling note. 'I could have some decent meals with this. I've heard the Pam-Pam is very good!'

128

Chapter 13

Pat wore her Sunday-best dress – navy cotton with a fine pinstripe – that she hoped would look slimming. Her coat was a little heavy for the time of year and she secretly hoped that, despite it being the end of May, it would be unseasonably chilly in Dublin.

On the train south they shared a carriage with a woman and her two children as far as Newry and exchanged no more than a few pleasantries. When they were alone, William cleared his throat. 'What did you tell your family about the trip?'

There was something in his tone that put Pat on her guard. 'I said it was government business.'

'You said that!'

'Well it is, isn't it?'

'Yes, yes, but you didn't tell them where you were going?'

'You told me not to.'

'And they don't know you're going with me?'

'I didn't tell them who I was going with.' She decided not to mention that they had presumed she was going with him.

'Just remember, Pat, that these negotiations with the Dublin government are, shall we say, delicate and you are bound by the Official Secrets Act.'

She had been so caught up in her desire to be alone with William that only now, with talk of delicate negotiations and secrets, did she wonder why just the two of them had been sent to Dublin. She detected, too, a nervousness in William's small talk, as though something was being left unsaid. They arrived at Amiens Street Station late morning and walked a short distance in the direction of North Strand to a modest-looking hotel.

William stopped outside. 'Pat, there's something you should know before we go in.' He didn't meet her eye. 'I've … ah … booked a double room for us.' He quickly held up a hand. 'Hear me out, please. It's a twin room, so you needn't worry–'

'William, you'd better tell me what's going on, or I'm getting the train home.'

'It has to seem as though we're a married couple but,' he hesitated, searching for words to calm her, 'of course we're not. This is a business arrangement.'

'A business arrangement!' Pat wanted to slap his face, but how could she? He might think she was insulted by the idea of a business arrangement because she had been expecting … Oh, she wanted to die of embarrassment!

'Just listen will you? It's complicated. No one must know that I'm here to negotiate with the Dublin government. It could jeopardise their neutrality if word got out. That's why it's just you and me – a couple taking a little holiday over the border. No one would suspect you of being involved with government negotiations, now would they?'

Pat opened her mouth to speak and closed it again. She couldn't begin to unravel the excitement and hope of the past few days and come to terms with yet another, perhaps the greatest, disappointment inflicted upon her by William Kennedy. The man had no heart!

She endured the checking in under a false name and the knowing smirk of the hotel manager. Her face was still flushed with shame and anger when they arrived in the room and William began moving furniture.

'See, I'll push my bed right over here as far away from you as I can.' William looked towards the ceiling, 'Maybe I could rig up a curtain with one of the sheets.'

'Will you stop?'

'What's wrong?'

'What's wrong? What's wrong? For a start, I thought you needed me here to help you and because you wanted to spend time with me. Now it seems I'm here just to make this trip look like some seedy affair.'

'No, no, it's not like that at all. I do want to be with you. Remember what we discussed when we were in the Pam-Pam? You agreed to be my colleague and to help me do what needs to be done.'

'I did, but I thought coming here would bring us closer together.'

'Do you want me to move the bed back?'

Pat grabbed the nearest heavy object and threw it at him. The pitcher of water smashed against the wall, narrowly missing William's head. The shock seemed to bring him to his senses. In seconds he had crossed the room and wrapped his arms around her. She struggled to be free, weeping with frustration, but he would not let go. When all resistance was gone, he lowered them both on to the bed and stroked her hair and kissed her wet cheeks.

'Help me, Pat,' he whispered. 'Tell me what you want me to do and I'll do it.'

What happened next was completely out of character, but the closeness of William and the pleading in his voice were more than she could bear. She pulled him towards her. 'Kiss me,' she said.

Their first meeting was at one o'clock in a lawyer's office in a Georgian town house on Merrion Square. They were shown into a grand room with a marble fireplace and ox-blood leather chesterfields. On a stand behind the door hung black robes. A collection of legal wigs was arranged on a nearby bookcase.

'Just get as much of the conversation down as you can and make sure you get the exact wording of what is agreed,' William reminded her.

There was the sound of whispered discussion outside the door and two men came in. The first, a man in his sixties, formally dressed in a morning suit with winged collar and dark tie, went straight to William and shook his hand. No names were mentioned. The second man, younger, also soberly dressed but in a more modern style, crossed the room, sat on an upright chair and took a notebook and fountain pen from his pocket.

The discussions covered ways in which the Dublin government could give help to the north: supplying food to relieve growing hunger; caring for refugees from the north; help in clearing bomb debris. Time and time again the words 'to relieve the suffering of the population' were stressed. Then the emphasis shifted to defence – searchlights, barrage balloons and shelters. There was less agreement here, with everything seeming to be based on 'maintaining neutrality'. Pat carefully noted down everything.

After two hours the elderly gentleman suggested a break for refreshments, adding, 'Perhaps my clerk could take the young lady to the common room.'

Pat saw through this suggestion at once. He was to keep her out of the way while the serious discussions continued, that was obvious, but as she and the clerk drank tea she was surprised to find herself being closely questioned.

'Where are you staying?' he began.

Instinctively, she was on her guard. 'Somewhere past the railway station, I can't remember the name of the hotel.'

'Mr Kennedy must be held in high regard by the Stormont government to be responsible for such important talks.'

'I don't know Mr Kennedy that well. I'm just the clerk who collates the reports about civil defence.' He looked sceptical. She leant towards him, opened her eyes wide and whispered, 'Is that de Valera Mr Kennedy's been talking to?'

The young man laughed at her naiveté. 'No, that's not the Taoiseach! Let's just say he's been talking to a senior civil servant in the Department of Defence.'

Almost an hour later William poked his head round the door and, with a quick nod, indicated to Pat that it was time to go. Anyone watching Pat and William as they walked hand in hand exploring the city would have seen only a young couple, showing all the signs of being in love. William had spent three years studying at Trinity College and knew what Pat would find interesting. He took her

132

there first to see *The Book of Kells* with its beautiful illuminated pages. On O'Connell Street she listened in fascination as he told her the story of the Easter Rising and she touched the bullet holes in the walls of the GPO. They climbed the one hundred and sixty eight steps to the top of Nelson's Pillar and watched the people and traffic far below them. In between, they drank Guinness, ate fish and chips and wished the day would never end. And not once did they talk about why they were there.

Later in their hotel room, William was anxious to go through Pat's notes before the next meeting the following morning. 'I want to look at what he's likely to agree to and where I'll have to push him hard. He'll certainly agree to send medical aid if we're bombed again, but I'll need sound arguments to convince him to send us manpower for building shelters or supplying us with food at low cost.'

'What about your conversation when I wasn't in the room? Did he say anything significant then?' asked Pat.

William's tone changed. 'You don't need to know about that. Nothing important was said.'

'I just thought you might like me to add the details so that the notes are complete.'

'Not necessary.' He took the notebook from her and lay on his bed reading through it. It was as though he had forgotten she was there.

The daylight slowly faded until it seemed too dark to read, but he did not stir. In the end Pat drew the curtains and switched on the light. At ten o'clock she went down the hall to the bathroom and got ready for bed. When she returned he was staring at the ceiling. She went and knelt beside him and stroked his forehead. 'William, I'm sure it'll go well tomorrow. He was convinced by your arguments, I know he was.'

He rolled over to face her, his eyes level with hers. 'You've no idea what's at stake. We could change the course of the war. I have to find the words to persuade him.'

'And you will, you will, but it's time to go to sleep now.' She took the book from him and went to put it on the dressing table.

'Pat, come here.' At the urgency in his voice, she turned to see him staring at her. The cotton nightdress reached to her ankles, covered her arms, the neckline was not low, but her shape beneath the thin material was clearly visible. With a sweep of his eyes William suddenly saw what he had previously only dreamt of: full breasts, narrow waist, the curve of her hips. Puzzled, she crossed the room and took his outstretched hand. He pulled her on to his bed and into his arms.

The following morning when William and Pat arrived at the barristers' chambers the clerk was waiting for them in the entrance hall. The meeting would not be minuted or recorded, he told them, so the young lady would not be needed. If William was surprised by this, he didn't show it.

'I understand,' he said then took Pat to one side. 'Don't worry, this looks very promising. Things are moving, I know it, but it might take a while. Do you remember Bewley's Café in Grafton Street that I pointed out to you?' Pat nodded. 'Wait for me there. I could be two hours or more, but you must stay there until I come. Do you understand?'

'Yes,' she said and briefly touched his arm, 'be careful, William.'

Pat didn't go directly to Bewley's. Instead she wandered towards the Liffey and stood looking down into the dirty brown water, trying to collect her thoughts. She understood that William's mission to gain help for Belfast was important, but this morning anxiety seemed to have gripped him – he ate no breakfast and had barely spoken to her. He always pushed himself hard and constantly worried about what could be done to protect Belfast, but now he was filled with a mixture of excitement and desperation as though something more hung in the balance.

Last night his behaviour had been erratic. When he had pulled her on to the bed she had been frightened by his caresses and passionate words, then suddenly he was on his feet pacing the room talking again about a chance to change the course of the war and asking forgiveness for treating her disrespectfully. But, in truth, she was sad when he told her to go back to her own bed and she had lain awake for hours, sick with love and longing to have his arms around her.

'You're troubled, I see.' An old woman was standing a few yards away watching her. Her swarthy face was criss-crossed by deep lines, her head was covered with a black scarf. Pat walked away, but the woman called after her. 'He's a fine man, but he needs you to be his eyes and ears.'

Pat turned. 'What do you mean?'

Sensing Pat's uncertainty, the woman moved quickly towards her, her hand open. Another time in familiar surroundings Pat would have walked away. Instead, she took a sixpence from her purse. The old woman smiled and leaned in close. 'Ach sure, he's easy deceived. It's up to you to watch over him.'

Pat stumbled backwards from the words and the whiskey breath.

In the café Pat chose a window seat to watch the street, hoping the coming and going would calm her. The gypsy had caught her off guard. What nonsense it was to be frightened, but she was glad that she'd given the woman money and avoided adding a curse to everything else she had to worry about. She ordered tea and it arrived on the table in an elegant flourish of silver pots and fine white china. The tablecloth had a fine weave and Pat reflected on how far she'd come from the Ulster Linen Works where she had painted designs on linen just like this. Now here she was in Dublin, a civil servant taking tea off the finest damask.

The teapot grew cold and there was no sign of William. The relaxed morning customers were replaced by the busy lunchtime crowd. She called the waitress and ordered more tea and a toasted teacake and went back to watching passers-by. She was struck by the dowdiness of the people compared to Belfast, but very occasionally she noticed someone of wealth and style, the exception to the rule, like the woman looking in the window of the jewellers down the street. Eau de nil dress, probably silk, a fitted navy jacket cinched at the waist. As Pat watched, the door of the jewellers opened and a man emerged. She caught her breath. William! The woman turned to watch him cross the road and as she did so she was joined by a man with his hat pulled low over his brow.

William arrived in the café looking more relaxed than she had seen him in weeks. 'Have you eaten lunch? I'm starving.'

'No, I've been waiting for you.'

'I wasn't too long, was I?'

'No, not too long.' Pat would have waited all day, three hours was nothing. 'It went well?' she asked.

His smile said it all. 'Better than I could ever have hoped.' He leaned across the table and whispered, 'The papers outlining the agreement we reached are being drawn up. I'll have them to take back to Belfast tomorrow morning.'

Pat wondered why there was a delay. Surely the agreement could have been drawn up this afternoon, but she didn't want to dampen William's elation.

'So, we've the rest of the day to ourselves,' he said and reached across the table to take her hand, 'in fact we have the rest of our lives.'

The afternoon was glorious with clear blue skies and some warmth to the sun. They caught the tram to Phoenix Park, where they found a quiet grassy spot and spread their coats on the ground. They sat quietly for a while. William seemed distant and Pat was content to watch him as he no doubt turned over the events of the morning in his mind.

When he eventually spoke his words startled her. 'Hard to believe that this was the scene of such brutal murders.'

Pat wondered if she'd heard him correctly. 'Murders?'

'In 1882 the chief secretary for Ireland and his permanent undersecretary were stabbed as they walked to that building over there. The murders changed the course of history. Some say they put an end to the Home Rule Bill that might have given a united Ireland a peaceful transition to independence.'

Pat examined the impressive building and thought how randomly history is written – important plans so carefully laid could be obliterated in a moment. As she watched, a woman as indistinct as a smudge of eau de nil in an impressionist painting walked across her line of sight and sat on a bench under a towering oak tree.

'What are you thinking?' asked William.

She could have mentioned the woman, but what was the point of something so insignificant when she knew William expected something more? She needed to find a way to speak of this strange and wonderful time they had spent together before it was gone forever. The intimacy of it all had both frightened and thrilled her.

'Do you remember when you said you wanted to run away with me to Donegal? I never dreamt it would be like this.'

'That's because we're in Dublin!' he laughed.

'I'm being serious,' she chided. He put his arms around her and pulled her close and she was glad to be able to lean on his shoulder and speak her thoughts without him seeing her face. 'When we're at work I'm never sure what's happening between us. Oh, I know we have to be formal and we're dealing with sad things all the time, but sometimes I long for a smile or a kind word, anything to show you like me. I see that you're furious with what's happening in Belfast and I want to tell you I understand, but I'm scared you'd just turn away thinking I know nothing of what you're going through. But I do, I see it in your eyes and the way your shoulders tense and your voice cracks with anger.'

'Oh Pat, don't you know? I couldn't have got through these last months without you. If I didn't show how I felt about you it was because—'

She put her finger to his lips. 'It doesn't matter, not since we were so close together in that little room all night. I lay there listening to your breathing and knew I'd only to cross the space between us and I could creep in beside you and feel your warmth. But I didn't because that would have seemed …' She knew of no words to explain what others would surely think. She willed herself to be bold and reached up to stroke his cheek. Bolder still, she spoke of the moment when she understood what love could be. 'Last night when you took me into your bed and held me, I was frightened, but I know now that I shouldn't have been.'

William took her hands and kissed both palms. 'Pat, these last few days I've been entranced by you. I've been sitting in the meetings and, Lord knows, they're so important, but I find myself struck by an image of you lifting your hair up from your face and letting it fall, or that sudden smile you give when you're unsure. And today the memories of last night … it was wrong to do what I did and I'm glad I came to my senses before—'

'I love you, William.'

'Do you really? After all—'

She stopped him with a kiss.

When he spoke again, his voice was full of emotion. 'And I love you, Pat, more than life itself.'

They had dinner at the Gresham Hotel: Dublin Bay prawns; steak au poivre; and a bottle of Cabernet Sauvignon. Pat was unaccustomed to such fine food and elegant surroundings, but she felt somehow that this world had been there waiting for her and now she was a part of it.

William had chosen each course, but when the dessert menu arrived he said, 'Why don't you choose for both of us.'

Pat read from the menu, 'Peach Melba: a concoction of peach, meringue and raspberries, created and named for the famous Australian soprano. That's the one I want.'

William laughed, 'Perfect! For tonight you and I are Susanna and Figaro.'

'Don't tell me we're singing for our supper!' Pat laughed.

William was suddenly serious. 'You're so beautiful when you laugh. Aah, Pat, will you be Susanna to my Figaro?'

'Of course I will, I love singing their opening duet with you,' and she hummed the first few bars.

'I was thinking more of the finale to act four,' and softy he sang 'La voce che adoro'.

Pat looked uncertain. 'You mean—'

'Pat, will you to marry me?'

The impact of his words was physical: her heart leapt, the room full of people seemed to disappear and there was only William's face, full of love. He spoke again, as though she hadn't heard, 'I'm asking you to be my wife.'

Pat knew she had only to nod her head or whisper one word and William would be hers. She closed her eyes and held the delicious moment of exhilaration like the most perfect top C for as long as she could, then opened her eyes. 'Yes,' she whispered, 'yes.'

'Oh Pat, my darling, I promise I'll make you happy.' He placed on the table a small green box and inside, nestled on green satin, was a beautiful solitaire diamond ring.

Chapter 14

They finished the wine and drank champagne in the hotel lounge. Pat, unaccustomed to alcohol, was grateful to lean on William's arm as they walked back to their hotel. The evening had turned chilly and the stars were sharp pinpoints of light in the clear night sky.

'I hope there's cloud over Belfast and not a bomber's sky like this one,' said William.

They turned into the hotel's quiet street and William slowed to a stop.

'What is it?' asked Pat.

'I'm not sure – listen. Is there a sound, something different?'

She heard nothing, but a sudden movement caught her eye. 'William,' she whispered, 'there's a man across the street watching us.'

He turned to look, but the man had already faded into the shadows.

'Don't be silly, darling. Let's get inside,' he said.

It felt like coming home, being back in their room again. Was it only yesterday that she had come here furious and embarrassed at the prospect of sleeping in the same room as a man? Now she longed for such intimacy with William who loved her. Emboldened by the wine and champagne she reached up and pulled him towards her. She had no idea how long they stood lips on lips, body to body, until he pulled away from her.

'There's something happening outside.' He took her arms from his neck and went to the window. 'I don't know what it is. There are people on the road. I'll go and have a look, you stay here.' And he was out the door and away, before she could argue.

It was already after midnight and Pat thought about changing into her nightclothes, but decided against it. If there was something going on she'd be better able to deal with it fully dressed. She lay on the bed and wondered what had possessed him to go out into the street in a strange city at this hour?

He returned twenty minutes later, full of excitement. 'The air-raid wardens have been ordered to their posts – there's one at the end of the street. It seems a lot of planes have been flying over at high altitude.'

'Germans?'

'Yes, I think so; they often fly over Dublin to reach British cities. The planes that bombed Belfast would have come right up this coast.'

'But why have they called out the ARP? They won't bomb here, will they?'

'I shouldn't think so, although …' he hesitated, not wishing to alarm her. 'Although back in January they did drop some bombs to the south of the city.'

'But why would they do that when Ireland's a neutral country?'

'True, but the Germans got a bit anxious that Ireland might be tempted to help the British by letting them have naval bases in the south.'

'So was it a bit of a warning to the Irish to stay out of it?'

'Hmm,' said William and sat on his bed, deep in thought.

Pat heard it first and looked up at the ceiling, William did the same. It was a noise anyone from Belfast would instantly recognise – the drone of German planes low overhead. Seconds later, there was a loud whoosh followed by a bang and the room was bathed in light. William ran to the window, Pat followed and together they watched arcs of light flying upwards into the Dublin sky.

'It's all right,' said William, 'they're just flares to tell the German pilots they're over neutral territory.'

'There'll be an air-raid alert, won't there, if there's any danger?' asked Pat.

'I wouldn't count on it. Remember how long it took in Belfast – the bombers were practically over our heads before the sirens sounded.'

Pat went lay down on her bed again and watched William silhouetted in the window. She must have dozed off because she awoke to the unmistakable sound of a bomb exploding some distance away. She was instantly on her feet. 'Should we find a shelter?' she shouted.

'It's probably too late for that now, best to stay here rather than be caught on the street. Get under the bed; it's a strong metal frame and the mattress will protect you from flying glass. I'll push mine next to it and there'll be a wider canopy for you to shelter under.'

William grabbed her arm. 'Quickly now.'

'Wait a minute, are you not taking shelter?'

'No, I've things to do. I want you to stay here until I come back for you.'

'Where are you going?' she cried.

'To see if I can help.'

'Help?' Pat was incredulous. 'This isn't your responsibility. You're not in Belfast now! Leave it to those on duty.'

'Pat, those men at the ARP post haven't a clue. I can get them organised; the sooner they're sorted the more lives will be saved.'

'I'm coming with you!'

'You can't, you'll be in the way.'

'I'm not staying here on my own.'

'Yes you are. Now get under the bed. I'll be back as soon as I can.'

'William, don't go!' she cried.

'I have to, don't you see? It's what I do!'

Pat had no idea how long she lay under the bed. There were two more explosions, both of them further away than the first, and then, sometime after that, there was the terrifying sound of planes low over her head and, almost simultaneously, the deafening detonation of a huge bomb so close that it lifted both her and the bed off the floor. The pain in her eardrums was excruciating, and would have left her screaming in pain had it not been for the fact that the air had been sucked from her lungs. In a blind panic, struggling to breathe, she crawled to the blown-in window and lay there gasping for breath. When she had recovered a little, she pulled herself to her feet and looked out at the street. The sky was bathed in an orange glow.

Whether she would have followed William's instructions and stayed there or acted on instinct and left the hotel in search of him, she would never know, because at that moment there was a sharp knock on the door. When she opened it, a woman brushed past her into the room.

'You're Patricia Goulding, yes?' Her Dublin accent was refined and well-educated. She wore a tailored camelhair coat with a velvet collar, a cameo necklace just visible at her throat. Her hair and shoulders were dusted with ash.

'Who are you?' Pat demanded. 'I've seen you before, haven't I?'

The questions were ignored and the woman went on, 'Please get your coat and come with me.'

'Now look here,' said Pat, 'I'm not going anywhere with you. I've no idea who you are, or–'

'There isn't time.' The woman picked up Pat's handbag from the dressing table and pushed it at her. 'You're to come with me.'

'No! I'm waiting here for–'

'William Kennedy, yes we know that, but he won't be coming back.'

Pat's eyes widened in fear. 'Why, what's happened? Is he all right?'

'Get your coat and I'll take you to him.'

A dark saloon car was parked outside the hotel with its engine running and it moved off at speed as soon as they got in.

'Where are you taking me?'

'To the Mater Hospital.'

Pat grabbed the woman's arm. 'Has something happened to William? Is he all right?' Her voice rose in panic.

'I don't know.' It was clear to Pat that she did.

'Has he been hurt in the bombing?'

'We'll be there in ten minutes.'

The roads around the bombed area were clogged with emergency vehicles and people who were distressed and injured. Many injured people lay on the ground while others stood staring at the buildings that had been demolished or were ablaze. All the time Pat prayed, 'Please, God, let him be all right.'

At the hospital, ambulance men were juggling stretchers, passing the blood-soaked injured through the crowds. Inside, the walking wounded queued at the desk, but many more lay on the floor, incapable of moving or speaking for themselves – the lucky ones lay on trollies. Those whose injuries were life-threatening were receiving treatment in one of the handful of cubicles. Pat scanned the room in horror, taking in the dead and dying; the bloody and mutilated; family members and friends, distressed beyond measure at the suffering of their loved ones.

'William where are you?' she screamed, but her cries were lost in the chaos.

She felt the woman grip her arm and propel her into a small office where a tall man was standing with his back to the door. He turned. 'We meet again, Miss Goulding, but under dreadful circumstances.' It was the clerk from the Department of Defence.

'You?' Pat's brain reeled with questions. 'What's going on? Where's William?'

'I'm afraid, Miss Goulding, that Mr Kennedy died fifteen minutes ago as a result of injuries he sustained in a bomb blast in the North Strand area.'

The woman steadied Pat as she staggered backwards and helped her into a chair. If there were words to respond to the shock and panic Pat felt in the first seconds of grief she could not utter them. The only sound to escape her lips was a terrible strangled scream that came from her very core.

*

Pat remembered nothing of her journey across Dublin, nothing of the cold marble interior of the government building to which they took her. Weeks later she would recall the breakfast of egg, bacon and soda bread that they set in front of her and how she watched the fat slowly congealing until they removed it, untouched. She knew the woman had been with her for hours, but all she could think about was the emptiness within her now that William was gone. The morning wore on and she began to long for her mother. To be with Mammy wouldn't take away the pain, but to be circled by her arms and hear her say, 'Sssh now, Pat, sure I'm here, amn't I?' might bring some comfort.

The woman brought tea and sat next to her. It was then that Pat noticed that she had removed her coat to reveal an eau de nil silk dress. 'Would you like me to explain to you how William died?'

Pat nodded.

'He had been with an ARP patrol when a bomb fell near their post; a house was demolished. He organised the wardens and showed them how to clear the debris quickly. Several people were pulled out alive. He left them shortly after and we assume that he was on his way back to the hotel when he was caught in another explosion.'

Pat's head seemed to clear as she listened to the details of William's last hours and, turning to the woman, she said, 'Of course you know all this – where he was and what he did. You were following us all day – Bewley's café, Phoenix Park,' Pat's voice was devoid of emotion. 'You and the clerk. Only he isn't a clerk, is he? Who ever heard of a clerk with a notebook and fountain pen who never made a single note?'

The woman leaned in close and lowered her voice. 'These are dangerous times. Your country is at war and we felt the need to protect Mr Kennedy while he was here negotiating with our government. That's why we were following him, that's how we know what happened to him.'

'But you didn't protect him, did you?'

'We did all we could.'

'So what were you supposed to be protecting him from?'

The woman looked away.

Pat's thoughts raced on. 'You weren't looking after William, you aren't looking after me – this is about the agreement, not us! There's been something strange about all this from the start. It was more than shelters and searchlights wasn't it?' She stood up, suddenly aware of her surroundings. 'What is this place? Why are you keeping me here?'

'Please sit down,' the woman's voice was soothing, but Pat was in no mood to be placated.

'I want to see William,' she demanded and paced the room as her thoughts raced on. 'And I'll need to tell his sister and the people back in Stormont.'

'It's all been taken care of. Please calm yourself.'

'I am calm,' Pat shouted, 'and I'm going to see William!' But before she reached the door it was opened and the man who was supposed to be a clerk stood in the doorway.

'You can't leave yet, Miss Goulding,' he said. 'With Mr Kennedy's death you are now the only representative of the Northern Ireland government in Dublin who is aware of the negotiations that have taken place over the past two days. The papers outlining the draft agreement reached between Mr Kennedy and our minister of defence are being drawn up. It's your duty now to take them back to Stormont.'

Pat opened her mouth to protest, but William's words came back to her. 'We could change the course of the war.'

The woman took her arm and said gently, 'Come and sit down. It won't be long until the papers are here and we'll drive you home to Belfast.'

Pat leaned back in the chair, closed her eyes and let the despair take her. William had succeeded in negotiating something that would bring relief to Belfast and something more, but they had paid a heavy price; he was dead and she would never see him again. For a few hours the previous night she had loved and been loved in return and a future that she had only been able to dream of had lain before her. Now there was nothing but an ache that she hoped would kill her too. Time crept on and, outside, the fair morning turned grey. Soon rain was beating on the window. Towards noon the clerk returned.

'It's time to go,' he said and led her outside to the car. They crossed the river, rounded the Custom House and minutes later the car pulled up outside Amiens Street station. He handed her a ticket. 'A single to Belfast. I'll walk you to the train; it leaves in ten minutes.'

'But you said I would be driven to Belfast to deliver the agreement.'

'What agreement?'

'The one negotiated between William and the Minister of Defence; you said I was to take it to Belfast.'

'I think you've misunderstood, Miss Goulding. Mr Kennedy was in Dublin to discuss improving food supplies to the north, but nothing was decided.'

'But you said this morning that—'

'I think perhaps the terrible ordeal you've been through might have, shall we say, clouded your judgement.'

He got out of the car and took her suitcase from the boot. 'All your belongings from the hotel,' he explained then took her elbow and led her to the train.

On the platform Pat said defiantly, 'I know exactly what you said earlier this morning and I know important things were agreed.'

He thrust the suitcase into her hand. 'You know nothing, Miss Goulding. Now go home.'

In Belfast, dark clouds obscured the Cave Hill and rain was beating off the streets, soaking through Pat's coat as she walked from the station to the Carr's Glen trolley bus. It was as though some primitive instinct willed her to put one foot in front of the other. Her mind was numb, save for thoughts of her own home and bed. From that moment on, she would never be able to recall any moment of the traumatic journey from Dublin to Belfast.

Round the back of the house she came and found the key where it always was; under the scrubbing brush. The house was cold – the range was out – and it didn't smell right. She called out 'Anybody home?' but there was only the ticking of the clock high on the mantelpiece. She made her way slowly up the stairs, got out of her wet clothes and into a clean soft nightdress from the drawer, and crawled under the eiderdown. Sleep was slow in coming, images of William and her together rushed one after the other, ripping her sanity: the hotel room, the café, Nelson's Pillar, the restaurant where he had proposed. Suddenly, she was out of bed and reaching for her suitcase, emptying the contents over the floor. Searching. Searching. It was lost or stolen. How could she have been so careless as to have left it behind! Then she remembered the pocket in the lid of her case – there was something small and hard and square. The green satin box, and inside … She held William's ring up to the light, turned it full circle and saw for the first time the surprise he had left her. Inside the band was engraved a message to Susanna from her Figaro. '*La voce che adoro*' – 'The voice I love'.

Chapter 15

Irene stood at the bus stop in Ballyhalbert and watched the single-decker bus disappear into the distance. It was Saturday afternoon and there wasn't a soul in sight. She'd left home determined to be positive. He's your husband and it's right that you should be with him, she told herself, but as each mile had passed the doubts had grown. She set the little suitcase she'd borrowed from Betty Harper on the ground and leaned against the bus stop. Well, at least if she didn't like it, she knew where to catch the bus back to Belfast.

There was the sound of a horn and she turned to see a military lorry coming towards her. As it drew nearer, she saw Sandy leaning out of the passenger window waving at her. The door was open before the lorry had stopped and he jumped out and ran towards her lifting her off her feet and swinging her round. His excitement at seeing her was all she needed to chase away her feelings of apprehension and when he set her back on the ground she lifted her face to be kissed.

'The base isn't far,' he told her as he helped her up into the lorry. 'You remember Tommy, don't you?'

'How could I forget him? He was with you when we met in Stranraer.'

'And we danced at the Aldergrove concert,' Tommy reminded her.

Irene laughed. 'You're the best Lindy Hopper I know, Tommy!'

'I've got the rest of the day off in honour of you coming,' said Sandy. 'So we'll go to the NAAFI for something to eat and then I'll take you to see our house.'

Our house ... that sounded so good. 'I can't wait,' she laughed.

The Ballyhalbert base was not much more than a concrete strip of runway with half a dozen Nissen huts and a control tower. It had been hastily constructed, but the squadron of night-flying Defiants lined up on the runway was impressive.

They drove straight to the NAAFI, housed in one of the Nissen huts, where it seemed everyone on the base, including the three other wives, had gathered to welcome her. The lunch of mince and potatoes, followed by rice pudding, was just what she needed after two hours on a bus with poor suspension, and the lively conversation was enough to make her think that maybe she might enjoy Ballyhalbert after all.

The house was a little over a mile from the base, a pleasant walk now that the rain had moved northwards. Patches of blue sky hung in the sky like washing on a line. The lane was little more than a dirt track bordered by hawthorn in full bloom.

'Cast not a clout 'til May is out,' said Irene.

'What nonsense is that?' Sandy teased her.

'Last day of May today and the May flowers are everywhere – time to swap winter clothes for summer dresses.'

'Maybe I'll give that tradition a miss,' he said.

They rounded a bend and the land fell away. Brown and cream cows grazed in a lush green field to their left and a collection of roofs could be seen in the fold of the land below. They paused a moment to take in the patchwork of green that stretched as far as the eye could see. A cow appeared over the hedge lowing softly and high above them a circling curlew called.

'It's beautiful,' said Irene.

'It needs to be,' said Sandy, 'you haven't seen the house yet!'

Too small to be considered a hamlet, the row of three cottages, the farmhouse and barn were simply known as Road End, but 'back of beyond' might have been a better description. The end cottage, like its neighbours, was whitewashed and thatched and the door at the front was flanked by a two small windows. Sandy pushed the door open, swept Irene up in his arms and carried her over the threshold. He kissed her and set her down. 'Well, what do you think of the wee house?'

Irene inspected everything: the open fire place with a box bed to one side; the solid wooden table and dresser with its mismatched crockery; the ancient sofa covered with a crocheted blanket; and two bright rag rugs. Everything was clean and cared for.

'Will it do?' Sandy's voice was anxious.

Irene stood between two shafts of sunlight that shone through the windows and lit up the little room and grinned. 'It will.'

'Hello, anybody there?' A woman's face appeared at the window and seconds later she was at the door. 'You must be Irene. Welcome, welcome!' She was a small stout woman with grey hair and her smile was full and well meant.

'This is Mrs McCoubrey,' said Sandy. 'She's renting us the cottage.'

'Now, now, what did I tell you? Call me Jeanie.' She put a string bag on the table. 'Brought you a few wee things to be going on with: potato bread, milk, butter, eggs, bacon.'

'That's really kind of you,' said Irene.

'Not at all, not at all, sure we're neighbours now, aren't we? Now I'll leave the two of you to get settled and, if you need anything at all, just ask.'

'There's enough here for a feast,' said Sandy, unpacking Jeanie's bag. 'I'll fetch some water from the pump and see if I can get a fire going.'

'There's no hurry. After the big dinner we had, I'm in no rush to eat,' said Irene. 'Let's just sit for a while and you can tell me all about Ballyhalbert.'

Saturday night in the NAAFI was a noisy and raucous affair. The beer and cigarettes were cheap and the craic was good. Tommy owned a gramophone and half a dozen records so there was quite a bit of dancing. With the arrival of Irene there were now four women on the base, but they were still heavily outnumbered by the men and, by nine o'clock, Irene must have danced with at least half the airmen. She had just danced the Lindy Hop with Tommy for the third time, when she slumped into her chair next to Sandy.

'I can't dance another step. I'm exhausted.'

'Maybe it's time for something less energetic,' said Sandy.

He took a harmonica from his pocket and played the opening to 'Wish Me Luck As You Wave Me Goodbye'. Another airman with a harmonica joined him, playing the harmony, and soon everyone was singing along. Between them, Sandy and his pal had quite a wide repertoire of popular songs and when one or two people were confident enough to sing solo, their efforts were rewarded with loud clapping and cheering.

'What about you, Irene?' shouted Tommy. 'Will you not give us a song? One of those you sang at the concert.'

Irene blushed and shook her head, 'No I couldn't.'

'Of course you can.' Tommy took her hand and pulled her out of her seat.

'I'm used to singing with my sisters; I'm not that good without them.'

'Come on – you can do it,' Tommy insisted.

Irene looked at Sandy. He nodded and smiled his encouragement. 'I could sing "Kiss Me Goodnight, Sergeant Major",' she said. 'That's one I usually sing on my own.'

The opening bars were played and Irene came in on cue. This wasn't a performance for a concert hall, but a sing-song with friends and Irene was modest enough to leave out the bits of theatricality – like marching up and down between verses – that she and her sisters would have included in their act, though she did encourage everyone to join in the chorus. She held the final note like a professional and bowed quickly at the loud clapping and cheering before returning to her seat, still blushing.

Chapter 16

There were just a few neighbours up and about in Joanmount Gardens when an impressive black car with highly polished chrome headlamps and bumpers pulled up outside the Goulding house. Those who saw the driver emerge, dressed formally in a dark overcoat and bowler hat, might have wondered why a solicitor, or possibly an accountant, might be calling on the Gouldings on a Sunday morning. Peggy answered the door in her dressing gown with a piece of toast in her hand and, on seeing the middle-aged man on the doorstep, her first chilling thought was that he might be an undertaker.

'Good morning. I'm sorry to disturb you, but I'm looking for Miss Goulding.'

'Which one?'

'Oh, ah ... Patricia.'

'I think she might be upstairs.' Peggy didn't explain that she hadn't seen her sister for three days and that when she had got home the previous night from the Plaza it was only the sight of her sister's coat over the bannister that alerted her to the fact that Pat had come home. 'Why don't you go into the sitting room and I'll find her.'

Upstairs Peggy quickly shook Pat awake. 'Get up, get up,' she hissed. 'There's a very important-looking man downstairs. In a bowler hat no less!'

Pat rolled over and sat up.

'Oh my God!' Peggy gasped, seeing Pat's puffy face. 'What happened to you?'

'I don't want to talk to you, go away.' Pat turned towards the wall and pulled the eiderdown over her head.

'Your eyes are all swollen. You've been crying, haven't you?'

'Just go away, will you!'

'I could do that, but that strange-looking old fellow downstairs isn't going anywhere until he's spoken to you.'

'Who is he?'

'Looks like an undertaker if you ask me.'

Pat jumped up. 'What?'

'Bowler hat, little moustache, shoes you can see your face in.'

'Tell him I'll be down in five minutes. Give him a cup of tea or something.'

Sir John Andrews didn't often get to meet ordinary Belfast people in their own homes. He had toured a significant number of slums, pledging to build new houses when he was running for office, but this house was not like those. Maybe Miss Goulding was a different sort of working class. He noted the clean, neat room. The furniture was a little threadbare, but a Monet print on the wall and the sheet music for a Schubert song on the piano suggested at least some refinement.

'She'll be down in a few minutes,' said Peggy. 'Sit down if you like. I'll make you a cup of tea.'

'No, please don't bother. I just need to speak to Patricia in private.'

'Ah, right,' said Peggy, worried now about what this man wanted with Pat. 'I'll just be upstairs.' Sitting on the top step listening out for any sign of trouble more like, she thought.

Sir John stood up as Pat entered and offered her his hand. 'Are you Patricia Goulding, a clerk at the Ministry of Public Security?' Pat nodded and he went on, 'Do you know who I am?'

'Yes, you're Sir John Andrews. We've met before.'

153

'Have we?' He looked surprised.

'I sang in the choir at the Stormont carol concert last Christmas. My aunt, Kathleen Goulding, introduced us.'

'Of course, I remember.' His condescending tone disappeared. The girl had connections; this might be easier than he thought.

'You're aware, I take it, of my position at Stormont.'

'Of course I am.'

'Miss Goulding, I hope the fact that I have come personally and alone to your home to talk to you will lend weight to what I have to say and what I must ask of you.'

Pat was struggling to concentrate; her grief was still raw and she was stunned and incapable of engaging with anything. His words washed over her. William was dead and nothing else mattered.

He went on, 'As far as the government is concerned, Mr Kennedy took a break in Dublin. He had been working very hard and went away for a short holiday. He went sightseeing, dined in some fine restaurants.' He paused for effect. 'He was ... alone.'

'No he wasn't,' Pat corrected him. 'I was with him. He was on government business.'

He saw the anger flare in her eyes, but pressed on. 'You have been ill at home since Thursday. Your sick absence has been recorded on your record. In fact, you will also be absent next week to give you the chance to make a full recovery from your illness.'

Pat looked at him in horror. 'What are you saying? Don't you know that William is dead, killed by a German bomb while he was in Dublin trying to negotiate concessions to make life in Belfast better.'

Sir John looked uncomfortable; this wasn't the effect he wanted. He changed tack and spoke slowly as though to a confused child. 'Patricia, I know what happened and what you've been through, but Mr Kennedy should not have gone to Dublin and, quite frankly, neither should you. He was not authorised by me to negotiate with the Dublin government. He was acting on his own initiative and too much is at stake to allow what he was doing to become common knowledge.'

'But don't you know that he succeeded? An agreement was reached and the papers were ready to be brought back to you. I know he won all kinds of concessions regarding the provision of food and care of refugees, but there was something more, something very important. I don't know what exactly, but he told me it would change the course of the war. So don't stand there and try to tell me that William shouldn't have gone there!' Her voice had edged steadily towards the hysterical.

Sir John didn't reply straight away. Instead he turned to the window and stared out at the street. He had seriously underestimated this young woman. He had hoped to use his authority to persuade her to accept a new version of events. If necessary, he had intended to insinuate that she had been absent from work without permission. But he was struck by her genuine grief and passionate defence of Kennedy. Was it possible she was more than his clerk? She was certainly very attractive.

'Patricia,' he said eventually, 'am I right in thinking William meant a great deal to you?'

She bowed her head.

'Tell me, were you in love with him?'

'He asked me to marry him,' she said, her voice a whisper.

'Hmm.' This was a complication he hadn't foreseen, but it might still be possible … 'Patricia, can I trust you with a matter of the utmost importance on which the security of Northern Ireland depends?'

Pat lifted her head. 'You'd better not tell me something bad about William because, if you do, I won't believe it.'

'No, what I will tell you will show you what a good, brave and clever man he was, but I suspect you know that already.'

'Please tell me what we were really doing in Dublin.'

'William Kennedy was commissioned by the British government to negotiate the end of Irish neutrality. It wasn't the first time they had attempted to reach such an agreement. The plan was to bring Ireland into the war in a non-aggressive way. To begin with, Ireland would have refused German planes permission to fly over their country and would have permitted Britain to establish naval bases within its borders.'

'Why would the Irish suddenly have agreed to all that?'

'Because, as part of the agreement, Churchill would have reopened talks on the future of the six counties. You understand what I'm saying, Patricia? William brought the prospect of a united Ireland to the table.' He paused to let the importance of his words sink in. 'Now do you see why I wasn't told of his assignment until yesterday when it had already failed?' He couldn't keep the anger out of his voice.

Pat stared at him, realisation dawning on her face. 'Yes, because you would never have authorised negotiations that jeopardised the future of the six counties. You want Northern Ireland to remain British. But I still don't understand – an agreement was reached. Has the Irish government denied all knowledge of it?'

'The German bombing put paid to the whole plan. We think that the Germans got wind of what was happening. The bombing was a warning. You have to understand that Ireland would never recover from a blitz on a grand scale. So the agreement William negotiated was torn up. You could say that it was killed, as he was, by the German bombs.'

Pat could clearly see why the Irish had backed away from the plan. Absolute denial was the only way to save them from further attacks. 'And William?' she asked.

'He knew the Northern Ireland government would never have agreed to it. He risked the future of Ulster.'

Pat lifted her chin and spoke proudly, 'To save its people from suffering.' She held out her hand. 'Thank you for telling me the truth.'

'You're one of only a handful of people who know what really happened. If word of this were ever to get out–'

Pat didn't hesitate. 'I will never speak of it again.'

Standing at the top of the stairs, Peggy had not been able to make out a single word that had passed between the mysterious caller and Pat, so softly had they spoken. Nevertheless, she recognised an intonation in her sister's voice that was a sure sign of distress. The man had seen himself out and Peggy slipped into the front bedroom to get another look at him as he walked to his car. Then she waited a few minutes before going downstairs. Pat was staring out of the window, deep in thought.

'Well?' said Peggy.

No reply.

'Who was he then?'

'My boss from Stormont.'

'What did he want?'

'I'm to take a week off work on the sick.'

'What's happened? Are you ill?'

'Not ill, no, not really.'

There was a deadness in Pat's voice and a weariness about her that Peggy would never have imagined possible.

'Tell me what's wrong with you.'

'Not now, Peggy,' said Pat and she left the room and went back to her bed.

Around lunchtime, Peggy crept upstairs with a piece of toast and a scraping of butter and put her head round the door. 'Will you eat something now?' she whispered.

Pat was lying on her back staring at the ceiling. 'I'll try.' She pushed the toast round the plate, took a bite and set it down while Peggy sat on the edge of the bed watching her.

'Did something bad happen?' Peggy asked at last.

Pat nodded.

'To you?'

Pat shook her head.

'Do you want to tell me about it?'

Pat closed her eyes, but the tears escaped and ran down her face. Peggy took a handkerchief from her sleeve and wiped them away. 'What can I do to help you?'

'Nothing, go away.'

Peggy looked in again a few hours later. 'Can I get you anything?'

'No.'

'You have to tell someone.' The minutes passed. Peggy tried again. 'Is this about William Kennedy?'

Pat spoke in a voice so soft Peggy struggled to hear.

'What did you say?' and she leaned in close.

'William's dead.'

'Dead? William Kennedy's dead, is that what you said?'

'Yes.' Pat's voice caught in her throat and she began to sob. 'In Dublin … he was caught in the bombing … he died yesterday.'

'Dublin was bombed?' Peggy tried to make sense of what had happened. 'You were there with William?'

'I'm not supposed to talk about it.'

'But what were you doing in Dublin?'

'I'm not allowed to say.'

'Pat, if you and William went away to be together—'

'No!' Pat sobbed. 'It wasn't like that! We loved each other and now he's gone, I can't bear it,' and she began to weep uncontrollably.

Peggy reached out and pulled her sister close. 'There now,' she soothed. 'I'll stay with you, I'll help you.'

Pat cried until she fell asleep, exhausted, and Peggy lay next to her on the bed until teatime when she slipped downstairs to make some food. She boiled an egg, turned it out into a cup and chopped it up, then buttered a round of bread and took them up on a tray.

Pat stirred as she came in. 'You've made me egg in a cup,' she attempted a smile, 'just like Mammy used to give us when we weren't well.'

'I need to look after you, don't I? And you'd better eat it all because it's our last one.'

They sat a while in silence while Pat ate the egg, then Peggy spoke again. 'Do you want me to get Mammy home?'

'No!' Pat's eyes widened in fright. 'Nobody must know what happened. I shouldn't really have told you. You have to swear not to tell anyone!'

'But people must know William's dead. Your boss knows.'

'Yes, but nobody else must find out why he was in Dublin!'

'It wasn't just you and him going off together?'

'Of course it wasn't!'

'What will you tell people?'

'I won't tell anyone anything, because officially I was at home sick. William went to Dublin on his own and was caught up in the bombing. That's the story.'

'I could stay at home with you for a few days, if you like.

Mr Goldstein would understand if I said you were ill.'

'No, I'll be all right on my own.'

'Pat, I'm really sorry about all the times I was rude about William and for … you know … making fun of you both.'

'It doesn't matter.'

'But I feel awful.'

'I told you it doesn't matter. Nothing does any more.'

The piercing scream woke Peggy and she was out of bed and at her sister's side in an instant.

Pat was sitting bolt upright, eyes glazed, hands clawing at the air. 'Don't go! Don't leave me!'

'Wake up, Pat, it's just a dream. You're all right, I'm here.' And, as she had done for the past five nights, she held her sister until the terror subsided and the crying began. The nightmares and anxiety had increased in intensity and Peggy worried how, in just a few hours' time, Pat could possibly cope with William's funeral. Goldstein had insisted on driving them to the service and Peggy was grateful to have him there to help her support Pat.

'I understand the bond that develops between two performers who are able to create such passion when they sing together,' Goldstein had reassured her, when they locked up the shop the previous night, and Peggy was glad that he had mentioned only their passion for singing and not speculated that there might be anything more.

Peggy was ready and waiting when Goldstein arrived at ten in the morning. She shouted up the stairs to Pat, 'Time to go now!' Her sister appeared a few minutes later and Peggy almost wept at the sight of her. The dark blue costume she normally wore to work was hanging loose on her. Her beautiful auburn hair was dull and lank but, most strikingly, her face was devoid of any expression. At any other time, Peggy would have taken a few minutes to brush Pat's hair into shape and add a bit of rouge and lipstick to her face, but she knew instinctively that Pat would push her away. Besides, such superficial tricks would make no difference at all to a face etched with grief.

The church was packed and Goldstein nudged Peggy as several well-dressed men walked up the aisle and sat near the front. 'I see several senior members of the Stormont administration are present,' he whispered.

Pat saw none of this. From the moment she sat down her head was bowed and her eyes were closed. Peggy could feel the tension from her. The only time she seemed aware of what was going on was when she raised her head and stared at the ceiling during a piece from Mozart's *Requiem*, played by the Stormont string quartet.

Later, as people stood about outside the church, William's sister Helen came to thank Pat for coming. 'I really appreciate you being here,' she said. 'I hope you know William was fond of you and often spoke about how supportive you were.'

Pat looked into Helen's blue eyes, identical to William's, and it was all she could do to nod and shake her hand before moving away.

Goldstein had gone to fetch his car and Pat and Peggy waited on the pavement.

'Don't look now,' said Peggy, 'but that man who came to the house on Sunday morning is heading this way.'

'I don't want to speak to him,' Pat's eyes were wide with panic, but he was already at her side.

'Patricia, I'm glad you were able to come. I wanted to say that, should you need to remain on sick leave, we can manage without you a little longer.'

Pat didn't answer and Peggy, to avoid any embarrassment, spoke for her. 'That's very kind, thank you.'

At that moment Goldstein's car pulled up next to them and Peggy opened the door and helped her sister into the back seat.

'Good gracious,' said Goldstein to Peggy under his breath as she got in, 'do you realise who that was?'

'Pat's boss from work,' said Peggy.

Goldstein laughed. 'I suppose you could say that – he's the prime minister of Northern Ireland!'

Peggy's jaw dropped as she watched the man who had been in their sitting room on Sunday morning place his bowler hat on his head and stroll away.

A week later, Peggy arrived home from work and as she came through the back door, she could hear the sound of things being thrown around and Pat's angry voice at full volume. This wasn't the quiet stillness of grief that had hung over Pat since William's funeral. She ran upstairs to find Pat standing in the middle of the bedroom surrounded by the entire contents of the wardrobe and dressing table.

'Where is it? Where is it?' Pat screamed.

'What's the matter? What are you looking for?'

'My notebook, it's gone.' Pat turned on her. 'You've taken it, haven't you?'

'I don't know what you're talking about. What notebook?'

'It's here somewhere. I have to find it. It's got all the notes I made for William in it.'

'Pat–'

'Help me find it!'

'William's gone, Pat – the notes don't matter any more.'

'Yes, they do. I've still got the notebook, so I can prove what happened. They'll not get away with this!'

'Who? Who won't get away with what?'

Pat eyed her suspiciously, 'Never you mind.'

'Do you want me to help you find it?' Peggy asked, hoping to calm her.

They set to, Peggy retrieving each item and returning it to its proper place and Pat randomly picking things up and casting them aside.

'What's this?' Peggy asked, holding up the green ring box.

'Nothing.'

Peggy opened it and her eyes widened at the sight of the beautiful solitaire diamond. She took it out of the box and held it up to the light. 'Pat, where did you get this?' she asked, already knowing the answer.

'He gave it to me.'

'William gave you this?'

'Yes, he asked me to marry him then went and got himself killed.' Her voice rose again in anger. 'What kind of love is that?'

'He didn't mean to. How could anyone have known the Germans

would bomb Dublin? He was just in the wrong place at the wrong time.'

'That's just it, isn't it? The right place was with me, but he left me. Walked out the door when I begged him not to, but that was just like him wasn't it, putting work before me. He didn't love me at all!'

'But he did! He asked you to marry him and gave you this!' Peggy held out the ring to her.

Pat snatched it and threw it with all her might out the window into the long grass. 'I don't want a ring. I want him!' she cried.

Chapter 17

The end of June brought sunny weather that helped to lift people's spirits. Since the bombing in early May very few of the bombsites had been cleared and they remained as shocking as scars on the face of a friend. In Royal Avenue trade was still slow, especially in shops like Goldstein's. Gramophone records and musical instruments seemed to be the last thing on people's minds.

As was his custom on Wednesday, Goldstein took lunch at his club in Cornmarket leaving Peggy in charge of the shop. The first thing she did was to instruct Esther to sort out the delivery of sheet music while she went outside, ostensibly to draw down the awning to protect the window display, but really to enjoy the sun.

'Well if it isn't the shop girl.' It was Devlin.

Peggy didn't look at him. 'What do you want?'

'That's no way to speak to your boss.'

'You're not my boss. I told you I wasn't coming back after the last time, remember?'

He gave her his best smile, but she was determined not to be seduced by it. 'But I've got a job for you on Saturday night as—'

'Look here, you were out of order giving me that drink when I was sick. You should've sent me home – in a taxi!'

163

'Instead of keeping you safe in an air raid?'

'It was a false alarm!'

'So you don't want to know what the job is?'

'I wouldn't work for you if–'

'I need a pianist for a big, big event at the Plaza' – he swept his hand as though imagining a banner – '"Grand Dance Competition". Let's see if we can't chase away some of the misery around here.'

Peggy had dreamt of playing at such an event. It could be a big break for her, but she shook her head. 'I can't do it, sorry. My sister isn't well and I just can't leave her at night.'

'I'll pay you double.'

'No.' Peggy turned to walk away. Devlin grabbed her arm and pulled her back.

'You didn't refuse me last time. In fact you enjoyed yourself so much you stayed the night,' he leered. Peggy blushed scarlet. 'We could make a night of it again, you and me, after hours. Only we'll go easy on the brandy this time.'

'What are you talking about?'

'You and me, together all night.'

Peggy froze. 'Nothing happened between you and me that night and you know it!'

'Are you sure about that?'

'Absolutely,' and she pulled her arm away.

Devlin laughed. 'Well, maybe not, but there's nothing to stop me saying that it did. I'm sure old man Goldstein might be interested to know about you getting drunk and staying out all night, or maybe your mother should be told?' He was so absorbed in baiting her that the slap to the jaw caught him by surprise. The anger blazed in his face.

'Now listen here, I've spent a lot of money organising this competition and I'm damned if I'll see it ruined for lack of a pianist! You'd better be there.'

When Peggy came through the back door that evening, she was surprised to hear the sound of laughter coming from the kitchen. Pat and Betty from next door were sitting at the table and the room was filled with the smell of stew simmering on the stove.

'Ach there you are, Peggy. Just popped round with some stew we had left over and there are some vegetables and a couple of eggs on the draining board there.'

'That's so kind of you, Betty. What would we do without you and Jack?' Peggy's thanks were all the more heartfelt since there was next to nothing in the cupboard.

'Pat's been telling me she's not been too well. She could do with a good tonic, I think. You know, there are a lot of people under the weather at the moment. Sure, what else would you expect with all the destruction and disruption, and you've only to look in the shops to see there's nothing worth having, is there? Ah well, sure we just have to keep going.' Betty heaved herself out of the chair and headed to the door. 'Oh, any news from your mother?'

'Her and Sheila are fine the last we heard. We're hoping they'll be home any day. I thought she might have rung me at the shop before now, but maybe I'll hear from her tomorrow.'

'Sure she's probably better off there anyway. I could do with a wee stay in the country meself.'

When Betty had gone, Peggy ladled out the stew and they ate in silence until Pat said, 'I had a letter from Stormont today to tell me I'll be going on half-pay next week.'

'God that's all we need!' Peggy threw her spoon into her empty bowl. 'If it wasn't for those two next door we'd be on starvation rations. It's bad enough having to walk to work and back, without doing it on an empty stomach.'

Pat began to cry.

'Oh, I'm sorry,' Peggy knelt and put her arms around her sister. 'Don't cry, please. I shouldn't have said that. It's all right, we'll get you well again soon.'

Pat wiped away her tears. 'No, you're right. I'll just have to go back to work. Sure I've been off a month. I'll go in tomorrow.'

'No! You can't. You're not sleeping half the night and when you do you're dripping in sweat or crying out in a panic. You just need a bit longer. We'll manage, I promise you.'

*

'Peggy, will you stop giving off and listen for once!' Martha held the phone a little away from her ear and smiled nervously at the customers in the post office. She disliked strangers knowing her business, but most of them already knew she was the Belfast woman who had come in search of her daughter and had been there for the McManus family when they needed an extra pair of hands – sure, hadn't she served in the shop, got the messages and cooked meals so Bridie could spend time with Rose, the poor wee girl, they told each other.

'Peggy, it's time you girls started fending for yourselves, sure there's only you and Pat there anyway. No, I don't know when I'll be back … another week maybe… If you speak to me like that, my girl, I might take myself off altogether! I'm going now. I'll maybe speak to you next week. Don't forget to thank Mr Goldstein for letting you use the telephone.' Martha hung up the receiver and composed herself before turning to face the post office queue and walking quickly out the door. Sheila was sitting on the bench outside.

'Well, Mammy, can you stay?'

'Of course I can stay. I'll do what I want – those girls have no right to tell me what I can and can't do! It'll do them no harm to be make their own meals and wash and iron for themselves. No doubt the house'll be piggin' when I get home, but a good day's reddin' will soon put that to rights.'

'And can we go and help with the harvest?'

Martha took Sheila's hand and swung it as they walked. 'Why not, we're having a wee holiday, just you and me, aren't we?'

They were up at six the following morning to walk the three miles to the farm. Bridie's family kept twenty acres of arable land and needed two fields of oats gathered in within the week. The party numbered eight, Sheila and Martha filling in for Bridie and Rose who was still too weak for manual work. They left the sleeping town behind and walked in companionable silence under a canopy of soft blue sky. Other workers were already there – men stood about leaning on up-turned scythes; others spat on whetstones and sharpened blades; and a group of young men joked and smoked. The women sat in a circle chatting quietly. Nearby, a shire horse chomped breakfast from a nosebag. From a distance, the horse seemed deceptively small but up close Martha marvelled at its height and girth – she had never imagined a beast so big. Frank gave Sheila a long wooden stick and showed her how to hold a length of oat stalks upright while he scythed them down, before moving quickly forward to hold up the next row.

'The secret,' he said, with a wink, 'is not to get yer legs mixed up with the stalks.'

Behind them came Martha and Dermot who gathered up armfuls of stalks, tied them in sheaves and dropped them on the ground to be gathered up later. Time and again they reached the headrig and turned again into the sun … away from the sun … and Martha lost all sense of time and place. There was nothing in her mind save the ground strewn with oats and the rhythm of bending and standing and twisting the sheaves.

Shortly after midday a halt was called. The wives had arrived and spread blankets on the higher ground. They laid out bread and cheese and tomatoes, with little newspaper pokes of salt, and apple juice for everyone. Children played tig in the stubble and every now and again a shout would go up as a field mouse or frog was discovered in the devastation. Workers took their ease: some lying asleep, cap over their eyes, others sitting in groups smoking. Martha sat in the shade of a sycamore and held her hair up to let the wisp of breeze cool her neck. She kept her eye on Sheila and Dermot as they sat side by side with the other youngsters, his head inclined to hers as he listened to her chatter. She'd seen the way his eyes followed her in the kitchen and the yard and knew they sometimes left the house separately on their bikes in opposite directions only to meet up minutes later further down the road. He was a nice boy, gentle with his sister in her grief, but soon Sheila would return to Belfast and Martha worried about the pain of parting.

She sensed a shadow fall on her and followed the line of it to its owner. She let her hair fall and raised her hand to shield her eyes.

'Y'all right there, missus?' It was Vincent, Bridie's brother.

'Aye, I am thanks.'

'I'm grateful for you and the wee girl helpin' us out. An' Bridie told me what you done for her an' Rose.' He had an embarrassed look about him.

'Oh, it was nothing,' Martha protested. 'Bridie did much more for me when she took Sheila in.'

He made to sit down, then hesitated. Martha, seeing his confusion, moved over a little to make room. He hunkered down.

'How many days to harvest the oats?' she asked.

'Well now, a couple more good days like this one should do it. Then there is the grass seed crop to mow. Of course, if any other farm is strugglin', we'll give them a hand. All in all we should be finished in time for the ceilidh.'

'Ceilidh?' said Martha.

'Aye, a bit of celebration – dancin', eatin' …' he lowered his voice, 'and drinkin' for some eejits.'

'You don't approve of the drink, then?'

'Oh I don't mind a bit of celebration of hard work, but I'm a Pioneer.'

'Pioneer?'

'The Pledge.' Vincent noticed her blank look. 'Drink, I never touch it, it's the devil.'

Martha smiled, 'Aye, maybe you're right,' she said.

They sat for a few minutes looking out over the field to the low hill beyond. Eventually Martha spoke. 'It's beautiful here, so peaceful.'

'It is today, but imagine it in the winter when the black clouds scutter over thon hill day after day and ye've to be up at dawn seeing to the animals.'

'Even then it's beautiful, I'm sure.'

'Aye, I suppose it is,' he conceded, 'but we don't have the excitement of Belfast.'

Martha looked sideways at him and saw the twinkle in his eye. 'There's nothing exciting ever happens in Belfast,' she laughed.

'Not even with the war, the bombin' and the like?'

'Oh aye, we've had bombs on our heads, but that's frightening not exciting. I'll tell you something but, working in the fields is hard on the hands for a city dweller like me!' She held up her hands

168

to show the cuts from the sharp stalks. To her surprise, Vincent reached out and took both hands in his and examined them closely. Then he looked up at her and, realising what he had done, he released her hands and looked away.

'You needed to have washed them in vinegar before you started to harden them up. Try an' do it tonight even if they sting a bit.' He reached into his hip pocket and pulled out a pair of well-worn leather gloves and offered them to her. 'Put these on for now; they'll protect your skin.'

'No, I'm fine, honest. Anyway, you'll need them.'

'No, I don't really,' he laughed and added, 'they're more for show than anything!' Martha took the gloves and slipped her hands inside them. He nodded, satisfied, and stood up to survey the field. 'We'll have this finished by the end of the day, I think, if we get a move on.' He touched his cap and with long, purposeful strides he was off towards the horse and cart. As he passed, the workers stirred and within minutes the work had resumed.

Bridie had a big dinner of stew and potatoes made for them when they got back and Martha marvelled at the pleasure of sitting down to a meal that someone else had prepared. Her hunger satiated, exhaustion set in. She couldn't wait to take her aching limbs to bed, but first there were her hands to see to.

'Bridie, would you have any vinegar I could bathe my hands in?'

'Of course, let's have a look at them. Ach, they're not too bad.' She fetched the vinegar from the cupboard.

'They'd have been even worse if Vincent hadn't lent her his gloves to wear,' said Sheila.

'Is that so?' said Bridie raising an eyebrow as she passed the vinegar to Martha. Then she rummaged in the hot press and found an old pillowcase from which she tore two long strips. 'Soak these in the vinegar then wind them round your hands before you go to sleep.'

It was still light when Martha went to bed. She lay on her back waiting for sleep to come and thought about the strangeness of the day – the hard physical labour, the satisfaction that grew with each sheaf she tied. But as she drifted off to sleep, breathing in the smell of vinegar bandages, the image that stayed in her mind was of Vincent's kind face as he offered her his leather gloves.

Devlin had said it was going to be a spectacular affair and he had certainly transformed the tired and dated Plaza Ballroom into a stylish venue. A huge banner was strung across the entire façade proclaiming 'Grand Dance Competition'. On either side of the entrance, huge flower arrangements cascaded over fluted pillars. A broad-shouldered, uniformed doorman welcomed everyone as they arrived. In the ballroom itself the mustiness had been replaced by the smell of polish from the shiny dance floor. The stage was lit by coloured lights, the glitter ball was gleaming and the band were tuning up their instruments.

Peggy couldn't help but be impressed. The place certainly had class, as did the many people arriving for the evening. Despite her misgivings about asking Betty to sit with Pat for the evening, she was pleased to be part of such a grand event. Think of it as a professional engagement, she told herself, do what you have to do and leave. She was, as always, well-groomed and elegant, her hair swept up to give her a little extra height. There were pearls in her ears and around her neck. Her white blouse was bleached and starched, her black pencil skirt damp-pressed to look like new, her black high-heel court shoes polished until they shone. She lifted her chin and walked the length of the ballroom to the stage as though she was on a catwalk.

Devlin had his back to her and was talking to the band who, one by one, stopped listening as their eyes flitted in her direction. Devlin turned to see the focus of their attention and watched her walk to the piano.

'I knew you'd come.' He leaned on the piano and smiled.

'Really and how could you know that?' Peggy refused to look at him and played a scale to check the piano was in tune.

'Because you couldn't resist spending another evening, or should that be night, with me.'

'Don't flatter yourself. I'm here because you pay well.' She glared, intending to face him down, but she was distracted by the blueness of his eyes.

'In that case you'd better make sure you earn it, so keep off the booze and get the tempo right!'

Peggy stood up. 'How dare you speak to me like that!' But Devlin was already walking away.

The ballroom filled up rapidly. There was a queue of competitors registering to take part and the dance floor was packed. At eight o'clock Devlin went to the microphone.

'Ladies and gentlemen, welcome to the Plaza Grand Dance Competition. There will be four rounds – waltz, quickstep, foxtrot and modern. At the end of each round the judges will decide who should be eliminated. The final round will consist of only twelve couples who will dance three different modern dances. There will be prizes of £1 for third place, £3 for second and £5 for the winners!' The audience gave a huge cheer.

'And that's not all. In between the rounds, there will be dancing for everyone with spot prizes and prizes for the best-dressed man and woman.' More cheers. 'The competition starts in five minutes!'

At around ten o'clock, just before the final round, the band was given a break and records were played. Peggy powdered her nose and reapplied her lipstick then sat at a table drinking a glass of water.

'Sneaked in some gin and tonic, have you?' Devlin said sitting down next to her. Peggy ignored him, so he waved his hand to take in the whole ballroom. 'Good idea of mine, don't you think? This is just a start. I've loads of ideas to make the Plaza the place that everyone who's anyone wants to be. It's all about style really.' He touched his bow tie and pushed back his dark hair and Peggy saw a grace in his movements, an arrogance that compelled her to look at him and, despite her dislike, drew her admiration.

As if reading her thoughts, he moved his chair closer. 'You could be a part of this.' His voice was soft, persuasive. 'You have talent and looks. You might be just a member of the orchestra, but when you're on the stage all I see is you, all I hear is the piano.' Instinctively, Peggy leaned towards him and, with just inches between them, he whispered, 'I can make exciting things happen.'

There was a change of record and Devlin reached for her hand and pulled her on to the dance floor.

'I thought I wasn't allowed to dance on my break,' said Peggy.

'You are when I tell you to.'

Peggy could dance the foxtrot, but this was in the swing style. One circuit of the floor, though, and she had the measure of it. She followed Devlin's lead instinctively.

When the music ended he kissed her softly and said. 'Now get back to work, I'm not paying you to entice men.'

At the end of the evening Peggy queued with the rest of the staff for her wages. 'What's this?' she demanded when Devlin gave her ten shillings.

'Going rate for a pianist for an evening's work.'

'You said you'd pay me double for tonight.'

'So I did,' he replied, 'but you'll get the extra in next week's wages.'

'But I'm not coming next week. I told you my sister's ill! I only came tonight because …'

'Oi!' someone behind her shouted. 'Get a move on, some of us have homes to go to.'

'So I'll see you next week then,' and Devlin flashed his broadest smile.

Peggy had discovered two things quite by accident, the first being that if she gave up eating lunch every day she could save some money, and the second, that spending her lunch looking round the shops made her forget how hungry she was. She left Goldstein's at one o'clock as usual and headed towards the department stores intending to wander round some make-up counters.

She was walking towards the City Hall when she heard someone shout her name and turned to see Devlin running across the road towards her, dodging the traffic. He took her arm and put it through his, as if it were the most natural thing in the world, and Peggy was so taken aback that she let it rest there. As they walked he chatted about the coming Saturday night at the Plaza. Peggy was so pleased to be walking arm in arm along Donegall Place with such a handsome and well-dressed man, that she was reluctant to explain to him yet again why she wouldn't be there on Saturday and, by the way, he owed her money.

Devlin stopped suddenly in front of Robinson and Cleaver's.

'What is it?' asked Peggy.

'That.' he nodded at the window display.

Her eyes widened in surprise. It was the kingfisher cocktail dress, the one she had dreamt of wearing to play in a dance band. The one she had tried on the day she first met Devlin.

'You're the focal point of the band, eyes are drawn to you,' he was saying, 'but you shouldn't be in black and white like the men. You should be a splash of colour, of drama. That's why I'm going to buy you that dress.' And Peggy began to think that perhaps she might consider playing in the band again. By the time she emerged from the changing room in kingfisher blue and twirled in front of Devlin's admiring gaze she had decided she would.

While the shop assistant wrapped up their purchase, Peggy admired a green silk dress on a mannequin.

'You like that one too?' asked Devlin.

Peggy nodded. 'Oh I don't have my clothing coupons with me!'

Devlin gave a humourless laugh. 'Coupons? We don't need coupons,' and he produced a roll of banknotes from his inside pocket. As they left the shop Devlin took her arm again and turned towards the Plaza.

'Where are we going?'

'To the Plaza; you can try on the dresses again.'

'No I can't. Mr Goldstein doesn't like it if I'm late back from lunch. I'll try them on again at home.'

'That's not how it works.'

'What do you mean?'

'Well, strictly speaking they're my dresses. So I'll keep them at the Plaza and you'll change into them there when you arrive for work.'

That evening when Peggy arrived home, she could see at once that Pat had been crying again. On the table was a typed letter with the government crest. 'What's this?'

'Just read it.'

'Now they're going to stop paying you altogether? I thought you were entitled to sick pay – you're in this state because of them!'

'It's the rules. I can't argue.'

'But that's so unfair!' Peggy was outraged. 'After all you've been through.'

'It's no good. I'll have to go back,' Pat cried. Peggy tried to calm her, but Pat's breaths were coming faster and faster. Suddenly, she rushed to the back door. 'I can't breathe ... I can't breathe!' she shouted.

Peggy ran after her. 'You're fine. Don't panic. Breathe in ... now out ...' and she repeated the words over and over until Pat's breathing slowed.

Later, when Pat was calmer, Peggy again broached the idea of her seeing the doctor, something Pat had flatly refused to do. 'There's no point,' Pat argued, 'what's he going to say? Pull yourself together, that's all. And I know he's right and I am trying to pull myself together, but I just can't do it!'

'Pat, will you at least let me tell Mammy?'

'No!' Pat shouted. 'I'm not going to bring her and Sheila back here. They're safe where they are. What if they came back because of me and they died in the next bombing? It would all be my fault.' She covered her face and wept yet again and for the first time Peggy could no longer hold back her own tears. She cried for her sister in her grief and because of the strain of looking after her, but most of all because she knew what they both needed was their mother.

Chapter 18

The weather held, the oats were gathered in and the ceilidh was organised for the Saturday. Sheila was beside herself with excitement at the prospect of her first real dance and, although she wouldn't admit it even to herself, Martha shared some of the same emotions. It was over twenty years since she'd been to a dance. Dear God, she didn't even remember how to dance! But that didn't matter – she'd got to know everyone through the companionship of hard work and was looking forward to spending an evening with them. She hoped too that she'd have a chance to talk to Vincent. Each day in the fields they had chatted a little – simple exchanges to pass the time of day, nothing more than that, but as the days passed, she found herself looking forward to him appearing at her side underneath the sycamore. On the day after her hands were sore he'd come to ask her if the vinegar had worked and she confessed that the pain had gone, but that the smell would be harder to shift. She offered him his gloves back, but he urged her to keep them, and she had worn them every day.

On the night of the ceilidh the faded pink of the hay shed at Higher Farm paled into the shepherd's delight sky. Inside, the trestle tables, hidden under a patchwork quilt of tablecloths, were covered with all manner of platters and pots, bowls and pitchers full of all that the land could offer and the women could cook. There was no electricity so far out of the town, but hurricane lamps lit the scene. Bridie and Rose were treated like guests of honour and the best parlour chairs were set out for them. Bridie and Vincent's mother sat with them. The company was good and Martha couldn't remember being so free of worry since she was a girl.

After they'd eaten, the space was cleared and several of the men, whom she recognised from the fields, gathered in one corner with fiddles, penny whistles, a squeeze-box, a bodhrán, and even spoons. They started with a few reels and people tapped their feet as they chatted. The band moved on to a jig and some clapped, whilst a few took to the floor, confident in the steps learned in childhood. A few times, Martha caught sight of Vincent making his way round the gathering talking to neighbours and friends, many of whom had helped with the harvest. At one point, when he was over speaking to his mother, he looked in Martha's direction and inclined his head slightly. She spotted Sheila too, clearly enjoying herself. She had been one of the first on the floor to dance and had hardly stopped since.

After a while Bridie came to find Martha and handed her a drink. 'Have a drop of that,' she said.

It tasted of apples and something else. 'Is it cider?' asked Martha. 'It's not alcohol is it?'

'Not at all … not really,' said Bridie and grabbed Martha's hand. 'Come on, let's have a dance!'

'Ach, I don't know any of these dances.'

'They're easy. See yer man there, he's going to call out the steps. Listen to him and follow me, and you'll soon get the measure of it.'

And so it proved. Martha danced the jigs and reels and paused now and again to catch her breath and quench her thirst. At one point she noticed that Sheila was no longer in the barn and, feeling warm herself, she wandered outside in search of her. There was the sound of voices down the lane a little and Martha caught sight of a group of six or seven young people, sitting on the fence of a small paddock. She heard Sheila's laugh and, satisfied that she was safe, turned back towards the barn.

He was standing in the shadow of an outbuilding. 'Hello, Martha.' She jumped at the sound, but relaxed immediately because there was no mistaking his voice.

'Hello, Vincent.' The silence lingered between them.

'Are you havin' a good time?' he said at last.

'I am indeed,' she replied. 'I came out to make sure Sheila was all right.' She indicated the paddock. 'And to cool down – it's thirsty work this dancing.'

'Tell you what, would you like a taste of the coolest, sweetest water there ever was?'

Martha smiled, 'You know, I think I would.'

They walked through the farmyard to the back of the house. The well was surrounded by a low wall. Vincent took a bucket and lowered it carefully. She watched him lean over, head to one side listening for the soft splash of the bucket before he pulled on the rope to retrieve it. He dipped his hand in and put it to his lips.

'Straight from the Cappagh Mountain,' he said, 'sweetest in Ireland.'

He moved the bucket towards her and she plunged her hand into the water. It was icy cold in her mouth. She dipped her hand again and drank some more. It ran down her chin and she laughed. He reached out and wiped her lips with his thumb.

A moment of uncertainty.

'I'll show you the hill it runs from, if you like. You can see it just a wee walk up thonder,' he pointed.

'I'm not sure' – Martha looked in the direction he'd indicated – 'it'll be dark, won't it?'

'Not in this moonlight. It's such a sight to see.' His voice had a soft pleading tone.

All her life, she had never taken a risk, never done anything on a whim or without thoughts of the consequences. She had scarcely recognised a desire of her own, let alone succumbed to one. But what did it matter at her age, anyway? She took a deep breath and stepped into the unknown. 'Yes, I'd like to see it.'

The path was easy enough underfoot and there was light to see it rise gently before them. After a ten-minute climb, Vincent stopped at an outcrop of rock worn flat like a bench and they sat down.

'You'll see most of the farm from here,' he said. 'There's the two meadows and, beyond that, the field where we worked those first days. Over toward the house there's an acre of potatoes. They'll be ready in October.' The sound of a horse whinnying carried up the hill. He laughed. 'And that's Jinny in the paddock; she always has plenty to say for herself!'

'You're lucky to have all this, Vincent.'

'Indeed I am, but it's not really mine. I'm just havin' my turn at lookin' after it. It's the ma's farm and after me it'll go to Dermot.'

'You've none of your own to pass it on to.' It was a statement not a question. Bridie had discussed her bachelor brother quite a bit, lamenting his lack of a sweetheart when he was young and his lack of a wife as he got older. 'Married to Higher Farm, that's the problem. That an' the ma sayin' the girls were only after the land,' she had said.

'It's a lonely life,' his voice was low, each word tentative. 'Sometimes I think I should …' A low rumbling sound seemed to roll towards them from the other side of the hill. With each second, it deepened and became louder and louder. Closer it came, less a wall of solid sound now, and more like oscillating waves. Deafening. They were on their feet just as the plane screamed over the hill. The vast metal fuselage hung above them so close they could see the swastikas on its wings. Without a word, Vincent took her hand and together, slipping and sliding, they rushed down the hill to the barn.

'What direction was it travelling in?' shouted Martha.

'Northeast I'd say, to Belfast probably.'

'Oh dear God, not again! Where might those girls of mine be this time of night? Please God let them be at home under the stairs!'

They arrived in the farmyard to find the crowd had left the barn and were standing around discussing the plane, many of them still looking skywards.

Sheila was with Dermot, a short distance from the paddock where she'd been earlier. 'Mammy, Mammy, where were you? Did you see it?'

'I just went a walk to cool down. It came over my head.'

Vincent appeared at her side. 'I've just bin talkin' to Seamus. He knows about planes. He says it wasn't a bomber. It was a Henschel reconnaissance plane – no bombs, just high-powered cameras on their way to take photographs of Belfast. The pilot probably strayed off course and was trying to get his bearings. It's all right, Martha, Belfast isn't being bombed.'

'No, not the night, it isn't, but, when they've got all their photographs of the damage they did last time and the targets they missed, for certain they'll be back and God help us then.'

Whether it was the cider, the excitement of dancing, or the sight of the German planes that kept Martha awake half the night, she knew as dawn broke that it was time to go home. Sheila might want to stay; she enjoyed living in the country and there was her fondness for Dermot to consider. Martha too had mixed feelings. The stay in Dungannon had lifted her spirits more than she could ever have thought possible, thanks to the fresh air and good food, the companionship of Bridie and Rose and, she finally admitted to herself, her friendship with Vincent.

The previous night she had felt a stir of emotion so unexpected and unsettling that she was tempted to dismiss it as the effect of cider on a foolish woman, but what if . . ? Unbidden, Vincent's words immediately before the first drone of the plane came back to her: 'It's a lonely life, sometimes I think I should ...' He had reached out and touched her hand but she, startled by the noise above her, had stood up abruptly. Like random notes picked out on a piano, she sensed the tune his words might have become. Sheila might be happy to stay in Dungannon and what was to stop her staying too? Was that what he had been about to suggest?

'Ach, catch yourself on!' she said aloud. 'An oul woman like you!' But there was no doubt he had sought her out when they rested in the fields and he'd given her his gloves. She remembered his finger on her lips, the invitation to climb the hill, and the hand reaching out for hers. She had no inkling how courtship was carried on in middle age, but maybe these were indications that she was indeed being courted!

But later, in the grey dawn light, she reviewed the evidence again and found it circumstantial, inconclusive and deliberately put it to the back of her mind.

Martha left Sheila sleeping and crossed the yard to the kitchen, as she had done every morning since she had arrived in Dungannon, to make the fire and bake some soda bread.

It being Sunday, the McManus family ate a hearty breakfast then went to early Mass, leaving Bridie and Martha to prepare Sunday dinner.

They stood at the table peeling potatoes over a bowl of water, a relaxed silence between them, then Bridie spoke, 'We had a good night last night, didn't we?'

'We did sure enough,' said Martha.

'Ye had a bit of a talk with our Vincent then?'

'Aye, we walked up the hill to look at the farm.'

'You know he's taken a notion for you, don't ye?'

Martha hesitated, unsure how to answer. 'Maybe he has, I'm not sure.'

Bridie pressed on. 'And what about you, have you a notion for him?'

'To tell you the truth, Bridie, I like him, but sure I've no knowledge of what a man would be thinking. I'm not some lovesick young girl. I'm not sure I ever was. I remember when I first met Robert, it seemed like before I knew it I was married without being aware of any kind of decision being made.'

'Aye, I know what ye mean, but you're older and wiser and you must do what's right for you. I'll say this, though, our Vincent's a decent man. You could do a lot worse.' Bridie set the potatoes in a pan of fresh water and began scraping the carrots while Martha shelled the peas.

After a while Bridie put down her knife. 'Your Sheila was reading a book before you came, *Jane Eyre* it was called, about a young woman who seemed like she was pushed from pillar to post, who had to make a lot of decisions, some wise, some not so wise. But the thing is, she was true to herself and in the end that's what it comes down to. Life's a contract between us and God and He expects us to make the best decisions we can.'

There was a rattling of the yard gate, the back door opened and Vincent came into the warm kitchen.

'Speak of the Divil!' said Bridie.

'What? Were youse talkin' about me?'

Bridie laughed, 'If the cap fits wear it!'

Vincent, mistaking her meaning, quickly pulled off his cap and twisted it in his hands. 'What are youse doin'?'

'What does it look like? And what are you doin' not at Mass?'

'Oh, well, I borrowed Seamus's pony and trap and I thought you and Martha might like to come out for a wee jaunt.'

'We're just making the dinner, Vincent–' Martha began.

'Ach, never mind about that,' said Bridie, 'sure I'll get it done meself. Away you on out, the pair of ye. Come back in a couple of hours and we'll all have our dinner.'

'Are you sure, Bridie?' said Martha. In reply, Bridie gave her a look of mock disbelief and nodded towards the door.

Martha fetched her scarf and handbag and minutes later she was riding out in a pony and trap into the countryside.

Vincent had clearly decided where they were going and along the way he pointed out places that had some connection with his family or childhood. Martha was content to listen to the rise and fall of his soft voice, noticing now and again pronunciation and words that were unfamiliar to her. As he talked and handled the pony, she watched him from the side. He wore a white shirt, crisp with starch, tweed trousers and brown well-polished brogues. He'd taken his cap off and it hung over his bent knee. His hair was longer than you would see in the city and on the grey side, but dark flecks suggested the younger man. His high cheekbones had the ruddiness of a farmer; the rest of his skin, including the back of his hands, was the colour of hazelnuts.

They stopped at a ruined church at the front of which stood a Celtic cross. He tied the reins to the iron railings then helped her down, keeping hold of her hand as he pushed open the gate.

'Used to walk here after mass when I was a boy,' he said. The cross retained a faint outline of its original carvings though one side had been colonised by bright yellow lichen. They walked around it.

'Last night we didn't get the chance to talk,' he began. 'I've been thinkin' about you a lot, Martha. I know you're not long since a widow and maybe I'm rushin' in here sayin' something you'll not want to hear, but …' – he turned to face her and she felt his hand tighten on hers – 'I've really taken to ye … you've a lovely way with ye …' He bowed his head and spoke to the floor, 'I haven't the words to explain such things, to tell ye what I feel … but when you arrived in my fields and sat under my sycamore and gathered in the corn I'd planted … well, Martha …' He looked up suddenly and must have caught in her eyes a glimpse of understanding. His arms drew her in and he kissed her softly like something precious, something valued.

This is what it could be like, she thought … to be loved again. They sat in the shade of the church and he kissed her again. It seemed now he had found a way without words to explain what he felt. And she understood and kissed him back and touched the thick hair on the back of his neck and looked into his hazel eyes. And knew with absolute certainty that this was a moment stolen from a life that could have been, a moment that she would hide from prying eyes to uncover and marvel at down through the days of her life.

'You know I can't stay, don't you? I have to go home,' she whispered at last.

'Yes,' he said, 'I thought that might be the way of it.'

Chapter 19

The privet hedge needed cutting, the windows needed washing, and Martha was already rehearsing the tongue-lashing those slovenly daughters would get when she saw them. She was reaching down to get the key from under the scrubbing brush when Sheila said, 'Don't bother, Mammy, the door's not locked.'

Inside, there were dirty dishes in the sink, a pile of ironing on the draining board and the fire in the range was out.

'Right, Sheila, you get the fire lit while I take our bags upstairs.'

Moments later there was a startled cry and Sheila rushed to the foot of the stairs. 'Are you all right, Mammy?'

'Yes,' came the reply, 'Pat's up here.'

'Why's she not at work?'

'I don't know … away and get that fire going like I told you.'

Pat was lying on her bed staring at the ceiling and had jumped up in fright when Martha came into the room.

'Mammy, what are you doing here?'

Martha didn't reply, so shocked was she at the sight of her daughter. Pat's face was thin, her skin almost transparent, and her hair lay flat against her scalp.

'Oh Mammy, I can't believe you're home.' Pat's voice cracked with emotion and she began to sob.

'God save us,' whispered Martha and she took her daughter in her arms and hugged her close. 'There, there, it's all right.' This was not the time for questions or explanations; comfort the body then calm the mind was Martha's philosophy of healing.

When Pat had quietened a little Martha said, 'Now then, you tidy yourself up a wee bit and come down when you're ready. We've brought some bacon, eggs and fresh bread home with us to have for our dinner.'

Downstairs, Martha warned Sheila about the state of her sister. 'Just chat away about what you've been up to in Dungannon,' Martha told her. 'Expect no conversation, mind, just let her listen.'

By the time they'd finished eating, the range had heated the water and Martha ran a bath for Pat. 'You'll feel better when you've had a good soak and washed your hair. While you're doing that, Sheila'll tackle the ironing and I'll get this kitchen shipshape.'

Later, in the warm kitchen that smelled of fresh ironing and with *Workers' Playtime* on the wireless, Pat was settled in the armchair next to the range while Martha combed and teased the knots out of her hair. Pat tried to speak, but she couldn't manage more than a few words.

'Hush now,' Martha told her, 'sure you can tell us all about it later.'

Martha was alone in the kitchen when Peggy arrived home from work. Pat had gone upstairs to lie down and Sheila had offered to sit and read to her. It was obvious that Peggy was exhausted too and whatever had taken place had brought great sadness to both girls.

'You're home then?' was all Peggy said.

'I am.'

'You've seen Pat?'

'Indeed I have, but it's you I need to speak to. Sit yourself down.'

'Mammy, I can't talk about all this now.'

'Oh yes you can, my girl! I need to know why our Pat is in such a state and, more to the point, why you didn't tell me what was going on here.'

'I couldn't tell you.'

'Couldn't? Couldn't!' Martha's voice rose. 'I've a wee girl upstairs, the weight dropped off her, can't string a sentence together, who looks to me like she's had a nervous breakdown and should be locked up in Purdysburn!'

'It's not my fault!' Peggy shouted through her tears. 'I've tried to help her, but she just keeps crying all the time and I had to leave her to go to work, otherwise there'd have been no money. We've only just managed to pay the rent. If it hadn't been for what I earned at the Plaza and the food Betty gave us we'd have starved!'

'What? How long has she been off work?'

'Two months, they stopped her money.'

'Dear God, two months! And you never saw fit to tell me?' Martha was incredulous. 'We're getting to the bottom of this right now. You tell me what's caused this or I swear I'll take my hand to you!'

'I can't!' Peggy howled and sank to the floor.

Martha stood over her weeping with frustration. 'Tell me, tell me!'

'Leave her be.' Pat stood in the doorway. 'I made her promise she wouldn't tell you.' Pat went to Peggy and helped her up. 'She's taken care of me. I'd have gone mad without her so don't blame her, blame me.'

'But I'm your mother. Am I not allowed to know what put you in this state?'

Pat breathed deeply. 'William Kennedy was killed by a bomb in Dublin. I loved him and now he's dead. That's all there is to know.'

Martha could have left it at that, but the sooner Pat could speak of her grief the sooner she could begin to come to terms with it.

'I didn't always see eye to eye with William, but he was a decent young man,' said Martha. 'Why don't we sit down and you can talk to me about him.'

The following morning Pat received a letter from Stormont asking her to come for an interview about her future in the Civil Service.

'They want to dismiss me,' said Pat.

'Do you want to be dismissed?' asked Martha.

'No.'

'In that case we've got three days to get you looking and sounding like someone who could hold down a decent job.'

'How will we do that?'

'We'll start with a good breakfast then we'll clean this house from top to bottom. Tonight when Peggy comes home we'll cut your hair and sort out your clothes for the interview.'

They carried the rugs out into the garden, shook them and hung them over the washing lines: 'To let the air at them,' Martha said. They swept every room and used plenty of hot water and carbolic to mop the oilcloth. Pat black-leaded the range in the kitchen while, in the sitting room, Martha polished the fender with Brasso. The delft cupboard in the kitchen was emptied, the shelves lined with fresh newspaper and the washed crockery restacked gleaming clean. On and on they worked until they felt the pangs of hunger. The sun was warm enough to sit side by side on the back step with their tea and bread.

They ate in silence a while then Martha said, 'You'll have been thinking about him all the time.'

'Aye.'

'There's no harm in that. At first, when your father died, I went over and over what had happened … ' Martha sighed and shook her head. 'Asking myself the same questions day after day. Could he have been saved? What should I have done differently? A burst appendix, they said – if only I'd realised and done something when he first felt ill. But, you know what, all the questions and thinking get you no further forward than the moment you knew he'd gone.'

'Do those thoughts ever go away?'

'They have to or you'll never rest easy. Doesn't mean you ever stop thinking about him, but you have to find a way to let him be there with you, hear him when he speaks to you, ask him what he thinks.'

'How do you do that?'

'Sometimes at night before I go to sleep I walk with him again up the lane like we did every Sunday when we were courting. We sit on the hill and I tell him what's on my mind. Last night we talked about you.'

'You told him what happened?'

'Aye.'

'What did he say?'

Martha smiled. 'He said that you are the most sensible of our daughters.'

'He said that?'

'Hmmm.'

'That's all?'

'It was enough.'

On the second day, Martha collected her pension and sent Sheila to the McCrackens with a shopping list, while she and Pat set about the front garden. Pat borrowed some clippers from Jack next door and trimmed the hedge and Martha weeded the borders. The sun was hotter than the previous day and soon they were sitting on the front step drinking water.

'Well, did you tell William what was on your mind?'

Pat looked sideways at her mother, a little embarrassed, but after a moment she said, 'We were in the wings waiting to go on stage. I told him about the interview at Stormont and how scared I was.'

'What did he say?'

'He said that I was his most sensible clerk.'

Martha couldn't help but laugh and to her surprise Pat laughed too.

By the third day Pat's appetite had returned. Her hair had been trimmed and shaped, the skirt of her best costume had been taken in at the waist and her skin was glowing after a day in the sun.

'We'll tackle the back garden today – Jack's lent us his lawn mower,' said Martha. 'Don't worry, I'll push it.'

'No, I'll do it,' said Pat.

'Are you strong enough?'

'I think so.'

The grass was long and lush and the sun was hotter than ever as Pat laboured back and forth and with each step she whispered William's name. Let him be next to you her mother had said, but she had no sense of him there at all. Desperation gnawed at her as she pushed the length of the garden and back again and in her mind his name became an anxious plea. 'William!' He'd deserted her again … left her alone … when she needed him so much.

'William!' she cried and thrust the mower hard. It shuddered and the full force of her weight sent her crashing into it. A stone in the blade. She bent to remove it and there next to it sparkling in the sun was the diamond solitaire – his gift to her.

'You didn't have to come with me, you know,' Pat told her mother.

'I know, but I fancied a trip out to Stormont. Haven't been out this way in many a year. I'll walk around the grounds while you have your interview. You're sure you're fine with all this?'

'Look, Mammy, I need to get back to work because I know there's so much to be done. That's what I'll tell them.'

Pat was directed to a part of the building she did not know and left alone in a small windowless waiting room with a 'Careless Talk Costs Lives' poster on the wall. Time dragged and no one came. Steadily her heartbeat quickened and the panic rose within her. She had to get out … but the interview … her hands were on her chest, there wasn't enough air. Then she felt it. Beneath the thin cotton blouse on the chain round her neck was William's ring.

The man who interviewed her sucked on his pipe and shuffled the papers in front of him. 'You've been ill, Miss Goulding.' Pat couldn't tell if it was a statement or a question. She answered anyway.

'Yes I have.'

'And what was the nature of your illness?'

'Scarlet fever.'

'Really? A very dangerous illness; I trust you are fully recovered.'

'I am.'

'Unfortunately, during your absence we had, out of necessity, to replace you as clerk responsible for co-ordinating the air-raid reports. You were also, for a short period, I understand, clerk to the permanent secretary, Mr Kennedy, who is no longer with us.'

Pat nodded.

'I am able to offer you a position as a filing clerk.'

'Filing clerk?'

'Indeed.'

She had only to say 'thank you' and she would be back in employment with a wage every week. She hesitated.

'I don't think that would be right for me.'

'Miss Goulding, I am offering you a chance to come back to work in the Civil Service.'

'I'm very grateful for that, but I don't want to file bits of paper. I want to do more. When I worked for the permanent secretary, I saw people so frightened that they left Belfast in huge numbers to sleep rough in the hills and the countryside – wretched people, bombed out of their homes, half-starved and in rags wandering the streets.' She paused to gather her courage, to keep her voice measured and to hold back her tears. 'Sir, Mr Kennedy had plans to give these people back their dignity and our city its pride and I want to be a part of that.'

The man gave her a hard stare. 'Wait here please,' and left the room.

'Oh, William,' she whispered. 'I've done it now, haven't I?'

Martha paced up and down beneath Carson's statue. Why hadn't she insisted on going with Pat to the interview? She knew it would have been odd for a grown woman to have her mother with her, but she could have supported her. Instead, Pat had probably broken down – even now they were probably trying to calm her and any chance of keeping her job would be disappearing with every tear she shed.

'Come on, Mammy, let's go home.' Pat walked past her.

Martha scanned her daughter's face for any sign of the outcome. She noted only that Pat held her head high and that she walked in determined strides. Martha fell into step alongside her.

'Well?'

'The man who interviewed me offered me a job as a filing clerk.'

189

'Thank God for that.' Martha's relief was evident.

'I didn't take it.'

'What!'

'I told him it wasn't the job for me.'

'You told him!'

'Yes, and then he offered me a job as clerk to a committee being set up by Sir Basil Brook to plan Belfast's recovery because, he thought, I seemed like a very sensible clerk and ideal for such a position.'

Chapter 20

The cottage at Road End was everything Belfast wasn't. Irene got used to waking up to blue skies and the sound of sparrows in the thatch and to having the whole day ahead of her to do as she pleased. At first she took long walks down the lanes, occasionally meeting someone with whom to pass the time of day along the way, or she came across a village and called into a shop. One afternoon, after she had walked to Ballyhalbert for some liver for Sandy's tea, she popped into Jeanie's house for some fresh milk.

'Liver's very good for the blood, you know,' said Jeanie, 'especially for young women like yourself.'

'I'm not so keen on it.'

'Do you cook it with onions?

'Not too keen on onions either.'

'Come with me.'

Irene had not been round the back of the farmhouse before and was surprised to see a large kitchen garden. Jeanie marched up the path pointing out what was growing on each side. 'There's the salad comin' on. Over this side there are fruit bushes – gooseberry, raspberry, blackcurrant, all good for pies and jam. Here are peas and beans, then cauliflowers and cabbages, then onions, carrots and turnips and, all the way down to the fence, potatoes. Over the back there is the orchard with apples and damsons.'

'It's an entire greengrocers!' laughed Irene.

'It's better than that – ye pick it when ye need it and it's always fresh.'

'It must be great to have a garden like this, growing all these things to eat.'

'Aye it is, but it's hard work, mind ye. Now this is what ye want,' and she stooped to pull up two onion plants. 'They're not too strong and they're sweet fried in the pan. Put them with the liver and then come back and tell me if ye still hate liver.'

The next day, Irene was back in Jeanie's kitchen telling her how much she and Sandy enjoyed the liver and onions.

'So there ye are, another meal ye can cook for him.' Jeanie rolled out some pastry on the kitchen table as she chatted. 'What have you been up to the day?'

'Cleaned the house, washed some clothes.'

'Do ye find it a bit quiet in the country?' Jeanie put a dinner plate on the pastry and scored a knife round the edge.

'Ach, I don't mind a bit of quiet.'

'You've enough to pass your time, then?' Jeanie lined the plate with the pastry and sliced the baking apples into it, sprinkled them with sugar and put an upturned egg cup in the middle.

'I go for walks, read a bit in the afternoon.'

Jeanie settled the pastry lid over the apples and the little dome of the egg cup, then turned the plate with one hand while the finger and thumb of the other pinched the edges to seal it.

'Could you teach me to do that?' asked Irene.

'What?'

'Make an apple tart.'

Jeanie laughed and brushed the pastry with egg before putting the tart in the range. 'I'll tell ye what, why don't ye come round in the morning and I'll give ye a taste of what it's like to be a farmer's wife for a day?'

The weeks passed and under Jeanie's guidance Irene learned to plant and tend the garden. The sun turned her skin as golden as

Jeanie's shortcrust pastry. She fed the chickens and learned where to find their eggs each morning and, once she got the hang of it, helped with the milking. When the farm work was done she and Jeanie would pass the afternoon baking and making jam or homemade wine. Soon the world beyond Road End and Ballyhalbert seeped away like water in a ditch at the height of summer and even the letters she received from her mother and sisters seemed irrelevant. Until one evening Sandy came home and announced that Ballyhalbert airfield was set to become operational. His work there would be finished and his next posting would be to an RAF base in England.

'England? Why are they sending you there when you've been based over here all this time?'

'That's just the point,' explained Sandy. 'I've finished installing the wireless equipment in the planes and the control towers. It's all been tested and works fine. Now I have to go and do the same at another base.'

'But I've just got used to being here.'

'I'm sorry, Irene, but that's what happens. I'm in the forces and there's a war on. At least they're not sending me overseas. An airbase in England is a good billet. It'll be out in the country again, just like here. We can find another cottage.'

'But I don't want another cottage and I don't want to go to another country!'

'It's not another country.'

'It is to me!'

'Irene, you knew what it would be like. I have to go where I'm sent. You know the other wives, they'll be going too. You always enjoy it when we have a night out in the NAAFI with everyone. It'll be just the same.'

'No it won't!'

A party was planned for the night before the squadron was to leave RAF Ballyhalbert, and Irene had spent the morning baking a cake. Sandy, on the other hand, had spent the day in the NAAFI drinking and playing cards. Just after dinner Jeanie popped her head over the half-door. 'I was just down at the post office, collected a letter for ye.'

Irene examined the writing. 'It's from my friend Macy, the American, remember I told you.'

'The one who builds planes?'

'The riveter, yes.'

'Well, sure I'll leave ye to get on.'

Irene hadn't heard from Macy in a long while, not since she wrote to say she'd got a waitress job to tide her over until the aircraft factory started up again. The letter was short, but it was everything Irene wanted to hear: 'Great news, girl, Short and Harland are back in business. We start in a week, so get yourself back here.'

Irene sat at the table and stared at the letter, turned the cake out to cool and read it again. She wandered up the lane with the letter in her pocket and leaned on the gate for a long time.

Sandy had promised to return by five for something to eat and afterwards they would walk down the lane together to the party. His tea was still in the oven at six when she went upstairs to get ready. She chose her mauve polka dot dress with the sweetheart neckline and sat in front of the mirror to put on her make-up. She had never felt less like going to a party and the thought of telling Sandy about the aircraft factory reopening filled her with dread. At seven he arrived in a rush, with a flushed face and smelling of whiskey.

'Sorry, love, didn't realise the time. Got talking with the boys, you know how it is. Great you're ready, let's go.'

Irene went to the table to get the cake tin. Macy's letter was there beside it and she slipped it under the tablecloth.

They left the NAAFI when the hokey cokey started. Irene had felt the strain building all evening, listening to the chatter about the new base, trying to keep a smile on her face. Sandy would leave in the morning and she still hadn't told him about the letter.

'Look at that sky,' said Sandy as they walked the lane to Road End. 'So many stars tonight, one for everybody in the world and millions to spare.' He stopped at the five-bar gate overlooking the top meadow and pulled her towards him. 'Choose the most beautiful one,' he said.

At any other time she would have warmed to such a romantic notion. 'I can't, they're all the same.'

'No they aren't! You see the brightest star just there?' He put his cheek next to hers and pointed upwards. 'That's the North Star. It's fixed, you can always find it. Sailors use it to get their bearings. That's my star. I've known it all my life ever since my father showed it to me when he first took me out on the trawler. Even when I was in India, I would look for it and know the people back home could see it too. Look at the smaller star, just to its right. That'll be your star, always next to me.'

Sandy left early the following morning, promising to find them somewhere to live near the new base. 'Now, you're to stay on here where I know you'll be safe from the bombing and you'll have Jeanie for company. I'll try to find somewhere near the new base as quickly as I can, but you've got to promise me you won't go back to the city.' Irene promised and when he had gone, she packed her bag, said goodbye to Jeanie and caught the afternoon bus to Belfast.

Irene could hear the laughter coming from the back garden as she came up the side of the house. They were all there sitting on blankets that were spread out on the grass and she stood for a moment realising how much she had missed them.

Sheila saw her first. 'It's Irene!' she screamed and ran to hug her.

The others were quickly on their feet and lining up to do the same.

'Bless us!' said Martha. 'Here you are without a word to tell us you were coming! We thought you were staying on until Sandy sent for you.'

'I was going to, but when Sandy left …'

'You decided to come home,' Martha finished her sentence, 'and sure why wouldn't you.'

'My goodness, Mammy, look at the colour of you. I thought you went to Dungannon not Africa!'

'You're a one to talk! Have you been working in the fields like me and Sheila?'

'Been doing a lot of gardening,' said Irene and she held up a wicker basket. 'Brought some stuff home with me.'

They sat in the warm sunshine with the scent of tea roses all around them and caught up on everything that had happened in Ballyhalbert and Dungannon. Irene scanned the faces of her family. Martha and Sheila tanned by the sun and looking well fed. In fact, Irene was sure if Sheila stood up she would be two inches taller. There was also something about the way they spoke, the way they held themselves that suggested more subtle changes. Sheila seemed more confident, more grown-up and her mother less anxious, content almost. Peggy too looked different, older maybe, slimmer too and she had done something with her hair that made her look more sophisticated. Only Pat, sitting towards the edge of the blanket, gave Irene cause to worry. She had said very little since Irene's arrival. She was much thinner and her normally expressive face registered little emotion.

As the afternoon wore on, Peggy, Pat and Sheila went inside to cook tea and Martha and Irene sat side by side in the garden.

'There's been no more raids then?' asked Irene.

'No, praise be to God, though there are still too many alerts breaking up our night's sleep.'

'Awful news about William Kennedy, wasn't it? I couldn't believe it when I read your letter. What was he doing in Dublin?'

'No idea.'

'Didn't Pat know why he was there?'

'She was off sick when he was killed.'

'Sick? It's not like Pat to be sick. How did she take his death?'

Martha shook her head.

Irene answered her own question. 'Very badly, I would think. She always had a hankering after him, hadn't she?'

'I think it was a lot more than a hankering,' Martha lowered her voice. 'By the time I came home she was in such a state ...' Martha bit her lip. 'I can't tell you, I hardly knew her.'

'She's still not right, is she? I can't believe the change in her.'

'Well, maybe now you're back she'll buck up a bit. You talk to her, will you? See if you can help her at all.'

'I'll try. So it was just Peggy with her when she heard about William?'

'Aye, and I'll give Peggy her due, she tried so hard to help her. Strange, when you consider those two are always going at it hammer and tongs.'

'No it isn't, they're closer than you think, Mammy.'

'That's as maybe, but the trouble is Peggy's so caught up in this dance band nonsense at the Plaza, she's no time for anything else. Says she's in with a chance of becoming band leader. Keeps talking about this character Devlin, can't fathom what manner of man he is, but he's good at giving out orders and kicking up a fuss when things aren't to his liking.'

'She's met her match then.'

'God, I hope not.'

'Well at least she's got her wish to play in a dance band.'

'Be careful what you wish for, I always say.'

It felt so good to be wearing her trousers and turban again and to be crossing the Queen's Bridge on her way to the Short and Harland aircraft factory. Irene was looking forward to having money in her pocket and friends to have a laugh with. From a distance the bomb damage to the factory looked extensive, with huge sections of the roof burned away, but inside the Stirling bombers stood damaged, but not destroyed. The workers were told to go straight to the canteen where the manager was waiting to address them.

'I'll not lie to you,' his voice was grim and his face was etched with exhaustion. 'We're a brave way from getting this factory back to full production, but we're on site and our job now must be to clear the debris and salvage what can be repaired. Work on the burned-out areas is well under way and as soon as it's complete the raw materials will arrive and we'll be back in business.'

Irene was assigned to a team clearing the floor area under one of the planes while skilled workers began stripping away the damage from the fuselage.

When the hooter sounded for tea break Irene went in search of Macy and found her sitting in the sun smoking a cigarette.

'How does it feel being back to bomb sites and food shortages?' Mary asked her.

'Great!' laughed Irene. 'But shifting what's left of the ceiling off the floor is hard on the back.'

'Now what you need, Irene, if you're going to stay at Short's, is a skilled job.'

'That's not going to happen, is it? I'm not skilled at anything.'

'But you could be. Hell, once they get this mess cleared up, they're gonna increase production and that means more manpower, or in our case womanpower. They're gonna want apprentices and you have to apply!'

'I can't do that. I'm too old to be an apprentice and I think someone might notice I'm a woman, don't you?'

'No problem. You can be my apprentice. I've already spoken to Mr McVey. You know I'm one of his favourite workers, don't you?' Macy gave an exaggerated wink. 'I've told him training another woman would be a good idea.'

Irene looked at her friend, so strong and confident and almost believed her. What had she to lose? 'No harm in applying I suppose.'

Chapter 21

Peggy had talked of nothing else for weeks. The Summer Dinner Dance at the Plaza would be the social event of the year. With tickets at ten pounds a head, only the very wealthiest of Belfast's citizens could afford to be there. The whole idea had been hers from the start, of course. Devlin, with all his talk about making the Plaza the top venue in the city, hadn't built on the success of the dance competition. No imagination, was Peggy's verdict.

'You need to ask yourself what would draw the wealthy to a dance hall,' she told him.

'Champagne?' he suggested.

She rolled her eyes. 'They can get that at the Imperial Hotel round the corner. Now what can we offer that isn't available?'

Devlin shrugged his shoulders.

'John McCormack,' said Peggy.

'Who?'

'The greatest Irish tenor ever, a singing sensation, and if you can persuade him to come here, there'll be Bentleys pulling up outside and more diamonds than you could shake a stick at coming through the doors.'

Once pointed in the right direction, Devlin knew how to cut a deal. John McCormack had been touring England, giving concerts in aid of the Red Cross for several months, and had recently returned home to Dublin. He agreed to come north in exchange for a handsome donation to the charity. The caterers too were from over the border and promised the very best Irish beef in quantities unrestricted by rationing. Devlin applied for a drinks licence, the first time ever that alcohol would be sold at the Plaza.

In the weeks leading up to the event Devlin came to rely on Peggy more and more. He had entered the unknown in terms of such a high-class event and became increasingly uncertain when making decisions. Whereas Peggy, although she had never done anything like this before, seemed to know instinctively what was needed and grew in confidence with each passing day. Every evening when she finished work at the music shop she would walk round to the Plaza to discuss the latest plans with Devlin. He would report on the progress he'd made with the arrangements so far and they'd draw up a list of what he would sort out the following day. At times he would be frustrated by delays in supplies or angry about the cost of the event and Peggy would soothe him by reminding him of the expected ticket sales. Sometimes she was tempted to reach out and smooth his worried brow or to touch his bottom lip which he chewed when anxious, but he gave her no sign that he would respond to such intimacy. He had kissed her before in an aggressive way and another time fleetingly when they had danced but she had no sense that he really cared for her. Sometimes, before she went to sleep, she thought of the night she lay alongside him during the air-raid alert and wished she could remember what that felt like.

On the day of the dinner-dance Peggy called at the Plaza in her lunch hour. The dark blue carpet (red being common, according to Peggy) had already been rolled out across the pavement and matching silk ropes had been strung from chrome stands from the road to the entrance. The foyer was resplendent in blue and silver and a large poster of the smiling John McCormack proclaiming 'Here Tonight' hung from the ceiling. Inside the ballroom, circular tables, each seating ten people, had been arranged around a smaller than usual dance floor. In the centre of each table were tall silver vases filled with dark blue flowers and silver foliage that stretched in elegant arcs above the gleaming silver cutlery, wineglasses and napkins. Perfect.

'Peggy! I need a word with you quickly.' Devlin emerged from his office, his brow more deeply furrowed than she had ever seen it.

'Isn't it beautiful?' she called to him.

'What?'

'The tables, the flowers,' she spread her arms wide to encompass the entire room. 'Everything!'

'Yes, yes, it's what we agreed,' he said dismissively. 'I'm worried about Mr McCormack's music.'

She followed him into his office. 'Everything's fine. I told you, I've scored the songs he's to sing. The orchestra have rehearsed, you've heard them, they're very good.' Her voice was calm and soothing.

'But—'

'No buts. I said I'd look after everything to do with the music, it's my responsibility and you've got to trust me.'

'But I'm trying to tell you. I've just had a phone call from his manager to say he'll be late for his rehearsal.'

Peggy shrugged. 'It won't matter. He's a professional and so are we. It'll be fine.'

'It had better be! You know the money that's been spent on all this.'

'Yes, you've told me often enough and you've sold all the tickets, so what are you worried about?'

'I know, but I won't be happy 'til it's all over and people are going out the door saying it's the best night out they've had in years and asking when's the next one.'

She caught him by the arm. 'Look at all we've done here. In a few hours this room will be full of people dressed to the nines eating a dinner the likes of which they haven't had since the start of the war. They'll be entertained by one of the world's greatest singers then they'll dance the night away. For a few hours they'll forget about the chaos out there and it won't be long before they're coming back for more.'

His voice softened. 'You're right. I know I couldn't have done this without you,' and he leaned towards her and kissed her cheek. Peggy was thrilled at the look in his eyes. Surely later, she thought, when everyone has gone and we're alone …

'I've bought you something for tonight.' He took a large box from behind his desk. Peggy's eyes widened at the name in copperplate across the lid – the most expensive dress shop in the city. She opened the box and pulled back the tissue paper to reveal an exquisite full-length ball gown in midnight blue taffeta with silver chiffon ruched around the waist and tied at the side in a bow.

'It's wonderful,' she gasped and held it up against her. 'I don't know how to thank you.'

'I'm sure you'll think of a way,' he whispered.

It was late when Peggy locked up and left Goldstein's music shop. A customer had arrived ten minutes before closing time to buy a recorder for his daughter and couldn't make up his mind which one to choose or which 'How to play' book would be most suitable for an eight-year-old. By the time Peggy had dealt with him, cashed up and made sure everything was secure, it was already 6.30 p.m.

She had arranged to go straight to the Plaza where she would change and run through the final instructions with the orchestra before John McCormack's arrival. She was thrilled to be meeting such a star; her sisters were so jealous and she would enjoy telling them all about appearing on the same stage as him. She'd get him to sign her copy of the 'Ave Maria' sheet music as a souvenir. In fact, in a fit of generosity, she had decided she would also get his autograph for each of her sisters.

Devlin was pacing up and down in his office when she arrived. 'Disaster!' he shouted. 'A bloody disaster! I knew it would be!'

'Calm down,' she told him, 'it can't be that bad.'

'Oh, it is! I'm telling you.'

'What is it?'

'Star of the show, John bloody McCormack!'

Peggy caught her breath, 'What about him?'

'He's not coming!'

'But he's already here at the Imperial Hotel.'

'Aye, he's there all right, in bed with a dose of laryngitis and no voice to speak, let alone sing! His manager's just been on the phone.'

'Oh no,' Peggy could feel the panic rising in her chest – all those people getting ready, putting on their finest clothes, booking taxis. All that roast beef!

'We'll have to give all the money back. I'll get the sack!' Devlin wailed. Suddenly he turned on her, jabbing his finger. 'This is all your fault! You talked me into this. John bloody McCormack indeed! I should never have listened to you!'

'Will you shut up and let me think!' Peggy knew all the arrangements were good: the ballroom looked magnificent; the food would be excellent; the orchestra would play brilliantly for the dancing. The only thing missing was the star act. John McCormack might be irreplaceable, but nevertheless they had to replace him. They just needed an excellent, entertaining act and the sympathy of the audience to carry the night.

'I've an idea that might work,' said Peggy. 'I want you to carry on with the evening as if nothing's happened. Welcome everyone, get the dinner served, and for goodness sake smile, will you! I'll be back in under an hour.'

'An hour! You can't leave me with this mess. Where are you going?'

'To get us a show.'

Peggy had never been in a taxi in her life, but she headed straight for the rank outside the City Hall, shouted her destination through the window to the driver and climbed into the back. 'And make it quick! This is an emergency!' she yelled, just as she had seen it done in countless American films.

When the taxi arrived at Joanmount Gardens she told the driver to wait. 'Irene! Pat!' she screamed as she came through the back door. The kitchen was empty, so was the sitting room. 'Where are you?'

Pat met her halfway up the stairs, 'What is it? What's happened?'

'Where's Irene?'

'Gone to the pictures with Macy. Why?'

'Aaargh!' Peggy screamed with frustration. 'I need you and Irene to come to the Plaza. John McCormack can't sing and there's a hundred people sitting down to their dinner right now looking forward to a show.' She sank down on the bed, 'Oh God, what am I going to do?'

'Wait a minute, are you suggesting we sing at the Plaza?'

'Yes!'

'Instead of John McCormack?' Pat laughed at the absurdity of the idea.

'It's the only chance of saving the whole evening.'

'But we haven't rehearsed for ages, not since Irene went away to Ballyhalbert and we haven't performed since … I don't know when.'

'Irene's wedding. But it doesn't matter. We've sung the songs so many times – all those concerts with the Barnstormers, and the huge audiences at the army camps. We can do this!'

'Peggy, I don't think I can–'

'Please, Pat,' Peggy pleaded, 'just say you'll do it. You're the best of the lot of us. You can really make this work. Irene and I are nothing without you. Say you'll do it!'

'But we're no substitute for somebody like John McCormack.'

'But if we give our very best, people will enjoy it. That's better than sending them away with nothing. Please, will you? Will you just do it for me?'

Pat sighed, 'I might, but I have to say it's against my better judgement, and there's a problem.'

'What?'

'We're still a Golden Sister short.'

Pat remembered only that Irene was meeting Macy at the YWCA and they were going to see *The Philadelphia Story*. She had no idea what cinema. On the way back to the city centre in the taxi, with the hour almost up, Peggy wanted to call at the McCracken shop for Sheila, but Pat was adamant.

'She's no experience at all. She sang three songs with us at a concert and that was over a year ago. No, if we can't find Irene, that's it, I'm afraid.'

'But how will we find her?'

'Stop!' Pat shouted.

'What is it?'

She pointed to the paperboy on the corner shouting, '*Telegraph*.' 'We'll look at the cinema listings.'

There was a queue round the block for the second house at the Ritz when Peggy jumped out of the taxi. Along the line she went, searching every face. Irene wasn't there. She could have wept with frustration. It was almost eight o'clock and back at the Plaza she knew they would be serving the strawberries and ice cream. Then she noticed that some people were already in the cinema foyer queuing for tickets. The commissionaire stood in front of the doors. 'I need to find my sister,' she told him.

'Back of the queue please.'

'It's an emergency.'

'Back of the queue please, miss.'

Suddenly Peggy caught sight of flaming red curls, a woman as tall as the men: Macy. And just beside her Peggy could see Irene. 'She's just there, please tell those two girls. It's a matter of life and death!'

The commissionaire laughed. 'Well I've not heard that one before. You'd better go and get her then.'

The diners had finished their dessert and were being served coffee and petite fours when Peggy and her sisters arrived and went straight to Devlin's office.

'Where the hell have you been?' he shouted. Then he noticed she wasn't alone. 'Who's this?' he demanded.

'This is Irene and Pat and together we're the Golden Sisters.'

Peggy tried to look confident and added, 'The girls with the golden voices.'

Devlin gave a humourless laugh and shook his head. 'Are you joking?'

'Right now you've got a hundred paying customers waiting to be entertained and we're the only entertainers in the building so, no, I'm not joking.'

'But they're expecting someone famous not ...' He looked from one girl to another. They looked like they'd just walked in off the street – which of course they had.

'That's why you've got to convince them we're worth listening to.'

'And how am I supposed to do that?'

'You'll start by serving them a free after-dinner brandy, while we get to work transforming ourselves into three glamorous singers. Then you'll explain that John McCormack can't perform and give us a big introduction.'

Twenty minutes later, the girls were ready. Peggy's expertise with stage make-up had worked its magic and their hair had been brushed and shaped. Finally, Peggy produced the three beautiful dresses that Devlin had bought her. They didn't match, but they seemed to suit the girls' personalities: Peggy in the Midnight in Paris ballgown, strong, dark, and with a flash of creativity in the silver sash; Irene in the kingfisher silk, mercurial, lively; Pat in the emerald green, deep and sensitive. They looked like Hollywood starlets.

'Ladies and gentlemen,' Devlin remembered to smile. Peggy had warned him that he must hold his nerve and show the audience that he was confident that the rest of the night would be a success. 'Ladies and gentlemen, I hope very much that you have enjoyed the excellent dinner. At this point in the evening I know you are all anticipating the appearance of our guest performer John McCormack.'

There was cheering and banging of tables.

'Unfortunately, I have just been informed that he is unable to perform because he has laryngitis.'

The noise level in the room rose as people turned to each other

206

in disbelief, questioning what they had heard. There were shouts, demands, accusations …

Devlin held up his hand. 'Please let me explain.' The microphone ensured he was heard and slowly the audience quietened. 'At the last minute we have managed to bring you a wonderful act; three young Belfast women, who have made quite a name for themselves singing in concert halls and army camps. If you enjoy the music of the Andrews Sisters, I'm sure you will love these girls–'

A man near the front stood up, 'But we've paid good money to see John McCormack, that's the only reason we're here.'

'Give us our money back,' another shouted.

Devlin ignored them both. 'Please understand that it can't be helped. Mr McCormack is ill. No one could have foreseen that. Now I'm sure you'll agree you've had an excellent dinner and there will still be dancing later. So I hope you'll allow the girls to perform.'

There was some grumbling about wanting half the money back, but one or two people were calling out, 'Let's give them a chance.' Eventually the room quietened.

'Ladies and gentlemen' – Devlin's smile had slipped a little – 'all the way from the Oldpark Road, the talented Golden Sisters!'

They ran onstage, smiling warmly. Peggy went straight to the grand piano that had been moved centre-stage and Irene and Pat stood at the microphone alongside it. They'd decided which songs to sing as they had been getting ready. They'd begin with 'Zing! Went the Strings of My Heart' and Peggy would introduce each subsequent song so the girls wouldn't have to worry about remembering the order.

Peggy played the introduction and they smiled warmly and swayed to the music. On cue Peggy and Irene began to sing 'Dear when you smiled at me …' Instantly, they knew the sound was wrong – too thin, no depth. The harmonies were there, but the central melody, the power of the song – Pat's voice – was absent. Peggy brought it round again; another chance for Pat to pick up. Irene glanced sideways at her sister and saw her breathe deeply, shape her mouth to the words … but still no sound emerged.

For Pat, the Plaza had ceased to exist. Darkness was all around her, the only sound was the clump and crack of bombs. The old woman had told her to watch over him, but he was out on the streets, it would be her fault if … The explosion that killed William, discordant and deadly, filled Pat's head and there was no music or words to be found inside her. She turned and walked off the stage.

Chapter 22

The summer of 1941 was sweltering. The tar melted on the roads and small boys with sticks poked at it until their hands and clothes were stained brown. Outside the City Hall adults lazed on the grass: men with no hats, ties undone, sleeves rolled up; women, who hadn't worn stockings since the war began, exposed winter-white legs to the hot sun. Peggy ate her Spam sandwich and listened to the chatter of two women just behind her.

'I'm telling you it shut down overnight, no notice or anything. They say there was no money to pay the bills. It's a real shame. The Plaza was a great night out. I met my husband there, you know.'

Peggy threw her half-eaten lunch in a bin and headed for Chichester Street. The doors of the Plaza were secured by a heavy chain and on a cardboard sign behind the glass a scrawl of red paint proclaimed it 'Closed'. Devlin, no doubt, was gone. After the John McCormack concert that never was, his rage had been frightening, most of it directed at Pat. He had stood over her screaming, until Peggy dragged him away, and then ordered them off the premises immediately. They left, still wearing the beautiful dresses, while Devlin went alone to face the customers demanding their money back. Pat didn't say a word until they were safe at home then she broke down. It had been stage fright she said, but both Peggy and Irene knew that Pat was the least likely person to be struck dumb on a stage. Besides, she had shown no anxiety at all at the thought of performing. It was quite simply that when she opened her mouth to sing nothing came out.

Peggy peered through the Plaza doors. The blue silk ropes and chrome stands were lying on the floor, the poster of John McCormack hung skewwhiff from the ceiling. She thought of what might have been – the wonderful night she had planned to perfection, the romance she had hoped would blossom – but the tears that pricked her eyes were all for Pat and her lost voice.

Goldstein was waiting for her when she returned to the shop. 'Such a beautiful day, Peggy, so many people out and about. I think it's time for one of your impromptu concerts to encourage people to buy.'

Peggy sat at the piano. 'Do you know the Plaza's closed?' she asked.

'No, but you play it and I'll hum it!'

It wasn't like Goldstein to make jokes. He really must be in a good mood, thought Peggy. 'Mr Goldstein …' she hesitated, not knowing how to broach the subject. 'I know I've let you down over the last few months, playing at the Plaza on Saturday nights and not helping with the Barnstormers at all.'

He held up his hand. 'Not at all, Peggy, not at all, you saw an opportunity to play in a dance band and you were right to take it.'

'But it didn't amount to much, did it?'

Goldstein shrugged. 'But you have more experience. Did you not score the music for the band? Did you not organise a large event?'

'Ha! You mean the one that ended in disaster?'

'Do not be so hard on yourself. Is it your fault the star of the show did not turn up?'

'No but–'

'But nothing,' he insisted. 'I will be honest with you, Peggy, we have really missed the Golden Sisters at the Barnstormers concerts. We have nothing like your act and' – his eyes twinkled – 'your glamour! With the lighter evenings and the fact there have been no bombings since May we should attract bigger audiences for our next concert. What would you say to joining us again?'

'You mean the Golden Sisters?'

'Yes, you and your sisters and, now that Horowitz has left Belfast, I need a new assistant director. I think you would do a good job.'

'Oh Mr Goldstein, I'd really love to be your assistant director, but there might be a problem with us singing.' Peggy was unsure whether Goldstein would have heard about the sisters' disaster at the Plaza, but how could she pretend everything was fine with them.

'A problem?'

'Aye, when John McCormack couldn't perform, we were going to sing in his place, but we couldn't …' she hesitated, reluctant to reveal what had happened with Pat. 'When it came to it, Pat wasn't able to sing. She said it was a touch of stage fright.'

'Stage fright? Pat? Never!'

Peggy shrugged her shoulders. 'We were surprised too, but she just couldn't do it. '

'Couldn't sing?' Goldstein thought for a moment. 'I'm sure she'll be fine once she's had a chance to rehearse. Why don't all of you come along to our next rehearsal, Sheila and your mother as well, if they want to? Pat will be fine, I know it.'

Martha liked nothing better than waking up in the morning to a clear blue sky and the promise of a warm day. She especially liked it when it was pension day. Ten shillings wasn't much for a widow, but since her girls were all out earning, it meant Martha could afford a few treats now and then. Carson's beef sausages were always good quality – not full of fat and gristle like some she'd had – and she picked up a bag of gravy rings from the bakers as a nice surprise for the girls after their tea. She was coming out of the home bakery, when she ran into Vera Grimes, an old friend she hadn't seen for a while – not since that business with Vera's policeman husband Ted, who had bullied Irene over a friendship she had with a Catholic family.

'How are you keeping, Martha?'

'Fine. How's yourself?'

'Ach, I'm a martyr to the rheumatism.' She leaned in closer as though sharing a confidence, 'And you know my heart's not strong.'

'Aye, I know, but sure you're looking well,' said Martha.

'What about the girls?'

'Aah, they're great.'

'You're blessed, so you are, Martha.'

'Aye, I suppose I am.'

Martha walked back up the hill in the sunshine weighing up Vera's words. She was blessed – they were good girls – but she'd been a mother long enough to know there was always something to worry about when it came to children. Pat was working hard in her new job at Stormont. Never one to do things by half, she had thrown herself into her work, but she'd been hard hit by William Kennedy's death for sure. Sometimes Martha would catch a glimpse of the sadness she tried to hide, and longed to put her arms around her and rock her as she did when she was a child. Irene was happy enough, though God knows why she'd become an apprentice and a riveter at that. What sort of a job was that for a woman? And what sort of marriage had she with Sandy away in England and still no word of a house so she could join him? Well, at least Peggy was out of the dance hall and away from that Devlin character – it was no place for a respectable young woman. At one time she thought Peggy and Harry Ferguson might have made a go of it, but then he took himself off to England to join the army and she'd never mentioned him since. Then there was Sheila, growing up fast and turning into a real beauty. Yes, Martha knew Vera was right, count your blessings and make the most of every day.

She had just turned into Joanmount Gardens when she heard the bell of a bike behind her. Sheila was back from helping the McCrackens in their shop. Now if we can just find her a proper job, thought Martha.

'Guess what I've got?' said Sheila

'No idea.'

'A piece of Cheddar, just big enough to have for our dinner.'

They sat on the back step eating their cheese on toast, savouring each mouthful.

'What would you say to a wee trip out on Sunday, if the weather holds?' asked Martha.

'You and me?'

'No, all of us, the whole family together, a trip to the seaside to blow away the cobwebs.'

Martha was always excited by trains – billowing steam, gleaming engines, and the heavy clang of slamming doors all promised adventure. Who wouldn't want to be whisked away from ordinary life to hurtle through the countryside, leaning out the window until your eyes streamed and little smuts of soot smudged your face?

The railway station was heaving with people, even at nine on a Sunday morning, all anticipating a day in the sun at the seaside. A huge blackboard at the entrance advertised 'Bangor and Back for a Bob' and Martha parted with her five shillings and gave each girl her own ticket. Sheila and Peggy immediately rushed ahead to the platform to claim an empty carriage so they could all sit together.

In no time they were clear of the city and heading out along the south shore of the lough, past the gantries and slipways until they had a clear view out across the water to the far shore. At Holywood station several people left the train, no doubt heading for the small beach there, the first one along the coast.

'Your daddy and I came here to see the *Titanic* sail down the lough on its maiden voyage,' Martha told the girls. 'We could have gone down to the docks at the shipyard – thousands of people did – but Robert said he'd been right up close to the ship for so long while he was working on it that he wanted to see all of her just once, in her glory, leaving the city where she was built. It was like a Twelfth of July holiday down on the shore; people were all dressed up, from the poorest to the wealthiest, and were waving and cheering. Sure they would never have heard us on board, but it didn't matter, it wasn't about them. It was about us, we'd built it.' She sighed, 'Ah well, t'was others sunk it.'

At Bangor, they walked from the station with all the other Belfast people, down the hill to the sea front. They leaned on the wall to look at the little scrap of beach rapidly filling up with people.

213

'We'll away round the corner,' Martha decided. 'There's a better sandy beach there and less people.'

The girls had never owned a bathing costume each – there had been no need. They never went swimming together so they simply shared. But just for today, Irene and Pat had borrowed costumes from neighbours. When Pat emerged from under her towel there were howls of laughter. Mrs McKee's bathing attire had seen better days, probably in the 1920s. Pat took it all in good humour and pretended to model it as though she was some bathing beauty. Sheila, in her elasticated costume, ran straight into the sea, screaming as soon as she hit the freezing cold water, and one by one her sisters followed. Martha settled herself on the sand and watched their antics get rougher and rougher – splashing and pushing and taking turns to lift Sheila and throw her into the sea. Eventually they came back to sit in the sun, teeth chattering and shivering as their bodies cooled. The lemonade was passed around and some bloater paste sandwiches. Then Martha took a tin from her basket.

'I thought today should be a celebration, so I've got something special to eat,' and she opened the lid to reveal a sponge cake.

'What are we celebrating?'

'A birthday.'

'But it's nobody's birthday today.'

Martha laughed. 'I know it's not, but since poor Sheila's birthday is 29 February, she only gets to celebrate every four years and you ones always tease her about that, so I thought we'd give her a birthday this year and it's today!'

Sheila clapped her hands in delight. Martha sang 'Happy Birthday to You' and the others joined in. When the song ended nothing was said, but everyone was aware that Pat had only mouthed the words.

The sun rose higher in the sky and Irene and Peggy went looking for crabs in rock pools while Sheila attempted a sandcastle without a bucket or spade. Martha and Pat walked together along the edge of the water in their bare feet.

'It's hard to believe that only a few months ago we were in fear of our lives,' said Martha. 'You couldn't get a more peaceful day than this. Gives you hope, makes you think we could come out the other end of all this destruction and misery.'

'Mammy, I was there.'

Martha stopped, alarmed by the sudden anguish in Pat's voice. 'Where?'

'In Dublin with William on the night he died.'

'Dear God,' Martha gasped. 'You were there? When we spoke of his death I assumed he was in Dublin alone and you were just repeating what you'd been told. So, the two of you went off there together?'

'It wasn't like that! We went on business, I can't say why, but then ...'

'Then what, Pat?'

'He asked me to marry him, gave me a ring, then went out and got himself killed.'

'You must have been–'

Pat cut her off. 'I can't say any more, I can't bear to think of it, but I've wanted to tell you so much.'

Martha looked into her daughter's eyes and saw no tears, just aching sadness. She put her arms around her and held her close.

In the afternoon they strolled along the front and ate ice cream – sliders and pokes. Then, while Martha and Pat sat on deckchairs around Pickie Pool watching the children scream with laughter and fright at Punch and Judy, the others went off to the amusement arcade. They tried the slot machines, roll a penny and then Peggy put a farthing in a sinister-looking machine called The Hangman. At first nothing happened, then there was some screeching melodramatic music and a light went on in the box to reveal a scaffold with a hangman holding a noose. As they watched, a model of a man obviously on some sort of track chugged towards the scaffold where the hangman proceeded to put the rope round the man's neck. Only it didn't fit quite right and when the trapdoor opened the man fell right through, leaving the noose behind.

'I want my money back,' shouted Peggy.

'That was horrible,' Sheila shuddered. 'What's that got to do with amusement?'

'This is better,' said Irene pointing at a fortune-telling machine.

'But that's a waste of money too,' Peggy told her. 'You'll just get a card from the slot with some rubbish printed on it. I'd have a better chance of predicting your future!'

'Go on then.'

'You have to cross my palm with a thruppenny bit first.'

'No, let me,' Sheila shoved in front of Peggy. 'I'll do it for nothing!' she cried, and she took Irene's hands in her own and closed her eyes. Irene and Peggy giggled and made spooky noises, but Sheila seemed unaware of their antics. After a moment, still with her eyes closed she began to speak. 'You'll meet a friend, someone you haven't seen for a while, and they'll have news for you.' She stopped and thrust Irene's hands away, as the image of an empty noose flashed into her head. 'That's all, nothing else.'

'That's not much! Just as well I didn't pay thruppence for it!' laughed Irene.

Martha had one final treat for them before they caught the train home: fish and chips. 'It'll save us cooking when we get home. Betty told me the Jubilee Café is very good.' There was a queue out the door, but they didn't have to wait long and soon they were tucking into fish and chips with tea and bread and butter.

'This is the best birthday I've ever had,' declared Sheila.

'But you've only had four,' pointed out Peggy.

'I know, but now I think I should have one every year at this time with a trip to the seaside as my present.' She reached for another slice of bread. 'We don't have enough treats, do we?'

'That's because treats cost money,' said Pat, helping herself to more tea.

'The thing is,' Irene said, 'everything seems so miserable and sad, with all the bomb sites and people looking half-starved. We've been lucky. We still have a roof over our heads and we manage to get some food each day, but it's hard not to get depressed by it all sometimes.'

'I think it seems better somehow when the weather's good. Sunshine lifts the spirits, and so does a change of scenery,' said Martha.

'Like the song,' said Peggy. 'The blue skies chase the dark clouds far away.'

'Yes that's it,' said Sheila, 'and sometimes you have to make an effort to be happy. You might not feel like smiling, but you should do it anyway. It costs nothing,' and she gave the widest, happiest smile possible.

'And somebody might smile back!' Irene matched Sheila's smile and it went round the table.

Sheila was so busy chatting to Irene as she left the café that she didn't see the couple coming through the door. She collided with the man and in that instant the image of the empty noose flashed again before her eyes. She felt a moment of horror. Then she heard Irene call out and turned to see her speaking to the couple.

'Theresa! How are you?' Irene was saying.

'I'm fine. You remember Michael, don't you?'

Irene nodded at the handsome man with his arm around Theresa's shoulders. She'd met him before and he still wore the same sullen expression as he had done then.

'Are you still working at the aircraft factory?' Theresa asked her.

Irene nodded.

'And what about Sandy?'

'He's based in England at the moment. What about you?'

'Well the big news is,' she looked up at Michael and smiled, 'we're getting married.'

'Congratulations! When?'

'We haven't set a date yet, but it'll be sooner rather than later. I was going to invite you to the wedding.'

'I'd love to come. Have you heard anything from your brother?' Irene tried to sound casual. There wasn't a day she didn't think about Sean O'Hara and the last time she saw him before he fled the country.

'Oh, Sean's settled in America now, working in the building trade and he's got himself a girl!'

'I'm really pleased for him. Tell him–'

'Irene, come on we'll miss the train!' Peggy shouted.

'I'd better go. Great to see you, don't forget to let me know about your wedding.'

'Who were they?' asked Sheila.

'That was Theresa – I used to work with her at the linen mill. I don't really know Michael.'

The train was packed, but they managed to squeeze into a carriage with another family. The guard blew his whistle and they chugged out of the station, everyone sleepy after a day in the sun.

'We'll meet again …' Irene sang softly and one or two voices joined her to the end of the verse. 'Till the blue skies chase the dark clouds far away.'

The light was fading as they approached Belfast and Martha looked at her girls who were all now dozing: Sheila with her head on Irene's lap, Peggy leaning on Pat who rested her head against the window. 'Count your blessings,' Vera had said and Martha did just that: one, two, three, four.

Chapter 23

The fierce heat of August faded rapidly and September turned chilly enough to warrant a small fire in the sitting room in the evening. Martha was sitting quietly doing some sewing for Betty, turning a wooden orange box into a bedside cabinet by making an elasticated skirt to go round it and covering the top with a matching piece of material.

'Who ever thought of doing that?' said Peggy.

'Well, I learned it off a next door neighbour when I was first married. It's what they call "Make Do and Mend" these days. Sure, when you have nothing, you make do with what you have.'

'What?' Peggy giggled. 'Mammy you say the daftest things sometimes!'

Martha looked up from her stitching and saw all four daughters laughing at her. 'Ach away on with you, you know what I mean. You should be doing the same. Away and get those jumpers I knitted that are too small for you now and unravel them. Then you'll have enough wool to knit something else.'

'Ach, sure we're better singers than knitters,' said Peggy. 'Which reminds me, does anyone fancy running through a few songs for the next Barnstormers' concert? Did I tell you I'm the new assistant director?'

'Yes!' they chorused. 'A hundred times!'

Peggy sat at the piano and played a few bars of 'We'll Meet Again'.

'I thought you hated that song,' said Irene.

'I do,' said Peggy, 'but Goldstein has me playing lots of Vera Lynn to bring the customers into the shop, so he'll probably want a few in the next concert. Sheila, you sing as well if you want. Come on, everybody on your feet, you too Pat.'

'I don't think—'

'Oh come on, it's only us.'

Reluctantly Pat joined her sisters round the piano and Peggy played the introduction. Martha pretended to continue sewing, but sneaked a look at Pat. The introduction ended and Pat opened her mouth to sing. Her sisters' voices rang out strongly, but all of them knew there was a voice missing. They sang to the end of the first verse and Peggy stopped playing.

'Do you want to try it again, Pat?'

'No,' Pat's voice was no more than a whisper.

'You can do it. Come on. How many times have you sung this song?' There was a touch of frustration in Peggy's tone.

Pat stiffened. 'I can't do it!'

'Of course you can.'

'Leave her be,' Martha was on her feet. 'Can't you see she can't?'

'If she'd only try—'

But Pat had already left the room.

Peggy had promised that the Golden Sisters would be at the next Barnstormers rehearsal, but she didn't specify which sisters. Irene and Sheila had practised with her every night, but it was clear that without Pat their distinctive sound could not be replicated. Instead, there was something, not off key, but slightly out of kilter about the blend of voices. When they arrived at the rehearsal hall it was already packed and the noise levels were high. She left Irene and Sheila chatting to Macy and went in search of Mr Goldstein. He had a good ear, maybe he could fix it.

When the Templemore Tappers arrived, late as usual, Goldstein called for silence. 'Our next concert will be in three weeks' time at the British Legion. They want to raise funds for the St John's Ambulance Brigade and, provided there is no more bombing between now and then, we can expect a sizeable audience. Peggy, our new assistant director' – the performers cheered – 'has drawn up a running order and I hope those of you who need accompaniment have already provided her with your music. Let us get started and don't forget – pace, pace, pace!'

The acts came and went and it was clear that Goldstein was determined to raise the standard. Those who thought they could get away with sloppy performances were given detailed notes on how to improve. Then it was the turn of the Golden Sisters, with Sheila replacing Pat in the line-up. On stage they looked every inch the professional performers and the first song 'I'll Take Romance' was lively, confident and engaging. Throughout it Goldstein leaned forward, his head turned to one side to better concentrate on the sound, and let them proceed without interruption. They took their bow and waited for his comments. He said nothing.

They waited and eventually Peggy spoke, 'Mr Goldstein–'

He held up his hand. 'The first verse again please.'

Once more he listened intently and when they had finished he said, 'Same again, but this time just Sheila.'

Sheila glanced at Irene who nodded encouragement. Sheila sang. Goldstein listened.

'Now sing it again, Sheila,' he said, 'only this time without accompaniment and sing it the way you would if there was no one listening.'

The rest of the performers, curious to know what was going on, stopped chatting and focused on the solitary figure on stage. Sheila bowed her head, raised it, took her breath and began to sing. Slower this time, unclouded by harmonies, the beauty of her voice and the way in which she interpreted the melody revealed the emotion of each phrase.

It was well past six when the girls arrived home, disturbing the tranquillity of Martha's evening with their chatter and laughter.

'Oh, Mammy, you'll never guess what's happened!'

Martha looked up from her knitting. 'I'm sure I won't, so why don't you just tell me.'

'Our Sheila's going to sing solo in the next Barnstormers' concert,' announced Peggy.

'You'll never believe the way she can sing – all sort of jazzy and … and … different!' said Irene.

'She's to learn a whole new repertoire and I'm to decide on the songs,' Peggy's voice rose with excitement. 'I'll be her musical director and we're going to have some Ella Fitzgerald and Billie Holiday–'

'Just hold your horses a minute,' Martha cut Peggy off in full flow. 'What's all this about? I thought Sheila was just standing in at the rehearsals until Pat felt up to singing again. Now you're telling me she's going to be the star of the show. Learning new songs, is it? Well, I'll tell you something for nothing. Sheila's got more important things to do than spend her days learning songs – like finding herself a job!'

'Mammy, you don't understand,' Peggy explained. 'Mr Goldstein says Sheila has a rare talent and she could go far in the business.'

'Ach, catch yourself on, Peggy Goulding! I'll not have you filling Sheila's head with a load of nonsense.'

At that moment Sheila spoke up. 'Mammy I want to do this. When I stand on the stage on my own and sing the way I want to sing, it just feels so … so right.'

'Sheila love, that's all very well, but you're only young and your first priority is to get a job.'

'But I have a job at the McCracken's shop. I can do that and still sing.'

'That's not a proper job – a few hours a week. You're the one said you wanted a good job in an office or something like that.'

'But everybody there today said I was very good. They said I could sing professionally – maybe get a job with a dance band.'

Martha hit the roof. 'God give me strength!' she shouted. 'Not another one with her head turned. I never thought I'd hear the like from you, Sheila.' Martha stood up. 'I despair of the lot of you!' She flung down her knitting and headed for the door. 'I'm away out of here.'

'Away where, Mammy?' asked Sheila.

'Church,' she shouted over her shoulder, 'to ask God to give me patience, for I'm in sore need of it!'

The following morning Martha did not get up early to make the girls' breakfasts. There was bread and butter and porridge, if they could be bothered to make it, or they could go to work hungry. She lay in bed and listened as each one left the house, rising only when she heard Sheila wheel her bike down the path. From the bedroom window, she watched her pedal off down the street, on her way to do a few hours' work at the McCracken's.

She wandered into the bedroom Peggy and Sheila shared and stared at the unmade bed, the clothes on the floor, make-up on the dressing table. She shook her head and left, closing the door behind her. In Pat and Irene's room the scene was much the same, with the addition of two dirty cups on the dressing table. Instinctively, she lifted them, changed her mind, set them down again. That's when she saw the envelope: British Forces franking mark, a Ballyhalbert address in Sandy's writing, crossed out and, in another hand, redirected to Joanmount Gardens. She picked it up. It had been opened. She hesitated, set it back on the dressing table and went downstairs.

Dressed in her Sunday coat and hat, Martha caught the trolley bus to the city centre and walked the ten minutes to May Street National School. She crossed the empty playground and paused in front of the closed doors while she found her handkerchief and wiped her face. That was the trouble with her sister-in-law, Kathleen Goulding, she always made Martha nervous. She was what Martha would describe as well-to-do with her big house on the Cregagh

Road and her position as headmistress. Right from the start, Kathleen had disapproved of her brother marrying the daughter of a blacksmith and over the years she had kept her distance. But Martha knew that Kathleen, though she would never admit it, had a soft spot for Pat. Maybe because she recognised something of herself in her, the soprano voice, a love of opera, the auburn hair.

A bell sounded and the door swung open leaving Martha startled as dozens of noisy children ran past her into the fresh air.

'Good heavens, Martha, what on earth are you doing here?' Kathleen had followed the children out into the playground.

'Hello, Kathleen, would you have a few minutes to talk to me?'

'I suppose I have, but it'll have to be outside – I'm on duty today,' and she began to walk around the perimeter of the playground, her eyes trained on the children. Martha hurried after her, trying to match her long stride.

'I wanted to talk to you about the girls–'

'You, boy, stop that at once!'

'Well, it's Pat really that's the problem.'

'Pat's a problem?'

'No … yes … Look, I know you've helped Pat in the past with her singing.'

'Some voice training, yes.' A child rushed up to them. 'No, Edith, I can't watch you just now, I'm speaking to this lady.'

Martha collected her thoughts and started again. 'You heard about William Kennedy?'

'Indeed I did, from acquaintances at Stormont, a terrible tragedy.'

'Well, it's hard to explain, but since William's death Pat hasn't sung a note. I don't know whether it's because she can't or she won't. Kathleen, you know what singing means to her and it breaks my heart–'

'Martha, if you've come here in the middle of the school day expecting me to explain why Pat has stopped singing, then I'm afraid you've had a wasted journey. I have no experience of such matters.'

'Oh, I just thought …' Martha sighed. 'I'm sorry to have bothered you,' and she turned away.

'Where are you going?' Kathleen snapped. 'I was about to say that I have, however, heard of children who have stopped speaking as a result of experiencing a tragic event.'

Martha brightened. 'Maybe you could–'

Kathleen held up her hand. 'All I'm saying is I'll give the matter some thought.'

They walked a while in silence and stopped to watch some girls play three-ball against a wall.

'You think rearing them is hard,' said Martha, almost to herself, 'but letting them go is harder.'

'You said "girls".'

'Sorry?'

'You wanted to talk about the girls, not just Pat.'

'Yes, the truth is I'm worried about Sheila as well. She's finished school and she needs a decent job. She's bright, you know, did very well–'

'I'm sorry, I can't stand here chatting,' Kathleen interrupted her. 'I have to go and sort out those boys over there before someone gets hurt,' and off she went, striding across the playground. 'Stop that immediately, do you hear!'

That evening around the tea table, Irene announced that she'd been invited to Theresa's wedding reception on Saturday night. 'You remember we met her in Bangor. It's in her uncle's bar, and there's going to be food and music. She was waiting for me tonight when I came out of work to tell me about it. I was with Macy and she invited her along too, so I wouldn't be on my own.'

Martha laid down her knife and fork and stared at Irene. 'Would this be the same bar you were in when you collapsed and ended up in the Royal Hospital at death's door?'

'Mammy, that was over two years ago. And you're not being fair. It wasn't Theresa's fault I got blood poisoning; it was because I cut my hand that first day at the aircraft factory.'

Martha gave a thin smile. 'Oh yes, but it was Theresa who was the cause of you losing a perfectly good job in the linen mill and having to find another more dangerous job in the aircraft factory.'

'The linen mill sacked Theresa because she's a Catholic. I couldn't stand by and let that happen. It was a matter of principle!'

Martha ignored her. 'Away you girls into the front room. I want a word with Irene in private.'

When they'd gone, Martha turned again to Irene. 'So, we're talking principles are we? Well, what kind of principles is it that makes you think deceiving your husband is the right thing to do?'

'Deceiving? What do you mean?'

'I mean letting the man think you're still in Ballyhalbert, when clearly you're not!'

Irene looked as though she'd been slapped in the face. She opened her mouth to reply, but nothing came out except a scream of frustration and she ran out of the kitchen, through the front room and up the stairs. Martha followed her, but Pat caught her arm.

'Stop this, Mammy.'

Martha shrugged her off. 'No, I'll have this out with her.'

She made it as far as the turn of the stairs. Irene was standing at the top, Sandy's letter in her hand.

'How dare you read my letter!'

'I didn't read it – why would I? It's private.'

'Well, that's never stopped you before! Sure, didn't you write to Sandy the last time he was away without telling me. I'm fed up with it! You're always interfering in our lives.'

'I was trying to help.'

'But it's none of your business! I'm twenty-three. I'm a married woman!'

'Then you'd better start acting like one!'

Chapter 24

They could hear music from the end of the street, and with it the babble of voices and sudden raucous laughter. The door of the bar was open and light spilled out onto the pavement in defiance of the blackout. Outside some men stood around, glasses in hand. As Macy walked into the pool of light there were whistles and shouts in her direction.

'I told you you'd cause a stir dressed like that,' said Irene. 'I doubt if they've ever seen a dinner suit around here, let alone a woman wearing one.'

Inside was crowded, but they found Theresa standing at the bar dressed in a cream lace wedding dress and matching mantilla.

Irene hugged her friend. 'Theresa, you look lovely. Your dress is beautiful.'

'It was my mother's. She always said I would wear it one day. Mind you, it's been in the pawn so many times it'll find its own way back there on Monday.' Michael appeared at her side, smiling for once and shook hands with Irene and Macy.

'And this is my brother Finn,' he said. Irene and Macy looked from one brother to the other. 'Yes, I know, we're the spit of each other.'

'You're twins?' asked Irene.

'No, I'm the oldest by a year,' said Michael.

'And I'm the smartest by a country mile,' said Finn, with a glint in his eye. 'And who have we here?'

Theresa introduced them. Finn shook Irene's hand, but his eyes never left Macy's face.

'Hi, glad to meet you,' Macy held out her hand and Finn took it and pulled her towards him.

'Macy with the smiling face, will you dance with me?'

'But the music's stopped.'

'I can change that.'

Finn, with his arm around Macy's waist, guided her across the room to where the fiddler was enjoying a drink. After a brief conversation with Finn, he started playing again and moments later Finn and Macy waltzed out the door and into the street to the strains of 'My Wild Irish Rose'.

'Well, I'll leave you two to have a gossip,' Michael winked, 'but keep an eye on your friend, Irene.'

'Maybe you should go after her,' Theresa suggested.

'No, she'll be fine. She's a big girl,' said Irene. 'Anyway, tell me about today. You had good weather, didn't you?'

'Aye, it's been a lovely day. I only wish my mother could have been here to see it … but I'm thankful for small mercies; my father was there to give me away.'

'They released him from prison?'

'I think in the end they had to. It wasn't as if he'd committed a crime. The internment was to get suspected IRA men off the streets in case they'd somehow help the Germans. I suppose they realised that wasn't going to happen.'

'So what about Sean, will he be able to come back now?' Irene held her breath.

'No, he'll never come back. He's still officially a wanted man, even though there's no evidence against him. He's better off in America anyway. He loves it there.'

The musicians had gathered again around the fire and began a lively jig.

'Come on,' laughed Theresa. 'The hooley's about to begin!'

The tables were pushed back and soon the floor was crowded with dancers including Macy, easily spotted towering above the other women and still in Finn's arms. Irene danced with several partners and it seemed to her that the pace of the music speeded up with each tune until her head was light with all the spinning around.

When the dancers were tired and the musicians thirsty, there was a break. Irene found her way back to Theresa who nodded towards two women who were now standing in front of the fire and facing the crowd.

'Lilters,' she whispered. 'They're famous round here, Kitty and Nora, been doing it since they were wee girls.'

Three taps of their feet and they began to sing, but it was like no singing Irene had ever heard. There were no words only strange melodious sounds that made the heart soar and Irene smiled in delight.

Theresa touched Irene's arm, 'I'm going to say hello to some people who've just arrived.' She leaned closer, 'and if I was you, I'd go and rescue Macy. She's surrounded by the sort of fellas she should be stayin' well away from.'

Irene found Macy seated in the midst of several young men. 'There you are.'

Macy raised a glass of porter in Irene's direction. 'You're sure missin' some great craic from these guys.' Her eyes were bright, her smile huge.

'I think it's time for us to go,' said Irene. 'We don't want to miss the last bus.'

Macy moved even closer to Finn to make room for Irene to sit down. 'Come and join us. Hey, you haven't got a drink. Someone get Irene a drink.'

'No it doesn't matter, we're going now.'

But Macy, her voice too loud and shrill, insisted. 'Sit down and have a drink, Irene.'

At that moment a man began to sing, unaccompanied, a song about a boy caught up in some heroic deed. The tune was poignant and the words heartbreaking, and those around her joined in the chorus. Surrounded by strangers, Irene suddenly felt overwhelmed by the smell of stale beer and cigarettes, by the unfamiliar music and the tragic tale of Kevin Barry.

'Macy, we've got to go, it's getting late.'

'But there's gonna be more dancing.'

'But I have to go and I don't want to leave you here,' Irene was close to tears.

'I'll be fine, you go on,' said Macy. 'Finn's gonna walk me home,' and she nestled even closer to him.

'I don't know,' Irene hesitated.

'She'll be safe with me.' Finn stroked Macy's hair, whispered in her ear and she threw back her head and laughed.

Outside, a full moon the colour of straw lay low in the sky – a bombers' moon. Irene pulled her coat tightly around her and took a headscarf from her bag. She kept her head down and walked as quickly as she could along the pavement's edge away from doorways and alleys. At least there was light enough to see where she was going. At a corner further down the road a group of men were standing and as she passed they called out to her. She didn't respond and, although they continued to shout after her, they didn't follow her.

On the main road she heard the sound of a bus and realised there was a stop just yards in front of her. The bus slowed to let someone off and she hopped on, sitting just inside, close to where the conductor was standing. In the centre of the city, she was relieved to find a trolley bus going as far as Cliftonville Circus, leaving her with a ten-minute walk home. Nothing to worry about, she'd be safe in her own area.

It was late when she got home. No one was up, but Irene knew her mother would be awake and listening. She felt for the key on the string behind the letterbox. It wasn't there. Had Martha in her disapproval locked her out? Round the back of the house, on the drain, under the scrubbing brush she found the back door key. Inside the house, it was pitch-black, not a chink of moonlight came through the blackout curtains. Irene felt her way past the sink and round the kitchen table to the door. She went into the front room and got her bearings, china cabinet on the left, arm of the settee on the right.

'Argh!' She touched warm flesh. 'Mammy is that you?'

'Irene?'

'Sandy!' She sensed him swing his legs off the settee and stand up. She reached out to touch him. 'Sandy, is that you?'

'Yes it's me. What time is it?'

'I don't know – not too late.'

'Where have you been?'

She didn't answer. Instead, she felt her way across the room to the light switch.

He blinked rapidly in the bright light and rubbed the sleep from his eyes. Irene caught her breath at the sight of him, stripped to the waist, his shirt and air force tunic over the back of the armchair. He ran his hand through his thick auburn hair, his brown eyes looked so sad – her husband, her handsome husband.

She moved towards him, her arms outstretched. He stood quite still, arms by his side.

'You left Ballyhalbert,' he said.

'I needed to come home. I couldn't–'

'You left without telling me.'

'I didn't want to upset you.'

'Upset me!' he raised his voice. 'I went there to find you. They said you left the same day I did.'

'Sssh, sssh,' Irene tried to quieten him. 'You'll wake everyone.'

He shook his head in disbelief, but when he spoke he lowered his voice and spat out his words, 'You made me look stupid!'

There was the creak above them and instinctively they both looked towards the ceiling. 'Someone's on the landing,' said Irene. 'Get your coat on. We'll go for a walk.'

They left by the back door, closing it softly behind them, and didn't speak again until they got to the bottom of the street and turned right towards the corner shop. They took shelter in the doorway.

'I didn't want to stay in Ballyhalbert without you. I get lonely. I need company.'

'You had Jeanie, you and her got on really well together.'

'Yes we did. She was good to me and reminded me of Mammy, but don't you understand? It's not the same. I wanted to be at home with my family. I wanted to go to work and have a laugh.'

'Why didn't you write and tell me?'

'I thought you'd be angry.'

'And what do you think I am now!' he shouted. 'I follow you here and you're away out somewhere. Next thing you come sneaking in, in the middle of the night, stinking of cigarettes and beer! I don't know where you've been. I don't know who you've been with. I don't know what you've been doing.' He breathed deeply and sighed. 'In fact, Irene, I feel like I don't know you at all!'

'It's not the middle of the night and I've been to my friend's wedding reception where, strangely enough, people were having a drink and smoking. And it sounds to me like you don't know me, but maybe that's because every time we start to get to know each other better, you leave.'

'Don't get clever with me! I can't help it if I get posted. There's a war on.'

'Yes there is and that's another reason why I don't want to sit in Ballyhalbert on my own when I could be in the aircraft factory helping to build bombers!'

Sandy left the doorway and stood on the pavement, his back to her, looking up at the moon. Irene watched him: his broad shoulders, the tilt of his head. Her heart had lifted when she saw him standing in her own front room. She left the doorway and put her arm in his.

'I've been posted to Enniskillen.' His voice was calm, but still he didn't look at her. 'A big new airbase, something to do with the Atlantic convoys and protecting them from the U-boats. It'll be a long posting, probably – till the end of the war, whenever that is.'

'When do you go?'

'Tomorrow.'

'Tomorrow!'

He took her arm from his and held both her hands. 'I came to get you. We need to be together or this marriage won't work. Enniskillen is two hours on the bus from Belfast. When you need to see your family, you can come back and visit them. They can come and visit us.'

Irene's eyes were fixed on the ground. He put his finger under her chin and raised her head. 'Irene, my darling, come away with me.'

Chapter 25

'Will you sit still, Sheila?' Pat's hand shook a little as she moved the eyebrow pencil to the outer corner of Sheila's eye. In her head, she could hear Peggy's instructions – 'Just a little upwards flick will widen the eyes, but not too much. We want her to look natural.'

'I can't, I'm so nervous. I don't think I can even remember the words of the songs.'

'Of course you can. You've practised those two songs every night for the last three weeks and always remembered them.'

'But it's different being in front of an audience.'

'Yes, it is different' – Pat dusted a tiny amount of powder across Sheila's nose – 'but it's so much better. Once you're standing up there the audience will lift you and you'll sing like you've never done before.'

'I hope they like me.'

Pat showed Sheila how to pout her lips and with the lightest of touches applied the soft coral lipstick. 'They will love you.' Pat stood back and nodded. 'That looks great,' and she went to fetch Peggy's kingfisher cocktail dress, the one Devlin had bought her, from the hanger.

'I'm worried about that change of key in the second verse. I've been going over the song in my mind and every time I get to that bit I can't remember it – it just goes!'

'Hands up, bend forward,' Pat slipped the dress over Sheila's slim figure. 'Don't dwell on it and don't even think of it when you're on the stage, just sing and before you know, you'll be singing it.'

'But I've lost it – I don't know how to do it.' Sheila gripped Pat's arm. 'How does it go? How does it go? I can't get it!'

Pat took Sheila's hand. 'Calm down and listen to me. You've rehearsed and rehearsed and the song is lying there ready – it's waiting for when you need it. Now sit quietly a while and concentrate on your breathing, that's how you'll prepare.'

In the hall beyond the dressing room where Sheila sat, the audience was beginning to arrive. Martha chose a seat not too near the front, over to the right-hand side, where she hoped to go unnoticed. Sheila had asked her not to come – 'You'll make me nervous, Mammy' – and Martha knew she was right, because she would be feeling the same way. Yet here she was at the British Legion, twisting the programme in her hand, having noted that 'Sheila Goulding – young singing star' was the fourth act on the bill. She turned towards the end of the row to the sound of a commanding voice asking to come past and watched in amazement as Kathleen made her way along to the empty seat next to her.

'I thought it was you,' Kathleen's voice was school-teacher loud. 'I saw the concert advertised in the *Belfast Telegraph* – thought the girls might be singing.'

'No, just Sheila.'

'Sheila?'

'Well, Irene's gone to Enniskillen with Sandy, he's been posted there and,' Martha couldn't keep the annoyance out of her voice, 'if you remember, I told you Pat's stopped singing.'

'Pat's still not singing? Oh dear.'

The music began, the curtains opened and the Templemore Tappers filled the stage with colour as they began their tap-dancing routine. They were followed by the compère who told a joke about an old woman from the Shankill who lost her way in the blackout that Martha didn't find funny, but that had the audience in stitches. Then he introduced a magician, who seemed to have so much bunting concealed about his person that he looked a stone lighter by the end of his act. Lizzie, the accordion player, was next with 'a lively selection of reels and jigs', but Martha heard none of them, she was so nervous for Sheila. Her hands felt clammy as she gripped the handbag on her lap and she wished she'd had the forethought to remove her handkerchief from it before the show began.

'And now, ladies and gentlemen, a real treat, the Barnstormers' newest star – Miss Sheila Goulding!'

Martha didn't hear the applause; she was too busy staring at the young woman who strode confidently across the stage to the microphone, smiling broadly. The music began and Martha closed her eyes. She had heard Sheila rehearse the song, 'Can't Help Lovin' Dat Man', a hundred times at home and knew every note, every nuance of meaning, every gesture. She had thought then that Sheila sang the song well, although the song itself wasn't to her taste, but hearing it now as a member of the audience in a packed hall, she felt as if she was hearing it for the first time and sensed its power to move. Into the second verse, past that difficult change of key, Martha opened her eyes and marvelled at her youngest daughter transformed into a beautiful young woman.

The second song, 'I've Got My Love to Keep Me Warm', was much more up tempo and the audience clapped along while Sheila moved effortlessly to the beat. She took her bow to loud applause and left the stage to sounds of cheering. Martha paid scarce attention to the rest of the acts in the first half and when the interval was announced she and Kathleen made their way to the tables at the back of the hall where tea and biscuits were being served.

'I have to say, Martha, I would never have recognised Sheila.'

Martha might well have said the same thing.

'The last time I saw her would have been at Robert's funeral – what's that, just over two years ago? Seeing her on stage, I thought she had a look of him around the eyes. Although I must say, I can't imagine what my brother would have made of his youngest girl singing like that in a show.'

There was something in Kathleen's tone that made Martha bristle. 'What do you mean?'

'How old is she, fifteen? She looked twenty. It's all very well the older girls singing, but at Sheila's age who knows what it could lead to? I tell you, Martha, I think you were right to be concerned about the fact she hasn't got a proper job. I hope she doesn't think she can make a living singing like this.'

'Kathleen, I–'

'No, Martha, it's as well you came to see me about finding her a position and how fortunate it is that I have heard of a job that would suit her. Indeed, I hoped to run into you tonight – save me the trouble of writing to you. A junior clerk is required to assist the secretary at Belfast Royal Academy, a fine institution. I am acquainted with one of the senior masters through my work with the Board of Education, and he mentioned the vacancy. Naturally, I recommended Sheila, told him she was my niece. The interview is next Friday at four o'clock. Please tell her to report to the school office. Now if you don't mind, Martha, I think I'll slip away. I've had a look at the rest of the programme and there's a bit too much vaudeville there for my taste.'

Martha, eyes blazing and fists clenched, watched her go. How dare Kathleen imply that Robert would disapprove of Sheila singing and insinuate that, as her mother, she should have put a stop to it. How little Kathleen, a spinster, knew about bringing up children: the constant give and take, allowing them small victories, like Sheila singing in a show to raise money for the war effort, but being prepared to dig your heels in if it went beyond that. The bell rang for the start of the second half and Martha returned to her seat. It was true, the show was a bit too vaudeville, but the audience loved it and Martha could quite easily see why. Kathleen was altogether too quick to look down on decent people.

Sheila's face lit up when she saw her mother waiting in the entrance hall at the end of the show. 'Mammy, Mammy! You came to meet us!' She flung her arms round Martha. 'It was wonderful, so it was. I was so nervous, but when I got on the stage, I … Oh, it was the best thing ever.'

'You sang beautifully and I was so proud of you.'

'How do you know?'

Martha smiled. 'Because I was there.'

'You came! I didn't see you. Where were you sitting?'

'Oh, I had a good seat, so I did. I heard and saw everything and it was all wonderful.'

Martha left it until the next day before telling Sheila about the interview – one thing at a time was Martha's way. Let Sheila enjoy the excitement of performing, before she thrust the reality of a job interview on her. They were at the sink washing the breakfast dishes when Martha told her Kathleen had been at the concert.

'She's says she's found a job that would really suit you.'

'Why would she find me a job? She doesn't know me that well so how does she know it would suit me? What kind of a job is it anyway?'

'Questions, questions,' Martha rubbed away at the porridge pan with the dish mop. 'Sure isn't she your aunt? She heard about a job as a junior clerk from somebody she knows and she spoke for you, that's all there is to it.'

'What does a junior clerk do?'

'Ach, filing, running errands, adding up – that kind of thing.'

'But I won't know what to do.'

'Don't worry, they'll teach you. You'll be in an office and they'll pay you a regular wage.'

'And where is this office?'

'Just down the road at the Belfast Royal Academy.'

'Ach no, Mammy! I've just left one school and you want me to work in another one.'

'Sheila, stop putting obstacles in the way. This is a great opportunity for you. Be positive and, once you've passed your interview, we'll buy you some smart office clothes. Pat'll help with that.'

'An interview! You didn't say I'd have to have an interview. I won't know what to say.'

'Don't worry, Pat'll help with that too.'

Sheila moped about in her bedroom all morning and Martha left her be. Around lunchtime she came into the garden where Martha was hanging out the washing.

'If I get this job, does that mean I can't sing anymore?'

Martha couldn't hide her exasperation. 'I'll tell you this for nothing, Sheila, no daughter of mine will ever make her living singing in a dance band, so you can get rid of that notion right away.'

'But if I get it can I still sing with the Barnstormers like I did the other night?'

Martha gave Sheila the impression that she was considering the question carefully. 'You're very young to be doing that on a regular basis and I'd worry about who you might be mixing with.'

'Aaah, Mammy, please. I'll do my best to get the job, but can I not sing as well?'

'I'll have a word with Pat, see if she'll keep an eye on you at the concerts like she did the other night.'

Always give them a small victory.

Sheila emerged from the Belfast Royal Academy just in time to see a trolley bus disappearing up the road, but it didn't matter. She felt shivery and hungry and excited all at the same time and couldn't bear to stand around waiting for the next one. The walk home was just what she needed to calm her down after the interview and she set off with the words of the headmaster's secretary still ringing in her ears: 'We would like to offer you the position of junior clerk.' She couldn't wait to tell Mammy.

She would be just like her sisters, going to work and earning money, but that was only the half of it. She would be a singer too, in a beautiful dress alone in the spotlight. Sure hadn't Bridie foretold it and wasn't Mr Goldstein going to make it happen?

Martha was ironing when Sheila arrived home and her heart sank when she saw the look on her face. 'Well?' she asked.

Sheila slumped into the chair. 'My feet are killing me. That's the last time I'm wearing Peggy's shoes!' and she kicked them off.

'What about the job?'

Sheila's smile said it all.

The following day Martha had even more reason to be grateful to Kathleen when a letter arrived for Pat.

'Who would be writing to me?' wondered Pat.

Although she had recognised the handwriting, copperplate with all the flourishes, Martha said nothing, but busied herself in the kitchen while Pat took the letter into the front room. Minutes later, Pat was back.

'It's from Aunt Kathleen, asking me to come to her school when I finish work tomorrow. What do you make of that?'

Martha shrugged her shoulders.

Pat raised an eyebrow. 'Strange that she's taking such an interest in her nieces lately,' but she said no more.

When Pat arrived home the next night, she was barely through the door when Martha, wreathed in smiles asked, 'Well, what did Kathleen want?'

'She was waiting for me with fifty children. "I've a challenge for you," says she, then proceeded to tell me that the school choir has been invited to sing at the Stormont Christmas concert this year. But, lo and behold, she didn't really have the time for all that and would I, with all my experience of being in choirs, like to train them.'

'Really,' Martha acted surprised. 'What did you say?'

'I told her that was the last thing I wanted to do.'

'You said that to Kathleen? And what did she say?'

'She reminded me, no doubt in case I'd forgotten, that it was the same concert William and I sang at last year and she thought maybe I'd like to be there again in some capacity.'

Martha hardly dared ask, 'And what did you say?'

'I told her that's the last place I'd want to be and I'm telling you, Mammy, that I know you mean well, but you have to stop interfering in other people's business.'

Chapter 26

November 1941 was a hard month to endure. Bitter winds blew in from the north, rattling the slates on the roof and blowing soot down the chimney. Every day Martha wrapped herself in layers, ration books in hand, to join the seemingly endless queues at shops with precious little to sell. At night they went to bed early with hot water jars and, without fail, Martha would wake up in the early hours to retrieve the stone-cold jars from the bottom of each bed and refill them with hot water to keep the girls warm and cosy until it was time to get up for work. She'd learned to be thankful for small mercies: the air-raid warnings were a rare occurrence and, since those terrifying nights in May, there had been no more bombings. The reason was clear from the news on the wireless. Hitler was too busy with the Russians and it was a comfort to know that cold winds in Belfast would mean Arctic conditions on the Eastern Front.

During the summer, Jack from next door had helped her to dig over a patch of the back garden and given her seeds to plant. 'You're diggin' for victory now, Martha,' he'd joked and she had good reason to be thankful for the crop of winter cabbages, onions and turnips she could pick each day to make a bit of meat go further.

She put the neck end of lamb in the pan with the vegetables and water and left it to simmer while she made herself a drop of tea and sat down to read the *Belfast Telegraph*. The girls had been chatting about a carnival that was in town and on the front page was a picture of it set up in what they were now calling Blitz Square – a cleared bomb site where Arnott's department store used to stand. It was unusual to have a carnival come to town in the winter months but this one, according to the paper, had come over the border 'to cheer people up'. The girls were planning to go on Saturday and there had been endless talk about dodgem cars, chair-o-planes and helter-skelters.

There was a rattle of the back door and Betty called out, 'Are ye in, Martha?'

'I am, come on in.'

Betty had a jar of damson jam in one hand and a piece of knitting in the other. 'There you are – there's been a great crop of damsons off that wee tree of ours, so I thought you'd like some jam.'

'That's very good of you, Betty' – Martha nodded at the knitting – 'and is that for me as well?'

'Ach, you know I'm useless at these patterns. I can cast on and do the rib and crack on with the stocking stitch, but you see when it gets to the decreasing for the sleeves? Well, it has me beat.'

'Let's have a wee look.' Martha took the knitting. 'There's tea in the pot if you want it.'

While Martha unpicked the mistakes in the knitting and started the decreasing, Betty chatted. 'You've been reading about the carnival coming, I see.' She pointed to the paper on the table. 'We could do with a bit of fun for a change. I was just saying to Jack we should get wrapped up and take a trip down the town – see what's going on. I haven't been down there for months.'

'You would go to a carnival?'

'Aye, why not? You could come with us.'

'Away on with you! The girls are going, but I'm ...' She was about to say, I'm too old for the likes of that, when she looked up from the knitting and saw the excitement on Betty's face. 'Oh, why not,' she said, 'sure, we never go over the door except to queue for rations.'

When Martha announced that night that she would be going

to the carnival the girls howled with laughter. 'I couldn't say no to Betty,' she tried to explain. 'After all, she brought me damson jam,' and they laughed all the more.

Though the blackout was still in force, no one in authority had the heart to demand that the strings of coloured lights strung around Blitz Square should be taken down. Added to that, several people who thronged around the stalls and rides carried their own torches. The wind had dropped, but there was sleet in the air and the caravans selling hot drinks and the man roasting chestnuts over a glowing brazier did a roaring trade.

They wandered around looking at all there was to offer in the way of entertainment and diversions, reluctant at first to become involved. Betty suggested the hall of mirrors; she'd been in one years before on a day trip to Portrush. Martha weighed up the price and the likelihood of embarrassment and decided to risk it. She and Betty went inside, leaving Jack to join a group watching a man move three playing cards around at great speed and encouraging his audience to 'find the lady'. The girls had already gone off in search of something more exciting and found the ghost train.

'I'm not going on that,' said Pat. 'You never know who's in such places. I've heard that some of these fellows try to take advantage in the dark.'

'Ach, Pat, that's nonsense,' said Peggy. 'It's only a bit of fun.'

But Pat was adamant and waited outside for them, listening to the shrieks and screams and easily picked out Peggy's, the loudest of them all. Sheila and Peggy eventually emerged, arms linked and giggling.

'Oh, Pat, you missed the best laugh ever! Didn't she, Peggy?' But Peggy wasn't listening, she was staring across at the rifle range.

'What's the matter with you?' laughed Pat. 'You look like you've seen a real ghost.'

'What?' Peggy shook her head. 'It's nothing.'

Sheila linked arms with her two sisters. 'Let's get in the queue for the chair-o-planes, and this time, Pat Goulding, you're not going to say no!'

The ride was a popular one. Individual wooden chairs hung from chains that were attached to a carousel-type structure. The girls climbed the steps to a platform ten feet above the ground. As a chair came level with the platform they were helped into it and a chain fastened across for safety. When all the chairs were full, the steps were moved back and far below two strong men cranked the mechanism to set the carousel in motion. Faster and faster it spun, until the chairs tilted and swung out with centrifugal force and the girls screamed, terrified and thrilled. When the carousel stopped, they remained suspended above the ground, disorientated and shivering, until their chairs came level with the platform again and it was their turn to be released. Peggy tried to focus on something below her to stop her head from spinning – a wooden tower with a huge brass bell, a soldier swinging a heavy mallet with all his might, the clang of the bell, the man's laughter. She held him steady in her gaze, while she waited to be released. Once out of her chair, she was off down the steps, turning to shout to her sisters, 'I'll be back in a minute!', and she pushed through the crowds to the bell tower. But the soldier was gone.

She plunged into the crowds again. Someone grabbed her arm and pulled her between two stalls.

'Well, look who it is – cloakroom girl or should that be failed musical director? I'm glad we've run into each other again.'

'Devlin!' Peggy tried to pull back from him, but he held her fast. 'I heard you'd left the Plaza.' She tried to keep her voice light.

'Not so much left it, as escorted from the premises by the police who wanted to charge me with fraud.' His fingers tightened round her arm. 'You walked out and left me to face all that.'

'I didn't! You threw us out. You were horrible to Pat and it wasn't her fault she couldn't sing.'

'You were responsible for that whole disaster – it was your big idea. I lost everything because of you.' He pulled her closer and wrapped his arms around her like a vice. 'You owe me.'

His whiskey breath disgusted her and she dropped all pretence at politeness. 'I owe you nothing!' She tried to pull away from him, but still he gripped her.

'Oh come on, you were after me from the moment we met, you know you were,' and suddenly his lips were on hers, his hands pulling at her clothes. She twisted away from him, but he lifted her off her feet and lurched towards the darkness behind the stalls.

'Let me go!' she shouted, but his mouth stifled her screams.

Then there was shouting. Devlin was being pulled away from her, but still he held on. She tripped and fell on the hard ground. She felt someone tall and powerful grab Devlin, heard a fist connect with Devlin's jaw and floor him. Then the man picked him up and hit him again.

Devlin backed off. 'That's enough,' he shouted, 'I'm going. I'm going.' He spat out blood at her feet. 'You're welcome to her, the bitch!'

'Are you all right?' Her rescuer picked her up and drew her close, stroked her hair. 'Don't worry, you're safe now. Did he hurt you?'

Peggy was shaking and close to tears. 'No, but I was scared. He was so strong.'

'Well, he's gone now and he won't be back.'

'I saw you ring the bell and I was trying to find you, but he–'

'Sssh, Peggy, I'm here, you've found me.'

'Why didn't you tell me you were home?'

'It's a long story. Why don't we find a warm bar where we can talk.'

'Give me two minutes,' her voice was breathless with excitement.

Her sisters had come looking for her. 'I've met someone I know,' she said. 'Tell Mammy I won't be late,' and she ran back the way she had come.

'What's that all about?' asked Sheila.

Pat pointed towards the tall soldier with a look of Humphrey Bogart about him who had put his arm around Peggy and had bent to kiss her. 'It's Harry Ferguson, he's home.'

The Belfast entries, a series of interconnecting back alleyways, cut across the main city streets. There, among the sleazy bars and brothels, was the oldest inn in Belfast – White's Tavern. Peggy and Harry came in from the chilly night into a fug of tobacco smoke and the warmth of a blazing fire. He ordered hot toddies and they found a quiet corner away from prying eyes where for several minutes they alternated between gazing at each other in amazement and holding each other close. Where to start a conversation that had ended so abruptly months before when Harry fled Belfast on the day of Irene's wedding?

'I've missed you,' he started

'Why didn't you write?' Peggy asked.

'Ach, you know me, I'm a talker not a writer.'

'Are you home on leave?'

'Not exactly. My father died, we buried him today.'

'Oh, Harry, I'm sorry to hear that.'

'Aye well, it's the rest of the family I feel sorry for. It'll be hard leaving them.'

'How long are you here for?'

'I got two days leave. So I'm back on the boat tomorrow.'

'When you left you said you couldn't come back – you owed Dessie all the money you'd borrowed to set up the bakery.' A look of horror crossed Peggy's face and she caught her breath. 'What if he finds you?'

'It's all right. I was talking to some fellas at the funeral and they said Dessie was doing six months in the Crumlin Road Gaol for black-marketeering. But never mind all that,' his voice softened and he caressed her cheek and kissed her tenderly, 'what about my best girl in all the world?'

She smiled shyly. 'Oh I'm fine now I've seen you, but these last months have been hard, with the bombing and the rations and everyone so miserable.'

'Ach sure you'll have cheered them up with all the singing and the concerts.'

'That's just it. There's been no singing.' She told him about William dying in the Dublin bombing and the terrible time with Pat and how she hadn't been able to sing since. 'And Mammy and Sheila were away in Dungannon for ages and we've hardly seen Irene since she started trailing round air force bases with Sandy.' Her lip trembled and tears welled in her eyes and when Harry wrapped his arms around her she laid her head on his shoulder and let them fall.

'And did you not have some fella to take care of you and make you laugh and take you out dancing?'

Peggy squeezed her words out through the sobs. 'No, no, there was no one. I've been all alone.'

'And what about that eejit you were wrestling with back there?'

'He's been pestering me for a while, but I never gave him the time of day.' She sniffed and raised her head. 'What about you? The uniform suits you and I bet there's been plenty of girls chasing you, like there always was.'

'Aah, Peggy pet, sure there's no one for me but you, only you.'

She almost believed him.

Outside, with the moon obscured by the clouds, the blackout was total. Harry took a small torch from his greatcoat and shone it on the pavement. 'I'll see you home,' he said.

'Well that's better than the last time we had a drink in White's.'

'I never took you to White's.'

'No, you asked me to meet you there one night after a concert. When I got there you forgot you'd asked me and that you'd promised me a lift home.'

'Don't remember that.'

'Not surprising – you were drunk and I had to walk home in the blackout!'

'I wasn't very reliable, was I?'

'No,' Peggy laughed, 'but you were always good fun.'

They started walking, hoping a bus would come past but none did. They walked quickly in an attempt to keep warm, but every now and again Harry would pull her into a doorway out of the wind, open his coat to wrap her close and kiss her until she was warm again.

Neither of them had a watch, not that they would have looked at it anyway – when they were together, it felt as though time didn't exist. The walk was long, but all too soon they were in Joanmount Gardens.

'I'll go with you to the back door,' said Harry, 'just in case you can't get in.' The door was unlocked and as they stepped into the back hallway they could see the light was still on in the kitchen.

'Is that you, Peggy?' Martha's voice.

Peggy put her head round the door. 'Yes, Mammy, I've someone with me. '

'Who? Who's with you at this hour of the night?' Martha's voice was sharp.

Peggy came through the door, drawing Harry by the hand behind her.

'Mercy me!' shouted Martha. Peggy held her breath, but she needn't have worried.

Harry stepped forward, his hand outstretched and with a broad smile said, 'Hello, Mrs Goulding, how in the world are you?'

'Mr Ferguson, you're a sight for sore eyes, so you are!'

Peggy stood amazed as her mother reached up and hugged Harry, who tipped a wink at Peggy as he returned the embrace.

'No, no, remember you were calling me Harry when I was last here?'

'Aye well, Harry, you certainly suit the uniform. Now give me the coat or you'll not feel the benefit later. Pull that chair up to the range, why don't you, and I'll make you a hot drink.' As Martha busied herself with cups and milk, she kept up the constant chatter. Peggy was astonished at her mother's pleasure in seeing Harry.

'How long are you home for?' asked Martha.

'Just for my father's funeral. I'm going back tomorrow.'

'Oh, I'm sorry to hear about your father.'

'Thank you.' He took the cup of tea Martha handed him. 'I'm sorry to say I've brought you no cake this visit.'

Martha laughed, 'I tell you, your cakes were the best, better than the Ormeau bakery. You don't still bake, do you?'

'Indeed I do. I'm in the catering corp. When we can get the sugar, a well-risen Victoria sponge can raise the morale of the whole battalion!' he joked.

When Harry was warmed and ready for the long walk back home, Martha shook his hand and told him he'd always be welcome. 'Now I'll away to my bed and, Peggy, don't you be long,' and she left them to say their goodbyes.

Harry took Peggy in his arms and kissed her until her head was light and her heart pounded with excitement. She had thought she loved Harry once long ago, but tonight she understood that those feelings had been just the first stirring of passion. Now her love consumed her and she wanted all of him for ever and ever.

He reached up and took her arms from round his neck and eased his body away from hers. She opened her eyes and saw he was smiling down at her.

'Peggy,' his voice no more than a whisper, 'are you still mine?' She nodded. 'Then say it, say it.'

'I'm still yours.'

'And?'

A moment's hesitation and she knew the answer. 'And I love you.'

He released the breath he had been holding and took Peggy's beautiful face in his hands. 'And I love you, Peggy Goulding.'

Chapter 27

Peggy stood shivering outside Goldstein's shop, stamping her feet on the pavement, blowing on her bunched fists and silently cursing her boss. At last, half an hour late, she spotted Esther hurrying down Royal Avenue towards her.

'Where's your uncle?' she shouted when Esther was still ten yards away.

'He went out early to a meeting. I've had to come on the bus.'

Once inside they locked the door behind them and went straight to the office where Goldstein kept a one-bar electric fire for his personal use.

'We'll leave the shop blinds down and get warm in here for a bit,' said Peggy, pulling Goldstein's comfortable chair round to the front of the fire. 'What's this meeting he's gone to?'

'I'm not sure, but it must be very important. He had on his best suit and shirt with his favourite dicky bow and' – Esther paused before delivering her conclusive evidence – 'he was whistling while he cooked his breakfast!'

'Are you sure he isn't off somewhere to negotiate the sale of a grand piano? That usually puts a spring in his step.'

'No, if that was it, he'd have said where he was going. No, this is definitely something mysterious, something exciting.'

'Oooh!' Peggy laughed. 'You don't think he's meeting a woman, do you?'

'What, during business hours? I don't think so, do you?'

Peggy stretched out her legs to toast her freezing feet in front of the fire.

'You'll get chilblains,' said Esther.

Peggy ignored her. 'Do you want to hear something really exciting?'

Esther caught the change in Peggy's voice and pulled her chair closer.

'I went to the carnival on Saturday night and I met someone there ...'

'Who was he?'

'How do you know it was a "he"?'

'It wouldn't be exciting if it wasn't.'

'It was ... it was ...' Peggy wished she could orchestrate a drum roll. 'It was ... Harry Ferguson!'

If Esther felt a stab of envy, she hid it well. She had fallen for Harry's charms during one of the many occasions when he and Peggy had fallen out. Of course, he'd been using her to make Peggy jealous and his plan had worked. They had got back together leaving Esther brokenhearted. Looking back, she knew it had been a silly infatuation but even now, when she had Reuben to love her, her heart leapt at the sound of Harry's name.

'Can you believe it?' Peggy was rushing on. 'I spotted him in the crowd. Oh Esther, I can't tell you how handsome he looks in uniform.' Esther had no trouble imagining. 'We went to a bar and talked for hours, then he walked me home and he came inside with me ...' Peggy's voice trailed off.

Esther's eyes widened. 'What happened?'

At that moment there was a loud banging on the shop door and Peggy jumped up, knocking over the little fire. 'Who do these people think they are?' she shouted. 'It's a music shop for goodness sake, how desperate can you be for some sheet music?'

Esther had gone to unbolt the door and Peggy heard the sound of Goldstein's voice. 'What's going on? Why is the shop not open? Get these blinds up right away!'

She quickly moved the chair back and was just switching off the fire when he appeared in the doorway.

Caught off guard, Peggy tried to explain, 'I'm sorry–'

'Never mind all that. Come into the shop. I have amazing news to tell you.' Peggy had never seen him so animated.

'I had a telephone call last night inviting me to a meeting with Basil Dean, no less.' He looked at the girls' blank faces and tutted. 'Basil Dean,' he repeated, 'the impresario who runs ENSA. You know what that is, don't you?'

'Of course I do,' said Peggy, 'I'm a member. It's the organisation that puts on shows for the troops.'

'Quite right and Mr Dean is here in Belfast to set up some concerts with a big star from England.' He grinned at the two girls, no doubt expecting to see his excitement reflected in their faces. 'Do you not see? He needs someone here, on the ground so to speak, who has the experience to make it all happen. That someone is me. He wants local talent on the bill and has asked me to provide it.'

Peggy saw the possibilities and understood why he was so excited. 'So you'll be in charge of it all?'

'Yes indeed and you two are going to help me. Peggy you will be assistant director and Esther you will be my personal assistant. We have only six weeks until the first concert. Mark my words, this will be the biggest theatrical event ever seen in Northern Ireland. We'll need to choose our best acts to show these English people what we can do!'

'Just one thing, Mr Goldstein,' said Peggy.

'What's that?'

'Who's the big star from England?'

He pursed his lips, considering. 'I'm not supposed to tell anyone yet, but as you are my production team I will tell you in confidence.' He paused for effect. 'Our star is none other than George Formby!'

He watched as the two girls danced around the shop pretending to strum ukuleles and singing 'When I'm Cleaning Windows' at the top of their voices.

Goldstein spent the rest of the morning in his office making plans and phone calls. When Peggy brought him his afternoon tea he was kneeling on the floor surrounded by lists of performers, venues and set designs.

'Peggy, if we need ten Northern Ireland acts to support Mr Formby, who would you choose?'

As she began to name her chosen performers, Goldstein ticked them off, or added them if they were not his own list.

'Hmmm,' he mused when she had finished. 'You hesitated when you mentioned Sheila. Do you worry that it would be too much for her?'

'No, I think she's got a great voice, but it's a tour with lots of concerts. She's just started a new job at Belfast Royal Academy and I'm not sure they'll let her take time off to do it. And, to be honest, I'm don't think my mother would agree to it.'

'Ah yes, Martha worries about her girls. I noticed you did not include the Golden Sisters in your list of acts?'

Peggy didn't hide her frustration. 'Pat'll never sing. I can't tell you how often I've talked to her about it, but either she can't or she won't. Whatever's going on, you'll not get a note out of her. And don't forget Irene's away in Enniskillen. I'm sorry to say it, but the Golden Sisters are finished.'

'Hmmm.' He stared at his list for a while then handed it to her. 'Right, we will include all those I've ticked. Send them a postcard asking them to get in touch – just say it is a big new show, do not mention anything else. In the meantime, I'll get on with contacting these military bases.'

In the days that followed, Goldstein was like a man possessed as he inspected army camps to assess their suitability for hosting a concert, all the time making copious notes about staging, dressing rooms and distances from Mr Formby's base in Belfast. He drew up a demanding rehearsal schedule of evenings and weekends for the local performers. At his side, Peggy caught some of his fervour and, after the disaster at the Plaza, she was determined to taste success.

At the end of their first gruelling week of rehearsing Peggy asked, 'Mr Goldstein, do all the shows have to be in military camps?'

'Well, George Formby is here to entertain the troops; he offers his services for free and the camps are happy to host the concerts.'

'But what if there could be a show in a big theatre like the Empire. That would be something special, wouldn't it?'

'You mean charge people to see the show? I doubt he would agree to that.'

'No, but the money raised at our concerts always goes to charities like the Red Cross. A lot of performers donate the money from ticket sales. Could we ask him? It would be so exciting for everyone to perform in a big theatre.'

Goldstein could see the appeal, but he wasn't sure whether George Formby would agree to it, or if he could persuade a theatre like the Empire to give them a night in the middle of the pantomime season. 'I will think about it,' he said. 'Now let us discuss what needs to be done this weekend – we have less than four weeks of rehearsals before the first show.'

Martha awoke on the first Sunday in December to a milky sky and a glittering frost. There was ice on the inside of her bedroom window and her slippers and dressing gown were cold to the touch. In the kitchen the cinders in the range were still glowing and she carefully placed some firewood against them so that, by the time the girls got up, the room would be warm and they could all have a hot breakfast before church. The girls were going to rehearsals straight after and they probably wouldn't be back until evening.

She had agreed to Sheila taking part in weekend concerts, but only if Pat was with her at all times. She had to admit that the prospect of these concerts had raised their spirits. Peggy, especially, was full of beans. Although she never mentioned it, Peggy had been upset about that business at the Plaza, but now she had an important role to play in this new show. Added to that, Harry Ferguson showing up out of the blue meant that she was being pleasant to everyone. If only something would come Pat's way. She had been through hell but, credit to her, she went to every rehearsal to keep an eye on Sheila. How hard that must be for her – to be there and not be able to sing. Martha was grateful to her.

Towards evening, Martha settled down to crochet a little Peter Pan collar to brighten up Sheila's plain blue jumper. At seven o'clock she switched on the wireless just in time to hear the chimes of Big Ben introduce the news.

'It has been reported in the United States of America that an American naval base at Pearl Harbour in the state of Hawaii has today been the target of an air attack by the Japanese air force. There are, as yet, no confirmed reports of damage or casualties.'

Martha was puzzled by the announcement. It was clearly significant – why else would it be the first thing on the news, but what had Japan to do with the war and why bomb the United States when they were not at war with anyone? There would probably be more details in the main nine o'clock news, she thought, and she went back to her crocheting still wondering where exactly Hawaii was.

The girls came through the back door, laughing about the antics of the Templemore Tappers and their attempt at a cancan.

'You should have seen them, Mammy. The music got faster and faster and when they were kicking their legs up, somebody's shoe flew off and hit Mr Goldstein on the head!' Sheila convulsed with laughter and could say no more.

Peggy took up the tale. 'They all started laughing and, of course, they couldn't keep time and in the end they were just running round the stage making right eejits of themselves. It was a geg!'

'I'm sure you've that man's head away,' said Martha. 'I don't know how he keeps up with you all. Now, there are some farls there that you can toast with a wee bit of cheese on top. I'm just waiting for the news; there's been an attack at an American air base.'

At the ominous sound of Big Ben they fell silent, the fun of the Tappers forgotten, and listened to the report of the terrible strike on Pearl Harbour that had killed thousands. Their hearts went out to the people there – they understood completely what they were going through. Pat fetched her old school atlas and they stared at the tiny green spot of Hawaii in the vast blue of the Pacific Ocean.

'How could that happen?' asked Sheila. 'Why would the Japanese do that? The Americans aren't even in the war.'

'Ach, their blood's up,' said Martha. 'There's no telling what some of these countries will do – they're like drunks when they see a scrap on a Saturday night and wade in fists flailing.'

'Well, they've picked a fight they can't win,' said Pat. 'How long, I wonder, before the Americans throw the next punch?'

Listening to the wireless the following day, Martha heard the President of the United States say that the bombing of Pearl Harbour was 'a date which will live in infamy' and he declared war on Japan. Three days later Germany and Italy declared war on the United States and within hours this was reciprocated.

On the Thursday before Christmas Pat was in a meeting all afternoon, finalising transport arrangements for evacuees who wanted to return to their families. The room was stuffy and she felt the beginnings of a headache drumming in her temple. She left her desk in time to catch the early bus, but as she was passing the Great Hall she paused to look at decorations for the Stormont carol concert that evening. Boughs of holly hung from the banisters of the wide staircase, and the landing at the top was dominated by a huge Christmas tree, resplendent with red velvet bows and gold baubles. Rows of elegant gilded chairs had been set out in neat rows.

She should not have come this way. What was she thinking of? Tonight the choir would be singing here, but William would be missing from the tenors and she from the sopranos. Pat felt tears sting her eyes and turned away. As she reached the main door, it opened and a crocodile of children marched in – a raggle-taggle bunch, all chattering and laughing, swivelling and pointing.

From outside there was a sudden shout – 'Stand still children! Remember, best behaviour at all times!' – and Pat watched in amazement as Aunt Kathleen swept through the door.

Without thinking, Pat called, 'Aunt Kathleen,' and immediately wished she hadn't.

'Good gracious,' said Kathleen. 'I didn't expect you to be here to welcome us.' She removed her hat and handed it to Pat, then went and stood in front of the children. 'Remember you have come to your country's parliament and you must show respect. And what must you not do?'

'Run in the building,' they chorused.

Kathleen nodded, satisfied. 'Now, I want the third row of the choir to go and sit on the third step up on that very grand staircase. Second row, second step; first row, first step.' When they were seated, she beckoned Pat to come forward. 'This lady is my niece and she is also called Miss Goulding,' she explained, 'and we're going to sing for her.'

Kathleen indicated to Pat to sit down and to the children to stand up. She gave them the note and counted one … two … 'Away in a Manger' they sang, as only a choir of children can. The sweet sound filled the hall and Pat looked from shining face to shining face and felt at once uplifted.

When they had finished, Kathleen nodded, satisfied. 'Do it just like that tonight,' she said, 'now sit down and chat quietly to the person next to you.'

'Well, what do you think, Pat?'

'I think they sang beautifully. How do you get children like that to—'

'Children like what?' The look on Kathleen's face pulled her up short.

'I didn't mean …'

'Children are children, Pat. It doesn't matter what their fathers do for a living or how many petticoats their mother has. If you give them music they will give it their hearts.'

'I know that, I'm sorry Aunt Kathleen.' Pat felt awkward. 'I'm sure they'll be wonderful tonight. Look, I have to go or I'll miss my bus. Good luck,' and she turned to walk away. But before she reached the door there was a sharp cry behind her and Pat turned to see Kathleen slump to the floor.

The children clustered round their teacher. 'Get back,' Pat shouted, but they didn't move. She clapped her hands. 'Back to the steps all of you,' and they reluctantly moved away. 'Aunt Kathleen, are you all right? Can you hear me?' There was a low groan. Pat scanned the rows of children. 'You there, the big boy at the back. Yes, you. Go down that corridor, there's a man on the desk. Tell him to come here quickly.'

Kathleen's eyes flickered open and she tried to sit up. Her face was plaster white.

'No, stay where you are for now, I've sent for help.' Pat took off her coat, rolled it up and put it under Kathleen's head.

'I need to sort the children.'

'They're fine, be still.'

The man arrived and together he and Pat helped Kathleen to her feet, but her legs went from under her again and they sat her gently on a chair.

'I think I'm going to faint again.' There was a grey sheen to her face.

'Put your head between your knees,' Pat told her.

'There's a nurse in the building, I've sent for her,' said the man.

Kathleen lifted her head. 'Don't fuss, I'll be all right in a minute. I have to be. I'm responsible for these children and they have to perform tonight.'

'Aunt Kathleen, do you think you're well enough for a concert? What if you faint again when you're up there conducting?'

'The children have been practising for weeks. I won't let them down!' She stood up, swayed and sank again to the chair.

'Can we get them back to the school?' Pat asked.

'No, they are to have their tea here with the other performers. Their parents are coming to collect them later.'

The nurse arrived and after a quick examination decided Kathleen should go to hospital.

'I'll come with you,' said Pat.

'No, stay with the children,' Kathleen doubled over and let out a low moan. 'Can you take them out of here?' she whispered.

The man from the desk nodded towards the corridor. 'Committee room number four, they're setting up the tea things now.'

'But I don't want to leave you, Aunt Kathleen.'

'Pat, you're in charge of the children now.'

'But I can't–'

'You can't let me down.' There were tears in Kathleen's eyes.

Pat nodded, embraced her aunt briefly, then crossed to the

257

stairs where the children were sitting, quiet as mice, watching the goings-on.

'Miss Goulding is unwell,' said Pat, sounding more confident than she felt, 'so I'm going to take you now to the room where you'll have some tea and I'll stay with you until your parents come to collect you.'

'What about our singing?' asked the older boy who had helped earlier.

'I don't think there'll be any singing tonight,' said Pat and with a last look at Kathleen she led the children down the corridor to the committee room.

There was no one there when they arrived, but the door was open and inside the large committee table was covered with a white tablecloth on which were set platters of sandwiches and slices of Madeira cake. At one end stood a trolley with a tea urn and cups and saucers. For a fleeting moment she thought the children might rush at the food and she wouldn't be able to control them, but they almost crept into the room, one or two talking in whispers, the rest silent.

'Sit on the chairs for now,' said Pat. 'The other performers will be here soon and then we'll all have something to eat.'

They sat in silence, looking around them, taking in the grand room with the huge fireplace, the twin chandeliers, the portraits on the walls. The large ormolu clock on the mantelpiece measured the silence and Pat watched the children, wondering if she should say something, do something. A tiny girl with eyes as big as a marmoset's put her hand up.

'When are we going to sing, Miss?'

Pat saw all eyes were on her, each child waiting for the answer. They'd come here to sing. When would they be singing? Pat cleared her throat. 'I'm afraid,' she hesitated, 'I'm sorry you won't be singing because Miss Goulding isn't well.'

'But we have to sing. Miss Goulding said it would be the chance of a lifetime and we would remember it always.'

Pat could hear the echo of Kathleen's voice. That was exactly what she would have said to them. 'But Miss Goulding isn't here.'

The child replied as if Pat had not quite grasped the point, 'But we're here and you're here.'

'Yes, but Miss Goulding isn't here,' repeated Pat, her voice a little sharper.

'But you're a Miss Goulding too,' said the child.

The logic defeated Pat and as she struggled to explain, the older boy turned on the girl. 'Don't be stupid – she's a different Miss Goulding, she can't conduct a choir!'

The girl burst into tears. 'But I wanted to remember it always,' she sobbed and then another child began to cry, then another. Pat realised in horror that in seconds the whole choir could be in tears.

'Stop! Stop!' she shouted and quicker than she thought possible they were quiet and looked at her, waiting for her to tell them what to do.

'Put up your hand if you want to sing.'

All hands went up.

'Put up your hand if you can sing just as Miss Goulding taught you, even though she's not here.'

All hands went up, but the boy said, 'As long as someone conducts us.'

Pat took a deep breath and looked again at their expectant faces. 'I can conduct you, but you have to promise you will sing your very best and make Miss Goulding proud of you.'

At seven o'clock the children lined up quietly in the corridor outside the Great Hall. They were to perform first. Pat stood with them and smiled to encourage them. She had no idea how they would perform in front of an audience and wondered what on earth had possessed her to take Kathleen's place. Then the door opened and Pat led the children out into the splendid setting to take their places on the stairs in front of Belfast's most prominent citizens.

She scanned the choir and saw that they had followed the instructions to focus on her. Pat counted them in, 'One … two …' But nobody sang, they just stood looking at her, expectant, silent. In the first row the girl with the marmoset eyes calmly mouthed the word 'note'. They needed their note! So well-trained were they, so disciplined, they would not begin without it. Pat was horrified. The children waited, the audience waited. Just one note from her lips was all it would take. Kathleen's words flashed in her brain – 'You're in charge of the children now' – and Pat opened her mouth and sang one note, the only one that mattered, a pitch perfect C.

Chapter 28

On Christmas Eve morning Martha cleaned the house and put clean sheets on the beds. She was in the middle of digging up vegetables for the Christmas dinner from the garden, when the postman came round to the back of the house.

'Hello there, Mrs Goulding, I've a quare parcel for ye here.'

'Lord bless us!' said Martha. 'What on earth is it?'

'I'm guessing it's livestock,' he laughed. 'Although by the amount of blood seepin' out of it, it's surely dead. I've a letter from Enniskillen too.'

Martha slipped the letter into her apron pocket and took the parcel inside. She put it in the sink to unwrap it. Some sort of fowl, all gutted and plucked for the oven, thank God. She spotted a bloody envelope and inside that, also bloody, was a long letter from Bridie McManus. The goose was a present from the family because, she said, 'I know you'll not get anything like this in Belfast.' Martha silently thanked her friend for her kindness and turned her attention to the other letter. She had not had a letter from Irene for two weeks, not since she 'd let them know that she wouldn't be home for Christmas. Inside there were just four words, 'Coming home Christmas Eve.'

Martha spent the afternoon hurriedly crocheting a lace collar and matching cuffs, identical to the three sets she had already made, so Irene would have a present to open on Christmas morning. And all the time she smiled to herself knowing that the bleak Christmas she had dreaded had been banished by the prospect of a roast goose dinner and a daughter returned home.

When Sheila and Peggy arrived home from work they looked at each other in amazement at the sound of their mother singing.

'You're in a good mood,' said Peggy.

'And why wouldn't I be, sure haven't I had two lovely surprises today. You can see the first one in the sink.'

'Is it a turkey? Where did you get it from?'

'It's a goose – a present from Bridie McManus.'

'And what's the second surprise? A plum pudding?' laughed Sheila.

'It'll be here later,' said Martha.

'Did Bridie send a letter as well?' asked Sheila. 'Is Rose back serving in the shop? What about Dermot?'

'Yes, yes, the letter's on the mantelpiece. Now away in the sitting room, the fire's lit. We'll have a late tea when Pat comes home.'

'Is she not home yet?'

'No she's gone straight from work to see if Aunt Kathleen is all right. She came out of hospital yesterday.'

'What was the matter with her?'

'She'd a fever and low blood pressure.'

The seven o'clock news had just finished and Martha was thinking about getting the tea started when Pat put her head round the sitting room door.

'I'm home and guess who I've brought with me.'

Martha was on her feet in an instant, her face eager with anticipation. 'Come on in, come on in,' she shouted and Pat came in followed by Aunt Kathleen.

'Hello, I'm sorry about the intrusion, but Pat insisted,' said Kathleen.

Pat saw the split-second hesitation on her mother's face just before good manners prevailed. 'I've invited Kathleen to spend Christmas with us,' Pat quickly explained.

Sheila looked confused until Martha flashed her a look. Then she was all smiles. 'Aunt Kathleen, what a surprise. Did you get my letter saying I got the job?'

'Indeed I did, Sheila. You'll have to tell me all about it.'

'Come and sit by the fire, Kathleen,' said Martha, 'and I'll go and make us all something to eat.' Pat followed her mother into the kitchen.

Martha spoke in an urgent whisper. 'What were you thinking of, inviting Kathleen? You know I don't really get on with her.'

'Mammy, her house was freezing and there was no food in the larder. What was I to do? She's always been good to me you know.'

Martha looked a little shamefaced. 'Aye, I know, it's just that … Well, never mind, a little Christian charity at Christmas is good for the soul. Have you thought where she's going to sleep?'

'In Irene's bed, of course.'

'Oh, but—'

At that moment the back door opened and Irene came in carrying a suitcase. The loud voices and laughter that greeted her brought Peggy and Sheila into the kitchen.

'What are you doing here?' asked Peggy.

'We thought you couldn't come,' said Sheila.

Irene set her suitcase down. 'Things have changed at the base; there are so many people there now, especially since the Americans arrived.'

Peggy's eyes widened. 'Americans?'

'Aye, it's all unofficial I think, but they're there to service the planes protecting the Atlantic convoys. So no billet for the likes of me.'

'And Sandy couldn't come with you just for Christmas?' asked Martha.

'No, all leave's been cancelled since Pearl Harbour.'

'So will you be home for a while?' Martha couldn't keep the excitement out of her voice.

'Until things calm down, then Sandy and I'll find somewhere to live off base.' Irene took off her coat and headscarf. 'I'm famished,

Mammy. I left at ten this morning and I can't tell you what a journey I've had. I need something to eat and then I'll be ready for my bed.'

'Oh dear,' said Pat, 'I've just given your bed to Aunt Kathleen.'

'Aunt Kathleen!'

After tea Martha took charge of the sleeping arrangements: Aunt Kathleen would have Irene's bed and Irene would sleep with Martha in her double bed.

'I think I'll go up now,' said Irene.

'I'll carry your case,' said Pat.

'You don't need to–' but Pat was already heading for the stairs.

While Irene unpacked her case Pat sat on the edge of the bed. 'Irene, can I tell you something?' The hesitancy in her voice caused Irene to stop what she was doing, a cardigan in one hand, a coat hanger in the other.

'What is it?'

'I think I might be able to sing.'

Irene's eyes widened. 'You can sing?'

'I managed a note and then I've been singing little snatches to myself, but I've no idea if I could sing in front of an audience.'

'Have you told the rest of them about this?'

'No, I'm really nervous about it and you know what Peggy would be like – she'd want me to rehearse and then I wouldn't be able to do it and I'd be back to where I started. I don't know what to do.'

Irene sat on the bed opposite her. 'What can you sing?'

Pat gave a half-hearted laugh, 'Away in a Manger.'

Irene smiled. 'Very seasonal. Look, why don't you just sing a bit for me. I'll be your audience. Go on, give it a go.'

Pat fixed her eyes on the wall and began to sing, soft and low, the first two lines were pitch perfect.

'How was that?' asked Irene.

'Fine.'

'Now try to keep going,'

Pat began again, managed the first verse and stopped, but Irene immediately started the second verse and nodded to Pat to sing with her. Steadily the strength of Pat's voice came through and by the final verse the rich sound filled the room. Pat held the final note and suddenly from outside the bedroom door came the sound of clapping and everyone crowded into the room, all excited and talking over each other, 'You can sing!' … 'Your voice is back!'

Martha hugged Pat. 'Thank God my prayers have been answered – what a wonderful Christmas present this is.'

Pat's ability to sing again sent everyone to bed in good spirits and when the family sat down to dinner on Christmas Day, Martha said grace for the food on the table and the surprises that had brought joy to her family. The goose was delicious and Aunt Kathleen turned out to be good company. After dinner they listened to the king's speech on the wireless and ate the chocolate bars Irene had brought with her, presents from the Americans on the base. Later, Goldstein and Esther arrived to spend the evening and Jack and Betty from next door made up the party. As usual, Peggy took her place at the piano and the first song she played was 'Away in a Manger'.

At the sight of Pat singing, Goldstein gasped in delight and at the end he shouted, 'Bravo Patricia, I will expect you to be singing at the next rehearsal and Irene too. The Golden Sisters are back in business!'

George Formby arrived in Belfast in a blaze of publicity with no fewer than nine ukuleles then took a drive in a jaunting car, as though that's what you'd see in Belfast. The tickets for the show at the Empire in aid of the Red Cross had sold out quickly and Goldstein's performers, re-named Stars for the Troops, had rehearsed to within an inch of their lives. Pat had gained confidence during the rehearsals singing with Irene and Peggy. Her voice was almost back to its best and it was decided the Golden Sisters should sing two songs in the show. Sheila would also have a two-song spot.

There had been quite a bit of discussion about what they should wear. Peggy had shown Goldstein the three beautiful dresses that Devlin had bought her, in the hope he would see the opportunity for some glamour, but he was unconvinced. He pointed at the kingfisher dress. 'That is the one Sheila wore at the Technical Institute concert, is it not?' Peggy nodded and Goldstein went on, 'She can wear that but, for the Golden Sisters, I prefer a trio to be dressed identically.'

'In that case, could I make a suggestion?' asked Peggy.

The dressing room backstage at the Empire was cold and shabby, with distemper flaking off the walls. Down one side of the room was a row of dressing tables each with a mirror and lights, several of which didn't work. By the time Pat, Irene and Sheila arrived the tension in the room was palpable.

Peggy wasn't there. She had gone after work to the dressmaker's shop off Shaftesbury Square to collect the new dresses. It had taken a lot of persuasion for Goldstein to agree that they should be specially made for them and Peggy had made sure her sisters knew what she had done.

'I'm not going to tell you what they're like, but just wait till you see them; we'll look wonderful!' she had told them.

Pat had lost patience with her. 'You and dresses again! Why can't we just wear what we usually wear – our black skirts and coloured blouses?'

'Because this is the biggest show we've ever been in and Mr Goldstein wants us to look like stars.'

'You might want to look like a star, but some of us would rather concentrate on our singing.'

Pat was restless and couldn't concentrate in the noisy dressing room. She needed to clear her head and to find a place where she could warm up her voice.

Sheila found her sitting on a trunk in a room full of props. 'Peggy's just arrived,' she said, 'she's brought the dresses.' When Pat didn't answer, Sheila sat down beside her. 'Are you all right?' she asked.

'Yes, I'm fine. I just want to get out there and do it.'

'I know how you feel. I'm so nervous. At least you've got Irene and Peggy out there with you.'

'No, it's easier on your own, you don't have to worry that Peggy

266

might do something to throw you off balance.'

'She wouldn't do that, not tonight.'

Pat looked sceptical. 'I wouldn't put it past her to pull her usual trick and play the introduction to a song that isn't in the programme!'

Sheila put her arm through her sister's. 'Don't worry. You've dealt with that plenty of times. Let's go and see what the Golden Sisters will be wearing.'

Back in the dressing room, Peggy was unwrapping a large brown paper parcel. 'You're just in time!' she shouted and pulled back the paper to reveal the emerald green material. 'They're all the same. We had two copies made from my Plaza dress,' and she handed one each to Irene and Pat and held the remaining dress in front of her, showing it off.

There was a howl of rage from Pat. 'How could you! How could you! I'm not wearing that!' and she stormed out the door.

'What's the matter with her?'

'You've no idea, have you?' Irene shook her head in disbelief. 'Of all the stupid things …'

'I don't understand. It's a beautiful dress and she's worn it before.'

'I suggest you sit here and think about why Pat might be upset at the thought of wearing the dress she last wore at the Plaza!' and Irene went off in search of her sister. She found her in the props room, crying softly.

'How could she do that to me?' cried Pat.

'She just doesn't think – you know what's she's like.'

'I'm not wearing it, Irene.'

'The last thing anyone wants is to upset you after everything you've been through. You've been so strong these last couple of weeks and worked hard to bring your voice back to what it was.'

'I wanted so much to sing tonight, to prove I could go on a stage in front of an audience. I promised myself … I promised William …' She covered her face with her hands.

There was a knock at the door and Goldstein came into the room. 'There you are, Patricia. I hear there is a problem.'

Irene explained, 'The dress is the same one Pat wore when she lost her voice at the Plaza concert. She can't face wearing it again.'

'Aaah,' Goldstein nodded and went to sit on a trunk opposite Pat. 'Irene, would you give us five minutes?'

Goldstein sat a while, listening to the muted sounds of the orchestra tuning up. Soon the show would begin. To have come so far with this company … they had been through so much and he looked on all the performers as his friends. But the Goulding girls and Martha, they were something more, they were like his family.

'Do you remember after the last bombing when my shop was almost destroyed? I wanted to give up when I saw it. The grand piano was covered in dust, plaster, broken glass. I was numb inside. I remember opening the piano lid and there were the keys, gleaming and pristine, just waiting to be played. Mozart, Puccini,' he laughed, 'even "We'll Meet Again". Right there and then I vowed to carry on entertaining people who had been through a nightmare. Something told me that as long as there was music …'

'That's when William and I found you.'

'Indeed, and do you remember what he said?'

Pat nodded, 'William said, "That's the spirit, Mr Goldstein. I wish we could bottle that." And then you said we'd be the stars of the show – Belfast's Sweethearts.'

'Just so, just so.'

Pat didn't even look at Peggy when she returned to the dressing room. She simply put on the green dress and sat down to add the finishing touches to her makeup, all the time listening to the voice in her head that told her, 'That's the spirit. That's the spirit.'

Martha had been past the Belfast Empire many a time, but had never been inside. She would have liked to have seen some of the big names that had played there over the years, but Robert had never been keen. 'We've more important things to spend the money on,' he'd say. 'Wait'll these girls are reared, before we go gallivanting.' Aye well, their family was long reared and Martha wasn't sure what he would make of his girls on the stage and her gallivanting off to see them.

She had been delighted when Goldstein had sent her three tickets and decided at once that she'd ask Betty and Jack to go with her. They'd been the best of neighbours for many years. Time and again when she had been down on her uppers they had been there to support her. Indeed, the food they grew had saved her family from hunger pangs often enough.

Quite a crowd had gathered outside the theatre and at first they were unsure whether it was a queue to get in but, as they stood there, several cars drew up in quick succession and men in dinner suits and women in floor-length organza, satin or brocade spilled out, and swept through the entrance into the dazzling lights of the foyer.

'Come on,' said Jack, 'this is the way.'

'I don't think so,' said Martha, 'sure, this isn't the door for the likes of us.'

'Of course it is. We've tickets for the front stalls and you've four daughters performing,' and he offered an arm each to Betty and Martha and, three abreast, they entered the theatre.

There were so many people milling around inside, all of them chattering excitedly. Jack squeezed Martha's arm and pointed to a large board on an easel. In the middle was a picture of George Formby with his toothy grin and, around that, photos of the other performers. There was no mistaking the smiling Golden Sisters above his left shoulder – sure hadn't she stitched those colourful blouses herself. Jack led them towards a door above which was written in gold leaf 'Front Stalls' and they passed into the auditorium. Martha caught her breath at the sight of the rows and rows of seats upholstered in red velvet that descended to the stage and its matching red velvet curtains with gold tassels and braid. Somewhere beyond those curtains her girls were waiting. Please, God, look after them tonight, she prayed. On down the aisle they walked, closer and closer to the stage.

'Here we are,' said Jack at last, 'row G, right in the middle. Best seats in the house!'

From where she sat Martha could see the boxes on either side of the stage and their occupants. It was easy to pick out the mayor, with his gold chain, in one of them and next to him a woman in a peach-coloured, off-the-shoulder evening dress and long white evening gloves. In another box were several military officers in dress uniform.

Jack nodded towards them. 'If I'm not mistaken there are a few Yanks in that party. What would they be doing in Belfast do you think?'

In one of the boxes on the opposite side a group of young well-to-do people were laughing and passing round a hip flask. The sound of a violin being tuned made her start; she hadn't noticed the orchestra pit with its subdued lights highlighting the silver and brass and illuminating the music stands and starched shirts.

After what seemed like an age, the house lights dimmed, the leader of the orchestra appeared on his podium and the overture began. How strange to hear snatches of George Formby's most popular songs played as though they were introducing a symphony and not a variety show. The applause was enthusiastic, but almost immediately the curtains opened to reveal a wonderful painted backdrop of Belfast City Hall gleaming against a starry sky and, at the sight of it, there was loud cheering. On to the stage came the Templemore Tappers, lined up one behind the other and with their hands resting on the waist of the girl in front as they high-kicked in unison, first one side and then the other. Their routine was lively and well coordinated. Martha knew that Macy had inspired them to try to new ideas, but it was the memory of Myrtle's dusty tap shoes in a coffin in St George's Market that filled her mind.

The dancers were followed by a baritone, a middle-aged man, slightly rotund, who put some strain on his bright red cummerbund when he reached for the high notes. Then there was a female impersonator, not something Martha expected to enjoy, but soon she and the rest of the audience were roaring with laughter at his antics. He left the stage to run after a trolley bus, skirt hitched up to reveal red flannel drawers.

The stage was plunged into darkness and there came the haunting sound of a saxophone, then a solitary spotlight picked out the head and shoulders of a woman standing centre stage. Her head was bowed, but Martha had recognised the introduction of 'God Bless the Child' and knew it was her child standing there. Sheila raised her head and began to sing softly. Martha had heard it rehearsed so many times at home that she almost sang it with her, sensed how perfectly the volume and pace were controlled, how moving the lyrics. The applause was enthusiastic. Betty and Jack leant across.

'Wonderful, just wonderful!' said Betty, her face flushed with pleasure.

'Who'd have thought wee Sheila could sing like that?' said Jack.

Sheila's second song was an Ella Fitzgerald number, 'A-Tisket, A-Tasket', completely different in every way to the first. The spotlight grew and Sheila clicked her fingers and moved to the beat as the kingfisher dress rippled with colour. She seemed so confident that Martha relaxed a little in her seat. Sheila took her final bow and her face lit up with pleasure at the applause. Martha had never seen her so happy or so beautiful.

Macy was next and she looked stunning in a Ginger Rogers-style dress – figure-hugging, powder blue and scattered with sequins. She danced to 'Cheek to Cheek' from the Fred Astaire film *Royal Wedding*. She used the whole stage, skipping across it at speed one minute and then slowing down to turn elegantly, her whole body conveying grace and precision. As she took her bow, the officers in the box were on their feet applauding and cheering.

The other acts seemed to race by and each was of such quality that it was hard to believe they were amateurs. The Golden Sisters were the final act before the interval – the second half being entirely devoted to the top of the bill, George Formby. Martha felt a tightness in her stomach. They had rehearsed so much at home in addition to Goldstein's rehearsal schedule and were note-perfect, but Martha knew well enough that counting chickens was a fool's game.

They were introduced as Belfast's answer to the Andrews Sisters and ran on stage smiling and waving. The dresses were beautiful, complimented by the City Hall behind them bathed in green light to mark the finale of the Irish half of the show. Peggy was quickly at the piano and Irene and Pat stood just in front of it as the intro played. Three bars and they'd be into 'Chattanooga Choo Choo.' Pat would sing the first line before the other two joined in. Martha leaned forward and clenched her fists, her eyes on Pat. One bar and

Pat was moving in time with the beat, two bars and she smiled at Irene. Just like rehearsals. When it came to the third bar, Martha saw Pat stiffen slightly, eyes flitting to the side of the stage. The cue came and went without a note from Pat. Peggy improvised a few notes to smooth the way into repeating the intro. Still swaying, Irene reached out, took Pat's hand and swung it in time, maybe she squeezed it too for Pat looked at Irene and smiled back. Into the third bar, Pat turned to the audience, 'Pardon me, boy, is this the Chattanooga Choo Choo?' and her voice was strong and clear.

The second song went without a hitch and the curtain came down to rapturous applause. In the wings Irene caught Pat by the arm, 'Are you all right? I thought–'

'Yes, I'm fine. I just–'

'Did something distract you?'

'Sort of, I thought I saw something … someone in the wings.'

'Nobody should have been moving in the wings! I'll tell Goldstein.'

'No, Irene, I've told you. There was nothing. Come on let's get back to the dressing room.'

All the performers had crowded into the ladies' dressing room and Goldstein was going round speaking to each of them in turn. 'I'll have to sit down,' said Irene, 'my legs are like jelly.'

'There's a seat over there out of the way – you grab it and I'll get us some water.'

When Pat returned Irene was bent over clutching her stomach. 'I feel a bit strange, nerves probably.'

Pat handed her the water. 'You look very pale.'

'Well, you did give me quite a fright out there.' Irene tried to laugh it off, but suddenly she was doubled over and groaning. 'I need to get to the lavatory.'

'I'll come with you,' said Pat.

'No, no I'll be fine,' and Irene struggled to her feet.

She had taken only a few steps when Pat called out, 'Irene, wait!'

'What, what is it?' In reply Pat pointed at the back of her dress and Irene twisted round to see a red stain seeping through the green silk.

272

'What is it? What's happening?' She felt for the chair behind her, eyes wide with panic. Seconds later her face contorted in pain and she doubled over.

'Don't move,' said Pat and she went quickly to Goldstein. Moments later he ordered everyone to move to the men's dressing room just down the corridor. Sheila passed by and asked Pat if she was coming.

'Yes, I'll be there in a minute,' she told her. Peggy was one of the last to leave and Pat caught her arm. 'There's something the matter with Irene. We'll need to get an ambulance. Can you find the manager's office? There's bound to be a telephone there. Phone the hospital and tell them to come to the stage door right away.'

'Why, what's happened? What's the matter with her?'

'Never mind that now. Just do it!'

When Peggy had gone, Pat persuaded Irene to lie on the floor with her legs raised and resting on the chair.

'Lie perfectly still,' said Pat. 'I've sent for an ambulance.'

Irene tried to get up. 'I'm not going in an ambulance, I feel much better,' and then another cramp seized her.

At that moment, the sound of the orchestra playing 'Chinese Laundry Blues' blared through the dressing room speakers and the compère announced: 'The star of tonight's show needs absolutely no introduction. He's one of Britain's most popular performers we're delighted to have him in the Empire Theatre Belfast – Mr George Formby!'

Irene lay shivering as the applause erupted. When it died down there was a moment's silence then, in his distinctive Lancashire voice, George Formby called out, 'Turned Out Nice Again!' and as howls of laughter echoed in their ears Irene and Pat looked at each other and smiled at the incongruity of it all.

While Formby sang 'When I'm Cleaning Windows' Pat made Irene comfortable with a coat under her head and another tucked in round her. Then they listened in silence to the play-acting and silly songs until the ambulance arrived.

Pat decided that she would go in the ambulance with Irene and she told Peggy to go and tell their mother what was happening.

Irene was suddenly agitated. 'We can't tell her now, not in the middle of the show.'

'It's not an ideal time, but if we don't tell her she'll be upset,' said Pat.

'And if she's told she'll insist on leaving the theatre and that will disturb everyone.' Irene was close to tears. 'I don't even want to go to the hospital!'

'Calm down, Irene, please.' Pat thought for a moment. 'Right, this is what we'll do. Peggy you tell Mammy at the end of the show that Irene had been taken to the Mater Hospital. Try not to worry her. She'll probably come straight to the hospital but, Peggy, it might be as well if you and Sheila go home. No point in us all cluttering up the place.'

Unaware of the drama backstage Martha settled down to watch the second half. George Formby was a lively character, smiling and laughing all the time. His songs were funny, although Martha felt one or two were a bit coarse. 'With My Little Stick of Blackpool Rock' brought howls of laughter and, although Martha was a little unclear of the meaning, she could sense the crudity in there somewhere!

The finale was a lively singalong with performers taking a bow front and centre stage before stepping back and joining in with the songs. Martha sat forward in her seat and watched Sheila come forward to take her applause. She was greeted with whistles and cheers – she'd done so well and, not for the first time, Martha felt not just pride, but wonder at her talent. She waited for the Golden Sisters to appear, but George Formby came on to take the final applause. Martha sat through the speeches that praised the work of ENSA, recognised the quality of the local talent, recognised the superb organisation by Mr Goldstein. By the time they stood for 'God Save the King' it was all she could do to mouth the words instead of rushing out to find out what had happened to the girls.

Peggy was waiting for her mother when the concert was over, but before she could say anything Martha demanded, 'What's happened?'

'Now you're not to worry, Mammy, but Irene's been taken ill.'

'What do you mean ill?'

'I'm not sure what's wrong with her, but she's gone in an ambulance to the Mater. Pat's with her.'

'Dear God!' Martha tried to collect her thoughts. Ambulance, hospital – it must be serious. 'Where's Sheila?' she asked.

'She's backstage collecting our belongings. Pat said I should take her home.'

'Yes, that's probably best. I'll go to the hospital right away. I'd better tell Jack and Betty.'

'I'll do that. You go on.'

Waiting outside the Mater Hospital, Pat watched Martha hurry through the gates and was struck by how much she had aged over the last few years. Daddy's death and the hardships of the war had taken their toll on her. The same felt hat she had worn for years had slipped a little and a wisp of grey hair had escaped from the bun at the back of her head.

'Where is she? What's happened?' Martha cried.

Pat took her arm and led her to a low bench in the waiting area. 'She's going to be all right, Mammy. You're not to worry.'

'What's the matter with her?'

'She's been haemorrhaging–'

'Bleeding, you mean?'

'Aye. Mammy, Irene's had a miscarriage.'

Martha shook her head, went to speak, stopped; she had no words to speak of such things.

'She's being taken care of,' said Pat. 'We can wait here and they'll let us see her when … everything is sorted.'

Martha gave a heavy sigh – perhaps she had been greedy and taken too much from this day. It had begun with such anticipation and brought excitement, success and pride, but now … now she needed to take care of Irene and help her with the sadness to come.

Chapter 29

During the night the temperature plummeted and Martha woke up shivering. She got out of bed and looked in on Irene. The coat that had been draped over the blanket to provide some extra warmth on the cold winter night had fallen to the floor and Martha gently replaced it.

'Is that you, Mammy?' Irene whispered.

'Sure who else would it be checking on you in the middle of the night?'

'I'm freezing.'

'I know. I was going to refill your hot-water jar.'

'I can't sleep.'

'There'll still be a bit of warmth left in the kitchen, so give me a few minutes to get the fire going again then come down and sit while the kettle boils to fill the jar.'

Soon they were sitting next to the range wrapped in their eiderdowns sipping tea.

'You'll need to start sleeping through the night when you go back to work next week, Irene.'

'I know, but maybe it'll be better then. I'll have other things to concentrate on. You can't let your mind wander when you're riveting.'

'Are you sure you're strong enough to go back to all that?'

'Macy says they're working flat out at the factory. They've a big new order for Sterling bombers so they need everyone they can get. I might as well make myself useful because there's no chance I'll be back in Enniskillen for a while, not with all the extra staff there to protect the Atlantic convoys.' Irene's defiant tone broached no further argument; they'd been over all this before.

They sat a while staring at the glowing coals, both aware that the sad event on the night of the concert had not really been discussed. Peggy and Sheila had been told only that Irene had suffered a haemorrhage and would need a week off work. Pat and Martha had not spoken of it either together or with Irene. But tonight, in the warm kitchen by the light of the fire, Irene felt able to talk.

'I was very frightened. I didn't know what was happening to me, didn't even know there had been a baby, until they told me it was lost. I keep thinking it should be here still. I would feel it growing every day. I would write to Sandy and tell him and he would be happy ... I would be happy.'

In the range, the coals shifted in a spray of tiny sparks.

'It just wasn't to be,' said Martha, 'but there'll be others.'

'But there'll never be this one. This one is lost. I'll have to write to Sandy and tell him.'

'You don't have to.'

'But ... how can I not?'

Martha shrugged. 'Sometimes it's better not to know. Sometimes it's for a woman to grieve alone.' The silence stretched between them until eventually Martha spoke again. 'When you were very small, before Pat was born, I had a baby ... a boy. He lived only a few weeks. I never imagined a man would grieve so hard. I always thought it was the woman who bore the brunt of it, but your father felt the loss of that wee boy all his life.'

Irene stared at her mother, who continued to look at the fire, and saw her now in a different light. She saw clearly what had always been there, behind and beneath – that her mother expected little and was grateful for small mercies, and that she would always worry about her children and find it hard to let them go.

'What was he called?'

'Robert, after his daddy. Ah well, they're together now I'm sure.'

There were other reasons why Irene was glad to be going back to work rather than whiling away her life at home with her mother. Being a riveter was hard and, truth be told, dangerous work, but she loved the sense of achievement in doing the job and there was nothing better at the end of a shift than casting her eye over the rows of perfectly flush and aligned rivets along the carcass of a bomber. Best of all, there was the company of Macy and her other friends in the aircraft factory and the craic in the canteen during their breaks.

Throughout January rumours were rife that the US Army was on its way to Belfast. Outside of her family, Irene had said nothing about the fact that a small number been in Enniskillen for some time.

Then one morning in the canteen, a woman who worked in the stores came in singing, 'The Yanks are coming! The Yanks are coming!' at the top of her voice. 'You'd better get behind me in the queue, girls, for I'm havin' first pick off the boat!'

'How do you know they're coming?' asked Macy.

'Because me brother works down on Dufferin Quay and he knows for a fact that an American troopship is going to dock there later today. So it's not hard to guess where I'll be after work.'

The long anticipated arrival of American troops was discussed up and down the factory. Expectations were high that their involvement in the war would be the beginning of the end for the Germans.

'After more than two years, it could be all over by the summer,' someone said.

'I hope there's time to get to know the Yanks before they go back home,' said another.

Irene wasn't so sure. 'It's taken nearly three years for the Germans to spread across Europe, it could take the same again to send them back where they came from.'

When the hooter sounded to end the shift, the workers rushed through the factory gates. Some went home for their tea but a good few, the majority of whom were women, headed for the dockside to see if they could catch a glimpse of the Americans. The late afternoon had turned misty and a light drizzle had wet the streets, but the crowd was good-humoured. Lots of the girls linked arms and chatted and laughed, caught up in the excitement: 'They say they're very tall.' … 'Sure they'll look like film stars, so they will.' … 'I'm on the lookout for Clark Gable, myself.'

The gates to Dufferin Quay were closed, but the word was that the Americans would march out, so the crowds waited outside. Those near the front could already see the ship approaching and as it came nearer they caught sight of hundreds of men lining the decks as eager to see what awaited them at a British port as the crowd lining the pavements were to see them.

It was a long wait while the ship docked, but no one minded. They shouted out greetings to each other and waved. One girl, with sharper eyes than the rest, spotted a soldier on the top deck and screamed in delight. 'It's a black man, look! Look! A black man!' and those around her began waving and shouting too.

When the ship was secure and the gangplanks fastened the troops began to disembark. As they did so the band of the Royal Ulster Rifles, waiting on the quayside, struck up 'The Star-Spangled Banner' and from outside the gates a lone voice sang along, accent and word perfect; a young woman with flaming red hair proudly welcoming her fellow Americans to Northern Ireland.

The troops marched through the gates to the sound of clapping and cheering and boarded the trucks waiting to transport them to army camps all over the Northern Ireland. Only then did the crowd become aware of the unmistakeable thud of heavy anti-aircraft guns in the distance, synchronised with the tramp of marching feet.

As her apprentice, Irene worked alongside Macy all day taking direction and advice on simple riveting and assisting her with the more complicated jobs. The one characteristic that set Macy apart from Irene's other friends was that she was open and direct to a fault. She cared little about what others thought of her and always spoke her mind and at length. But when Irene returned to work she thought it strange that Macy didn't mention Finn.

'Are you still going out with him?' she asked.

Macy glanced in the direction of the men working a little distance away then flashed Irene a look. 'No, never see him at all.' And she bent to her work again.

Later in the canteen Irene spoke to her about it. 'What was all that about back there when I asked about Finn?'

Macy leant towards her and whispered, 'Finn doesn't want me to mention him to anyone. He said it would be better if no one knew I was going out with a Catholic.'

'I don't think they'd care, would they?'

Macy shrugged. 'Finn said they would.'

'So is it serious between you?'

'He seems to think it is.'

'And you?'

'I don't know.'

'Well, maybe you should keep your options open now that there are so many Americans around,' Irene laughed.

Over the Easter holiday Irene travelled down to Enniskillen and stayed with Sandy in a bed and breakfast for a few nights. She was a little nervous about seeing him again after four months, but he seemed even shyer than she was. They went to Lough Erne for the day.

He had brought a picnic from the NAAFI and when they'd eaten he said, 'Come on, I'll teach you how to fish.' He'd brought his own fishing line. 'I fish on my day off,' he told her. 'It gets me off the base for a few hours and out in the fresh air.'

He showed her how to bait the hook and cast the line then she stood for a while on the little jetty watching the red and white float drifting on the water.

'Nothing's happening,' she shouted after a while.

'Och, have you no patience, woman?' and she smiled at his soft Scottish accent. He came to her and kissed her briefly before taking the line and checking the bait. She sat with her feet dangling over the water and watched him recast. This was how she first fell in love with him that day in July 1939 on a day trip with her friend Theresa to Stranraer. She had taken a walk with him along the harbour wall to where some wee boys were fishing and he'd helped them with their lines. Now here they were, married a year, and there was that same shy smile that made her heart skip a beat.

When Irene returned to work after the Easter break, the talk was all about the shooting of a policeman in the Lower Falls area.

'D'ye see them uns,' said one of the skivvying women from number four hangar, 'they're a disgrace, so they are, running round burnin' food warehouses when this country is fighting for its life and the men on them supply boats is riskin' their lives so we don't starve altogether. Now they're armed and shootin' policemen! They should lock up those bloody IRA men and throw away the key!'

'You don't know it's them,' said Macy.

The woman glared at her. 'Are you stupid or something? Who else in this city shoots policemen? Bloody Yank, what do you know? Unless you're one of those Irish Americans tryin' to bounce us into the Free State?'

Around three in the afternoon the foreman marched into hangar four flanked by two policemen and went straight to the plane where Macy and Irene were working. They halted at the bottom of the steps and one of the policemen called out, 'Police! Miss Macy come down here immediately!'

A few moments later Macy appeared at the door of the plane. 'What do you want?' she asked.

'We need you to come to the police station. We believe you can help us with our inquiries.'

'What inquiries? I've done nothing wrong.'

'It would be better for you if you came with us now. We're investigating a serious matter.'

At that moment the woman who had argued with Macy in the canteen shouted, 'There ye are, didn't I tell ye she was a republican!'

Macy began to climb down the ladder and Irene called after her, 'I'll come with you.'

Macy turned. 'No you won't, Irene. I'll not have you dragged into this mess,' and she let herself be led down the steps and out of the building.

It was two days before Macy returned to the aircraft factory. In the meantime, Irene had listened to the rumours become more and more outrageous: Macy was a member of the IRA; a German spy; she wasn't an American at all. Some people turned on Irene, 'You're her friend – you must know what she's done!'

To which Irene simply replied, 'She's my friend and I know she wouldn't do anything wrong.'

Shortly after the day shift began on the second day, the policemen returned to hangar four, this time accompanied by Macy and the managing director of Short Brothers and Harland – a man only ever seen arriving and leaving in his Rolls Royce.

He addressed the workers: 'Miss Macy is returning to work today. She has been assisting the police with some vital war work, so important that they are unable to say what it involved. But be clear about one thing – she is an American citizen who came to Northern Ireland to help with the war effort by using her considerable skill as a riveter. She is an honest and brave woman and we are lucky to have her here.'

The workers seemed to accept the explanation, after all Macy was popular in the factory, but Irene caught sight of the woman who had accused Macy of being a republican. She stood in the middle of her friends, arms folded, with a face that could sour milk.

Chapter 30

'But I don't understand, sir. I'm needed out there in the bombed communities. We've done so much to resettle people and they still need help to get things back to normal. I'm just in the middle of arrangements to bring more evacuees back home.'

Cyril Wood, Pat's superior officer, understood that she was reluctant to leave the important work she was doing, but he was certain she was the right choice for this new post. 'You've done exceptionally well Pat, but there are other members of staff who can take over your role. On the other hand, I have no one else who has the experience and knowledge for this task. You must see that.'

'What, making sure the Americans enjoy a full social life by organising concerts for them during their stay here? I hardly think that's important war work!'

'We have no idea how long the Americans will be here, but we're beginning to understand the sort of impact they might have on our community. We need to find off-duty activities for them. They need to be kept occupied, entertained.'

'But what's this got to do with me?'

'Because you come highly recommended. There was an advance contingent of American officers sent over here in early January to look at facilities and potential bases. It seems they were taken to a George Formby concert and they were mightily impressed: so much so that they contacted the organiser, Mr Goldstein.'

'So why don't they ask Mr Goldstein to do it?'

'Because he has business commitments, and in truth we would prefer to have one of our own staff involved. We, ah, would like to keep an eye on what the Americans are doing – socially, I mean – while they are guests in our country. So, imagine how pleased we were when Mr Goldstein recommended you, one of our civil servants.'

'It's all very well me having experience of the sort of concerts Mr Goldstein organises, but I've no idea what American troops would want. Besides, there must be lots of other things needed to keep them occupied.'

'Exactly, that's why your job will be Community Liaison Officer.'

'Really?' Pat didn't hide her dismissive tone. 'And who exactly am I liaising with?'

'Follow me.' He led her to an office just down the corridor and ushered her inside. 'Miss Goulding, I would like you to meet Captain Farrelly of the 5th US Army Corps,' he said, and Pat found herself looking into the face of the most handsome man she had ever seen.

His handshake was firm, but he did not smile. Instead he went behind the desk and stood with his back to Pat staring at the picture of King George VI on the wall.

'Well, I'll leave you two to get started,' said Wood, heading for the door.

Pat stood in the middle of the room waiting for Captain Farrelly to speak. Her eyes wandered over the immaculately pressed shirt stretched across his broad shoulders and up to the closely cropped dark hair flecked with grey and squared off above his collar. Once he moved slightly as if to speak, but turned again to the picture. A full two minutes passed, during which Pat's opinion of Captain Farrelly went from interest to annoyance – the man clearly had no manners. She was about to leave when he swung round.

'Let's get this straight, lady. I didn't ask for this job and I certainly didn't ask for no assistant.' He spoke quickly, his accent pronounced. 'There are over thirty thousand American personnel in this combat zone with plenty more arriving every day and I ain't about to turn these army bases into some kinda vaudeville theatre! As far as I'm concerned, what these men need is additional physical-fitness drill and advanced combat training. Do I make myself clear?'

Pat drew herself up to her full height. 'Perfectly clear, if somewhat misguided. I too did not ask for this job and I am certainly not your assistant. I'm an officer of the Northern Ireland government whose time would be better spent helping alleviate the suffering of families who have been bombed out of their homes rather than pandering to huge numbers of American servicemen who don't know what it's like to go without.'

She paused for breath and was encouraged by the surprise on Captain Farrelly's face. 'I've been asked to liaise with you because I have seen how good entertainment can lift morale. Sometimes people have to be taken out of themselves and given the chance to forget about the war, but clearly that's not something you understand.' Pat knew her voice had taken on a strident tone, that she had gone too far, and there was nothing else for it but to leave the room. At least she managed not to slam the door behind her.

When Peggy and Irene arrived home for their tea that evening, Martha was frying sausages in the pan and singing 'All Things Bright and Beautiful'.

'You're in good form, Mammy,' said Peggy.

'That's because I've been spending our coupons very wisely today. We've Carson's finest beef sausages with onions and gravy, and a rhubarb tart for pudding. Sure you wouldn't get better fare than that at the Carlton restaurant. Now get your hands washed and this table set and then you can read your letters.'

'Letters!' they said in unison.

'Waiting for you on the mantelpiece – once the table's set.'

Irene was surprised to find a five-pound postal order enclosed in Sandy's letter. He'd been sending her a little money now and then, but when she'd seen him at Easter he'd told her he wanted to save up so they would have some money at the end of the war to start their new life together. His letter was tender and full of the same endearments that had thrilled her when they were last together and he told her he could not wait to be with her again in July. She hid the postal order in her drawer and put the letter under her pillow to read again later.

Peggy's letter was from Harry Ferguson. He had written a few times since they met in November at the carnival: friendly letters full of jokey accounts of what he'd been up to at the training camp in the south of England. Well, at least he hadn't been sent overseas yet, but Peggy wished his letters had been more about the two of them and not him and a battalion of soldiers.

When Sheila and Pat arrived home they sat down to eat and by the time the rhubarb tart was on the table the talk turned to the Barnstormers concert that Goldstein had arranged at the Grosvenor Hall.

'We'd better fit in some extra rehearsals for ourselves,' said Peggy. 'We could do one tonight and try out that new Andrews Sisters' song "Don't Sit Under the Apple Tree". I've got the sheet music. Everyone's talking about it.'

'Great title,' said Pat.

'Great tune,' said Peggy.

'Sorry, can't rehearse tonight' – Irene reached for the custard – 'I'm going to the pictures with Macy. It's her birthday.'

'Well, that's just great!' snapped Peggy. 'I thought you said she was off work.'

'She was, but she's back now.'

'Talking of Americans,' said Pat, who'd been looking for a way to tell them about her American encounter, 'I met a captain from the 5th US Army Corps at work today.'

They stopped eating.

'This rhubarb is really good, isn't it?' said Pat, knowing all eyes were on her.

'Pat!' shouted Peggy.

'What?' said Pat.

And her sisters bombarded her with questions.

'How did you meet him?'

'What was he doing there?'

'What was he like?'

She finished her pudding, set down her spoon and, knowing she held the stage, took her time and made the most of it. 'The uniform is very smart – especially when you see it up close – a sort of olive green colour, I would say.'

'Never mind that,' said Peggy, 'what was *he* like?'

'His manners were none too good.'

'Manners!'

'But I soon put him straight.'

'Was he young, old, tall, short?' asked Irene.

'What colour was his hair and were his teeth really white?' asked Sheila.

Peggy leaned in close. 'And what was his name?'

'Captain Farrelly was quite tall, broad shoulders and he had dark hair. Couldn't tell you about his teeth – he never smiled. I'm supposed to be working with him, but I think I've put paid to that idea. And before you ask, no, I didn't think he was attractive and, anyway, he was far too old for me.'

When Irene met Macy outside the YMCA she was surprised to see her dressed up and her hair in a French pleat with curls carefully arranged on the top of her head. 'You're a bit overdressed for the pictures, aren't you?' laughed Irene.

'That's because I'm going dancing, honey, and so are you!'

'But look at the state of me.' Irene was dressed in her trousers and a jumper.

'Hey, you look great. I've decided I don't wanna spend my birthday at the movies. I promise you we won't stay late.'

The Kingsway, a dance hall off Castle Street, had a good resident band for dancing, but it was also a well-known fact that the management didn't mind if those dancing liked a drink or two. Macy had a bottle of Yates's Australian wine in her handbag and she wasted no time in heading to the toilets to drink it.

'What have you got that for?' asked Irene when she saw it.

'Because after the week I've had I need a drink. Here, it's for you too.'

'I don't want it. I don't mind dancing, but I'm not drinking.'

Macy took several mouthfuls then put it in her handbag and headed for the door. 'Come on then, let's have a dance.' Just then the door opened and the woman from the aircraft factory who had had the argument with Macy came in.

'Well, well if it isn't the Yankee republican! Enjoy your time in Mountpottinger police station, did ye? Ye didn't fool anybody – helpin' the police with important war work, my arse!'

'Get out of my way,' said Macy and pushed past her.

'You'll get what's comin' to ye all right,' the woman called after her.

'Best give her a wide berth,' said Irene.

'Sure will,' said Macy, 'with a butt that big.'

Inside, the dance hall was dimly lit. Coloured spotlights were dotted around the room and there was a small spotlit stage at the far end with a three-piece band: piano, snare drum and double bass. Tables and chairs were arranged round the edges of the dance floor. Irene barely noticed any of this, for it was no different to any other dance hall, but her heart skipped a beat at the sight of thirty or more American soldiers lounging at the tables or standing at the edge of the dance floor. They were making a noise loud enough to drown the band. It took only seconds for them to notice Macy who stood out because of her height and style and, by the time she and Irene reached the counter where drinks were being sold, they were surrounded by Americans clamouring to buy them a drink.

One soldier had pushed himself to the front. 'Hey guys, take it easy. As the highest-ranking GI in the room' – he pointed to the stripes on his arm – 'I get to buy these ladies a drink. What'll it be, orange juice or lemonade? That's all they got!'

Macy gave him her dazzling smile. 'Jeez, the guy's from Brooklyn! How about that?'

The sergeant looked confused. 'You been practising the accent?'

'Been speaking it all my life, born in Queens overlookin' the East River.'

'Well I'll be darned,' he shouted, 'she's one of us!'

The evening wore on and Irene and Macy remained the centre of attention. They danced with every GI at least once and laughed and chatted with them every time they sat down. There were other women there, including the woman from Shorts and her friends, but although the GIs danced with them too, it was clear that it was Macy and Irene they wanted to be with.

By ten o'clock Irene was getting anxious. She was supposed to be at the cinema and would be expected home no later than half past.

'You stay,' said Irene, 'I'll be fine.'

But Macy insisted she was leaving too. Outside they stood for a few moments in the light of the doorway.

'We can come back another night. It'll be just as good,' said Macy.

Irene went off to catch her bus while Macy had only to walk the short distance to the YWCA. Within a few yards Irene heard shouting and the sound of a scuffle coming from behind her. She looked round and could just make out a group of figures and flickering torches. She hesitated, uncertain what to do, but at the unmistakeable sound of Macy screaming, she ran back. Macy was on her knees, her face illuminated and someone was standing over her.

'It's her all right!' a voice said.

There was the flash of a blade and Irene screamed. Behind her the dance hall door was flung open, flooding the street with light, and several GIs rushed out and began to fight with Macy's attackers. Irene skirted round them in search of Macy and all at once her blood ran cold. Macy was sitting on the ground, head bent forward, and all around her lay her beautiful red hair which had been shorn from her scalp.

'Oh my God, Macy!' Irene put her arms around her friend. 'Are you hurt?'

'No, I'm okay,' but Irene felt her shaking.

In the poor light, it was impossible to make out Macy's attackers.

'Who are they?' asked Irene. 'Is it that woman from work?' Her thoughts raced on. 'It's because we were with the Americans!'

There was the sharp blast of a police whistle, and the sound of running feet. Someone shouted, 'It's the peelers, so it is!' and Macy's attackers fled, leaving the GIs shouting after them.

When the police saw the Americans they immediately ordered them back into the dance hall. 'Brawling again? Over some slut was it? Get inside so we can call the military police.'

'They should be getting an ambulance for you. I'll tell them!' shouted Irene.

But Macy grabbed her arm. 'No, I'm not hurt. I don't want any fuss. It's my own fault.'

'No it isn't, those people attacked you. Look what they've done to you!'

'Stop it, Irene. You don't understand. It's not about the Americans. If it had been you'd be the one who lost her hair, not me. No one would get angry about me, an American, fraternising with GIs. No, this is much worse.'

'How could it be worse?'

'This is about the policeman who was shot dead.'

'What's that got to do with you?'

'It's to do with Finn. He was taken into custody with other suspected IRA men after the shooting. He gave me as his alibi, said I was with him all night. When the police came to the factory and took me away it was because they thought I was involved. But I wouldn't lie to the police. I told them I wasn't with him. They didn't believe me at first, but on the night of the shooting I was in the YWCA as usual; people saw me in the dorm and after lights out I sat up half the night with a girl who was ill. Do you see, Irene? His alibi was false and, because I wouldn't lie for him, that was my punishment. I recognised one of those people. I'm lucky to be alive.

'There's something else you should know. I saw your friend Theresa at the police station. They arrested Finn's brother Michael as well.'

Irene looked at her friend's beautiful face and the ugly scraps of hair on her skull. 'What are you going to do?'

'First thing, I'm going to buy a turban. After that I'll carry on building planes.'

'But your lovely hair,' Irene was close to tears as she picked up a handful, but Macy knocked it to the ground. 'It'll grow back,' was all she said.

Chapter 31

When Pat arrived at Stormont the following morning she went straight to her desk in the Ministry of Public Security with every intention of finishing the list of evacuees due to return home the following week. She had been there no more than half an hour when she looked up to see Captain Farrelly standing at her desk.

'Okay, lady, time to go.'

'I beg your pardon?' Pat was aware that the other clerks had stopped work at the sight of an American officer, curious to know why he was speaking to her.

'I've orders to tour the US bases to see if they're suitable for' – he struggled to find the words – 'social events, and you're to accompany me on the tour as a representative of the Northern Ireland government.' He couldn't have looked more annoyed if he'd tried.

'Oh yes,' said Pat, 'and would those social events include concerts?'

'I'm told that might be possible.'

'Only possible?'

'Depending on the facilities on the bases.'

That would do to be going on with. Pat took her coat from the back of her chair and a notebook and pencil from her desk and followed Captain Farrelly out of the office and into the warm May sunshine where a US Army jeep was parked with its engine running.

They drove south and neither said a word until they were out into the country where the hawthorn hedges were in full flower and the whin bushes in bud.

'We didn't get off to the best start yesterday. I'm Tony Farrelly.' Without taking his eyes off the road he held out his hand and she shook it.

'I'm Patricia Goulding.'

'It seems our governments are expecting the pair of us to keep the US Army entertained until they're sent off to fight. Like I said yesterday, that's thirty thousand US troops and counting. I'll be straight with you – I don't think a few concerts will cut it. Physical exercise is the key – it gets them fit and tires them out.'

'And that's your solution, is it?'

'Well, it's more than that. I'm going to get a baseball league going with teams from the different companies. I'll be looking for a field at each base that's suitable for conversion to a baseball ground.'

'I'm not traipsing round the countryside with you looking at fields! I've told you I'm expected to get concerts organised.'

'Oh yeah and how often are they likely to happen?'

'How about every time you have a baseball game?'

They drove on and the morning sun grew warmer. The captain took a pair of sunglasses from his shirt pocket and put them on. Pat observed him as he drove, noticed his skin had a glow about it as though he'd spent some time in the sun. This close to him, she realised he might be younger than she thought. They arrived at the first camp around lunchtime and met with a major there. He seemed anxious to get some social events organised.

'Bored soldiers get soft – lose their discipline,' he told them. 'We'll go eat, then you can take a look around, talk to the men if you want. Let me know what you can do.'

The mess hall was a good size, filled with long tables and folding metal chairs. There were windows down one side and, high above them, rafters made from steel girders and a corrugated iron roof were visible. As they queued with the soldiers for their lunch, Pat was surprised at how informal it all was. Officers chatted and laughed with ordinary soldiers. Several of the men smiled at Pat and called out 'Hi!'

There was so much food to choose from – some of it Pat didn't recognise.

'Meatloaf is always good. You should try it,' said Captain Farrelly and passed her a portion.

She did recognise ice cream even though she hadn't had any for a few years. Finally, he reached out and grabbed two bottles of Coca-Cola, flicked off their tops and handed one to her. She had seen the distinctive bottle so many times in films and often wondered what a Coca-Cola would taste like and now she had one, ice-cold in her hand. Just wait till her sisters heard about all this!

The major was keen on the baseball league idea and said he would take them to see a suitable field, but he warned it would take some money to get it playable.

'Don't worry,' said Captain Farrelly, 'whatever it takes; the budget is big.' Pat caught his eye and smiled.

The major turned to Pat. 'Now tell me about these concerts, Patricia.' She was flattered that he had remembered her first name and had chosen to use it. Captain Farrelly had not called her by any name – either Miss Goulding or Patricia – since they met.

'I've been involved in concerts since the war started,' she told him. 'Variety shows, you know, singers, dancers, comedians – lots of different acts. They're very popular with the civilians and the military – the British Army, I mean.'

'We really need something like that. The men get to see films, but they're often out of date or so British that the guys just don't get what's going on. Newspapers and radio don't have any relevance to them either. I'll be honest, Patricia, the guys have money to spend, but nothing to spend it on but drink and dames and both of those usually lead to trouble.'

'A few concerts won't stop that,' said Captain Farrelly.

The major shook his head. 'Maybe not, but we have to start somewhere. Baseball games and concerts sound good to me, and if you can solve the problems we have to deal with when soldiers are in Belfast on one- or two-day passes, that would be even better.'

'What sort of problems?' asked Pat.

The major looked a little embarrassed. 'They get into trouble in the pubs and dance halls, trying to pick up girls mostly. The local guys don't like that so they get into fights. Before we know what's happening they're being picked up by the police – does a lot of damage that kind of thing.'

On the way back to Stormont, Captain Farrelly talked enthusiastically about the baseball field and how easy it would be to level the ground and maybe construct some seating – bleachers he called it.

'And what about the concerts?' asked Pat. 'The major seemed very keen to get them started.'

'I ain't so sure they'd work. A mess hall is hardly suitable.'

'Nonsense!' said Pat. 'With stage blocks and decent sound and lighting it would do very well and of course we'd have to find a piano.'

'That all sounds expensive.'

'Well, like you said, the budget is big.'

'But you heard the major, he thinks stuff over here isn't relevant to our guys. Some Irish baloney ain't gonna keep them entertained.'

'Why are you always coming up with reasons why there shouldn't be concerts? You've no idea what they're like!'

'I can guess.'

'Why don't you do better than that? Why don't you come to the next concert I'm involved in?'

'I just might do that!'

'I'll get you a ticket,' Pat snapped back.

They didn't speak another word until the jeep pulled up in front of Stormont. Pat climbed out and was about to walk away when Captain Farrelly leaned across and handed her a brown paper bag.

'I got you these,' he said and in a moment he had swung the jeep around and driven away. It was four bottles of Coca-Cola.

That evening after tea Irene was writing a letter to Sandy and Sheila and Peggy were reading some magazines that Betty had passed on to them.

'What are you doing, Peggy?' asked Pat.

'What does it look like?' said Peggy without looking up from the magazine.

'We need to get rehearsing – the Grosvenor Hall concert's next Saturday.'

'That's a bit rich coming from you isn't it? Plenty of times I've wanted to rehearse and you lot have always had an excuse not to.'

'It's a big concert. Important people might be there,' Pat argued.

'Like who?'

'Like a captain in the US Army for a start.'

Her sisters stopped what they were doing and stared at her.

Peggy laughed. 'Don't tell me, Captain Farrelly, who never smiles and is too old for you, is coming to see the show.'

'He's not that old,' said Pat.

'Ooooh, had a change of heart, have you? Persuaded him to come and watch you sing? Maybe that'll put a smile on his face.'

'Don't be so silly! There's a chance the Barnstormers could be invited to sing at some American bases, but they need to see the show first and it has to be very good.'

'Wouldn't it be great to perform for the Americans?' said Sheila.

'Imagine the spread they would have for us in the officers' mess!' said Irene.

'I can assure you it's excellent,' said Pat, 'particularly the meatloaf.'

'Meatloaf?'

'Yes, and the Coca-Cola is very good too.'

'You've tasted it?'

'Of course, I had it today when I visited one of their bases.'

'What did it taste like?'

Pat fetched the four bottles from her bag. 'You can have one each when we finish rehearsing.'

There were whoops of joy and Peggy burst into a chorus of 'Drinkin' rum and Coca-Cola … Workin' for the Yankee dollar'.

The following day Captain Farrelly was waiting for Pat when she arrived at work. 'Hi,' he said with a hint of a smile. 'Are you okay to visit a few more bases?'

'Of course, Captain Farrelly,' and she too attempted a smile.

As they walked to the jeep he said, 'I'm not sure we got off on the right foot you and me, how's about a new day, a new start?'

'All right,' said Pat.

'My name's Tony. What should I call you?'

'Patricia, Pat … I don't mind'

'My sister's Patricia, we call her Patti at home. How'd you like to be Patti?'

And to her surprise Pat found herself saying, 'Why not?'

The miles flew by in Tony's company with his stories about life in the army. He'd joined up straight from college. When the war in Europe broke out he hadn't expected to fight, but the bombing of Pearl Harbour had changed everything. She could see how determined he was to be involved. His frustration at being assigned the job of organising the leisure time of the US troops was evident and slowly she came to realise that it wasn't her that he resented, but the prospect of spending the war behind a desk. By the end of the week they had visited all the US camps within driving distance of Belfast and had set in motion the work to prepare the baseball fields. Pat had made detailed notes on everything that was required and left copies with the officers in charge. Her notes were equally detailed about the concert facilities, but she and Tony agreed to wait until after the concert at the Grosvenor Hall when, together with Goldstein, they would decide on the most suitable acts for an American audience.

'Can you get me a couple of extra tickets for the concert?' he asked. 'Me and the guys thought we'd make a night of it in Belfast – dinner, the show, some drinks maybe, just like back home.'

'I think that could be arranged,' said Pat, 'if in exchange we can borrow three US Army uniforms – the smallest you have.'

'Sounds kinda interesting. What are they for?'

'You'll have to wait until Saturday.'

The atmosphere backstage at the Grosvenor Hall was electric. Knowing that three American officers would be watching the show was very exciting, but the thought that their performance tonight could lead to regular concerts for the US Army was enough to ensure that even the most seasoned performers found it difficult to remain calm.

When Pat arrived with three GI uniforms and hung them up on pegs at the back of the dressing room, everyone crowded round, anxious to see them up close.

'They're such good quality,' said Irene fingering the material. 'No expense spared for the Yanks, eh?'

Peggy picked up the cap and put it on her head at a jaunty angle and saluted.

'Leave them for now,' said Pat. 'It's not time.'

Goldstein arrived just then in the dressing room and also went to look at the uniforms. 'Excellent. Excellent – something a bit special for the final act,' he said. Then he climbed onto the upturned crate set out for him, clapped his hands and called for order.

'Time for one of his stirring Churchill speeches,' Peggy giggled.

'Sssh!' Pat snapped. 'Try and behave yourself.'

'Pardon me,' said Peggy. 'Here's me a mere assistant director, while you have the ear of the entire US Army!'

Goldstein regarded the company standing before him – his Barnstormers. He seemed to take his time as though collecting his thoughts. He looked into each and every face until he was satisfied they were calm, focused, ready.

'There have been so many significant moments in the history of this company, some overwhelmingly exciting, others so sad we could hardly bear to perform. Tonight is, in effect, an audition and we must rise to the occasion. The Americans are now in this war and have chosen Northern Ireland to begin their campaign. We deserve to be a part of that, but we must show them our mettle and our talent. The Barnstormers is a superb company and can bear comparison with the finest the USA has to offer. So I want to tell you that your final rehearsal on Sunday was the best show I have seen, but tonight you will do even better.' With a flourish, he raised his arm high in the air. 'Tonight you will excel!'

The opening music for the concert was 'Yankee Doodle Dandy', performed by a small orchestra that Goldstein had put together to accompany the acts. When the curtains opened the Templemore

Tappers marched on stage in stars and stripes costumes. They paraded with precision, shaking their pompoms, following a girl tossing a baton. Throughout the first half, Goldstein stood at the back of the hall, observing each act closely and trying to imagine the performances seen through American eyes. It soon became apparent that the comedy routines would need different material. Jokes about the Belfast experience of wartime that brought hoots of laughter from the local audience, would fall flat in front of GIs. The acts came and went – Sheila's Ella Fitzgerald songs and Macy's stylish tap routine in dinner suit and homburg, both American in origin, drew warm applause.

The Golden Sisters had their usual spot as the final act of the first half. They stood in the wings in their US Army uniforms. A bugle sounded the reveille and they marched on stage, turned and saluted. 'This is the Army, Mister Jones,' they sang. It was a lively tune making fun of a new recruit who had joined up, expecting home comforts. It brought laughter from the audience and Pat thought she could hear Tony laughing from his seat close to the front of the stage. For their second song, Peggy crossed to the piano at the side of the stage and Pat and Irene joined her to sing 'Rum and Coca-Cola' but at the end of the first verse Irene shouted, 'Stop, stop!' Her sisters feigned confusion and the audience wondered what was going on.

Irene went on, 'You can't move in Belfast without bumping into a guy from the good ol' USA. I bet there are some here tonight.' She put her hand to her forehead and scanned the audience. 'Is there an American in the house?'

There was a shout from the audience. 'Can you stand up for us?' shouted Irene. 'Can we get a spotlight on our American visitors?' Tony and his two friends were bathed in light and the audience clapped politely. 'No don't clap them, they haven't done anything yet!' she went on. 'I heard that it was the Americans who invented the Lindy Hop – would one of you like to come up and show us how it's done.' There was some shaking of heads and embarrassed refusals.

'Can't do it without a partner!' said the tallest GI.

'No problem,' said Irene and she went down the steps into the

298

audience and took the GI by the hand. 'What's your name?' she asked when they were centre stage.

'Dwight,' he said.

'Right, Dwight! Tell me have you ever been to John Dossor's?' The audience laughed at the reference to Belfast's famous dance hall. Dwight looked confused, but Irene took his hand and slipped it round her waist and took his other hand in hers. 'Let's go!' she shouted and Peggy belted out the fast-paced 'Rum and Coca-Cola' with backing from the orchestra while Pat sang.

Dwight grinned and entered into the spirit of the performance. He had clearly danced the Lindy Hop many times and was soon swinging Irene round, trying different lifts, and at one point danced away from her to show off a few moves never seen in Belfast. Irene stood back and clapped along, while the audience cheered him on. They finished with a spectacular lift and Dwight set Irene back on her feet and leaned over to kiss her as the curtain came down.

Backstage, Goldstein and Pat discussed the first half.

'I didn't think there was enough glamour,' said Pat.

'I agree. We're missing something like Macy's Ginger Rogers' routine.'

'We could put that back in for the second half.'

'We don't have the dress, do we?'

'Yes, it's in the trunk,' said Pat.

'But they'll see her shaved head.'

'Not if we can cover it up. I'll think of something.'

'Well you had better be quick.'

Goldstein went to find the crooner to ask if he could sing an extra Bing Crosby song at the start of the second half that would give them more time to sort Macy.

'But I'm a bit rusty with that second one,' said the crooner.

'Not as rusty as the orchestra are, so you had better show them how it goes!'

Peggy, as Pat had hoped, took on the challenge of Macy's hair.

She eyed up Macy as she stood in the dress. 'We'll take the chiffon that's round the neckline and–'

'You can't do that. It'll make it way too low.' wailed Macy.

'Nonsense,' said Peggy. 'These strapless dresses are designed not to move; the chiffon's just for show. Anyway, what did Goldstein say? We need more glamour! Then we'll trim off some of this stiff petticoat underneath. It's the same colour as the chiffon. Pat, go and collect some jewellery from the Tappers. They're always covered in that cheap sparkly stuff. And while you're about it, shoot that bloody crooner – he's murdering that song!'

'No need to swear,' said Pat.

As the strains of 'Cheek to Cheek' began, Peggy was in the wings with Macy. 'Just be careful not to dip your head too quickly. The petticoat material is wrapped round tight, but the chiffon is only attached to it by the brooches. Macy nodded, hoisted up the dress and swept onto the stage.

She was a picture of elegance, moving effortlessly to the music, so light and graceful. The dress clung to her curves and her beautifully fashioned turban glittered in the spotlights. As the final bars played, Macy finished statue-like centre stage, her arms gently lifted upwards. There was a burst of rapturous applause and she smiled her thanks. Then the audience began to cheer and Macy swept into a deep curtsey and bowed her head. The turban, top heavy with the Tappers' brooches, tipped forward and in a flash Macy reached upwards and caught it. Too late, she felt the top of the dress slip – there was a gasp from the audience and the men stood as one and roared their approval.

The Imperial Hotel on Donegall Square had recently been refurbished and was attracting well-to-do Belfast couples as well as businessmen from further afield. The walls of the lounge were panelled in pale oak and the dark blue upholstery with gold trimmings gave it an air of luxury. Goldstein, anxious to impress, had reserved a cosy corner area for the after-show discussions and had ordered coffee, brandy and cigars.

He had anticipated meeting the Americans with Pat as liaison officer and Peggy as assistant director, but when all four sisters emerged from backstage together and everyone was introduced,

Tony Farrelly insisted that they should all come along. On the way to the hotel Peggy fell into step with Tony and every now and then Pat, who was walking ahead with Goldstein, caught the sound of their laughter.

'The thing is, Peggy, you guys are real friendly, but Ireland's so different, you know. In the camp it's just like being in the US. The food and bunkhouses are the same, we mix with the same guys, but when we come away from that, like into the city, well it's all kinda strange. We tried to find a restaurant tonight, but to be honest pretty much everywhere was closed and then we found a little place but ...' he laughed. 'Let's just say, it wasn't what we're used to. Same with the room we got for the night.'

They came in through the hotel's revolving doors and Tony was clearly impressed. 'Wow, wish I'd known about this place.'

'Maybe there should be restaurants and hotels just for the US Army – like a home from home,' laughed Peggy and nothing seemed more natural at that moment than for Tony to step aside and usher her past the huge coffee table towards the comfortable sofa and, just as naturally, when she sat down Tony sat next to her. Pat ended up opposite them and watched in disbelief as her sister flirted and Tony fell under her spell.

The coffee was served and Goldstein began. 'First of all I must apologise for the unforgivable incident with ... ah ...' – he searched for a polite form of words to describe Macy's indiscreet revelation – 'the décolletage mishap with Ginger Rogers' dress.'

All three officers looked at each other and couldn't contain their laugher.

'Jeez,' said Dwight, 'is that what it was? Where I come from we'd call that–'

'Easy, buddy, there are ladies present!' said Tony, but by this time the girls had given up any semblance of modesty and were rocking with laughter too.

Goldstein tried to continue. 'Obviously there will be no such burlesque in future performances.'

'You mean the guys back at base won't get to see that?' Dwight feigned disappointment.

'It ... it would be entirely inappropriate,' Goldstein stuttered.

'Don't worry, sir,' said Tony. 'He's pulling your leg. Now let's get down to business. We think your show was great.' He looked at his fellow officers, who nodded their agreement, 'and we'd love to have you perform for our men, but I'm afraid a few of the acts would have to go.'

The girls looked anxiously at each other.

'We are glad you liked it,' said Goldstein. 'Pat and I also discussed a few adjustments.'

'The fact is,' Tony went on, 'the gags weren't funny at all and the whole thing needs a compère who can chat to the boys between the acts, tell a few gags, get them in the mood. You know the kind of thing?' Without waiting for an answer he went on. 'The ventriloquist and the magician would also have to go and a few other things as well.'

By now the post-show excitement had faded and the girls sat glum-faced.

'Was there anything you did like?' asked Irene.

'Sure, there was. We loved everything that reminded us of home: you girls with all the familiar songs; the dancers and Macy; the crooner too.'

'So where do we go from here?' asked Pat.

'Well, Patti, you and I will have to find some home-grown American talent to fill the gaps. There are plenty of wise guys in the camps.'

On the way home there was excited talk about the prospect of touring the US bases, but Pat spoke not a word and Irene, squeezed next to her in the back of Goldstein's car, could sense that she was seething.

Once inside the house, Peggy couldn't resist teasing Pat. 'He's very handsome your captain, isn't he?'

'He's not my captain.'

'No, of course not, he's not your type. Though I must say, I found him very easy to talk to and great fun.'

Pat opened her mouth to reply, thought better of it and took herself off to bed.

'Goodnight, Patti!' Peggy called after her.

When the house was still and quiet and everyone was in bed, Irene whispered across the room to Pat, 'Are you still awake?'

'Yes.'

'You shouldn't let Peggy get the better of you.'

'But she deliberately sets out to annoy me.'

'Because you let her – every time. You walk straight into it. She could see you didn't like her chatting to Tony so she started flirting with him.'

'Am I that obvious?'

Irene yawned. 'Pat, men are simpler than you think. You should try taking a leaf out of Peggy's book.'

Chapter 32

By July 1942 the American concerts by the newly-named Stars and Stripes Show were in full swing and several camps were involved in the baseball league. Around the same time Martha became aware of changes in Pat: something about her hair that emphasised her cheekbones; her clothing coupons all spent; her smile wider. Martha didn't know what had brought about the changes, but she told herself that if anyone needed a wee bit of happiness, it was certainly that child.

Pat had been working late every night for a week, telling her mother, 'I'll have my tea warmed up when I get home.' She told Irene she was working on a new project, 'Something really exciting Tony has come up with, but I can't say anything yet.'

Then on Sunday evening while they were all listening to the wireless, Peggy suddenly announced, 'I'm meeting Tony Farrelly tomorrow.'

They looked at her, then at Pat, who appeared not to have heard.

'Why are you meeting him?' asked Irene.

'Oh, I made a suggestion to him a while ago – the night he came to the Grosvenor Hall concert – about opening a place in Belfast for GIs. We're going to discuss it.'

Pat whipped round and glared at Peggy. 'What are you talking about? That's our idea – mine and Tony's – nobody's supposed to know about it!'

'I think you'll find it's something Tony and I discussed ages ago. Anyway, I'm taking him to see some premises that might be suitable.'

'Premises!' Pat snapped. 'What premises? Tony would have told me if–'

'Well clearly he didn't.'

Irene stood up. 'Now stop this right now, Peggy! You're just doing this to–'

'What premises?' Pat asked again.

Peggy smiled. 'The Plaza Ballroom.'

Pat let out a yell of frustration and ran out of the room.

In Stormont the next day there were more raised voices.

'No, it wasn't her idea … well, not really,' said Tony.

'Not really! Was it or wasn't it?'

'Let's say she got me thinking–'

'I'll bet she did!'

'Listen, will you? She just said it would be good for GIs to have places to go that were just like back home.'

'Well, there you are! Next thing you're having lunch and looking at premises. We've been working on this together, now all of a sudden it's you and Peggy!'

'Is that what this is all about? Your sister?'

Pat opened her mouth to shout and closed it again. And the tears began to prick her eyes. 'Don't be ridiculous.'

'Patti, will you let me explain?'

She slumped into a chair and stared at the floor.

'On Saturday I ran into Goldstein on Royal Avenue,' Tony began. 'You and I had talked about the sort of premises we'd need for a GI club. So I asked him, on the off chance, if he knew somewhere. He suggested the Plaza; he said he knew the realtor and would arrange for me to see it. Next thing I'm in his shop and he's organised everything, even suggests that I should take Peggy with me because she knows the building well. I was going to tell you this morning so you could come with us.'

'Come with you! Me? Set foot in the Plaza again? Never!'

Pat spent the rest of the morning organising transport for a concert to celebrate the opening of the new US base at Langford Lodge on the shores of Lough Neagh, but the thought of Tony and Peggy at the Plaza was never far from her mind. By the afternoon she had made a decision and left her desk to walk the length of the corridor to the office of the staffing manager.

When Tony returned it was as though their conversation in the morning had never taken place. 'Oh Patti, you should've been there! The place is incredible, just what we dreamed of. We'll make it a real home away from home for the guys visiting Belfast – a bunkhouse, dance hall, restaurant. Everything! And we can swing it with the money. I'm talking about ripping it out and making it fabulous.'

'Well, I wish you good luck,' said Pat, without looking up from her paperwork.

'What do you mean, you wish me good luck? We're doing this together – you and me.'

'I told you, I'm having nothing to do with the Plaza. In fact, I'm having nothing more to with US liaison. I've requested a transfer to another post.'

'What the hell! A transfer? Why?'

Pat shrugged her shoulders.

'But you can't do that, not after–'

'Yes I can,' and she put on her coat and left.

That night Pat went to bed early, rather than sit in Peggy's company. It was late when Irene came upstairs so she undressed in the dark and slipped quietly into bed.

'Pat, are you awake?'

'Umm.'

'I've been talking to Peggy about her trip to the Plaza today.'

'I don't want to know, Irene. It has nothing to do with me.'

'Oh, but it has. All Tony did was talk about you – how glad he was that he had you working with him – your energy, your ideas. He said that you'd know how to make the club a success. Pat, are you listening?'

'I've asked for a transfer.'

'Ah, Pat, why do you do this to yourself? I saw the way he looked at you on the night of the concert. He knows how beautiful and talented you are—'

'Ha,' said Pat, 'you mean Peggy, don't you?'

'No! Peggy was just being a flirt. He had to look at her, she gave him no choice. Give him a chance, a moment, and you'll see all that I've told you right there in his face.'

Tony was leaning against the side of the jeep when Pat arrived for work the following morning.

'Please, Patti, will you just do one thing for me?' There was an anxious air about him that she had never seen before. 'Come and look at the Plaza and, if you don't think that it's right, I swear I'll forget all about it.'

They drove in silence. Pat shivered as she stepped out of the bright sunshine and into the chill air of the Plaza. The interior was dark, lit only by a small window high above them. She looked around her. She recognised nothing.

'Wait here,' said Tony. 'I'll turn on the electric and we'll have a look around.'

Had she come through this entrance hall the night of the John McCormack concert? Tony called out to her and she crossed the foyer and came through the double doors into the dance hall just as the lights came on. The air was stale – the same trapped air she had breathed that awful night. She shuddered at the memory of it, the shame of it. She took a few slow steps and looked up at the nicotine-stained ceiling and the suspended glitter ball dulled by dust. She did not know this place.

She walked across the scored and stained dance floor to the stage – how small it looked. Part of the curtain had come away from its rail and lay draped on the piano. Was this where she had stood?

The sense of hopelessness she had experienced after William was killed came rushing back and she remembered too the dark time when she couldn't bring herself to sing. But it was here in this dance hall where she truly lost her voice. Lost it ... like those who danced here might lose a scarf, a handkerchief, their inhibitions, their heart.

'Patti, are you okay?' Tony was at her side.

'Yes.'

'You look kinda sad.'

She turned to him, saw the concern in his eyes and something else on his face. 'No I'm not sad,' she said. 'It's this place that's sad.'

'You hate it?'

Pat shook her head. 'No, I don't hate it. It means nothing to me.'

'Do you want to see the rest of it?'

'No, there's no need. Will we rip it all out and make it new?'

Tony nodded. 'Just like we planned – somewhere special for the guys. The ballroom will be beautiful, there'll be concerts. Maybe you'll sing here.'

'We'll see,' said Pat and together they went out into the warm sunshine.

Across the city Irene and Macy were in the aircraft factory canteen having their dinner break.

'So how was your weekend with Sandy. Did you miss the marching Orangemen?'

Irene stared dreamily into the distance. 'It was great. We stayed in a little cottage next to the lough. There was a boat and we rowed out to an island. We hardly saw a soul the whole time. I could have stayed there forever. Did I tell you we're saving up to buy a house? I've opened a Post Office account.'

But Macy wasn't listening, 'Have you seen that?'

Irene followed her gaze across the room to where one of the men was reading the *Belfast Telegraph*. The headline on the front page read 'Six Men on Trial for Police Murder'. Macy borrowed the paper and quickly scanned the details, reading under her breath. '"The men were named as" … no mention of Finn. Wait a minute. "Police are still seeking two other men, believed to be brothers, in connection with the case." Jeez, that'll be Finn and Michael! I know it!'

'What does it mean they're seeking them? If it's Finn and Michael they know where they live; they've arrested them once already.' Irene caught her breath. 'Unless … unless they've gone into hiding.' Irene closed her eyes. It was happening all over again. 'Poor Theresa. The same thing happened with her brother Sean. You remember I told you about him?'

'The boy you almost ran away with to America? You never told me what happened exactly. '

'A policeman was shot during a riot. Sean was there because the police had come to take his father to prison, to intern him, even though he hadn't done anything wrong. They tried to arrest Sean for the policeman's murder, but he got away and hid somewhere in Donegal. A few months later he sneaked back into Belfast because his mother was dying and he wanted to …' Irene bowed her head, remembering. 'I was at the house that night with Theresa when he arrived. It was as though his mother had waited to see him one last time. She took a turn for the worse and Theresa went to fetch the doctor. But the police had found out that Sean was there and raided the house. There was a way out through the roof space and the attics of the terraced houses. Sean and I hid up there … together … until his friends helped him slip away.'

Macy nodded. 'And now the same thing has happened to Theresa again, only this time it's her husband Michael who's on the run. That's tough.'

The Stars and Stripes Show had come a long way since the meeting at the Imperial Hotel. Once they understood that the GIs liked what was familiar or reminded them of home, they increased the number of acts to include some American soldiers. There was now a sergeant from Brooklyn who did a great comic routine, a trio of black tap dancers from Chicago and a small jazz band. Macy had even gained her very own Fred Astaire.

The huge new base at Langford Lodge, built for the repair and maintenance of US aircraft, and rumoured to have cost millions of dollars, had been chosen as the venue for the biggest Stars and Stripes concert so far. Pat had worked hard to coordinate all the arrangements for an evening show in late August. It was to be held in the open air with an audience of one thousand US soldiers. The only thing Pat had left to chance was the weather.

On the morning of the show she awoke to grey skies and fine drizzle and her heart sank.

'They say that Lough Neagh has its own weather; it can be beautiful one minute and blowing a storm the next,' said Irene.

'Well, thank you for that reassuring weather forecast,' said Pat. 'Sure, aren't you a ray of sunshine yourself!'

There was a heavy shower at around four as the bus was approaching the lough and Pat knew that when she got to the base she would have to consult with her contacts there about whether to move the show into the mess hall and reduce the audience by half. She need not have worried – by teatime the rain had stopped, and by curtain up the skies were clear. The specially erected stage was a good size and the sound, when tested, proved to be very powerful. The officer in charge of the technical arrangements assured Pat that it was more up to date than a Broadway theatre and cost twice as much.

Once the show was underway it was obvious that the acts had raised their performances to a new level. The audience response ranged from enthusiastic and lively to quietly attentive and, at some points, the soldiers were deeply moved. It was often the case that soldiers would send messages backstage to the performers they had enjoyed or to ask a girl for a date. The stage manager would collect the scribbled notes and leave them in the dressing room.

One of the Tappers was looking through them and shouted, 'Hey Irene, there's a message here with your name on it.'

'Are you sure?'

Usually the sisters got messages addressed to 'the Golden Sister on the right' … 'the left' … or 'playing the piano'. This message was addressed to 'Irene Goulding' – odd enough for someone to know her full name, but even odder that it was her maiden name. She thrust it into her pocket and after a few minutes stepped outside the dressing room to read it. There were two lines in the middle of the page. Her eyes widened – a shock, a memory, a leap of the heart.

It was usual for the performers to join the officers for a few drinks after the show. This gave the audience enough time to return to barracks. Irene went with her sisters to the mess and stood talking a while with Pat and Tony. She knew instantly that the relationship between the two of them was different now. She was struck by how beautiful Pat looked, how handsome Tony was in his captain's uniform and she envied them that tentative time, before love was declared, when the anticipation of what might be charged every moment together. She made an excuse and slipped away.

In the gathering twilight the stage was silhouetted against the sky. On one side Irene could see a GI pacing up and down and she headed towards him, her breathing quick and shallow. He turned and ran towards her. He held her then, tighter than she had ever been held, his face buried in her hair. They did not speak though there was much to say. At last, he unwrapped his arms from around her to look at her face in wonder.

'I can't believe it's you, Irene. There you were up on that stage singing and I wanted so much to shout your name. I can't believe you're here.' His voice had the traces of an American accent.

'I'm here, Sean, but you shouldn't be! Someone might recognise you.' His dark hair cut close to his head had altered his appearance a little and he seemed broader, stronger than he had been, but still recognisable as the boy who fled Belfast. 'What are you doing here? And in this uniform?'

'A lot of people I knew joined up after Pearl Harbour and I decided to give it a go. It sounded more exciting than working on a building site. I knew we'd soon be sent to fight, but I never dreamed I'd end up back here.'

'But the police, will they not find you?'

'No I don't think so. I haven't used my real name since I left here.

The army records show no trace of Sean O'Hara, but I wouldn't risk going into Belfast, just in case.' He pulled her close again. 'Oh Irene, it's so good to see you. There's not a day I don't think about you,' and he bent to kiss her.

'Wait,' said Irene. 'Wait, this is all too much. A lot's happened since you left. I can't—'

'Sssh! There's someone coming.'

They waited while a group of GIs went by laughing and calling out, 'You doin' okay there, buddy?'

Irene stepped back, 'I have to go now. We'll be leaving soon.'

'Not yet. We need to talk. This is such an amazing thing that's happened, you and me meeting up again.' He rushed on, words tumbling from him. 'There's so much I want to say. And I want to ask you about Theresa. I haven't heard from her in a while. Is she all right? But you can't tell her I'm here because—'

'Stop! I have to go, Sean.'

There was panic in his eyes and he gripped her arm. 'You can't just walk away! I have to see you again. Look, I don't have leave until next month – the last Sunday in September I'm scheduled to drive some officers to a planning meeting in Larne. Will you meet me so we can talk?'

'I don't know if I can.'

'I'll be there for most of the day. I'll wait for you outside the railway station. Say you'll come and meet me – it isn't far. Please, Irene, say you'll come.'

Irene hesitated. She knew she couldn't possibly meet him, but his grip on her arm and the look in his eyes was desperate to see. 'I … I just don't know. I have to go.'

But he pulled her towards him and his lips were on hers and his desperation made her shiver.

Macy had been a bit withdrawn all morning while she and Irene had worked on a cockpit door. True, it was a tricky job in a confined space, but usually Macy would talk Irene through what she was doing and then allow her to try a few rivets herself. Instead she had worked in silence leaving Irene to give her basic assistance. At dinner time they went and sat outside in the warm September sun and ate their sandwiches. It wasn't until they'd finished and Macy had lit up a cigarette that she spoke.

'They hanged that man today, the one who shot the policeman.'

'Yes, it said in last night's paper that it was happening today. The other five men they arrested were lucky, they could have been hanged too.'

'It could have been Finn or Theresa's Michael if they'd found them. Running away has maybe saved them from the hangman's noose. I wonder where they are now?'

It could have been Sean, thought Irene, if he hadn't got away. Could still be Sean if anyone found out he had come back. 'Do you think Finn was involved?' she asked.

'I don't think he'd kill anyone. I suppose he might have been caught up in something. You hear things about factories being set alight and equipment being sabotaged.'

Ever since the night of the concert Irene hadn't been able to get Sean out of her head. Every night she had tossed and turned thinking about his demand to meet him and the crush of his arms around her.

'Macy, if I tell you something you won't …' – she looked at her friend – 'no, of course you wouldn't.'

'What is it? Is something wrong?'

'You remember I told you about Sean?'

'Theresa's brother?'

Irene nodded and looked across at a group of girls laughing in the sunshine. 'I've seen him; he's come back.'

'Back from America? You saw him?'

'Sssh,' Irene hushed her and whispered, 'he was at the concert last week. He's a GI now. I spoke to him.'

'Wow. What happened when you saw him?'

Irene sighed. 'It was so strange, as though he'd never been away. He …' How much should she say? The way he held her, kissed her? 'He asked me to find out about his sister Theresa, wanted to know if she was all right.'

'But you haven't seen her in a while, have you?'

'I really should go and see her anyway. I don't know where she went to live after she got married, but I could go round to her father's house. It's off the Falls Road, not far. I might go after work one day.'

'Be careful, Irene, there'll be a lot of bad feeling after the execution. They won't want strangers asking questions. Look what happened to me for getting too involved.'

'I'll be careful, keep my head down. I'd like to make sure she's all right.'

When the hooter sounded for the end of dinner time, Macy finished her cigarette and ground the butt under her foot. They were well into their afternoon's work when Macy suddenly said, 'How will you let him know about his sister?'

In their Stormont office, Pat and Tony were poring over a set of architectural drawings. In the space of just a few weeks the US Army engineers had surveyed and drawn up detailed plans to convert the Plaza into an American services club. The proposal had been approved and the finances secured through the American Red Cross.

'I can't believe it,' said Pat. 'Do things always get done so fast in America?'

'Sure do,' said Tony. 'Throw some money and enough man-hours at something and it gets done real quick. We'll be able to have a grand opening in October.'

Pat leaned over the plans and tried to get her bearings. Starting with the entrance, her finger traced a route through to the ballroom with its bar and stage, on to the mess hall and kitchens, then upstairs to the sleeping areas and finally a lounge and library. Tony stood beside her, his head bent towards hers watching her finger wander through the rooms. Her hair had fallen forward and she caught it and shaped it behind her ear. That's when she became aware of his eyes on her. She turned. His face was so close to hers she felt embarrassed and straightened up. He did the same and she found herself looking at the weave of his tie. He reached out and took her index finger from the plan and brought it to his lips … a pause … she looked up as he kissed first her finger then her mouth.

All the way to Northumberland Street on the bus Irene convinced herself that she was going to see Theresa, not because Sean had asked her to, but because Theresa was her friend and she was worried about her. Her husband and brother-in-law had most likely fled the city and she might need someone to talk to, or to help her in some way. Then a voice in her head would chide, What kind of friend are you? You haven't bothered with her for months!

The street was just as she remembered it – rows of terraced houses opening straight on to the pavement on both sides of the road. In the light of the September evening some children were playing a game of tig in the road, others were swinging on ropes round lamp posts. Theresa's family home was towards the end of the street on the left, just beyond where a group of women stood chatting. Irene smiled at them as she passed. Their conversation halted and she felt their eyes follow her. As she came closer to Theresa's house she sensed something odd about it, but it wasn't until she drew level that she saw the windows were boarded up. Her steps slowed as she looked upwards and she gasped at the sight of the blackened brickwork and the collapsed roof.

There was a shout from one of the women she had passed, 'You need to be careful coming round here, love – there's been trouble. They're a good family but some around here have taken against them.'

'I'm a friend of Theresa's. Would you know where I could find her or the family?'

'No idea, haven't seen any of them since all that bother.'

At the corner of the main road she hesitated outside Theresa's uncle's bar where she and Macy had attended Theresa and Michael's wedding reception. She'd come all this way and achieved nothing. The light was beginning to fail and the more she thought about the burnt-out house the more worried she became. She searched in her handbag for a pencil and a scrap of paper to write on. It wasn't about having something to tell Sean – of course it wasn't – she had no intention of going to meet him.

The smell of stale cigarettes and the whiff of hops pervaded the dimly lit interior of the bar. A couple of old men sat in one corner nursing their half-pints. Irene's heart sank when she saw the heavily built man behind the bar – she'd had a run in with him once before when she had come looking for Theresa. He glared at her, but said nothing.

Irene spoke up, 'I'm–'

'I know fine rightly who ye are.'

'I need to find Theresa.'

'Aye, you and plenty of others.'

'Can you not just tell me if she's all right?'

He turned his back on her. In desperation she held out the piece of paper, 'Will you not just give her this wee message?' He walked away.

She put the paper back in her pocket and walked out. She'd done her best, but as she walked away the tears of frustration were stinging her eyes and she nearly didn't hear the call behind her.

'Missus, will ye wait!' One of the old men from the bar was trying to catch her up. 'If ye've a message for Theresa I'll try and get it to her. Her da's a friend of mine.'

Irene pressed the paper into his hand and felt in her bag for her purse. 'You'll take something for your trouble.'

'Ach no, missus, sure I couldn't do that,' and he tipped his cap and went back the way he'd come.

Chapter 33

Pat loved the newness of everything. Every morning when she arrived for work at the Plaza she looked forward to the sounds of sawing and hammering, the whistling of the workmen, and the smells of plaster, freshly sawn wood and paint. Every evening when she left she marvelled at the transformations the day had brought. By late September the most exciting part of the renovation was ready to begin.

The ballroom was the heart of the building, and pride of place in it would be its unique dance floor, made of specially imported Canadian maple. She had been astonished by the cost, but Tony had shrugged it off.

'It ain't so much,' he said, 'less than it costs to keep a battalion fed and watered for a couple of days.'

It took the best part of a week to lay it and as the maple slowly covered the floor, some of Tony's excitement began to rub off on Pat.

'I've never seen anything like it,' said Pat.

'It's real classy,' Tony said and crouched down to run his hand over the grain. The top of his head was level with her hand. She looked down at his short dark hair, a crew cut he called it, and she felt a sudden urge to touch it, to feel its sharpness against her hand. She saw too the glint of the dog tags around his strong neck and how his broad arms strained the material of his shirt …

'What do you think then, Patti?' He looked up at her, smiling broadly.

'It's beautiful,' she whispered.

It was early on a Friday evening that the floor was finally finished and, when the workmen had gone, Pat and Tony stood in the middle of the ballroom with all the lights blazing and the magnificent Canadian maple floor all around them.

'I can't believe it,' said Pat. 'I love it so much I want to stay here forever!' and she threw back her head and laughed.

Tony stared at her in amazement. 'I've never seen you laugh.'

'Yes, you have.'

'Not like that. Sometimes I wonder why you're sad.'

'Am I sad?'

'Oh, don't look serious again, Patti. I've got a surprise for you, fixed it up today.' He went off to the back of the stage, and returned to stand in front of her a few minutes later, empty-handed.

'What is it? What's the surprise?' said Pat.

'Just wait. Listen.'

Moments later there was the sound of violins and then 'The Blue Danube' waltz filled the room. Tony stepped forward, took Pat's hand and drew her to him and together they swept across the ballroom floor. His eyes never left her face and she studied him too – his gentle smile, the slight cleft of his chin, his kind eyes.

When the music faded, they danced on, the closeness of their bodies and the rhythm in their heads making every step faultless. The ballroom disappeared, the floor was forgotten. She was safe in his arms.

Gently he slowed them down until there was no reason to hold each other, but still he held her and she wished she could stay in his arms forever. His lips parted and she waited, her heart beating fast. He had kissed her once before and now she longed for him to kiss her again. But he straightened up and withdrew his arms.

'Hey, guess what? We're the first people ever to dance in the ballroom of the American Red Cross Services Club!' The spell was broken and Pat felt only embarrassment. It was time to lock up and go home.

The jeep was parked outside. 'I'll take you home,' he said.

'There's no need,' said Pat. He had never offered her a lift before and after what happened in the ballroom she didn't want to sit with him in the close confinement of a car. Besides, she had nothing to say to him.

Tony opened the passenger door. 'I insist, get in.'

His tone brooked no argument. She climbed into the seat and they drove out of the city, Pat staring out of the passenger window, Tony with his eyes on the road. For a while neither spoke.

'I'd like to see where you live,' he said at last and the sharp tone had gone. 'I grew up in a small neighbourhood and on warm evenings people would sit a while on the stoop, just chewing the fat. Kids would play on the sidewalk until it was time for bed. When I joined the army it was like moving to a new neighbourhood with a whole bunch of new friends. Then they assigned me the liaison job and, I'll not kid you, it was tough working with one girl instead of a platoon of guys!' he laughed, 'I guess what I'm trying to say–'

'This is it, on the left,' said Pat and the jeep pulled up sharply at the kerb in front of the grey pebble-dashed house with the neat privet hedge. 'Oh there's Mammy talking to Jack next door.'

'Oh, that's your mom?' and he was out of the jeep and walking quickly over to Martha, his hand outstretched. 'Hi, Mrs Goulding, good to meet you,' he said. Next he turned and acknowledged Jack – 'sir' – and shook his hand.

Then Irene was at the door, smiling broadly. 'Hello, Tony, come on in.'

Martha made Pat and Tony something to eat and afterwards they all sat chatting about the new club and she marvelled at the sight of a US Army captain in her sitting room.

It was after nine when Tony left, promising them all tickets for the opening of the club, and Pat walked with him to the jeep. He opened the passenger door.

'Come sit a while,' he said.

The twilight had gathered, but she could still see his face turned towards her as they sat side by side.

'I'm just a regular guy,' he began, 'I don't do clever talk, so I'll just tell it like it is.' He paused and Pat's heart beat a little faster. 'Patti, you know there's something between us. These last few months working together, I've got so used to you being next to me. I get up in the morning and I can't wait to be with you. I go to bed at night and it's like a movie where I remember the day – I see you in the clothes you wore and little moments like when you smile at something stupid I said. Or that little frown that appears when you're not sure about something, and your voice … Tonight, when we danced, it was beautiful and having you in my arms I wanted to kiss you so much and I think maybe you wanted that to happen too. But … '

'But what?' Pat could see the sadness in his eyes.

'But I couldn't. I know there's another guy, isn't there? And if he's away fighting somewhere … well, I just wouldn't do that.'

How could he think that? She'd never said anything to suggest that she had a sweetheart. 'Why do you think there's someone else?' she asked.

'I've seen the ring around your neck. It's something special. Seen you touch it sometimes too.'

She bowed her head. 'There was somebody, but he's gone.'

Tony raised her chin and saw the tears ready to fall. 'But you still think of him. You miss him, don't you?'

Pat closed her eyes in agreement.

'Do you still love him?'

She nodded and her tears fell on Tony's hand. He pulled her close. A hug to comfort – that was all.

The rain had set in early and the wind whistling around the house blew soot down the chimney and threatened to smother the wee bit of fire in the grate. The girls had already gone to bed leaving Martha to finish her bit of sewing. The news on the wireless earlier that evening had been all about the goings on in North Africa and had unsettled her. She wondered as she stitched how this war, that people said would soon be over, could have extended into the desert. Eventually the stiches began to blur, her heavy eyelids closed and, just as her head began to nod, there was the sudden metallic clacking of the front-door knocker.

'Who is it?' she shouted from the hallway.

'Does Irene Goulding live here?' A woman's voice, close to tears.

Martha opened the door and a figure slipped past her into the hall. Martha closed the door and switched on the light. A young woman who looked vaguely familiar stood blinking in the light, drenched to the skin and shivering.

'Who are you?' asked Martha.

'A friend of Irene's. Is she here?'

There was movement at the top of the stairs. 'I'm here,' Irene called.

'Thank God!' Theresa cried and slumped to her knees.

Between them Martha and Irene half-carried her into the sitting room and lowered her on to the settee. Awkwardly, she leaned back and her unfastened coat fell open.

'Mercy me,' said Martha and Irene gasped when she saw that her friend was expecting a baby.

Martha asked no questions, but sent Irene to fetch towels, dry clothes and a blanket while she put some coal on the fire then heated water for tea and a hot jar.

When Theresa was warm and dozing under the blanket, Martha whispered, 'Now tell me who she is and what she's doing here at this hour?'

'It's Theresa.'

'I thought I recognised her.' Martha's face hardened. 'She's the girl whose wedding you went to? What's she doing here?'

'How should I know? I haven't seen her for months.'

Martha gave her eldest daughter a long hard stare. She knew Irene was a great one for keeping things to herself. She wouldn't lie, but …

There was a sob from Theresa and she sat up. 'I'm sorry, Mrs Goulding, but I had nowhere else to go,' and she covered her face and wept. 'My own people are too frightened to help me.' She took a deep breath and looked at Martha. 'Irene's a good friend and she said if I ever needed her …' and she dissolved into tears again.

Martha pursed her lips. 'Hmm ... I think you'd best tell us the whole story.'

And Theresa told them about the shooting of the policeman, and the police taking Michael, her husband, in for questioning. She knew that he would never have been involved in something like that but others thought different. The police let him go because they had no evidence against him so then people said he must be an informer. Martha's face looked grim, but she said nothing.

He'd had no choice but to go into hiding, Theresa told them, but he wouldn't tell her where he was going and she hadn't heard from him since.

She cried a little then and said, 'It was after that I found out I was pregnant.'

With her husband gone she'd had no money for the rent and had moved back in with her family. Then when the man was hanged for the murder, a lot of people were very angry and that night someone threw a petrol bomb into the house. They were lucky not to be burned alive. A cousin on the Springfield Road had taken her in.

'Then today ...' her voice quivered and her eyes widened as she recalled the terror. 'Today, I was coming back from the shop and I was just cutting through an alleyway when a man grabbed me. I don't know who he was, but he threatened to kill me if I didn't tell him where Michael was.' Instinctively, she spread her hands over her stomach. 'I don't know what would have happened if two women hadn't come past. I pretended to know them, shouted for them to wait and hurried after them. I didn't go back to my cousin's house. I walked into Belfast and sat on a bench outside the city hall. I didn't know what to do – nowhere seemed safe – and then I thought of Irene.'

When Theresa had finished, Martha said nothing but looked at her long and hard. The girl looked like a good feed would kill her; she probably hadn't eaten much in weeks. Her clothes were shabby and her face was drawn and grey. One way or another, men were to blame for this, but as usual it was the woman who bore the brunt. Who knew whether the husband was guilty or innocent, right now it made no difference. He was gone and might never be seen again.

Martha chewed her lip and decided to deal with what was in front of her – a pregnant girl, frightened out of her wits.

'Theresa, you're welcome to stay here for a while. I doubt anyone would look for you in this area, but you'll need to be thinking about somebody else you can go to, a relative maybe, who's away from Belfast.'

'I've nobody but a brother in America,' she said, 'and I haven't heard from him in a long while. Michael and I thought about emigrating there once the war was over – we even got passports and enquired about the fare. A one-way passage costs thirty pounds and I don't have more than a few shillings.'

'Maybe he could send you the fare.'

'I don't think he'd have the money either and sure he's a wife to support.'

'Would your husband have gone over the border, to some of his people there? Or what about England?'

'I don't know of any. He told me nothing, you see, just in case …'

'Well, maybe you could write to your brother, sure you never know. You could do that and Irene'll post it for you. Won't you Irene? Irene, are you listening?'

In the weeks since she had met Sean, Irene had told herself that she couldn't and she mustn't meet him. But in her mind she would see him as he was that night – waiting for her in the dusk, so striking in his uniform – and her heart would quicken. She remembered too the crush of his lips on hers and shivered anew at the excitement of it. And now here she was, on the last Sunday in September, wearing her best dress and Peggy's elegant court shoes, and on a train to Larne. It was because of the letter, she told herself. Theresa had written to Sean but, Irene reasoned, what was the point of posting the letter. He wasn't in America. Really she had no choice but to deliver it in person.

She emerged from the railway station and for a brief moment she almost hoped that he would not be there – that he, unlike her, had realised the foolishness of their meeting.

He was in uniform, leaning against a US Army staff car and his face lit up when he saw her. 'Gee Irene, you're a sight for sore eyes, so you are!' and he went to put his arms around her, but she stepped back.

'Sean, I've come to tell you about Theresa. I've brought you a letter from her.'

He looked uncertain, took the letter but didn't open it. 'Has something happened? Is she all right? Tell me.'

'She wrote the letter to ask you if she could come to stay with you in Boston, if you could send her the fare.'

'Her and her husband want to emigrate?'

'No, her husband's gone.'

'What do you mean – gone?'

'It's a long story. Let's find somewhere quiet and I'll tell you all that's happened.'

They drove a few miles along the coast and stopped at a small town on a bay. They sat watching the waves as Irene told Theresa's story.

'And you're sure my father and the rest of the family have come to no harm?'

Irene nodded.

'And Theresa has no idea where her husband is?'

Irene shook her head.

'God, Irene, I don't have the money for the fare. I have to send my money back home.' He looked away then towards a man pushing a rowing boat down the sand into the sea and wading out after it until it was afloat.

'Sean, I know you're married. Theresa told me. But if she could find the money for the fare could she stay with your wife in America?'

He didn't look at her, didn't answer right away.

'Sean?'

'Yes … yes she can, but where's she going to get the money from?'

'I don't know, we'll think of something, but will you write to her at my house and tell her she'd be welcome in Boston? You'll need to tell her you've joined the army too, but best not to tell her you've been over here.'

'Is there anything else I should know?'

'Yes. Theresa is expecting a baby.'

He smiled. 'Is that it now, Irene, or have you got some more shocks for me?

'No that's it,' said Irene. 'Can you take me back to the station now? I'll need to get home.'

He reached out and took her hand. 'Why don't we stay a bit longer? I've a few hours before I have to drive the officers back to base,' and there was such pleading in his eyes.

What's the harm? she told herself.

He touched her wedding ring. 'You have a husband.'

'Yes, and you have a wife.'

He smiled ruefully. 'But I've always thought of you,' he said. 'Thought about what might have been, the road I couldn't choose. It's strange that we've met again just as I have to leave. Our training's pretty much finished here and we'll be shipped out soon. Don't think I'll ever be back this way again.'

They went down onto the beach and he took her hand to help her over the rocks. He didn't let go when they reached the sand and they walked along the shore. 'Anyone seeing us now would think: there's a GI and his girl spending the day together. Maybe they're in love and planning their future when the war is over,' and he looked sideways at her and smiled.

'What about it?' he asked. Irene looked puzzled. 'Just for today, will you be my girl?'

They chased each other in and out of the sea, found shelter from the wind, ate his chocolate and chewed gum. They talked of how they first met in the Ulster Linen Works, of dancing at John Dossor's and of the night they spent in the cold attic. And it was enough – it had to be. Sandy would have the rest of her life, but today she was Sean's girl.

He waited with her on the platform, his arms wrapped around her. They heard the guard shout 'All aboard!' but they didn't take their eyes off each other. She was leaving him and she wanted him to … he wanted to … but maybe that would be too much. His mouth was close to hers … should she let him? He stepped back.

The whistle sounded. Irene reached out, pulled him close.

One kiss to last a lifetime.

Until yesterday Pat had viewed her two-week recall to Stormont – to organise the return of the remaining evacuees to Belfast – simply as an unwelcome interruption. Then the staffing officer had informed her that, since the full programme of entertainment she and Captain Farrelly had planned would be completed with the opening of the club, she would be returning permanently to her post at Stormont.

She had spent every working day of the past four months with Tony. Together they had organised so many events – concerts, film shows, sporting competitions and now, their biggest project, this beautiful club in the heart of the city. And in that time they had shared so much – the difficult decisions, laughter, anger, frustration, the sheer excitement of seeing their vision come to life. She couldn't believe that in a week it would be over.

She passed under the red, white and blue American Red Cross Services Club sign that had been erected over the entrance and inside she was amazed at the progress made. Everything was on schedule to be ready for the opening night, just a week away.

'Patti, you're back!' Tony came into the entrance hall with a huge grin and hugged her. 'Wait'll you see all the finishing touches. I tell you it's going to be amazing. I've hired us a manager too. You just got to meet him, he knows so much about running a joint like this.'

They crossed the ballroom, where he pointed out all the finishing touches put in place during her absence, and made their way to the office. A man stood with his back to the door going through a sheaf of invoices.

'Patti, I'd like you to meet–'

The man turned when Tony spoke and Pat froze as she came face to face with Devlin.

'What's *he* doing here?' Pat spat out the words.

'I told you, I just hired him.' Tony looked from Pat's horrified face to the sneer on Devlin's. 'Do you two know each other?'

'I will not be in the same building as this man. Not after the way he treated me!'

'Now look here!' shouted Devlin, 'you're the one that lost me my job – you and your sister Peggy. I've been hired by the Yanks to run this place so you can sling your bloody hook. I'll not have you in any building I'm managing.'

In an instant Tony had stepped in front of Devlin. 'Hey, buddy, don't you speak to the lady like that. You've no idea who she is.'

'Oh, I know who she is all right. A useless excuse for a singer and a pathetic–'

The punch caught Devlin square on the jaw and he fell backwards, catching his head on the corner of the desk. Blood poured from his lip and he struggled to rise. Tony grabbed him by the arm, twisted it up his back and marched him to the front door.

'Hey, what's going on? You just hired me to run this place!' Devlin shouted.

'Yeah, and now I just fired you!' and Tony threw him into the street.

When he returned, Pat was sobbing. Tony held her close and soothed her with soft words, but she was crying and shaking, her tears soaking into his shirt. Eventually, she seemed to calm down and when she pushed her hand against Tony's chest, he released her.

'Patti, will you tell me what that was all about?'

She pulled the strands of damp hair from her face and pressed the heels of her hands to her eyes. Where could she begin? How much could she trust herself to tell? She sighed and raised her head.

'He was the manager of the old Plaza, before it closed down. Peggy worked with him for a while. We were to sing here at a big event, but when it came to it ...' Pat's lip trembled.

Tony caught her hand. 'What happened?'

'I couldn't do it. I was on the stage, all the people were there watching and my voice – my voice was gone.'

'Gone? What ... was it some kind of stage fright?'

Pat looked away. 'Yes.'

'And this guy, Devlin, what did he do?'

'There was a huge row. He said such terrible things to me.'

'Is that why you didn't want anything to do with this building – bad memories?'

Pat nodded.

She sensed a tension in his body and his expression hardened as he addressed his words to the wall behind her. 'There's more to it than that, isn't there? Why would you have stage fright? I've seen you perform; you're so confident. I know you're not telling me the truth, Patti!' His eyes widened. 'Wait a minute! Is he the one whose ring you wear around your neck? The one you're still in love with?'

It was too much. She couldn't bear it. William – a good man, an honourable man – mistaken for Devlin! How could Tony think she could have loved that self-serving, sleazy, low character he had just thrown out of the building!

'Don't be so ridiculous!' she shouted.

'Well if it's not him why don't you tell me who it is? This person you love so much who's never here!'

She pushed past him, but he caught her by the arm.

'Goddamnit, you must know how I feel about you. I can't bear it, being so close to you every day, knowing that there's someone else.'

'Well, you won't have to put up with me much longer,' she snapped. 'I'm being sent back to Stormont after the club opens.'

Tony recoiled as though he had been slapped and Pat could have wept again at the hurt in his eyes. The hurt she had caused.

It was Pat and Irene's turn to wash the dishes, while the others, including Theresa, relaxed in the sitting room listening to the wireless. Pat closed the kitchen door and Irene looked up from the sink – she knew that Pat must have something she wanted to talk about. Keeping her eyes on the dishes she was drying, Pat recounted what had happened at the club, the row with Devlin and Tony's mistake in thinking he was someone she'd been in love with.

'Let me get this straight. You'd already told Tony about William, but you didn't tell him he had died?' Irene shook her head in disbelief. 'Then today, Tony more or less tells you he loves you and

328

you still let him think that you're unavailable. Are you in your right mind?'

'But I loved William so much that I can't–'

'What did you just say? You *loved* William? Pat can you not see you're talking in the past tense. You loved him, but he's gone and maybe you need to think about how you feel about Tony – before it's too late.'

Irene washed and Pat dried in silence for a while and the conversation might have finished there, but Irene couldn't leave it. 'How do you feel about having to leave the club?'

'I'll miss it so much.'

'Pat get a grip! You'll miss *him* so much.' Irene sighed at the sadness in her sister's face. 'I'm sorry but, you know, a first love is so strong it never leaves you, especially if it's snatched away. You keep it in your heart, safe and pure, and you find love again. It's not the same, but it can be just as wonderful.'

'I don't know; I get so confused.'

'That's because you love them both. But it's not a choice between the two – William's gone and Tony is right here.'

Pat nodded, 'You understand my feelings better than I do.'

'And sure why wouldn't I?' and she scrubbed a pan furiously before adding, 'Amn't I your big sister?'

The following morning Pat and Tony drove to Windsor Park to check the arrangements for the final of the Uncle Sam Trophy baseball game to be played the following day. Pat had been nervous about facing him after the row about Devlin, but Tony behaved as though the events of the previous day had not taken place. He was buoyant at the prospect of the game.

'I'm sure we'll get a good crowd,' he said. 'It's not every day you get to see baseball in Belfast! Did I tell you I was playing?'

Pat smiled. 'Yes, I think you mentioned it a few times.'

A team of GIs was already there erecting huge tents for refreshments, putting up bunting, marking out the diamond on the pitch.

'Just like a county show back home,' said Tony. 'Only thing we need is the weather.'

But as the morning wore on, dark clouds appeared over the Cave Hill and by noon they were forced to run to the jeep for shelter. It seemed that Tony's mood had darkened too and, as the rain drummed on the canvas roof, they sat side by side in lonely silence.

'Tony, I'm sorry about yesterday.'

'Forget it.' He continued to watch the rain. 'I've sorted all that. A sergeant from my unit used to run a dance hall; he'll manage the club for now.'

'I don't mean that …' The sound of thunder made her pause – gave her a moment to reflect, to decide. 'You asked me to tell you something and I didn't, but I'd like to tell you now.' She glanced sideways at his face – jaw set firm, eyes staring straight ahead.

'His name was William, a civil servant. We sang together and worked together. For a long time there was nothing between us, but gradually we realised how we felt about each other. Soon after that we went to Dublin on business; he had a meeting with the government there. That's where he asked me to marry him, bought me a ring.' Could she finish the story? Say it! Say it! She willed herself to go on. 'That night Dublin was bombed. William was killed.' Her voice was a whisper. 'The next day I came home on my own.'

There were no tears; she was beyond that, there was just emptiness.

She felt Tony's hand on hers, heard the rain quicken on the roof and, after a while, Tony started the engine and drove her home.

Chapter 34

Theresa sat on Irene's bed with her head in her hands. 'I can't believe he's joined the army. Well, that's put a stop to the Boston plan.'

'No it hasn't.' Irene picked up the letter. 'He says here, "You have to get right away from Ireland. I'm trying to raise the money for your fare to America. It will take me a few weeks, but once you're there you can stay in our apartment for as long as you like."'

'But it might take ages for him to raise that much money and I can't impose on your family any longer.'

'He'll get the money, I know he will, and until then you're–' Irene stopped. 'Was that the door?' She went out on to the landing. Martha was in the hallway below talking to someone outside – a familiar voice. She crept back into the bedroom. 'Stay here, Theresa, nice and quiet.'

'Irene,' her mother called. 'Come down a minute, will you?'

The light was fading, but the dark green uniform of an RUC officer was unmistakeable. Ted Grimes, once a close friend of Martha's, was not welcome in her home, not since that bad business two years ago when he had threatened Irene. Martha had never found out the full story but she knew that it had something to do with Theresa's brother who had fled to America. Now Ted was here again and she had no intention of inviting him in. He could state his business on the doorstep.

'I'm here on official business, concerning Theresa O'Hara,' he told Irene. 'I know you've had dealings with her and her family in the past. We need to speak to her about the whereabouts of her husband – wanted for questioning about a serious crime – but she seems to have disappeared. A local informant told us she had gone to stay with a friend.'

'I don't know where she is,' said Irene, 'I haven't seen her for months.'

'Now look here, you've lied to me before.' He took a step forward and thrust his face into hers. 'If I find out you know where she is, your feet won't touch the ground on the way to the police station, my girl, and I'll see to it that they throw away the key!'

'How dare you speak to my daughter like that, Ted Grimes, you're not fit to wear that uniform. And, as for Theresa, you should be ashamed of yourself hounding a pregnant woman!'

'Ho ho, pregnant is she?' he sneered. 'Now, how would you know that?'

Too late Martha realised her mistake, but Irene was quick to jump in, 'A friend from the linen mill told me, of course!' and she slammed the door in his face.

When he had gone, Martha brewed a pot of strong tea and they all sat down to draw up a plan of action to get Theresa out of Belfast in a hurry.

Ted Grimes had been suspicious, but they didn't believe he had the proof to search their house for a woman who had not committed any crime. However, as Theresa pointed out, if the police knew she had gone to stay with a friend, the chances were that those who had bombed her out of the house and threatened her on the street would also know that and would be looking for her. The difference being that they probably did not know Irene and certainly did not know where she lived. Not yet.

They agreed that Theresa should leave for America as quickly as possible, but where would she get the fare?

'Sean will send it. I'm sure of it,' said Irene.

'It's not certain,' argued Peggy.

Pat spoke up. 'We can't sit around waiting. Theresa needs to be away as soon as possible. Did you say the fare was thirty pounds, Theresa?'

'Yes, when Michael and I checked that was the price for a single, Belfast to Liverpool then Liverpool to America.'

And they sat in silence contemplating the huge amount – more than any of them had ever seen at one time.

Eventually, Theresa spoke, 'It's just impossible. You've all been so kind, but I can't stay here any longer. I won't risk anything happening to you or your home. I'll go and get my things,' and she stood to go.

'Sit down,' said Martha. 'We've all night to think of something. Put the kettle on again, Sheila.'

Pat arrived late at the club the following morning and as she crossed the ballroom she heard Tony on the phone in the office. 'Yeah, that's swell, nine o'clock will be fine. Everything will be ready, don't worry. Good … good … can't wait!'

'That sounds interesting,' said Pat.

'Oh, just something about the band tomorrow night. It's sorted now. Is everything okay?'

'Yes, I just had some family business to sort out.'

'Well, Patti, just two more days and you'll be free from all us Yanks.'

'Maybe I don't want to be free of you. I've loved every minute of it – although a day of baseball could change all that!'

'No, you're gonna love it, especially when my battalion wins the trophy. Good day for it too after all that rain yesterday.'

It was already very busy when they pulled up outside Windsor Park. Every battalion had sent a lorry-load of supporters. Children from local schools had been invited to watch and some Belfast people not at work had come out of curiosity.

'There's plenty of time to eat before the game,' said Tony. In the refreshment tent they collected a tray of food and went to sit in the stand. 'The hamburger's good isn't it? You like the ketchup?'

Pat nodded, 'There's something about American food–'

'Yeah, it tastes good!'

'That'll be why you Americans are always eating.'

'Are we?'

'Yeah! Can I try that?'

'Chilli dog? Are you sure?'

'Remember that first day when you took me to look at the army bases?'

'Yeah, you ate two helpings of meatloaf!' he laughed.

'That was when you told me about New York, but you said you lived on Long Island.'

'Yeah, at Long Beach, 'bout forty-five minutes on the Long Island Railway out of the city.'

'What's it like there?'

'Oh, it's just a beach town built on a strip of sand with the ocean on one side and the bay on the other and about ten blocks in between. The houses are mostly timber-framed clapboard with shingle roofs. It's just a couple a blocks from our house to the boardwalk and the beach.' Tony leaned back on the bench and stared into the distance. 'Of course, summers are real hot. We go swimming in the ocean to cool off, then come back and lie under the boardwalk outta the heat. Winters are hard though, twenty below some days, and when a blizzard comes through and dumps four feet of snow, well we just cosy up to the stove.'

'I can just imagine it,' Pat said softly.

Tony turned towards her. 'Patti–'

'Hi guys!' It was Dwight, Tony's fellow officer. 'Game starts in thirty minutes, Tony – team captain's asking for you.' He nodded at Pat. 'Are you coming to watch? I'll sit with you, if you like, and explain the rules.'

'It's a bit like rounders, isn't it?'

Dwight laughed. 'I can see I've got my work cut out here!'

Two hours later Pat was bored stiff and completely confused by Dwight's commentary. Tony had been fielding and had had little involvement with the game, but now his side was batting and Dwight explained that the game hung in the balance. The batsman swung in a wide arc and the ball flew high in the air and plummeted downwards, straight into the hands of a fielder.

'Last man in has got to save the game,' said Dwight and Pat followed his gaze to see the unmistakeable figure of Tony walking purposefully to the batting position.

How strange all this was, thought Pat, watching this man, so strong and handsome, an American, playing baseball. What twists of fate had brought her here to this moment, the moment when she knew absolutely that she loved him.

The ball was pitched, Tony swung at it and it flew – away beyond the pitch, out of the ground, soaring high – a home run! The crowd were on their feet cheering, Pat too was jumping up and down. Surely now the game was won.

'Great game, great day,' said Dwight.

'And we still have the opening of the club tomorrow night to come. You'll be there won't you?'

'Sure will. It'll be our farewell to Northern Ireland party.'

'You're leaving?'

'Yeah, our battalion is shipping out in two weeks. We're up to strength and fully trained – time for us to make room for the new arrivals.'

Pat stopped walking and one look at her face told Dwight he had said the wrong thing.

'Aw gee, Tony didn't tell you?'

She waited for Tony after the game, watched him laughing with his friends. After a while he looked around and saw her. His smile was easy as he came towards her.

'Why didn't you tell me you're leaving?' she asked him.

His smile faded and he reached out to her. She stepped back.

'I wanted you to enjoy tomorrow night,' he tried to explain. 'You've worked so hard to make everything a success. I couldn't spoil that for you.'

'So you were going to wait until we were locking up to say, "By the way we'll never see each other again, nice knowing you." Was that how you planned it?' Her eyes widened. 'No, wait a minute – you weren't going to tell me at all, were you? Because on Monday I'd be back at Stormont anyway.'

'It wouldn't have been like that—'

'No? Well, how would it have been, Tony – tell me!'

'I planned to make it a special evening for you. I hoped that somehow …' He shook his head. 'God Patti, I love you, don't you know that? I can't bear the thought of leaving you.' The anguish in his face gave way to anger. 'What's the point anyway? You love someone else! And I can't bear to share you with anyone, so that's an end to it!' and he turned away.

Pat touched his arm. 'Tell me what you hoped would happen tomorrow night?'

'Gee, I would know that you loved me as much as I love you and I would ask you to marry me and you'd say yes. And God forgive me for saying it, but that guy you love and the solitaire around your neck would disappear forever.'

Pat took his hand and guided it to her neck before she spoke. 'I love you more than words can say and I promise you that you will not have to share me with anyone. Tomorrow night is going to be wonderful,' and Pat watched his face as he heard her words and realised the ring was gone.

'I'm telling you it's all organised,' said Pat.

'So we don't need the ten pounds I withdrew from the Post Office or the ten pounds Peggy borrowed from Mr Goldstein?' asked Irene.

'No, I had enough to buy the boat ticket with some to spare for Theresa to take with her.'

'Away on with you!' said Irene. 'You got all that money from the pawn?'

'No, from the jeweller on Royal Avenue who said it was an exquisite ring and would I take sixty pounds for it?'

Theresa stared in amazement at the ticket that would take her all the way to America. 'I never thought I'd see this,' she said. 'I don't know how to thank you all. Irene you're the best friend anyone could have and your family are the kindest people I've ever met. And Pat, I'll do my very best to repay you, even if it takes years.'

Pat shook her head. 'There's no need, Theresa. The ring was a gift to me and the ticket is a gift to you.'

Martha was just drifting off to sleep when there was a gentle knock and Pat put her head round the door. 'Are you awake, Mammy?'

'I am now,' said Martha. 'Switch on the light there.'

Pat was in her nightdress, her hair shining from the brushing she gave it every night before bed. Her face was flushed and Martha could see that, even though she tried hard not to, Pat couldn't keep the smile from her lips. The significance of selling the ring had not been lost on Martha and she sensed that there was more to come.

Pat sat on the edge of the bed. 'Mammy, this'll probably come as a bit of a surprise.'

Or perhaps not, thought Martha.

'You know Tony Farrelly, the American officer I work with? Well …'

'You're in love with him,' said Martha.

Pat gasped. 'How did you know?'

'Sure don't mammies know everything.'

Pat laughed. 'He's going to ask me to marry him.'

'Oh, is he now? And you, no doubt, are going to say yes.'

'I want to, but you know what that means, Mammy. I'll end up away in America.'

'That's the way things work, Pat. I would never have wished what happened to you on my worst enemy. More than anyone, you deserve a good life, a happy life and, if that means following this man to the other side of the world, I say seize it with both hands. I'll miss you sorely, but the balm for that is knowing you're happy.'

Martha settled down again to sleep but, truth be told, she wasn't surprised to hear another knock on her door. 'Come in, Irene.'

'How did you know it was me?'

Martha raised an eyebrow. If she had to choose a word to describe her eldest daughter over the past couple of months it would be 'blooming'.

'Mammy, you know Sandy is coming to the opening of the club

337

tomorrow. Well, I've got some news for him, but I want to tell you as well.'

'Is that so?'

'I'm going to have a baby.'

Martha smiled and nodded her head.

Irene laughed. 'You knew didn't you!'

Chapter 35

The magnificent ballroom was festooned with bunting and balloons and the glitter ball scattered prisms of light over the finest dance floor this side of the Atlantic Ocean. Just one couple, an American officer and his sweetheart, waltzed alone to the music in their heads. In less than an hour the club would be filled with the US Army top brass, local dignitaries and specially invited guests, but for now Pat and Tony were alone and they had unfinished business.

'Patti, you know how much I love you.'

'And I love you.'

'You know what's coming, don't you?'

Pat feigned innocence. 'No.'

Tony laughed and went down on one knee. 'Patti, will you marry me?'

'Yes, yes, of course I will.'

And Tony took her in his arms and kissed her tenderly. Pat felt so full of love she could hardly breathe.

'We'll announce our engagement tonight,' he whispered and we'll marry on my next leave.'

Pat shook her head. 'No, I want to marry now. I can't wait.'

'But it's only days until I leave; there's not much time to–'

'I want to be your wife now. I want to be with you every minute, day and night, until you leave.' And her words awakened his own desperate longing for this beautiful woman, his dearest friend, his Patti.

Goldstein was late. Sandy was late. Martha, Peggy, Sheila and Theresa sat in silence while Irene stood at the window watching the street. The plan was simple: Irene and Sandy would go to the American Services Club on his motorbike; Goldstein would drive the others to the club, dropping Theresa at the Liverpool boat on the way; and Pat would meet them all at the club.

Theresa had not left the house in over a month. She had been terrified that someone would find out where Irene lived and might, even now, be watching the house. It was Peggy who came up with the idea of disguising her as Pat.

'When you leave just keep your head down and walk between Sheila and me to the car,' Peggy told her, 'and if anyone is watching, well, you'll look just like a Goulding sister.'

'He's here!' shouted Irene and the others stood up. 'No, not Goldstein, it's Sandy,' and she ran to the door. Once inside, Irene introduced him to Theresa. 'Mr Goldstein's giving her a lift to the boat; she's going to England tonight.'

'It's good that you were able to get leave to come for the club opening, Sandy,' said Martha.

'To be honest, I never expected to be here. When I got the invitation, I applied for a pass and didn't get it. Then a few days later I was ordered to the squadron leader's office – thought I'd done something wrong – and he just hands me the pass and says "Seems you've got friends in high places".'

'I think Tony Farrelly, Pat's American friend, might have pulled a few strings,' said Irene.

'I don't care how I got it, I'm just so glad to be–'

There was a sharp knock at the front door. 'That'll be Mr Goldstein,' and Peggy went to let him in.

'Wait!' shouted Irene. 'There's no car outside.' There were two more sharp knocks. 'I don't like the look of this. All of you go upstairs and don't come down until I tell you to. Sandy, you stay here with me.'

In the hallway, Irene took a deep breath and opened the door just as Ted Grimes was reaching out to knock for a third time.

'I knew you were in there. I think it's time you stopped telling me lies and answered my questions.'

'Who's this, Irene?' Sandy appeared next to her.

'Ted Grimes,' she told him.

'Constable Grimes, Royal Ulster Constabulary,' he corrected her. 'And who might you be?'

'I'm Irene's husband.'

'Oh, are you now? Well maybe you'd like to know the kind of shenanigans she's been getting up to.'

'Hold on there, I don't like the way you're speaking about my wife.' Sandy took a step towards Grimes, who stepped back and at that moment Irene saw Goldstein's car pull up at the kerb. Quickly she stepped forward.

'All right, Mr Grimes, I'll answer your questions. Just come inside before the neighbours see you.'

'Irene, I don't think—'

'Don't worry, Sandy, it'll be fine.' And she stood back to allow Ted Grimes into the sitting room then turned and winked at Sandy.

She had just enough time to say, 'All right, I'll tell you what I know about Theresa,' before Goldstein knocked at the door.

'Just wait, I'll be back in a moment. Why don't you sit down Mr Grimes?' She indicated the chair with its back to the window and left the room to shout upstairs, 'Mammy, I'm just talking to Mr Grimes in the front room and Mr Goldstein's here to collect you, so hurry up!'

Martha came down the stairs and put her head round the door. 'Sorry, Ted, we can't stop – we're already late. Irene, you and Sandy need to get a move on too,' and she was gone.

'It's the opening of the American Services Club tonight and we're all invited,' Irene explained, but Grimes was turning round in his chair and Irene followed his sightline.

There was Martha and three daughters with their backs to him.

He would no doubt recognise Pat in her best coat and headscarf that she wore to church every Sunday, but he wouldn't notice that she was an inch or two shorter than the last time he saw her. Besides, he had more important business to attend to.

'Now you'd better start telling the truth. I know you went looking for Theresa O'Hara and when you didn't find her you tried to get a message to her. Isn't that so?'

Irene nodded.

'And you met her, didn't you?'

So he didn't know Theresa had been staying with them. Irene lowered her eyes and tried to look upset. 'Yes, I met her a fortnight ago down town. She was desperate to get away, people were threatening her. She told me she wanted to go to Mayo – said she had a relative there who would take her in – but she had no money, so I lent her some.'

'Whereabouts in Mayo?'

'She wouldn't tell me, said it was better if I didn't know.'

'How much did you lend her?'

'Twenty pounds.'

'Where'd you get that kind of money?'

Irene glanced at Sandy. 'We've been saving up.'

Grimes eyed Sandy. 'You knew about your wife giving money to this woman wanted for questioning by the police?'

Sandy looked confused. 'I certainly did not! Irene what's going on here? I thought this Theresa woman–'

'You thought she got the money from her family to go to Mayo – I told you that because I knew you'd be angry if you found out that I gave her our money,' and she began to weep uncontrollably.

Sandy turned on Ted Grimes. 'I don't know what's going on here, but I'll not have you upset my wife a moment longer. I think you'd better leave!'

Faced with Irene's hysterics and Sandy's anger, Ted Grimes decided to retreat. 'I'll make further enquiries about these Mayo relatives and by God if I find out you're lying …'

When Grimes had gone Sandy took Irene's hands from her face and, as he expected, found her smiling.

'She was going on a boat to England, not Mayo, wasn't she?' he asked her. 'She's wanted by the police and you gave her the fare?'

'It's a long story, Sandy, but I promise you she hasn't done anything wrong and I didn't give her any money.'

Sandy shook his head in despair. 'Irene, I can't keep up with you, for as soon as my back is turned … You'd better tell me right now if there's anything else I should know!

Irene looked up at him from under her lashes as she tried and failed to conceal a smile. 'Well, actually …'

The opening party was in full swing and the dance floor was packed. Even Martha and Goldstein took a turn around the floor. The bar was well stocked with beer and soft drinks and the running buffet boasted the finest food the US Army could provide. Irene and Sandy arrived and joined the rest of the family, including Tony and Goldstein, at a table near the stage.

'Well, did she get away?' asked Irene.

'Yes,' said Peggy. 'I went with her onto the boat and saw her settled in her cabin. She'll be safe there. She gave me this to give to you.' Peggy placed a silver and blue enamel holy medal in Irene's hand. 'She said you're to keep it with you until the baby is born and you'll both be safe, and then you're to pin it to the pram. So I'm guessing you have something to tell us.'

Irene laughed and turned to whisper in Sandy's ear. He cleared his throat to get everyone's attention.

'I've got an announcement to make. Irene and I …' He hesitated and reached for Irene's hand and she smiled reassuringly. 'We'd like you to know that we're expecting a baby,' and he sat down wreathed in smiles, while everyone round the table clapped and congratulated them both.

At nine o'clock the band left the stage and Tony introduced the Northern Ireland Base Section Commander.

Brigadier General Collins, tall and distinguished-looking, made his way to the microphone. 'It's a real pleasure to be here tonight at the opening of this wonderful club that symbolises the cooperation between the United States army and the government of Northern Ireland. But it seems to me that this club is about much more than that. It's about the Northern Ireland people and the way they've welcomed us to their country. It took a bit of time for us to get used to each other and I'm not sayin' that we haven't put a few backs up along the way – we have a tendency to do that, I know.' He paused as the audience laughed in agreement then went on, 'But I was heartened the other day to hear a politician say "Americans are difficult people to hate!" In reply I'd say, "You are easy people to love!" In fact, the first marriage of a GI and a Belfast girl took place within three weeks of us getting here.

'The exchange of cultures was a bit of a wake-up call. We brought you chocolate, chewing gum and nylons and you kindly gave us champ, stewed tea and gravy rings, though I'm sure we had them already!'

The commander's voice grew serious. 'Your city bears the scars of a terrible conflict and your brave citizens have endured so much. The United States is proud to join its allies to bring a speedy conclusion to this war and we thank you for being our hosts in your beautiful country.

'Now before I declare the club open, I would like to thank all those involved in the project. In particular, Captain Tony Farrelly of the US 34th division and Miss Patricia Goulding from the Ministry of Public Security who together are responsible for creating this home away from home for our troops. In a moment Captain Farrelly will also say a few words and I believe he has a very special surprise for us. So, please raise your glasses as I formally declare the American Red Cross Services Club open!'

When the clapping died down Tony stepped up to the microphone. 'I'd like to say a big thank you to Patti Goulding for her vision in seeing what the club could be and for her organisation and common sense. I'd especially like to thank her for seeing it through and putting up with me. Come up here, Patti, I have a gift for you!'

Pat blushed to the roots of her hair, but it was her smile that caught everyone's eye as she walked on to the stage. Tony kissed her cheek and produced a long thin box which he opened to reveal a string of pearls. He fastened them around her neck and whispered in her ear. She laughed and nodded.

'Ladies and gentlemen, earlier this evening I asked Patti to be my wife. She said yes, but I just had to check she hadn't changed her mind before I announced it! We'll marry next week, so I guess some of you will be back here with us then for the wedding celebration.

'Now the special surprise. They stopped over here today on their way to bases in Europe, and tonight they bring us another "String of Pearls". Ladies and gentlemen, please welcome Glenn Miller and his orchestra!'

The orchestra came onstage to loud applause and, when Glenn Miller appeared and the opening bars of 'String of Pearls' began, the cheering was deafening.

Tony and Pat stood at the side of the stage.

'I can't believe he's here,' laughed Pat. 'How did you keep this a secret?'

'Never you mind,' said Tony. 'Do you like your string of pearls?'

Pat's hand went to her throat. 'I love them. They're perfect.'

'And so are you,' he said.

When the music ended, Glenn Miller came to the microphone. 'It's wonderful to be here, thank you. Now, I've been told that there are some sisters in Belfast who like to perform my tunes and, tell you the truth, I could do with a bit of help tonight, so are the Golden Sisters ready to sing with the band?'

To loud cheering and clapping Irene, Pat, Peggy and Sheila got up onstage and formed a semi-circle round the microphone.

'You'll know this one, girls, it's "Don't Sit Under the Apple Tree". Then Glenn Miller counted them in. 'One ... two ... three ...'

Goldstein leaned back on his chair. 'Well, Martha, who would have thought in those dark days that we'd be sitting here surrounded by Americans and that your girls would be singing with the Glenn Miller Orchestra?'

'Aye, it's a miracle, right enough.'

'It certainly is, Martha, it certainly is.'